UNSINKABLE

Dan James is a pseudonym for a bestselling, award-nominated thriller writer and author of bestselling non-fiction books. He is an experienced journalist who has contributed to all the major national newspapers, including the *Guardian* and the *Daily Mail*. He is 39 and lives in London.

D0667758

DAN JAMES

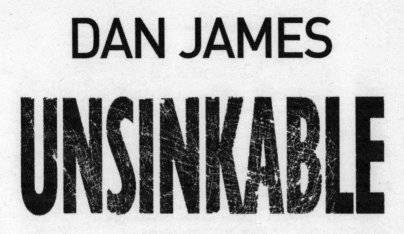

UNSINKABLE

arrow books

Published by Arrow Books 2012

2 4 6 8 10 9 7 5 3

Copyright © Dan James, 2012

Dan James has asserted his right under the Copyright, Designs
and Patents Act 1988 to be identified as the author of this work

This book is a work of fiction. Any resemblance between these fictional characters and actual
persons, living or dead, is purely coincidental.

This book is sold subject to the condition that it shall not,
by way of trade or otherwise, be lent, resold, hired out,
or otherwise circulated without the publisher's prior
consent in any form of binding or cover other than that
in which it is published and without a similar condition,
including this condition, being imposed
on the subsequent purchaser.

First published in Great Britain in 2012 by
Arrow Books
Random House, 20 Vauxhall Bridge Road,
London SW1V 2SA
www.randomhouse.co.uk

Addresses for companies within The Random House Group Limited can be found at:
www.randomhouse.co.uk/offices.htm

The Random House Group Limited Reg. No. 954009

A CIP catalogue record for this book is available from the British Library

ISBN 9780099558132

The Random House Group Limited supports The Forest Stewardship Council (FSC®), the
leading international forest certification organisation. Our books carrying the FSC label are
printed on FSC® certified paper. FSC is the only forest certification scheme endorsed by
the leading environmental organisations, including Greenpeace. Our paper procurement
policy can be found at www.randomhouse.co.uk/environment

Typeset by SX Composing DTP, Rayleigh, Essex
Printed and bound by CPI Group (UK) Ltd, Croydon, CR0 4YY

*T*he tall sergeant knocked firmly on the door. Behind him were four colleagues, wrapped in woollen overcoats against the winter wind whipping round the corners of the soot-flecked terraced houses.

They were better dressed for it than Beck was, in his suit and mackintosh. Not that he was cold after his run from Bishopsgate Police Station, just a few minutes away from this dead-end street in Houndsditch.

Houndsditch. The sort of intriguing name that London's past threw up. Once a protective moat around the old city where the Royal Hunt used to sling the carcasses of their dead hunting dogs. Beck loved all that stuff, the past of the benighted city. He knew that only a few hundred yards away lay Ripper Corner where Jack had once disembowelled another hapless victim. How Beck wished he could be the copper to catch that bastard.

That was all a long time ago now, though. He had to concentrate on the present. Sergeant Bentley, broad, moustachioed under his helmet, knocked again, more insistently this time.

As Beck had arrived, panting for breath, Bentley had looked him up and down, about to turn him away. Then he had introduced himself, mentioned Special Branch. Whispered that he was observing anarchists who might be linked to the Tottenham Outrage. Bentley's mood changed immediately: he nodded gravely, eyebrows twitching in recognition. A good policeman had been shot *and killed by robbers, immigrants, aliens – call them whatever you wanted. A small boy killed, too. Half a million had turned out for the victims' funeral. The two shooters responsible had been killed in the chase. But the word was out to keep an eye on all those associated or linked with them, a job that had occupied Beck for the past year, and that night had taken him to the warren-like streets around Spitalfields market.*

'Chief Inspector Hayes said there were some foreigners on the street here,' he had said to Bentley once he'd got his breath back.

Bentley had shrugged. 'Not sure of their nationality, sir. But we have reports of noises comin' from the rear of the property, bangin' and hammerin'. Heard it myself. There's a jeweller's shop on the next street. It backs onto the back of these houses. It sounds very much like the noise is coming from there.'

Beck had nodded. It was clear they suspected a heist.

'Chief Inspector Hayes told me to tell you he wants you to find out if the noise is coming from where the foreigners are. Have the neighbours said who lives there?' he had asked.

'Just a couple that moved in recently,' Bentley had replied. 'If the Chief's asked, we'd better knock and have a look. There's one of our chaps outside the front of the jeweller's and another stationed at the top of this road. No one has come or gone since the alarm was raised. Nowhere for them to go now, neither.'

The place was surrounded. It crossed Beck's mind to hold them back, to ask for more help. But until they knew more about who was inside it seemed unnecessary to delay them. There was no intelligence indicating that the anarchists were hiding out here. He should probably leave them to it. But something had made him stay.

'Mind if I tag along?' he had asked.

Bentley had shrugged his acceptance, and Beck had followed them to the door of number 11, a narrow terraced house in a street full of them. Along with Bentley, there were two constables, Choate and Strongman, and two other sergeants, Bryant and Tucker. As they'd approached the house their breaths had frosted in the icy night air.

Despite the gaslight flickering through the gap beneath the window shutter, suggesting that someone was in, there was still no answer to Bentley's knocks.

'One more time and if we get no answer we try and break in,' Bentley muttered and tried a third time. A rap that echoed down the street. He checked his pocket watch. It was just past 11.30 p.m.

At last there was a noise. The door opened; the rat face of a man peered suspiciously out.

'Have you been knocking about a bit inside?'

The man did not answer, just looked at them with the same sharp, blank expression.

'Don't you understand English?'

No answer.

Bentley put his gloved hands on his hips. 'Is there anyone in there who can? Go and get them if there is.'

The man paused a second, then closed the door partly, leaving them on the threshold. Seconds passed. No sound came from within. Standing behind Bentley's massive frame, Beck exchanged a look with Tucker – bearded, stout, a man of obvious experience. He raised his eyebrows, as if to say 'What now?'

They stood there on the threshold for a few seconds. Bentley sighed deeply. 'Come on, boys, let's go and take a look.'

Bentley pushed the door and it opened. He stepped forward, Bryant beside him. Over their shoulders Beck could see a flight of stairs. To their right was a small living room. A fire burned in the grate and on the table was some bread and tea. Of greater note, there was a blowtorch, a pressure gauge and some rubber tubing. Not your everyday equipment.

The room seemed empty. Then Beck heard Bentley speak.

'Is anyone working here?'

'No,' a voice replied quietly.

Beck crouched down to see who Bentley was talking to. Someone was sitting on the stairs, half-shrouded in darkness so he could see only a pair of feet.

Bentley continued his questioning. 'Anyone in the back at all?'

'No.'

'Can I have look?'

'Yes.'

'Show us the way.'

The man leaned forward, his face silhouetted in the gaslight. Was he the one who had opened the door? The shadows made it hard to tell, but he extended an arm and pointed to a door at the back.

'In there.' It was clear from his accent that he wasn't English.

Bentley and his men took a step forward. There was a loud thud. The door at the back of the room, which led to the yard, burst open. A man appeared in the frame: face round, a neat moustache, above it two eyes, dead and cold, bled of all emotion. He started to smile.

A face that Beck knew. A face he recognised though had never before seen in the flesh. The man they all spoke about in hushed tones.

A gun was in his hand. He walked forward, arm extended, still smiling. As he closed on Bentley he fired. A flash of light and a deafening crack. The man on the stairs fired too.

Beck crouched and flung his arms in front of his face instinctively. In front of him, on the threshold, Bentley went down, blood spurting from the wound in his throat, gargling and rattling as the life left him. To Beck's left Bryant lifted his hands in a futile gesture of self-defence. The man with the cold, dead eyes continued to fire and smile. Bryant stumbled back past Beck, through the door and into the street where he fell to his knees and into unconsciousness.

Beck leaned forward to check Bentley, to try to grab him and get him away, get help, raise the alarm. The sergeant's dying body was convulsing, slumped half in the house, half on the pavement.

As Beck bent down, a pain seared through his thigh, like a burn, and he was sent spinning, hitting the pavement. He opened his mouth in shock, as if to scream, but no words came.

He clutched his thigh and looked up. Tucker and Strongman stood frozen in shock, staring at their wounded, fallen colleagues. The force of the shot had left Beck lying in the road and when he looked up he could only see the barrel of a pistol pointing around the door. Then the man came into view again. That face and those coal-black eyes and curious smile. The pain came in waves and Beck saw the blood from his wound gushing onto the street, viscous, thick, pooling around his leg. He felt faint. He looked up at the man, waiting for the next and fatal shot, sure this was his end.

Time seemed suspended. The smell of gunsmoke was almost overpowering. The man raised the pistol and pointed it at Strongman. The constable stepped back instinctively as the muzzle flashed. But it was Tucker who stumbled, hit, his eyes wide with surprise. Strongman went to catch him, as another bullet slammed into Tucker. He fell into the road, got up, and staggered a few more feet before falling down a final time. Dead.

The firing stopped. The silence afterwards was profound.

Beck lay back, his head on the cold stone. He had not seen Choate. Was he inside? He turned to one side, energy draining from him. He was starting to feel the cold.

The man turned and called in a foreign tongue to unseen figures in the house, gesturing with his arm.

The gang had not seen Choate in the shadows. But he was there, lurking around the side of the door. As the first of them emerged – the pale rat-faced one who had answered the door – the surviving constable barred their way with his burly frame.

Ratface ran straight into him. The two began to wrestle. The pale man held a gun which he tried to fire in the constable's face. Choate proved too strong, forcing down his arm. Then the gun fired. Two shots hit Choate in the leg but still he kept his grip. Others were there now. Raining fists and kicks on the copper to make him release their friend. Still Choate held on. The moustachioed man appeared on the street, put his gun against the policeman's back and fired. As Choate fell he fired once more, but the policeman turned as he went, holding on to their friend. The bullet hit Ratface in the back.

More silence.

'You shot him!' a voice hissed incredulously, staring at the groaning body on the floor. 'You shot Gardstein.'

The smiling man shrugged calmly. 'Get him out of here.'

The men gathered up the wounded man and started to run.

The man with the moustache was the last to leave. Choate was breathing heavily, his blood slicking the pavement, mingling with Beck's and Bentley's.

Choate's glazed stare met that of his attacker.

'Goodbye,' the gunman said in his accented English.

He raised the gun and fired into Choate's supine body three times.

The policeman breathed no more.

Beck lay back, eyes closed, waiting for the bullet that would claim him.

Yet all he heard was the sound of fading scuffling footsteps, the faint noise of a whistle – and then the world turned black.

10 April 1912

The dream ended as it always did. With absolute silence. Beck had never known that the lack of sound could be so terrifying; the absence of light and noise as if he had been cast into the grave. Yet each time it came – and the silence always came, no matter what events preceded it – he woke covered in sweat, gasping for breath.

That morning, like others before it, the dream coincided with the dawn. He was thankful for that, at least. There would be no possible way he could go back to sleep after it. He sat up, waiting for his heart to stop hammering, doing all the things that the physician had told him to do: take deep breaths, look around the room, reminding himself of the here and now, forgetting the past and the troubles that lurked there.

There was enough light in the room for Beck to see that he was not in his own bedroom. A few seconds later he remembered where he was: Southampton. He had arrived at the South-Western Hotel late the previous night after taking the train down from Waterloo. Today was the day he was due to set sail on a voyage. Turning his back on the life he had once led and all its problems and dangers.

The same old questions about whether he was doing the right thing returned, and he was determined to banish them. Enough of prevarication, he thought. The decision was made; the course was set. There would be no turning back.

Then he remembered the vessel. It had been perfect darkness when he'd checked in. On the way to his room the bellboy asked if Beck had seen *her*. No, he said. It had been too dark. As he offered the boy a coin for hauling his luggage to his room, the boy nodded towards the window, draped in heavy curtains, so long that their hem sat piled on the carpet.

'This room looks right over Dock Forty-four,' he said. 'Make sure the first thing you do when it's light is open those curtains and have a look out, sir. She makes a remarkable sight.'

Beck smiled. 'Thank you for the advice.'

'No, thank *you*, sir,' he said, tucking the coin away in the top pocket of his waistcoat. 'Enjoy your voyage. I envy you greatly.'

As morning broke Beck glanced from his bed over to the thick curtains, light seeping its way around the sides. To hell with being decent, he thought. He was in pyjamas, three storeys up and it was barely 6 a.m.; he couldn't imagine there would be that many folk around. He stood up, testing the leg gingerly, because it was always stiff first thing, and half-limped across the thick carpet to the window. He pulled open the curtains.

The light, what there was of it, was watery. But the reason why so little penetrated his room wasn't poor weather. It was because the vast structure in front of him blocked so much of it.

Titanic. The biggest ship ever built. Her towering hull looming over the town like the side of a cliff. Even three storeys up Beck had to crane his neck in order to the see the tops of her black-capped funnels, like four huge fingers pointing victoriously towards the sky.

It was a few seconds before he remembered to breathe.

He dressed in a hurry, forgetting his plan to bathe before breakfast. There would be enough time for that in the languorous days to come. *Titanic* boasted Turkish baths, where a man could sweat away his troubles and then indulge in a massage, followed by a swim in the heated seawater pool. A swimming pool aboard an ocean liner? It sounded ridiculous yet enticing at the same time.

Once Beck was fully clothed, he hurried downstairs, taking the stairs rather than using the elevator, a machine he distrusted. He strode purposefully past the dining room and straight out of the revolving door at the front of the hotel and onto the street, immediately catching the cool fresh air in his face and the iodine tang of the sea. The sky was a light grey: it was too early to gauge whether the sun would bless the launch. In the distance he could hear the screaming of gulls, yet his eyes were focused solely on the ship. He was astern, a few hundred yards away, yet even from here it did not fit into his field of vision. It pointed at a ten-degree angle west, and his eyes followed its sleek lines all the way to the bow, which seemed miles away in the distance. In the morning air he could smell fresh paint on the north-westerly breeze.

He'd been wrong about the streets being empty. Men seemed to be converging on the ship from all directions, some in groups, others on their own: the general crew, eager to get on board and start work. The coal strike had rendered the shipping industry stagnant for the past six weeks, so this would be much-needed work for the firemen and engineers, along with a chance to sail on the biggest ship afloat. Beck rubbed his hands together, as keen as they were to board. The feeling of taking part in such a momentous occasion, of being a part of history, made him feel renewed. This was exactly what he needed.

Absent-mindedly, he pulled his cigarette case from his pocket, all the while never taking his eyes off the leviathan. It was now less than four hours until the first passengers could board and he decided then to be one of the first in order to explore as much of the ship as possible before departure.

'Horrible, ain't it?'

The voice was small and sounded almost withered. Beck looked down. At his side was an old woman, her hair ivory white, her face creased and mottled. She was smiling – at least, he thought it was a smile – revealing a set of blackened stumps. The odour emanating from her was far from pleasant. Some kind of tinker lady, he supposed, judging by the large sack she carried over her shoulder. As a copper, he had met this type of woman before. They were often useful, as little seemed to escape their notice. However, it was rare for them to be among nature's conversationalists.

'The ship? I happen to think she's quite beautiful.'

The old woman snorted her contempt, looking over her shoulder at the great mass of steel. She shook her head. 'You wouldn't get me going on something like that. And my Ernest, God rest his soul, spent his life at sea. Loved boats, he did. But he would have despised this 'un.'

Common sense told Beck to end their exchange, but he was intrigued. He couldn't imagine how any nautical man would have disapproved of such a miracle of engineering and workmanship.

'Really? Why?'

'It's unnatural,' she snapped. 'Something that huge shouldn't be floatin'.'

He should have known that her answer would be based on her sense of the uncanny rather than on the laws of science.

Beck shook his head. 'I disagree. I think it's a remarkable achievement, and one that should be celebrated. And I'm looking forward to sailing on her.'

The woman turned her gaze from the ship to him, fixing him with a stare for some time. A few more seconds than was necessary, he thought. It made him feel uncomfortable.

She hitched her sack onto her shoulder once more, and started to shuffle off. 'Good luck to you, then. Somethin' that huge shouldn't be floatin',' she repeated.

Beck watched her go, a vague sense of unease creeping over him. Then he looked back at the great ship, and once more his heart swelled. No superstitious old crone could darken his mood on a day of such promise.

The boat train that left platform 12 of Waterloo Station at 9.30 a.m. bound for Southampton Terminus and the *Titanic* carried on it some of the richest people in the world.

Martha Heaton was not one of them.

On feet still unsteady after more than a week of illness, several pounds of weight loss, and the disorientation that comes with being in a new country, on a different continent, she still managed to recognise a few of the more shimmering celebrities of the Gilded Age. They were, after all, the men and women who colonised the society columns of her newspaper. 'Ink eaters,' they were called because their every cough and sneeze devoured lines of newsprint. The society pages were not her beat. Thankfully. Though if they recognised Martha as a member of the 'sensationalist' press they would probably try and deny her passage on this highfalutin boat whose virtues they were all extolling.

Though, truth be told, she couldn't have cared less. Wealth was not something that appealed to her. All those people with their air of entitlement, and their belief that the world was run for their benefit, made her feel ill. Just like boats made her feel ill, albeit less metaphorically and more viscerally. Martha didn't have a problem with trains. Trains she could handle. Trains billowed acrid smoke, sure they did, but they didn't constantly sway and rock, make you walk like you had just drunk a bottle of bourbon, make you want to empty the contents of your stomach every ten minutes and generally make you feel like you wanted to die right there and then. As she fell into her seat, after tipping the porter who had ever so sweetly carried her bags on board, she shuddered at the recollection of her outward journey.

It had taken seven days to cross from New York to London. A week of nausea and vomiting, of lying in a room so small that you had to go outside just to breathe, not caring if the whole damn pile of steel went down to the bottom of the ocean. In fact, actively wanting it to, as fast as possible, because it would put an end to her misery.

There had been four days in London. Four days in which she had slept to get over the trauma of her outward journey. Martha had only just started eating again, just started to feel human once more, and now here she was, on a train – a steady, reassuring train – in order to catch another stupid boat for a further six days or more of torture. And why? Because the greasy schmuck she called an editor thought because some very rich people were going to sail on a very big boat, it was worth a line or two.

The train pulled slowly, gracefully out of the station into the fresh English air that she had been denied for the past few days. Martha had been looking forward to seeing London after hearing and reading so much about it. She had been brought up to believe the old place was the epitome of grace, manners and style – she was from Boston, which didn't go big on that stuff. But she had been too ill to experience it. And she doubted if she would return. Not until they invented a new way to cross the Atlantic, and she wasn't talking about the crazy Wright brothers and their dumb 'airplanes'. She was thinking more of the ability to click your fingers and arrive somewhere instantly. Until then, she was never leaving New York again. Not even for Philadelphia. Especially not Philadelphia.

Martha looked out of the window as they left London behind, trying to drink in as much as she could. She was furious at having been unable to explore more of the great old city. St Paul's Cathedral and the Tower of London had both passed her by. On her last day she had managed to crawl from her bed to see Big Ben and the Houses of Parliament, and had stood in awestruck wonder. The US did not do history like this. Her people's idea of heritage was venerating drunken cowboys who shot people in a bar fight.

From the window she saw the scenery change from urban to rural. It was spring and everything was lush and green. She appreciated the view. In a few hours' time all she would be able to see for most of the coming week would be endless water and sky. What the hell was this sort of assignment, anyway? Her newspaper, in thrall to J.P. Morgan and his cronies, impressed by the colour of his money, even hoping to get their hands on some advertising spend, had decided it would make a good puff piece for her to travel on the maiden voyage of the world's biggest ship, to write about its brilliance and luxury. Martha smiled. On the way out the only thing she'd noticed on her ship was the efficiency of the lavatory system, though that vessel had been a mere schooner in comparison with this one, so she had been told. *Titanic* was supposed to be an opulent hotel with an anchor. A floating palace for the upper classes, she thought. She would make a note of that phrase.

Of course, all this talk of luxury and hotels ignored the vast majority of the transatlantic clientele, the poor huddled masses in steerage, seeking a new life in the States. Little did they know about the reality of their dreams. One of the last stories that Martha had filed before leaving America had been about the terrible living conditions experienced by immigrants on the Lower East Side. It had been spiked. Too depressing, her editor had said. He wanted stories of hope amid the grime, triumph against the odds, 'that kind of crap'. The point of the story was vanquished hope, she'd explained, but he wasn't listening.

A few hours later she was in his office, being handed steamship tickets and given this assignment, being told to pack a 'fancy' frock because she was returning first class. The last thing he asked was that she should concentrate her efforts on the rich, 'the people our readers wanna read about', rather than the hard-luck stories of people in third. Despite her bringing him a steady stream of great stories, the sexist old pig still fed her a daily diet of fluff. Women in journalism were still few – she knew of only three others in the whole of the Big Apple – and most newspapers at best tolerated them. Martha had to work three times as hard as any male reporter she knew just to keep afloat. That meant going off-diary to break stories she sourced herself, as well as filing the fluff. Even then most of her stuff went on the spike, or appeared in the paper under a male reporter's byline, or under none at all. It was a good job she was the only hack in New York who didn't do it for the fame. She did it to expose the humbug and injustice of the rich and powerful – the sort of people she would be travelling with – and to give a voice to those whom fate chewed and spat out like her grandad did tobacco.

So, like she always did, she would give him what he wanted, but she would also seek out a few of those chasing the American Dream. Maybe even hook up with them in a year's time to see how it was tallying with reality. After all, she wouldn't be on this paper for ever. There were publications that were less besotted with the wealthy and glamorous. Or at least there used to be.

Martha must have dozed off, lulled by the gentle rhythmic sway of the carriage, because the next thing she knew the conductor was passing through, telling them that they were approaching Southampton Terminus, their last stop. Martha shook her head to rid it of sleep, and started to gather her things. Through the window she could see buildings and a few wheeling, tipping gulls, a sign that they were near water.

'Look!' she heard someone exclaim with excitement as she stood, smoothing her skirt. 'There she is!' the man said, taking his hat off and leaning forward to give himself a better view. Martha too leaned across the gangway. Straight away she could see the cause of the commotion. They were slowing, and behind a tall building was the clear sight of a ship at anchor. Not just any ship. A vast behemoth, sporting four enormous funnels. For a few seconds her cynicism deserted her, and she almost let out a whistle of amazement, which might have earned her a reproachful look or two from the gentlemen on board. As it was, the ship was soon hidden from them by the station building as they eased to a stop, but it had been a tantalising glimpse. An unfamiliar feeling coursed through her. It took her a while to identify it as excitement.

Maybe this wouldn't be so bad, Martha thought. The ship

looked beautiful, sleek and new, almost twice the size of the vessel that had brought her over.

Now if only they could do something about the endless-sea-and-sky thing.

It was 9:30 a.m. Beck was at the end of the gangway entrance to the first-class section, though its doors were still shut. The ship was ready to sail. The whole area was thronging with people, in groups, or alone like he was, some of them carrying huge cases and boxes. He wondered if the crowds, many of them without luggage, were all passengers, or were there just to witness the event? At breakfast his fellow diners had speculated about whether the locals would turn out in their hundreds to see the *Titanic* off. His heart sank as he remembered Sarah for the first time that morning, and imagined her at the dockside waving a goodbye. But there would be no one to see him off. Only one person even knew he was going. For everyone else it was a momentous event, stirring great emotions in them and their kin. Yet he was slipping from the country like a man nipping out for a glass of beer on his own. His mood slumped only for a second. He was there to look forward to the future, not to dwell on the past.

He could still revel in the ceremony and anticipation. The Blue Ensign at the ship's stern flapped in the morning breeze. While he waited for the doors to be opened for boarding, he had walked along the length of the ship, all nine hundred feet of it, a sixth of a mile. Crew members were scurrying back and forth, both on the dockside and across the decks above, trying to make the muster.

Beck walked beyond the liner's bow and turned to take in a

view from the front. It was as breathtaking a sight as he had ever seen. Now he could take in the full beauty of her, as well as her sheer size. They had named her well. His friend Alec, the only one he had told of his voyage – and better versed in the classics and mythology than Beck was – had scoffed at the name. The Titans, he insisted, were a group of deities who had been supplanted by another, the Olympians. Their fall, he claimed, hardly made *Titanic* a propitious name for an ocean-going vessel. 'Didn't Zeus strike the Titans down with thunderbolts, their final resting place in some limbo beneath the lowest depths of Tartarus?' he had said, eyebrows raised mockingly. Yet if he had been standing where Beck was now, gazing upon the mighty work of the shipbuilders, Beck was certain that Alec would have been less cynical.

He smiled at a dapper old gentleman – gleaming shoes, white hair tufting out from beneath his trilby hat – sitting on a low wooden platform only a few feet back from the dockside.

'Isn't she marvellous?' the man said.

Beck agreed she was. The man's excitement made a nice contrast to the old woman's scepticism earlier. 'Are you sailing on her?'

He shook his head ruefully. 'No, but I wish I was. I'm just going to sit here and watch it unfold. I work for the White Star Line. It's a proud day for us all.'

'I imagine it is.'

They both looked back at the ship. Again there was the smell of fresh paint, of newness, just about managing to mask the more pungent smells of a working dock. The foremast shadow fell across the gleaming white bridge. At its top flew the French flag; their first port of call was to be Cherbourg later that day, before steaming around to Queenstown in Ireland to collect the last passengers and some mail and then heading out onto the open Atlantic bound for New York. The idea of waking next Wednesday and to be sailing past the Statue of Liberty into a city of such legendary bustling energy fuelled Beck's excitement further. A fresh start, a new identity, a chance to escape the darkness of the previous year and a half.

Behind the foremast stood the mainmast, from which the White Star Line flag flew proudly. More eavesdropping at breakfast had told Beck that Ismay, the company's president, was a guest at the hotel and was planning to make the maiden voyage. Beck could only imagine the man's pride at having overseen such a magnificent feat of engineering, and of being on board as the liner made its stately way across the ocean for the first time. If he got the chance, he would introduce himself and offer his congratulations.

He said farewell to the smartly dressed old man and strolled back along the dock beside the liner's hull. The number of people milling around the boat appeared to have grown. The boat train from Waterloo bringing third- and second-class passengers had arrived and spilled a mass of people, many of them children now running back and forth, on the dock. Beck felt a tightness in his shoulders as a horrible memory returned, but managed to force it away. Above him, on a level of their own, away from the hordes, he could see that the first-class gangway doors were now open, just forward of amidships. At last he could board.

For a man leaving his home country to start a new life abroad, his one suitcase appeared rather meagre, but Beck had thought it best to travel light. The more he could leave behind the better. And he was thankful for its portability as he passed others puffing and sweating on the dockside with their chests and leather cases.

Beck stood at the end of the gangway, feeling hesitant for the first time. Few other passengers travelling first class seemed to be around. Their train from Waterloo wasn't due in until half an hour before the ship set sail. He admired the rich travellers' insouciance. There was no way he'd have wanted to cut it so fine.

He glanced down at his ticket, his palm starting to grow slick with sweat. The name 'Arthur Beck' written in the top right-hand corner, the White Star Line logo of a red flag, some legalese about the conditions in the enclosed contract, which he hadn't read, and a warning that liability for baggage was strictly limited. Then a line giving the date of departure and stating that it was for first-class passage on the steamship *Titanic*.

First-class, Beck thought. He had never travelled in such style in his life. It had taken most of his savings, and the sale of many of his possessions, to secure the ticket. A high price. But, if he wanted to walk into New York with as few questions asked as possible, a necessary one. There was also the fact that, because of the expense, the high-priced decks would be less likely to be full of families, of mothers and children, and therefore less liable to conjure the sort of memories that were forcing him to flee.

He walked up the gangway, where a crew member nodded a greeting and smiled. Beck held out the ticket but the man just waved him through. Was that it? he thought.

He was on the ship. And what a ship she was. The gangway took him through a large set of doors into a small entrance room.

From there he was ushered through an arch and into a huge reception room studded with tub armchairs and settees. Beck was not one for soft furnishings and mahogany fittings, but the detail and opulence thrilled even his philistine heart. That was merely an appetite whetter, though; as he took a few steps further into the ship, across a dark, thick Axminster carpet, he saw a sweeping staircase so grand that it could have come from a stately home. Natural light swept down it from an ornate dome directly above. On a pedestal, at the foot of the stairs, was a bronze cherub holding some kind of torch. On the landing halfway up the stairway was an even more elaborate decoration, a panel with a clock at its centre flanked by two carved female winged figures.

For a few seconds Beck forgot he was on a boat. Then he remembered that he should find his room and drop off his things before going to explore some more. From nowhere a crew member appeared at his side, causing him to jump. The crewman took his name, checked a list and gave Beck his berth, in the forward part of D deck. He went through a set of baize doors on the port side and found his cabin – one of the first he came across – on the right. Only a short walk from the first-class saloon and reading rooms. A mixed blessing. He had vowed to be good to his body and brain, to drink only with meals, to exercise as much as possible and get as much sea air as he could. But he was so close to the public areas that he might be able to hear the clink of ice on glass. The temptation to drink and stay up late might be too difficult to resist. More dangerously, it might loosen his tongue. No, it would be best if he kept as low a profile as he could.

It helped that his berth was as comfortable and well appointed as any hotel room he had stayed in, which meant that turning in early wouldn't be a chore. The room wasn't huge, but there was a comfortable-looking bed, a dressing table and a mirror, sink and lavatory, and the bathrooms were next door but one. The only thing missing was some natural light, but the outside berths on the ship were more expensive, and he would need some money left for New York.

There was a gentle knock on the door and a small head popped round. Its owner's hair was smoothed by wax, and he had a small neat moustache and soft blue eyes.

'Mr Beck, sir?'

Beck stood up. 'Yes,' he replied hesitantly.

'Mr Beck, I'm your steward,' the man explained, stepping stiffly into the room, and nodding respectfully. 'Donald is the name. Alan Donald. I'll be looking after you during your voyage.'

Beck offered his hand, unsure of how he was supposed to greet a steward. 'Pleased to meet you.'

That was the downside to travelling first class. So many unwritten laws and rules of behaviour that he was ignorant of, not having been born into the appropriate social stratum. Donald took his hand, slightly taken aback.

'You're on early, sir,' he said. 'Stayed in the town last night, did we?'

'Yes. I'm not one for waiting around. Couldn't wait to get on, truth be told. It's all new to me.'

'It's new to all of us,' Donald said, smiling. 'Can I get you anything? Some water? Perhaps a hot drink?'

Beck shook his head. 'I wouldn't mind exploring the ship, especially before she becomes too crowded.'

'Be my guest, sir. She's a glorious sight. Though be careful. It's like a rabbit warren.'

Beck smiled. 'Maybe they should give us a map.'

'They do, sir. It should be on the desk there. At least, a map of the first-class areas. Anything you need, just ask.'

'One more thing. How do I go about sending a wireless message?'

'Through the purser's office, sir.'

'Do you know what the range is? Of the wireless.'

Donald shrugged. 'I don't, sir. I don't understand how it all works, to be honest. Remarkable piece of machinery.'

Beck nodded. It certainly was. It would revolutionise communications across the world, this ability to transmit messages thousands of miles without wires.

'Anything else, sir?'

'No, that's all.'

'Thank you,' Donald said and with that the steward slipped out of sight.

The station platform was only a short walk from the dockside and the great ship. After Martha had found her ways off the train and battled for the attention of a porter – they seemed to consider her small fry among a more illustrious catch – the first impression made by the boat had diminished. All that interested her was its likely motion. If they'd promised her that it wouldn't make her ill, she'd have been prepared to take a tin tub back across the Atlantic.

While she waited for a porter, Martha took the opportunity to study some of her fellow passengers. The great and the good were there, lured by the promise of some sort of happening, as though it were a gala theatre premiere. Her gaze was immediately drawn to J.J. Astor, probably one of the wealthiest guys on the planet, buttoned up against the spring cold, his young bride at his side. She was nineteen, he was the wrong side of forty-nine, and on the crowded platform her sad, round face made her look as nervous as a kitten taking its first steps away from its mother. Probably the prospect of returning to the land where their marriage had created such brouhaha. And from the look of young Mrs Astor, and her shape, it looked like there might soon be an heir or heiress on the way. This was the sort of stuff Martha's editor would have given his best toupee for. However, if Colonel Astor, so-called because he financed wars rather than fought in them, knew she was there, she was likely to be pitched overboard. He was no friend of the press.

Among their possessions, and the coterie of people with them, was a dog – an Airedale, she guessed. Were they allowed on? Obviously they must be. Martha wondered what kind of world they lived in where third-class passengers had to undergo a series of medical tests before being allowed on board, while the dogs of the great and the good were allowed on without a second thought. And where did they go to the bathroom? The back of the boat? Maybe that was why they called it the poop deck.

The scandal-plagued Colonel Astor and his teenage bride could not have formed a greater contrast with another couple she recognised: Benjamin and Isidor Strauss. Benjamin was the founder of Macy's, worth uncountable millions. Martha also caught a quick glimpse of the theatre impresario, star maker, bon vivant and stretcher of the truth (he claimed to have discovered Lily Langtry), Henry B. Harris. She scoured her memory to see if there were any events where they might have met, but thankfully she could remember none. These faces heartened her, though. There would be sufficient glitz and intrigue to give her some sport while she sat at the bar and watched. All she needed now was someone to buy her a drink.

As if summoned by magic, a tall man appeared at Martha's side, doffing his hat. He had thick black hair and a moustache to match, and a smile that oozed self-satisfaction. 'I couldn't help but notice that you seem to be travelling alone,' he said, his accent revealing him to be a fellow American. 'Would you care to join me and make use of my porter?'

Martha flashed him her broadest, most sincere smile. 'Very kind of you.'

He clicked his fingers and a porter appeared, picking up Martha's bag and piling it onto an already well-stacked trolley.

'Heading for home?' the dark-haired man asked.

'Yes. You too?'

'Home is where I leave my hat these days. Business takes me most places.'

Martha laughed mirthlessly. God, a blowhard. That was all she needed.

'Have you been vacationing?' he asked.

'You could say that.'

'Wonderful country, England. Though a bit reserved for my tastes.' He leaned in conspiratorially. 'Shall we walk? I believe the entrance to the ship is just a short distance.'

I believe? Martha thought. You could see the tops of its funnels reaching high above the station building. Still, she nodded, took the man's arm, and they started to stroll. She decided to take the chance to get a bit of background.

'Do you know many of our fellow passengers?'

'Sure, some of them. The ones who travel regularly. I've seen a couple of familiar faces.' He turned and smiled. 'You must let me introduce you to some of them, Mrs . . .?'

'Heaton,' she said. 'Miss Martha Heaton.'

'It's a pleasure to meet you, Miss Heaton. My name is Darton. Lester Darton.'

The stream of people from the station was now a tide, swarming across the pier, porters rushing to and fro with great toppling piles of luggage, while others stood and smoked and gazed in silent awe at the vast ship. Martha noticed the first wisps of smoke wafting from the front three funnels of the boat.

'They're warming her up.' Darton's voice had risen due to his excitement. Even a seasoned ocean traveller like he was, or claimed to be, was being swept up in the event. 'We'll soon be on our way.'

Beck's tour of the *Titanic* had taken him along the maze of decks and passageways, of dining saloons and libraries and private rooms. His jaw dropped in the men-only first-class smoking room – where he vowed not to spend too much time – which was fitted out to resemble the Palace of Versailles. He walked along countless corridors and up and down several flights of stairs, yet had not even seen half the liner. The impression of being on a ship of unparalleled sumptuousness remained. Even the passengers in third class would be travelling in relative luxury. He passed many of them, all looking pleased and content with what would be their home for the next few days. He sympathised with the stewards who had to work on her; the ship was a veritable hive, a bewildering set of passageways so extensive that getting lost, taking a wrong turn, would be as easy as falling overboard.

Having had enough of exploring below decks, he headed for the cool air of the boat deck in time for the launch, and ended up wandering into the gymnasium. Some passengers were in there already, trying out the equipment; one woman giggling with excitement as she sat on a mechanical horse; a man in a full suit on some kind of rowing contraption. The instructor, McCawley, a great bear of a man as one might expect, his cheeks rosy with health, was proudly showing off the machines, drumming up business for the days ahead. Beck thought what a bit of swimming might do for him, but after a ride on one of the bicycle machines welded to the floor, feeling the blood pumping around his body and sweat on his brow, he decided to return. Who would have guessed that cycling nowhere could be enjoyable?

Back on deck he could see that the number of passengers had grown, most of them lining the port side nearest the dock. One man was holding a large camera, the new type that took moving pictures. Beck walked to the rail; some seventy feet or so below him, hundreds of people had gathered to see the ship off. A few were already waving handkerchiefs in farewell, their cries lost on the breeze. Some of those leaving might be gone for ever; this would be the last time many of them would see their kith and kin. Looking around at the calibre of his fellow first-class passengers, he guessed that most of those being waved off were in second and third class. Up here it seemed that a display of excitement could be uncouth. His palms were once again slick with sweat and a feeling of nagging doubt nestled at the back of his mind. But he managed to banish it. How spoiled by privilege could someone be to fail to be thrilled by such a glorious event? Others might not be impressed, but he was not going to allow cynicism to cloak his delight.

Beck glanced up at those funnels, the first three now beginning to churn out plumes of smoke, the gulls swooping through the thick black columns that rose into the grey sky. A stout man next to him began to laugh while nudging a lady friend. Beck followed his chubby pointing finger. A group of men hauling bundles of kit were at the bottom of a gangway on the dock, just aft of amidships. A petty officer was standing guard, making it clear from his gesticulations that they were not to be allowed on board.

The portly man wheezed with delight. 'They're too late!' The men, who were seeing the chance of valuable wages disappearing, did not share his joy.

They didn't give up easily, and while Beck couldn't hear what was being said, it was obvious that they were protesting loudly. In vain, as it turned out. All of a sudden the officer walked away and the gangway was gone, leaving the group of forlorn men abandoned on the dockside. He caught the twinkling eye of the portly gent at his side.

'Stayed in the pub too long, no doubt,' he said.

'The pub?'

'It's quite common for the firemen to have a few pots before getting on board. Thirsty work down there in the bowels, and they don't get a sniff of it until they get a day or two off at the other end. A lot of them make it for the muster, then nip off to The Grapes in town before coming back. This lot left it too late.' He laughed again.

Beck smiled, though part of him still felt sorry for the stokers, now sitting on their kit, heads in hands. That would be a difficult one to explain to their wives later that day. Probably best to head back to The Grapes and drown your sorrows, boys, he thought.

By now, even those on the boat deck feigning lack of interest seemed to be caught up in the growing excitement. The gangways were hauled up, the hawsers holding the ship to the pier were released, and, with three piercing blasts of her whistle, slowly but surely the great liner began to ease majestically away from her berth. As she moved, those on the dock moved with her, waving, some starting to run to keep up and shout a few last goodbyes. Beck expected some more noise and commotion, perhaps the sounds of bells and whistles from other ships at anchor, marking the maiden trip of this magnificent vessel, but there were none. The only sound he could catch, other than the growing rumbling of the ship's engines, was the sound of a mouth organ rising from a lower deck.

He watched the folk on the side gradually lose their race as the *Titanic* turned slightly to port and headed down the narrow channel that would take her out into the open sea. Anchored at the banks were several smaller liners, standing idle because of the recent coal strike, silent and passive, as if cowed by the sight of such a superior vessel.

The sound of gunfire echoed through the air. Two shots. Beck's heart began to hammer and he spun around, wondering where the noise was coming from. Not again, he thought.

The portly gent was staring at him.

'Gunshots!' Beck gasped. Instinctively he grabbed the lady at the man's side by her arm, as if urging her to take cover. 'Get down!'

He tried to pull her down as he fell into a crouch, the pain in his thigh stabbing, his hand reaching to his hip for a revolver that wasn't there. The woman wriggled free, though she looked shocked. Beck looked up at the man with her, whose face was twisted with anger.

'Let her be, man!' he said.

'Gunshots!' Beck said once more, louder this time. No one else seemed to be as shocked as he was, though all of them were starting to point and focus their attention off to port.

'Those weren't gunshots, you bloody fool! The ropes holding that steamer snapped.'

Beck looked back at the dock. A two-funnelled ship, little more than half *Titanic*'s size, had lost its moorings and its stern was swinging out into the water. He could hear a few gasps as he felt his cheeks turn crimson. He was about to turn and apologise when it became clear that the wake of the great ship was actually sucking the smaller one directly towards her, like a rubber duck caught in bathwater draining from a plughole. The boat carried on moving closer, as if pulled by some invisible string, and it became clear that *Titanic* did not have the speed to burst clear.

'Goodness me, she is going to hit our side!' Beck heard the portly man say. On the deck of the smaller vessel panicked sailors ran to and fro, paying out ropes over the side, one of which was caught by a small tug on the quayside, which then attempted to haul the ship back to dock. But the immense suction of the massive steamer's wake made their efforts futile.

The smaller ship was pulled closer and closer until a collision seemed inevitable. Beck and his fellow passengers stared speech - less, at the terrifying sight of the bigger vessel drawing the other one to its doom.

Then there was a surge, not of movement but of power, and the wash created as a result of what decision had been taken on the bridge pushed the smaller boat away from *Titanic*'s side. It glided away across her bow as the huge liner came to a slow stop.

There was silence as everyone took a breath and recovered their composure. The stout gentleman and his lady had forgotten Beck's earlier mistake. The man pushed his hat back on his forehead and smiled at Beck. 'Think that's enough excitement for one trip,' he said good-humouredly.

'I hope so,' Beck said quietly. 'I'm sorry about grabbing your friend. I honestly thought—'

The portly man held up his hand. 'Think nothing of it. Go and get a brandy – you look like you need it.' He glanced at his pocket watch. 'Come on, my dear,' he said to his lady friend. 'All that excitement has given me an appetite. Time for lunch. Good day to you, sir.'

Beck smiled and tipped his hat to the lady, only then noticing a tremor in his hands. Anyone watching him might have thought it was down to the near miss, but he knew better; it had been the sound of gunshots, two pistol cracks that took him back to a darker and more violent place and time. He drew in a deep breath just as the ship appeared to do likewise, its engines rumbling back to life.

Briefly stationary in Southampton Water, the estuary of the river Test that led them out into the Solent and away from England, Beck couldn't help but turn and look back towards land, suddenly apprehensive. He thought about Sarah – and about London, his home city, encrusted with the damp grime of the ages, shrouded in thick fog and choking smoke, barely warmed by a weak and pale sun, and felt a yearning to be back there.

The anxiety and doubt that he had smothered earlier now broke over him. What the bloody hell was he doing, running away like this? Why was he taking such a step? He had only told one person and he'd thought Beck was mad. All of a sudden Beck agreed with him: it felt stupid, wrong. He was a coward, a quitter. But he knew he could not go back. Not for a long time.

Maybe not for ever.

Considering she was on a boat and would be for the greater part of the next week, Martha felt in a surprisingly good mood. An hour into the voyage and already she was sitting down to lunch with a decent appetite. Other than the noticeable vibration caused by its motion, the ship was steady and stable; there was the sense of a slight lean to the left, but that might just have been her. What pleased her most was the lack of rocking or lurching. The real test of the *Titanic*'s steadiness would come when they were out in the open Atlantic, but for once she could believe the hyperbole: off deck, away from the sight of the sea, in one of the lavish reception rooms, it was almost possible to forget you were afloat and not a guest in some swanky hotel.

The other reason for her good mood was the near-collision when they were leaving Southampton, with a ship she'd been told was the *New York*. Imagine the irony, she thought, of a liner heading for New York crashing into one bearing that name. The drama would at least give her finished article some narrative drive and incident, rather than it being simply a dry list of the ship's luxuries and charms – though Martha had to admit there were many of those: her berth boasted a bath and thankfully no view of the sea, and the bed was just that, a bed and not a bunk.

Finally, Darton had turned out be a nautical buff and pretty well connected. He was also slimier than dripping oil, all smarm and wandering hands, and had attached himself to Martha like a barnacle to a hull. But as he seemed to be a fount of maritime knowledge, his attention's were a price worth paying. She would have to find some time to burst his balloon over the coming days, but a slow puncture would serve best.

It turned out that he had sailed on several previous voyages captained by Edward John Smith – 'Smithy' he called him, as if he were an old acquaintance – and described him as an affable, friendly sailor, popular with the regulars of the transatlantic crossing. Darton had been talking with a crew member after the near-miss, one of the senior officers he also knew from previous journeys, a Scot named Murdoch, and reported back that the captain had avoided the danger by making one of the propellers surge, an action which had created the wash that had pushed away the smaller vessel.

They sat down in the dining saloon for lunch – Darton said, to Martha's unconfined joy, that by happy chance they were to be seated at the same table in the dining saloon for the whole voyage – accompanied by two other single lady travellers, one of them a vivacious, forthright woman named Hardee to whom Martha took an immediate liking. There were also two couples, one with their single daughter in tow, a girl who remained silent and sullen throughout the meal, as did a young German baron, whose only contribution to the proceedings, other than a look of pure arrogance, was to slurp his soup extremely loudly.

Each of them gave the floor to Darton to waffle on about nautical matters, while Martha took mental notes. Darton had no idea what she did for a living since he hadn't asked, simply assuming that a woman travelling first class was a lady of leisure. Normally that kind of presumption would have annoyed her, but here it was in her best interests to let it slide.

The waiters, all seemingly Latin men, brought the women their chosen meals of fillets of brill, while the men seemed to have gone for Chicken à la Maryland (Martha wondered what a staple food of the poor in the US – fried chicken – was doing on the first-class menu of this ship of dreams) or the corned beef. Darton held court. Glancing around conspiratorially, speaking often in a stagy whisper, he started to talk about Captain Smith.

'Thing is with Smithy, he's been at this game for a long time now,' he said, putting a forkful of chicken in his mouth before laying the implement back on his plate. Martha thought it was a good job there were only Yankees like her at the table; any Brits would probably have been horrified.

'Which is all very reassuring for we passengers, who like a familiar face, particularly when it's as friendly and as avuncular as Smithy's.' Martha had caught sight of the captain shortly after the launch, peering over the side of the bridge. He had a white beard and a grandfatherly air. The sort of calm presence you wanted at the helm of such a powerful vessel. Darton took a large sip of his wine and leaned forward.

'However, I have it on good authority this is to be his last trip. I'm not sure if he's chosen to go, or whether he was asked to leave, if you catch my drift. But taking *Titanic* on her maiden voyage is his swansong.'

'Well, given his record of service, I can't imagine they forced him out,' said Kimball, one of the other men, who owned a piano company in Boston.

Darton tilted his head to one side, smirking. 'You might think that. However, today's incident was not his first brush with danger.'

'You're talking about the *Olympic*, I presume?' Kimball said. Darton nodded. 'I thought that was the fault of the pilot leading her out of Southampton?'

'Forgive my ignorance,' Martha said. 'Some of us aren't as familiar as others with some of the ships you mention.'

Darton nodded in a rather patronising fashion. 'Of course. *Olympic* is *Titanic*'s sister ship. Almost the same – I sailed on her maiden voyage too – but not quite as big, nor quite as well appointed. Much of the detail she lacked has been added to *Titanic*. But I digress; on her fifth voyage, in September of last year, she struck a naval cruiser. Due to the extent of the damage caused, the voyage was cancelled and she returned to Belfast for repairs. A similar sort of fate would have befallen us to today had we not avoided the danger, I guess. Mr Kimball is correct in saying that it was the pilot who was at the helm, but he was under Smithy's direction. There was some confusion over the course, I was told.'

He drained the wine from his glass, his third by Martha's counts. She could only imagine how unbearable Darton might become when he was drunk. He continued: 'My point is that these ships have become so huge, and their engines so powerful, that it takes a special skill to steer them safely. Smithy grew up on ships half the size of this. It's more about the law of physics now than the law of the sea, the way these vessels can suck others towards them because of their sheer heft. It's a whole new game. I think Ismay and his boys realise this, and want a younger, perhaps more modern guy, to lead the fleet.'

Kimball didn't look convinced. 'I was told the navy ship rammed *Olympic*. That it was no fault of the liner at all.'

Darton held up a finger, his eyes bright. 'That's the story White Star would have you believe. It's hardly excellent publicity to proclaim the fallibility of your most senior and respected skipper, is it? I also think that's the story Smithy tells himself. He refuses to accept any culpability, which might indicate another reason why they are rather keener to see the back of him than they might ordinarily have been: overconfidence. He has little doubt of his abilities, or the abilities of his ship.'

Miss Hardee let out a huff of derision. 'I'd rather have a captain who is confident than one who's fearful.' There was a murmur of agreement around the table.

Darton shrugged. 'Perhaps. That's just what I've been told. Don't get me wrong, I like the man. I have no problem with him as a captain at all. I merely tell you all this because it shows how far we have advanced. Captain Smith came through the school of hard knocks. The first ships he sailed on *had* sails. It's a different world now. Look at this,' he said, moving his arms apart to indicate the whole room. 'How far can it go? How big can these ships possibly get? And look!' Here he pointed to his wine glass, recently refilled. 'She doesn't spill a drop, or cause so much as a ripple! Remarkable.'

These ships could double in size and still not be as big as your head, thought Martha. Yet she couldn't deny the exchange had been fascinating, as was the question that Darton had posed: just how far could engineers and inventors go in their quest to provide the human race with comfort and convenience? Surely a ship such as *Titanic* was the pinnacle of their achievement?

There followed a conversation between the men about 400-kilowatt steam-powered generators and dynamos and boilers and revolutions, during which Martha concentrated on her food, which was too rich and buttery for her taste. She tuned back in when the discussion turned to speed and how long the journey might take. Kimball said he wondered if the owners had hopes for the Blue Riband award for the fastest crossing, currently held by a Cunard ship.

Darton dismissed the idea with a wave of his hand, his reddening cheeks hinting at his growing drunkenness. 'Ships like this, for all their ample power, cannot hope to match the Cunards for speed. The whole appeal is luxury and size. Plus, as it's her maiden voyage, I doubt they will yet know how fast *Titanic* can go. I'm told that they hope to beat the time it took for the *Olympic* to make her first crossing. It would make good publicity and we all know how much Ismay likes publicity. Though today's brush with danger wouldn't have been the kind he is after.'

From that point on, the discussion splintered and Martha found herself speaking with Miss Hardee, who had turned away from the German baron in disgust at an ungallant comment of his. 'I'm going to ask the chief steward if I can be seated elsewhere,' she whispered.

'I didn't realise you could change tables,' Martha whispered back. 'I may well do the same.'

A look of surprise appeared on Miss Hardee's face. 'Are you and Mr Darton not travelling companions?'

It took a while for her to realise what she was hinting at. 'Oh God, no,' she said, rather too loudly, her 'blasphemy' bringing a dark look to Mrs Kimball's face. 'We just met at the train station. He helped find me a porter.'

'Good. Keep a close eye on him if you don't move tables, though. You seem like a woman who can handle herself and you need to be able to on these voyages. There are sharps and scoundrels everywhere, and not just at the card tables.' Miss Hardee raised her eyebrows and leaned in closer. 'Though there are other men on board who make fine escorts.'

Sten-Ake Gustafson lay on his bunk, alone in the cabin, the sound of his blood pumping in his ears drowned by the vibration from the great ship's engines. The others must all be at lunch, he thought. He did not feel like eating – but then, he rarely did these days, which explained why his trousers were increasingly difficult to keep up. Not that he cared much about that. Or about anything else, for that matter, other than reaching the United States and having the chance to see Katerina, his daughter, her husband and his grandchildren for the first time. Given his worsening health, it would probably also be the last.

Gustafson had meant to seek out a steward and in his faltering English ask for a new berth. But he was just too tired. The journey from Gothenburg to Hull had been exhausting enough for a man of his age and condition. But then the train journey to Southampton had taken the best part of ten hours. He'd been squashed into a seat, his spine twisted and contorted, the pain in his abdomen from the cancer growing ever more unbearable. He had left his morphine in his luggage, thinking that he could last a few hours without it. He had been wrong.

Since boarding the *Titanic* he had been asleep, or trying to sleep, while the drug did its best to push the pain to the edge of his awareness. He had heard everything. The engines growling into life, and the great shuddering that accompanied the liner's departure and which soon subsided to a smooth hum, reassuring to someone seeking the comfort of sleep, a sound to focus on to distract him from the intermittent agonies. Then the ship had seemed to stop and start and stop once more. Only later did Gustafson hear why, from the gabbled remarks of his fellow steerage passengers – or at least the ones who spoke a language he understood – passing by in the corridor. There had almost been a collision. Then there was an hour's wait as the boat that had been sucked into the great vessel's path was rounded up and towed back to its berth. Now they were off again.

What a ship. Gustafson was a fisherman by trade, and had spent some time in the merchant navy, so he knew the sea. But never could he have imagined a ship of this size and beauty. As he had hobbled along the dock, leaning on his stick, he'd been forced to stop and stare for a few minutes at the *Titanic* to take in all its glory. If only his friend and old partner Klaes could have seen it. But Klaes was gone. As was his beloved Malin. There had been no one and nothing left for him in Gothenburg. So he had sold off what little he had, taken the cash and stitched most of it into his jacket lining, collected the few possessions he had left and booked his passage to the United States. Then he'd sent a letter to Katerina informing her of his estimated time of arrival in New York. He did not expect her or her husband to meet him. He would take a train to Harrisburg, where they lived, on the same day as his arrival and they could meet him there.

His doctor had warned against it. 'You are dying, Sten-Ake,' he'd said. As if Gustafson needed telling! A few months ago, when he'd still had an appetite but the weight had been falling from him like leaves from a tree in autumn, he'd known that something was wrong. Then had come the pain. He'd needed the doctor for relief, rather than information or advice. 'Stay here and die in your own home,' the doctor had urged. But Gustafson wanted to see his grandchildren, and his only daughter, to say goodbye properly and hand her the sum of his life savings.

'I fear you might not be well enough to survive such an arduous journey,' the doctor had added, in a low sonorous voice.

'Well, if I die, then at least I shall die trying,' Gustafson said. 'Rather than sitting here alone, waiting for death's hand on my shoulder.'

The doctor had nodded slowly. 'Then I will pray for you to make a safe crossing.'

'Save your prayers for those that want them,' Gustafson had responded. 'I do not believe in any God. Not any more.'

The doctor's face, long and drawn, had become ever more concerned, presumably at the prospect of a man dying without knowing the comfort of the Lord. Sten-Ake could live without his pity.

The medical examiner at Southampton had been far more his type. Before getting on board each steerage-class passenger was checked to see whether they were carrying any infectious diseases along with their luggage, an inconvenience foisted only upon their category. The young examiner, brisk and humorous, could see straight away that Sten-Ake Gustafson was ill.

'What is it?'

'Cancer.'

'That's all right. It's not contagious,' the examiner said, smiling sympathetically yet without any false pity.

And Gustafson was allowed on board.

Yet his Swedish physician had been right. He was spent, exhausted, and there was still a week's sailing to come. At least he had a bunk. Maybe with rest some appetite might return, and with food might come strength. Compared to the battered old liner on which he had crossed from Sweden, and the cramped train, this berth's soft mattresses were the greatest luxury. Yes, he would rest now. When he felt up to it he would go on deck and get some sea air. He loved that saltwater smell, had known it all his life. It never failed to revive him.

The only problem was his fellow occupants. There were six berths, and all the other five were taken. All of them by Finns. All men. Young at that, full of excitement and chatter at the prospect of a new life in America. Not the companions that a dying old man needed on a long journey. They would be drinking – Gustafson had known some Finns from his time in the merchant navy as a young man and they'd had a thirst that would have made the Sahara proud – and talking about their dreams and hopes, their plans and expectations well into the night. It would be churlish to fault them for that, on the cusp of a new life, but he required rest and it might be in scant supply. He wondered if there might be another room, with people nearer his own age, or even one that was empty – there was talk that the boat was not filled to its capacity, though the crowded docks appeared to make a lie of that. Yet the rigmarole of finding a steward, making his case in an unfamiliar language, then moving his luggage and weary body to another berth, perhaps even one in another part of this enormous ship, was too much of an effort. He would stay put and hope the young Finns were not so rowdy.

Some chance, Gustafson thought. And tomorrow they would be picking up the Irish, who were hardly renowned for their temperance. He managed a smile as a memory flashed across his mind, a recollection of landing at an Irish port more than forty years ago, of being ashore and a night of dancing and merriment with a couple of the most beautiful fun-loving girls he had ever seen or met. Yes, if his body allowed, he would like to go on deck and see that green land once more. It would be for the last time, after all. Then he let out a sigh.

His house, the old town of his birth, his neighbours, now this ship, and finally the sea: much of what he was seeing would be for the last time. But then, what was life if not a series of losses?

With that thought, along with other hazy memories, distant and more recent, of all that had been lost, Sten-Ake Gustafson fell into a merciful sleep.

Beck had decided against lunch. The incident with the *New York* and the 'gunshots' had ruined his appetite, so he went back to his cabin and read, not wanting any company. The excitement, the drone of the ship's engines, his underlying exhaustion, all meant that he was soon dozing soundly on his bed.

When he woke it was past five in the afternoon, and he was hungry, though dinner was still a few hours away. Rather than order something to keep him going, he chose to make do with a cigarette and a brisk walk on deck. They were due into France soon to collect more passengers and he wouldn't mind watching those people come aboard.

Beck wandered up the Grand Staircase, drawn to the dome above the stairs and a huge gilt-framed chandelier that had recently been switched on and now flooded the whole area with bright light. He passed a few of his fellow voyagers so entranced that they were standing still, staring upwards, admiring, unaware of other people passing. At this rate every passenger would reach New York with a cricked neck, he thought.

The early-evening sun was still glinting off the calm sea as Beck stepped out onto the long wooden promenade deck that was open to the darkening skies above. He chose the port side to walk along after asking a crew member which might give him the best view of land. In the distance he could see twinkling lights and behind them a looming dark mass. Cherbourg, and beyond it France, he thought. The edge of a whole continent.

Behind him he heard an excited scream that made him jump. He was still easily startled, jumping at nothing. It was exhausting to live your life on a knife edge.

Beck turned around. A small girl, maybe no more than seven or so, was playing a game of chase with another. She was smiling, at the excitement of being on a boat and of having the run of the deck, at the sheer joy of being alive. It brought back an awful memory. A prickling sweat broke out on his brow and his breathing became shallow and constricted. The girl smiled at him but he couldn't bring himself to smile back. He kept thinking over and over of a girl of a similar age, lying across her bed, the life stolen from her . . .

'Cara!' The girls' mother was calling. She came and scooped her up. 'It's dinner time,' she scolded. She flashed an apologetic smile at Beck. It turned to concern when she saw his perspiring features. They hurried away, leaving him, drenched with sweat, a pounding headache brought on by tension spreading slowly across his head to the backs of his eyes.

He tried to breathe normally. Gradually, the panic subsided. He lit a cigarette and looked out over the sea, wanting something, anything, to distract him.

Beck smoked away, leaning over the liner's steep side, forward at the furthest end of the first-class promenade, as far as he could go without having his view blocked by a big white lifeboat. Thankfully there were only a few of those; his detective's eye spotted the empty davits that were meant to secure them. Someone must have been certain they wouldn't all be needed.

He watched the waves created by the ship some seventy feet below as the land and its scattering of lights grew near. A few other passengers joined him at the rails, though the fading light seemed to discouraged most. Gradually the ship came to a halt a mile out to sea, unable to enter the port because of its size. Towards land, through the dusk, he could see two tenders making their way out to the ship's immense side.

Beck strolled aft along the deck, glancing over at the two boats as they neared. One appeared to be making its way to the starboard side, the other towards the stern of the port side where he stood. He reached the point where the division separated the first-class promenade from the smaller second-class area. Over the barrier he watched a young boy bounce merrily along the deck, being chased by his father. Beyond that he could see the third-class outdoor space, at the furthest part of the stern. How appropriate, he thought, that those in first could look down on those in second, while both loomed above the passengers in third. In more usual times, he would have been down there, in second, even third. Would he have preferred that? Perhaps. He knew that those in first class, their money aside, were no better than him, but the whole ambience was exclusive and it made him feel uncomfortable. Thank goodness for the brash Americans who slurped their soup, boasted of their wealth and injected some much-needed common sense to the mix.

Lost in these idle thoughts, Beck watched for a few moments before lighting another cigarette and walking to the side to see one of the tenders unload its cargo.

The boat had stopped, and a gangway had been fixed between

it and the entrance below. A crew member made his way across to the tender and soon after the passengers began to board. Despite the gathering gloom, Beck could see them stepping precariously off the boat and onto the walkway. From their clothes and Mediterranean appearance he could tell they were steerage, no doubt on their way to the United States in search of a new life. Seeking a fresh start in a strange land. Still, Beck was not leaving behind grinding poverty, or relentless toil, just a bunch of regrets and mistakes.

A steady stream of people came aboard, some of them families, the occasional woman travelling alone, but mainly men, swarthy, some looking bold and eager, others timid and unsure. Many of them might have come from landlocked places where the sea was a distant rumour and ships like this could not be imagined even in dreams. No wonder a few wore looks of outright terror, casting fearful glances up the towering dark walls of steel hanging over them. But even more people were looking up in awe.

One by one they shuffled aboard, their faces illuminated in the gloom. Young and old, some taking their hats off as if they were entering a stranger's home. Beck watched as one young man, little more than a boy, suffered a funk and baulked at the end of the gangway. He hurried back towards the tender, only to be bundled aboard by two men behind, his histrionic protests rising up for all to hear. Steerage would be one boisterous place – all those different cultures. With the Irish yet to board. Beck smiled. Maybe first class wasn't so bad after all. With each passing hour it was looking like money well spent.

The flow of passengers was slowing, and he could see the crew on board the tender preparing to load great sacks of mail. His gaze went back to the last few to board who were now approaching the ramp. Among them was a family that included a small girl holding a red balloon.

The little girl seemed to stumble climbing up to the gangway. As she did she lost her grip on the balloon. She let out a plaintive cry as it floated upwards. An older boy attempted to jump up and grab it but it had risen out of reach. The passengers waiting behind all seemed to be looking up at the red balloon, intrigued by the commotion it had caused.

There was a cry from below in a language that Beck didn't understand. The balloon was rising fast, bumping against the ship's side. A man was shouting and gesturing for him to catch it. It was almost within his grasp, but as it reached the level of the boat deck it was caught by a breeze and floated out of reach, out to sea. He watched as it drifted away, the sobs of the child from below now heart-wrenching. Beck cursed himself for being unable to help.

Then his gaze caught someone. A man watching the balloon. A handsome face.

A face he knew too well.

Beck's heart froze.

No.

Could it be?

It had happened so quickly, a glance of no more than a second. Beck turned away from the rail, not noticing the blaze of lights coming from inside the ship or the wafting smell of food that signalled dinner was about to be served. He stumbled away as if he had seen a ghost.

He went straight to a door which opened onto a flight of steps. As he raced down them, he tried to calculate how many decks he might have to descend. The entrance the passengers had embarked through was at sea level. He was on B deck. Perhaps two decks below that? Three? His heart started to beat hard as he continued his descent.

What were the chances, Beck thought as he raced down more stairs, of *him* being on board? The rumour was that he had fled to Europe. Other reports indicated that his ultimate destination was the USA. Those had come in only a few weeks before. The coal strike had delayed many ships bound for the States in the past six weeks; *Titanic* had been one of the first to set sail for some time, so it was not impossible that the man was one of the passengers.

There was a door at the bottom of the stairs. Beck opened it and found himself looking down long corridor. By the furnishings he could see that it was still in the first-class section. Maybe if he followed this route it would take him along to the Grand Staircase, via which he could reach the lower decks. But then, what about the bulkheads? How high did they reach, and how would that affect his route? The map in his room showed only the first-class areas. His tour of the ship earlier that day had taught him how confusing the layout of the ship was. To go charging off would be a sure way to get lost.

A steward emerged from a room, steam from a running bath billowing behind him. A towel was folded over his arm and his face was red and sweating, as was Beck's after his sprint downstairs.

'What deck is this?'

'C deck, sir.'

'The passengers who just embarked from Cherbourg – where would they have got on?'

The steward gave it a moment's thought. 'Aft, starboard. E deck, I believe, sir. Many of them are just making their way to their rooms via the second-class areas.'

'No, not the first-class travellers,' Beck said impatiently. Sweat continued to pour from his brow and his chest tightened. 'The steerage passengers.'

'Steerage? Not entirely sure about that, sir. But I think it might be aft E deck, portside. I can't be certain, though. My area is first class. Is there a problem?'

'I need to get to steerage. Which is the quickest way?'

The steward gave out a small mirthless laugh. 'Not sure I could say, sir. I don't know the ship very well yet. There are third-class sections forward and aft.'

'Aft,' Beck said. Though it dawned on him that the passengers only entered the ship towards the stern and could have been taken through to their accommodation in the bow.

'I'm not rightly sure, sir. Is there someone in particular you need to contact there? Only I—'

This was hopeless, Beck thought. By now the crowd that had boarded recently would have dispersed and be on their way to the berths. 'How many steerage passengers are there?'

Again the steward thought. 'She can hold upward of a thousand but I'm not sure how many are booked on this crossing, sir. Are you sure I can't help?'

'No, it's quite all right.' Beck's heart rate was returning to normal, the rush of adrenalin subsiding; running blindly around a ship so vast would be pointless. He needed a plan, some clear thinking, and a guide. 'Who should I see about getting access to third class? It may be a matter I have to speak to the captain about.'

'Purser McElroy is the man you need to see, sir. His office is next to the enquiry office on C deck, just by the first-class entrance there.'

McElroy. The name was familiar. Then Beck remembered why. It was written on an invitation that had been slipped under his door that afternoon, asking for his company at the purser's dinner table. While this wasn't a suitable subject for discussion over dinner, he might find a chance to ask for McElroy's help afterwards, and the purser might be more willing to help if he had dined with Beck and knew his name.

Beck thanked the steward and hurried back to his room to dress for dinner, his anxiety giving way to calm assurance. If the man he'd seen getting on board was who he thought, then the fellow was trapped, regardless of how big the ship was.

Beck smiled. Could it be that the most wanted man in England, public enemy number one, was finally cornered?

Martha was beginning to wonder if there was anything else to do on a steamship except eat and sleep. After lunch she had read, slept for a while, then walked on the covered deck, all the while trying to avoid Darton. She would be spared his company that evening because she had been chosen to dine with the chief purser. She wasn't sure if this was an honour, or if the captain dined with the debutantes while the purser ate with the wallflowers.

After taking some time to get herself ready – thank goodness she had brought a few good outfits, as all the women were in elegant gowns and the men in smart evening dress – she took her invitation to the dining room, feeling awkward and self-conscious; it seemed as if everyone knew each other.

Even more of the gilded few had boarded at Cherbourg, fresh from trips to the pyramids of Egypt and the boutiques of Paris. Martha had bought an evening gown on expenses and was wearing it only because convention said she should. The receipt was back in her apartment on the Upper West Side, and if she got through the voyage without spilling any soup on it, or snagging the damn thing on a table or chair, then she planned to take it back and retrieve her money.

The rest of the women in the dining room that evening were rather less calculating. They owned hundreds of these gowns, Martha guessed, and only the newest and best were getting an airing tonight. As if they were saying, 'This dress cost me a thousand bucks and I'm going to show it off.' If she'd been the type to be bothered by that sort of thing, she would be in her room now, mascara running down her face, vowing never to leave her room. As it was she didn't care. To Martha it was like playing a part.

Looking around, she had to suppress a smirk when she saw another of her newspaper's staples, Benny Guggenheim, in deep conversation with a fellow moneybags. What was this? Some kind of ship devoted to people embroiled in scandals? Benny, or 'The Silver Prince' as her paper referred to him because he had made a mint out of selling and buying silver or something, was a happily married man. So happily married that he had a mistress, a French actress. A woman who, if Martha wasn't mistaken, was at his side this very second. Man, this was like shooting fish in a barrel. She shook her head. On her return she would be making a good friend of the gossip columnist. A short, squat man who doused himself in bad cologne and cheap booze, he needed some stories to keep the editor at bay – and she needed someone to keep her supplied with Martinis.

Despite the new arrivals the saloon was little more than half full. Still, there were enough people milling around to create a lively hubbub as they bobbed up from their tables every five seconds to greet another old acquaintance. She passed and nodded a greeting to Darton, who was with the same group as lunch, minus Martha and Miss Hardee, who had been good to her word and found another table. Martha could see her in a far corner, deep in conversation with a tall, handsome man – presumably one of the escorts she had mentioned.

Eventually Martha reached the purser's table and saw that she was the last to arrive. The purser, a tall, burly man with a doughy yet handsome face and a pair of twinkling blue eyes, greeted her warmly and introduced her four other dining companions, four men and another female, all seemingly single travellers. It crossed her mind fleetingly that this might be some kind of introduction agency for the perennially lonely. The names passed by her in a blur as McElroy, in an accent she found hard to define but thought was close to Irish, listed them. Martha nodded and smiled at each in turn before taking a seat and asking the waiter, hovering attentively, if she could have a Martini straight up with an olive. A minute later it was there, shimmering in a glass in front of her. There were obvious benefits to dining with the staff. She took a sip. Perfectly mixed. Buoyed, she was able to take a better look at her dining companions, all hanging on the purser's words, laughing and smiling at each comment.

The other woman, sitting directly opposite, smiled at her awkwardly, looking somewhat relieved, and sipped a glass of iced water, so plummeting instantly in Martha's estimation. Great, she thought, you sip your water demurely and watch me get loaded. Next to her was the purser, amply filling his chair. To his right and Martha's left were four gentleman. One, called Harrison, a musty-looking character whom she guessed to be in his mid-forties, seemed to be familiar with the purser. Two of the others were father and son, called Williams, who had just boarded at Cherbourg. Last of all was an Englishman named Beck. Tall, his dark hair neatly cropped, clean-shaven, he was serious-looking but had a smile that lit up his whole face when the purser told a story about how he was once asked to care for a female passenger's lapdog that had developed a rather unfortunate illness.

In between spinning yarns, the purser spent much of his time jumping up to greet familiar passengers. During one of those interludes, when the other people at the table had to speak among themselves, Martha turned to the Englishman at her side. In a corner somewhere out of sight, the ship's orchestra was trying to compete with the growing rumble of conversation and was losing.

'I find it remarkable that everyone seems to know each other so well,' she said.

Beck nodded. So far during the meal he had seemed slightly on edge, as if eager to get it over with, and he had barely touched either the soup or the fish course – though he was less controlled with his wine. 'I know exactly what you mean. It's like being invited to a party where everyone else there is acquainted but you don't know a single person.'

She smiled. 'That's exactly how I feel. I take it you're not a regular on these crossings?'

'Goodness, no. It's the first one I've ever been on. It's been an eye-opener so far. How about you?'

'My second trip on a liner. The first one was the crossing to England.'

'Going home, then?'

'Yes.'

'Where would that be?'

'New York. How about you?'

'London.'

'Vacation? Sorry – holiday?'

Beck smiled. 'It's all right. I speak fluent American. I've worked with *a few swell guys*,' he said with what he hoped was a New York twang in his voice.

His accent was actually appalling, making him sound Welsh, but Martha appreciated the effort. 'Very good. Is that the reason you're heading west? Work?'

'Not really. I just fancied a trip to New York. I've heard good things about it.'

'I'm sure they're all true. If you like crowds, spending lots of money, noise and mayhem. But since you're from London, I assume you do. How long are you staying?'

Beck paused for a few seconds, as if it was a difficult question. 'Just a couple of weeks,' he answered eventually. 'Was your trip for pleasure?'

'No. Work.' He seemed friendly, charming and, unlike many of the stuffed shirts around here, unwilling to take himself so seriously.

'Really? What sort of work?'

Martha paused. She did not know this guy, though she already felt she could trust him. But with other flapping ears in the vicinity, she thought it best to be discreet. 'Just gathering information for a project.'

'Sounds rather mysterious,' Beck replied. That had not been Martha's intention. She'd aimed to deflect rather than invite any curiosity. But then, she was a lousy liar, a flaw which would probably be her journalistic downfall, where being able to tell the greatest whoppers with the straightest face seemed to be the most valued skill.

'Not really. What about you? What's your line of business?'

'Funnily enough, I'm in the information-gathering business too.'

'Now who's being mysterious?'

He shrugged. 'Touché.'

'Look at us,' Martha said, lifting her drink, the light glinting from the clear liquid. 'To information gathering.'

Beck raised his wine glass and nodded his approval of the toast.

'What sort of information do you gather?' she asked.

'You tell me and I'll tell you.'

'I could tell you,' she said, knowingly. 'But then I'd have to kill you.' The effects of the Martini were beginning to kick in.

'You're only making me more curious.'

'Maybe that's my intention,' she said.

They were interrupted by the waiters bringing their main courses, an interval during which the purser seized the chance to embark on one of his stories. Martha looked at the food in front of her and felt she wouldn't be able to eat another thing. She was still sated from lunch. From the corner of her eye she glanced at the young Englishman. He was watching the purser and acting as if he was listening to him, but something told her his focus was elsewhere and that he couldn't wait to get away. Shame, she thought. Still, the voyage was not yet a day old.

It had certainly just got a damn sight more interesting.

After finishing his main course – the purser didn't have the figure of a man who wasted food – McElroy stood up, apologised for having to leave because he was on duty, and wished them a pleasant voyage.

'Don't hesitate to come and see either me or my staff at any time, no matter how trivial the matter.' With a small, gracious bow he left.

Beck had barely touched his beef, but immediately got to his feet and followed the purser, feeling guilty for deserting the rest of the table, not least the intriguing and beautiful American woman he had spoken to briefly. Despite the distraction of what he had seen at Cherbourg, or believed he had seen, and which had kept him on edge all evening, when he had been speaking with her it was as if nothing else had mattered. She was so unstuffy, not at all like the buttoned-up women he was used to. Still feminine, but her gaze and manner were direct. He had enjoyed every second of her company. Yet now he had more pressing business.

At the saloon entrance he caught up with McElroy. 'Purser, please excuse me. Your offer of assistance?'

There was an amused twinkle in the other man's eye. 'So soon, Mr Beck! Was the food not to your liking? Only I noticed you hadn'd eaten very much of it.'

'No, it was fine. I just don't have much of an appetite. Still finding my sea legs. But I have an urgent matter that I may need your assistance with. Perhaps even the captain's.'

The sparkle in McElroy's eye faded. 'Oh really, sir? That sounds ominous.'

'Is there anywhere we could speak privately?'

McElroy glanced at his watch. 'I was about to conduct my rounds of the other saloons. But I could hold on a little longer. Follow me.'

They left the saloon and went upstairs, along the corridor to the forward grand staircase. Across from the entrance where Beck had boarded the ship that morning, beside the enquiry office, McElroy unlocked a door. 'Come in,' he said.

The room was as well appointed as the rest of the ship, with a large mahogany desk and a small chaise longue. Beck's eyes were drawn to a large metal safe at the far end. A Ratner safe. Pretty secure. It was mounted on an oak stand with two iron bars attaching it to the ceiling. He wondered what they kept in it.

'Now, how can I be of assistance, Mr Beck?' There was a tone of weariness in the purser's voice, as if it was too late in the day to be dealing with passenger complaints, though perhaps that was Beck's imagination. In any case, sizing up McElroy, he decided to be forthright and honest.

'I am a Scotland Yard detective – Special Branch. While my passage on this ship is not connected with my work, a matter has come to my attention that I may need to deal with, and I may need the assistance of the crew.'

McElroy's eyes glinted once more. 'Well, makes a change from being asked to look after someone's canary. What sort of matter are we talking about?'

'On the promenade deck earlier this evening, while we were stopping to pick up passengers at Cherbourg, I believe I saw a man boarding your ship who is wanted in the UK.'

McElroy let out a whistle this time. 'You believe?'

'Yes, I believe. I can't say for certain. It would be wrong of me not to investigate further, however.'

'I can see that it would be.' The purser's fingers danced on the desk. 'What sort of assistance are we talking about?'

'To begin with, I'd like to see a copy of the passenger manifest, or at least the one for those who embarked at Cherbourg. Then I'd like permission to move freely about the ship, starting with the steerage area.'

McElroy's large fingers continued to drum out an insistent beat on the desk. 'I see.' He paused for a while longer, clearly deep in thought. 'I think you're right: this is a matter you need to take up with the captain. Is this man dangerous?'

Beck did not want to create panic. If he told the truth – that the man he might have seen was a cold-blooded killer who could pose a grave and murderous threat – he would do exactly that. 'Not at the moment. If indeed it *is* him. The first thing I need to do is confirm that fact.'

McElroy nodded slowly. 'All right, sir. Here's what I think we should do. I will go and have a word with the captain. You wait here. Once I have had a chance to speak with him, I'll report back to you. Do you have any kind of official identification with you that confirms your position? I don't mean to sound rude, but we do occasionally have people report things to us which turn out to be hoaxes. Though I'm sure that's not the case here.'

'No, of course – no need to apologise,' Beck replied. His mouth had dried, and the vague sense of unease returned. Coming forward like this hardly fitted with his plan to remain anonymous, to slip quietly out of the UK and into the USA. But there was no way he could erase what he had seen earlier that evening from his mind. Or thought he had seen.

He fished in his pocket for his identity badge before passing it on to McElroy. The chief purser looked at it for a few seconds before handing it back.

'Very good, sir. I will speak to the captain and ask if he's able to see you. Given the time, while he might be able to see you tonight, I doubt whether you'll be given permission to tour the steerage area this evening. Men and women are requested to turn in down there at ten-thirty.'

'I thought it was midnight.'

'In first class, sir – in the smoking room at least. Eleven-thirty in second class. But we try not to encourage people in steerage to stay up too late. It can cause . . . problems, particularly if they have a drink inside them, if you catch my drift. We actually request that female passengers are off the decks by nine p.m. – ten p.m. at the latest – to discourage any unseemly behaviour.'

Beck nodded. He understood. 'I can start my inquiry in the morning. Of course, I'll be as discreet as possible.'

McElroy ceased his finger drumming, and started to leave.

'One more question, Mr McElroy. Is there any chance that I can send a message via the Marconi Room?'

'Of course, sir.' The purser disappeared through a connecting door into the adjoining office and returned with a form. 'If you fill that in, sir, then it will be sent up to the Marconi Room for dispatch. Can you excuse me for a few minutes?'

Beck nodded, glad of the privacy. He sat at the desk and pondered his words. Eventually he scrawled out a note:

Detective Alec Dunston
Metropolitan Police
c/o Scotland Yard
10 April 1912

ALEC. SUSPEC PP ON BOARD TITANIC. ANY INTEL TO CONFIRM? AB

A few minutes passed during which he recalled the image of the man looking up at the drifting balloon and wondered again whether the chain of events he was about set in motion was justified.

McElroy returned. Beck handed over the message, offering a silent prayer that Dunston was on duty and not off on holiday. The purser said: 'The captain is able to see you. He just needs to pay a visit to the bridge. Then he will see you in Cabin B-52, Mr Ismay's room. It's on B deck.'

'Ismay?'

'The president of the White Star Line, sir. He accompanies all the ships on their maiden voyages.'

Beck knew who Ismay was. But he was surprised to learn that he would attend the meeting, though since it was his company he supposed it was the president's business. As long as he could be trusted to keep his mouth shut, Beck didn't mind. Although experience had taught him that businessmen like Ismay were the worst blabbermouths.

'Thank you, Mr McElroy.'

'Don't mention it, sir. I'm here should you need me. Would you like me to show you to Mr Ismay's suite?'

'Is it difficult to find?'

'Not at all, sir. Simply take the Grand Staircase up one floor, and just aft of the staircase on the port side, the opposite side to us now, are a set of baize doors. B-52 is the first door on your right after you pass through those. Mr Ismay will be there expecting you and the captain will be along presently.'

'Thank you.' Beck turned to look at the safe. 'What do you keep in that?'

'Passenger valuables.'

'Cash?'

'Yes. And jewellery.'

'Jewels?' Beck's eyebrows rose. 'To what value?'

'We have on board some of the richest people you could hope to meet. More than one has placed their jewellery in my care,' McElroy said.

'Are we talking hundreds of thousands of pounds?'

'I'd say so. Maybe more. Do you see a problem?'

'Not really. It's a Ratner safe. It should do the trick. I just thought such a collection of priceless items would be rather more . . . hidden. Out of the way.' Beck shrugged. 'Ignore me. It comes with the territory.'

'The office is locked at all times. There are other valuables on board elsewhere.'

'Really. Such as?'

'The jewels aside, probably our most prestigious item of cargo is the *Rubaiyat of Omar Khayyam*. It's a book of translated ancient poems.'

'A book?'

'Its cover is studded with rare jewels, sir. The only one of its type.'

'Where's that kept?'

'It's in the cargo hold. In a locked box. Do you think your man intends to commit theft?'

If he didn't, he'd be changing the habit of a lifetime, Beck thought. But he said: 'Probably not. Just make sure this room and the one next to it are locked at all times, and never let the key to that safe out of your grasp. That's a steel-plated Ratner, isn't it?'

'Yes.'

'Good.'

Beck thanked McElroy once more and left. To allow himself more time to plan what he was going to say to the captain, he went up to the boat deck for a smoke. The air was clear and cold and the only sound was the great wash and churn of the ship's propellers ploughing onward through the dark sea.

After casting his cigarette stub overboard, he went back down the stairs. Dinner was over and people were returning to their rooms for the night, leaving the smoking rooms, cafe and à la carte restaurant to the night owls and hedonists. Beck straightened his jacket and bow tie and knocked at the door of suite B-52.

The door opened. The man standing there was reasonably tall, still in evening dress though his bow tie had gone. He had dark wavy hair and a well-tended moustache, above which a pair of clear brown eyes peered out with a mixture of concern and amusement.

'Beck?' he said briskly.

'Yes, sir.'

'Come in. I'm Bruce Ismay.'

'Pleased to meet you, sir.'

Beck stepped not into a berth but a sitting room. Decorated in grand style, with wooden panels everywhere and an ornate fireplace to his right; a clock sat on the mantel showing that the time was approaching ten. It was hard to imagine there was a more luxurious suite on the whole ship, which was saying something. In front of him were sliding doors which appeared to lead out to some sort of private deck.

As soon as the door had closed behind him, there came another knock. Ismay opened it without speaking. In bustled the ship's captain, in full uniform, cap under his arm, formal, almost regal, yet with his snow-white beard giving him a friendly look. He was tall and broad, yet Beck had imagined that he would be younger. He must have been sixty or more, and was it Beck's imagination or did he detect an air of weariness about the man? Perhaps because he'd been snatched from the bridge at such an hour.

Ismay introduced them and they nodded to each other. Neither the captain nor Ismay appeared in the mood for conversation. Ismay walked to the fireplace and leaned against it, while Captain Smith remained by the door.

Beck expected the captain to lead the meeting, but instead

Ismay spoke first. 'Purser McElroy tells us that you suspect there's a villain on board the ship.'

'That's correct.'

'And the reason for this suspicion is that you saw someone alighting at Cherbourg who fitted the description.'

'Correct.'

'The tenders didn't load passengers until dusk,' the captain interjected quietly. He looked doubtful.

'It was getting increasingly dark, I agree. However, the lights from the portholes offered some illumination,' Beck said.

'Enough for you to identify this man positively?' Ismay asked.

'Enough for me to see that he closely resembled him.'

'Is he a man you know well?'

Beck paused. 'Yes – I have seen him in the flesh, sir.'

Ismay and the captain exchanged glances. 'Forgive me, Detective – I trust that's the correct title?' Ismay replied. He was obviously the spokesman here. Beck nodded that it was. 'But are you telling us that you have positively identified a man from seventy feet above, in the growing darkness?'

Beck knew now that the look in Ismay's eyes wasn't amusement: it was sourness. Ismay was restless, not a man at ease, and Beck guessed that this was usually the case and not a result of his own presence. The contrast with the calm, cool assurance of the captain was marked.

Beck grew irritated. He knew that his news wouldn't be popular – no commercial cruise liner's senior crew would wish to learn that a wanted man was on board – but Ismay's attitude was lacking in respect. That was why Beck had wanted to speak to the captain.

A man like Ismay was incapable of seeing past pound and dollar signs.

'With respect, Mr Ismay, I haven't claimed to have made a positive identification. I'm on this ship for recreation. I saw someone who closely resembles a person I know a great deal about. I only seek permission to investigate further, so that I can say definitely whether the man I saw is indeed the one I have been seeking.'

Ismay held up a hand, his expression softening. 'Forgive me, Mr Beck. It's not my intention to show you any disrespect. As I'm sure you can understand, it's the first day of the *Titanic*'s maiden voyage and it's been long and not without incident. To receive news like this is a bit of a shock, to say the least. I apologise.'

'No need to, sir. I understand.'

Ismay took a deep breath. 'What did this chap do – if it *is* him?'

Beck had his answer prepared. 'I think, for everyone's benefit, it's best for the time being if I keep that to myself. I don't doubt the discretion of either of you, but if word got around that there was a criminal on board, regardless of what he has done, there could be panic, which would do you and me no good whatsoever.'

He could tell that Ismay was itching to know but did not want to appear too curious.

'So what do you propose?' Ismay asked.

'I propose that life on board the *Titanic* carries on as normal, with no changes to any schedules or the like.'

Ismay smiled for the first time, a peculiarly mirthless grin. 'Thank goodness for that. We stop at Queenstown tomorrow. I was afraid you might ask us to disembark the steerage passengers, which could cause all manner of delays. And hold-ups of any kind are not good for business.'

'That won't be necessary.' Beck knew a move like that would only arouse the suspicion of his quarry, if he was on board. 'What I would like is the freedom to roam the ship, in particular the steerage areas.'

'I don't see a problem with that,' Ismay said.

'It may cause a problem with quarantine when we reach New York,' the captain added.

'Only if we tell them,' Ismay replied. He turned to Beck. 'The reason we have strict demarcation between first and second classes and those in third isn't just to please those who wish to pay more and keep clear of the riff-raff. There are reasons of public health. Many of those in steerage are emigrants, and the American Immigration authorities ask by law that they are kept separate in order to prevent the spread of infectious disease to their country. We could always ensure you get a check-up from one of our doctors if that's a consideration.'

Beck shook his head. He had patrolled and worked in some of the most desperate and poorest parts of London, and been had attacked and even shot at by a whole host of rogues and villains, so the threat of illness, no matter how virulent, was not going to discourage him.

'Are you travelling second class?' Ismay asked.

'No. I'm in first.'

Beck could detect a hint of surprise in Ismay's expression.

'Captain Smith, could you see that Mr Beck is given some form of card or notice which allows him to go where he pleases?'

'I'm sure Purser McElroy could arrange that.'

'I'm very grateful,' Beck said. 'If possible I'd also like to have a look at the passenger manifest.'

'I'm sure the purser can arrange that, too. I'll make sure it's available for you to inspect first thing in the morning,' Ismay said. 'He'll also be able to find you someone who can show you the various steerage areas and the quickest routes between them. I hope you'll be able to keep us posted and let us know of any developments, or any other ways in which we can assist you.'

'Of course. I'll keep you updated. Just out of interest, how do you go about maintaining discipline on board?'

'You mean handling troublemakers?'

'I do. Drunks, fights, damage – that sort of thing.'

Ismay looked towards Smith for an answer. The captain spoke. 'We have two masters-at-arms whose job it is to control the passengers – and the crew, should it come to that. They ensure people keep to their designated areas, watch out for thievery, or investigate any reported theft. One patrols during the day, the other is on duty at night. Would you care to meet them, Mr Beck?'

'Not yet. As I said, I want the people who know about this to be kept to an absolute minimum. Just us three and Purser McElroy. But that's useful to know. One more question . . .'

Beck paused, knowing that his next question would hardly put the two men's minds at rest. 'Do the masters-at-arms carry firearms?'

Ismay's eyebrows looked as if they were about to leap from his forehead. The captain spoke again. Once more Beck noticed the quiet calm he exuded. 'There are firearms on board. They are locked and kept in a safe place.'

'Let us hope it remains that way. Thank you, Captain.'

Beck said his farewells. The captain stayed behind, no doubt to discuss with Ismay what he had said.

As Beck passed through the baize doors, he was hit by a sudden wave of exhaustion. He needed to sleep. It seemed an age since he had woken up in his hotel room in Southampton that morning. Mingling with his weariness was another feeling that he recognised as guilt. Not for scaring Ismay and the captain unnecessarily. But for not scaring them enough.

Because if his suspicions were right, then a ruthless killer was on board their ship. It was vital that Beck discovered the truth, but even more crucial that the man should not find out he had been spotted. Because Beck knew he would be no danger to anyone if, like a sleeping wild beast, he was left undisturbed. Yet if he was woken, and felt himself trapped, he would kill rather than be caught, taking as many with him as he could.

Beck was an atheist, unusually enough for a man of his time, but he still hoped, in the name of all that might be holy, that he was wrong.

The sheets were soaked with his sweat but Sten-Ake Gustafson was too tired to move, or even to shift his sleeping position. Late that afternoon he had been moved to a new cabin, the act of a kindly steward who had seen that placing an ill old man in a room with raucous, drunken Finns was tantamount to torture. He had the new room to himself, though he was told another man might join him when they reached Ireland because this was an area of third class exclusively for males travelling alone. To shipping companies, third-class passengers were no more than uncouth sexual incontinents: segregating the sexes and enforcing curfews were the only ways to avoid full-blown orgies, they reckoned. In reality, Sten-Ake guessed, these prim divisions and petty rules served only to increase the passengers' ardour, fuelled by ample drink and the liberating happiness of being on a ship at sea, miles from home and disapproving eyes.

He was thankful for the brief respite, even though his new berth was well forward, in the starboard bows, surrounded by the crew quarters and the third-class lavatories, and the noise of people coming and going had been incessant. Now, as midnight approached, it had grown quieter. Yet even the constant toing and froing in the corridors had been welcome; it was silence he feared most at the moment. There was also a porthole, something to gaze out of, just above the level of the sea, compensation if he was unable to make it out on deck.

The journey from his previous berth to the new one had been exhausting, requiring a slow shuffle along almost the entire length of the ship. But what a walk! The steward had said he would take him the 'scenic' route, whatever that meant. Sten-Ake's English did not extend to colloquialism.

It turned out to be a route along an enormous passageway, as long and busy as he remembered the streets of Stockholm to be. Scotland Road, the steward said the crew called it, named after a street in Liverpool, where many of them came from. It buzzed with low-paid workers and immigrants. As they made their way along it Sten-Ake forgot his pain and marvelled at what he could see. What he would have given for a place such as this on some of the cramped coffins he had once sailed on. It was like a world of its own.

It was here that the stewards, the cooks, the waiters, those who washed the dishes, the pantrymen, the storekeepers, the small army responsible for keeping the passengers fed and watered were all berthed. Yet, more than a place to sleep, it was an artery where other crew – the engineers and trimmers and firemen responsible for keeping the ship moving, came and went at all times of the day and night. At one point Sten-Ake and his steward were passed by a man carrying a cello, its spike bumping noisily across the decking floor.

The walk seemed to last for ever, the corridor to be never-ending. When they finally reached his berth, Sten-Ake needed the rest, yet he remembered to thank the steward for his kindness. He tried to reach into his pocket for some coins to give as a tip but the man refused to take it, telling him to get some rest and get well, calling him 'old timer'. He smiled and fell onto a bottom bunk and into a deep sleep. When he woke it was dark but he couldn't guess the hour. Time was ceasing to have any real importance to him now.

Yet again Sten-Ake's rest was fitful as he drifted in and out of consciousness. All the time, he heard voices, men talking on their way back from a shift or on the way to and from relieving themselves. Nearly all the talk was in English.

The first conversation he overheard was between two crew members. The words had caused him some alarm before he had slipped back into slumber, at least those he could understand.

'You look like shit, Jack,' one gruff voice said.

'Been horrible work, ain't it?' The other voice was reedier, but still recognisably male.

'Is it out?'

There was a silence that followed during which the second voice must have responded with a gesture of some kind.

'What they gonna do about it, then?' the gruff voice said. 'Bit queer to keep sailing on with a fire burning.'

'It's been blazing since before we left!' the reedy voice said. 'There's a team of lads on it. It's the coals on fire. They think they can put her out as it burns lower.'

'Good luck to 'em,' the gruff voice said. 'That's coal we might need if they're going to open her up and see what she can do later on.'

'They're not going to do that yet, I reckon. Ease her in gently, get that fire out and increase the revs as we go. It ain't gonna spread.'

The conversation ended there, as the two voices drifted away.

Stuck here in the bowels of a great ship whose size he could barely conceive, knowing that somewhere a fire burned, Sten-Ake felt a momentary twinge of panic. On the old sailing vessels he had known, a shipboard fire was a catastrophe. But they were made of wood, and they didn't carry coal. His fear ebbed as he realised where he was, and the ship's immensity gave him some comfort. A blaze in one hold of a ship this big was a mere nuisance.

He recalled another conversation, overheard as he had boarded earlier that day. The young woman ahead of him was seeing off relatives who had accompanied her on board. All of a sudden she had broken down, her features crumpled, though not in sadness but in fear.

'I don't want to go!' she said between sobs, clinging on to a male friend, who seemed both embarrassed at and concerned by her outburst. 'Please. I don't want to go. What if something happens? I can't swim.'

A steward, aware that she was unsettling some other passengers, stepped forward to reassure her.

'Ma'am, nothing can happen. She's the safest boat there's ever been,' he counselled in a soft voice. 'Practically unsinkable. Not my words. The words of *Shipbuilder* magazine. They know what they're talking about, ma'am.

The poor woman would have none of it. 'But she's never been tried out!'

'That's why she'll never be as safe as on this first trip, ma'am. The officers will be extra careful with her. Everything is shipshape. She's passed all her tests. Why, she was only just inspected and passed by the Board of Trade this morning. She is the safest boat afloat.'

Accompanied by the nods and agreement of her guests, the words seem to settle the woman completely. She even ended up apologising for causing a scene, which Sten-Ake found odd. But then, the ways of the English often baffled him. At last she said goodbye to her party and only a few seconds later he heard her telling one of her fellow passengers, another woman, how safe the ship was, how privileged they were to be on board such a remarkable liner on her first voyage when everyone would be taking extra-special care. It was as if she was trying to convince herself.

Sten-Ake had been at sea for many years. He did not think it was possible for any liner to be unsinkable, because he knew the ocean and its vagaries. Yet after only a day on this remarkable craft he was beginning to concede that he might be wrong.

When the first grey streaks of dawn finally came Beck was tired, hungry and so cold that he couldn't feel either his fingers or his toes. Yet the surge of expectation kept him going, dulling the throbbing pain in his leg. He should have been home convalescing, allowing his wound to heal. There was no chance of that, though. On Christmas Eve, the day after he was discharged from hospital, he was back at work. He wanted to be part of the hunt, to be out there tracking down the murderers. He hadn't slept since. He hadn't needed to. Every thought since that night in Houndsditch focused on that bastard with the dead eyes and the cold murderous smile. He never even felt tired. Rest wasn't an option.

Today would be the day he could set it straight. This snow-spattered January morning in east London, the second day of the year, when the men behind the murders of three policemen, the worst of its kind in history, would be apprehended and a great wrong would be on its way to being righted. And Beck had led them here.

His informer, Mart, a man he had cultivated with kind words and encouragement, meals and drinks, the odd gift, over the past fourteen months, had given him the information. This time, though, there had been none of those niceties. Beck had picked Mart up by the scruff of his neck and threatened him with a bullet of his own unless he told them where the gang were. He had meant it. The result was information that two of the gang, possibly three or even more, *their leader among them, were in the house. Then he told Mart to make himself scarce for a long time. That bridge was burned, anyway. Losing him from his network wouldn't matter as long as the report was correct.*

During the bleak hours of darkness the officers had moved quickly, silently, emptying number 102 and the surrounding houses of their occupants. Leaving behind only the killers, asleep, unaware of the massing ranks of officers and riflemen in the streets around them. The uncertainty of how many of the gang were in there stirred some doubt. Not helped when a colleague, aware of the chance they were taking, said the whole operation could make them a laughing stock. But Beck believed Mart. Daylight would reveal whether that belief was well founded.

Beck was facing the house at the end of an alley that led on to Sidney Street. Around him policemen gathered, stamping their feet to keep warm. One of them, Leeson, a tall and amiable sergeant, joked to his mate Wensley about all the places he would rather be than here. 'In bed with the wife.' He paused. 'With anyone's wife, come to think of it,' he said, and the whole group laughed.

Control of the operation had been taken from Beck. There was nothing he could do but stand and watch, with this group of men he didn't know but whose company he appreciated. The wanted men were armed; police riflemen had been positioned on the roofs opposite their hideaway. Their guns were antiquated affairs, so a request had been made to send soldiers, who were now taking their place at each end of the street as well as in the houses facing the back of number 102.

There was no possible escape. If the gang tried to shoot their way out, as Beck feared they would, only one outcome was likely: their destruction. Despite what had been done to him, he wanted to see the killer in the dock to face justice, then to be hanged for his terrible crimes, for the widows he had created and the poor children who had been left fatherless. Death in a hail of bullets would allow him to be martyred, rather than revealed as the police-killing barbarian he was.

Seven a.m came but the day was still bled of all colour or warmth. Bizarrely, in the wind, Beck caught the sounds of a brass band. What could that possibly be? Life beyond the cordon thrown around Sidney Street carrying on as normal, he thought. The soldiers lay prone on the wet cobbled streets, their guns cocked and ready. The noise of the band faded. There was silence. No sound at all. As if the whole area and everyone in it was holding their breath in anticipation of what was to come.

The sergeant sprinted across the soaked street, his boots splashing as he went, to the front of the house. He rapped loudly on the door before running back into the shadows.

Nothing.

Beck looked along the street, at the officers in charge, trying to guess what their next move might be. A small conference, heads nodding. The same officer who had knocked before emerged from the group. This time he was holding something in his hand. He edged into position, pulled back his arm as if to throw . . .

There was a smash of glass. Beck was uncertain whether it was the object thrown by the sergeant, but then he saw that the policeman was still holding it and was standing frozen to the spot. He looked up. A pane in one of the windows on the third floor had been smashed.

The muzzle of a gun was pointing through, directly at him and his group.

Shots rang out. Beck dived to the ground, his face pressing into the winter slush. He counted six reports, hearing the bullets ricocheting off the cobbles and walls.

'Jack I'm hit!' he heard someone say.

Beck turned. The tall sergeant was reeling, staggering backwards, towards the yard behind, away from the snipers' bullets. Where was the returning fire? Beck wondered. He jumped to his feet. The firing halted briefly. He ran towards Leeson, just as another volley rang out.

The wounded policeman was slumped against the rear of a van, face pale, eyes glazed. Another officer was ripping open his clothing, soaked with blood, exposing his chest and a bullet wound. Beck felt sick to his stomach, certain that another good man was going to die.

Wensley was pressing a cloth to the wound and offering soothing words. 'You'll be all right, old son.'

The injured one shook his head, gasping. 'I am done for, Wensley,' he said weakly. 'My heart. They've shot me through my . . . my heart.' He gasped. 'Give my love to the children.'

Beck turned away. Rage burned inside him. Not again, he thought. There was a roar of gunfire. The soldiers had started their riposte. Good, he thought. Had the anarchists been there in front of him, he would have killed each of them with his bare hands. Justice be damned. He wanted those animals and all trace of their existence wiped from the face of the planet.

11 April 1912

Beck rose early, woken again by the dream, and went to the boat deck in time to see the remnants of a glorious eye-popping sunrise off the *Titanic*'s starboard side, its light like diamonds on the calm water. He smoked and watched the coast of Ireland come into view, counting off the minutes, waiting for the ship's occupants to wake so that he could make his way down to steerage.

In his hand was a Marconigram. From Alec. It wasn't helpful: Alec seemed more interested in how Beck was feeling and in telling him to take it easy. He obviously didn't believe Beck's suspicions.

Beck cast his mind back across the previous sixteen months and all that had happened. Would they ever trust his word again? Even his greatest friend appeared to doubt him. He didn't blame them, either.

He was holding another completed form. One with a message that had not been sent. Last night, before turning in, he had gone to the smoking room for a whisky. As he had feared, being so close to the bars was a temptation. But he knew he wouldn't sleep, that the face he had seen would haunt his night-time thoughts like it always did, and he'd hoped a few drinks would help to knock him out. Warmed and melancholic from the liquor, he had picked up a form from the enquiry office. Back in his room, he had written a short message: 'Please think again. AB x'. Then he'd addressed it to Sarah. He had left it on his desk and finally slept. Now here he was on deck, the form in his hand. In this air, under this sun, a day ahead and a job to do, he was ashamed of his weakness. He took the form, folding and tearing it into eight pieces that he scattered into the sea, feeling stronger as he watched the breeze take them. Soon they were behind him. Like so much else.

'They have garbage bins for that,' a voice said, startling him. Female and American. He turned. Miss Heaton, whom he had met at dinner the previous night. She was smoking a cigarette, no holder. She exhaled coolly from the side of her mouth and smiled.

'Another early bird.'

Beck recovered his composure and nodded a greeting. A woman smoking in public so brazenly was frowned upon. At least, it was in most of the circles he moved in. There were one or two ladies he knew who might light up in their own home, or among friends. Never one who strolled about so openly, and without a holder or even a glove.

'Good morning,' he said. 'New bed. Difficult to sleep.' He didn't want to mention his recurring nightmare.

'Tell me about it. I was out like a light but I woke up just before dawn.' She took a drag and flicked the rest of the cigarette over the side. 'The throb of the engine is good for lulling you to sleep, but not so good when you wake and need to get back. I need coffee.'

Coffee too? This woman wasn't like any other he had met.

'What's so funny?' The question wasn't accusatory, more intrigued. Beck didn't realise he had been smiling. His cheeks reddened with embarrassment.

'Sorry.'

'What for?'

He shrugged, wondering why he was apologising. 'For showing amusement.'

Martha laughed, tilting back her head as she did, a full-throated roar, the sort of laugh that could stop an omnibus. She shook her head. 'You English have a very different social code to us.'

'I'm sorry . . .'

'There you go again. Apologising. What for? The behaviour and actions of your countrymen?' She took a deep breath. 'There's no need to apologise. Though it's actually rather sweet that you did.'

Beck merely shrugged again, uncertain what to say. That was the exact feeling she created within him: uncertainty. 'I'm so— forgive me, I was just smiling because, well, I haven't come across many women like you.'

Martha appraised him coolly. 'I'm taking that as a compliment.'

'Oh, you should,' he said, perhaps too eagerly. 'We're a nation crippled by restraint and conformity. It's nice to meet someone so . . . free of all that.'

'We have a conformity of our own in the States. Have no fear of that. Just a different type. I think we could learn some of your British restraint. Though it's too late for some of us. What were you throwing over the side there?'

'That? Just some notes.'

She nodded. Beck could see that she didn't believe a word. 'Obviously a note you didn't like. I saw your face when you tore it up.'

He said nothing, but the burning sensation in his cheeks returned. A part of him wanted to tell her the truth. That it was a wireless telegram to his fiancée. His former fiancée. Asking her to reconsider her decision to end their engagement, and if she did then he would come back to England face whatever punishment awaited him, as long as he had her at his side. Something about this American woman made him want to tell her everything, the whole story about the most recent year of his life, and the fruitless hunt for the man he now suspected was below decks. Yet he remained silent.

Again Martha seemed to sense what he was thinking. Seeing his awkwardness, her eyes turned away from him and glanced across the Irish Sea, to the looming mass of land growing less murky in the distance. In profile, Beck thought she was even more beautiful. 'Ireland, presumably,' she said.

'You're a reporter, aren't you?'

She flashed back a look, part surprised, part impressed, though she said nothing. 'And you're law enforcement,' she replied eventually.

'What newspaper?' Beck asked.

'Does it matter? I'm here to write about the voyage. Hardly my most taxing or interesting assignment.' Martha paused. 'Where are you staying in Manhattan?'

Beck ran through a few memories, snippets he had collected during his limited research of New York. All he knew was that he was going to present himself to the Pinkerton Detective Agency and ask if they had any work for an experienced Scotland Yard investigator. Beyond that, he had few other plans, not even for a place to stay. He just wanted to feel there was a new beginning, with the past vanquished. He had no sense of a future. He hadn't had any such notion for a while. There were times he couldn't even contemplate it. Just reaching the end of each day was an achievement.

'I thought I'd find somewhere when I arrived.'

Martha raised her eyebrows. 'Some vacation. You book the boat but not the destination.'

'Sailing on *Titanic* was my prority. At the other end, I'm less fussy.'

She shook her head. 'Uh-uh. It's nice, very nice, but it's still just a big ship and you don't strike me as a nautical buff. No, I reckon you're either working—'

She stopped abruptly.

'Or?' he found himself asking.

'Or you're running away from something.' She tilted her head to one side. 'Or someone. And that note you threw over the side might be from them. Or her.'

'Wrong,' he said. 'On all counts.'

'I'm nought for three. But I'll keep swinging.' Martha must have sensed Beck's puzzlement. 'Baseball term. If it's the former, and you *are* working, then you can count on me being very discreet. I protect my sources. And Lord knows I could do with a distraction. Oh look, now I've scared you.'

Beck had checked his pocket watch, seeing that it was almost 7:30, the time he had arranged to meet the purser. 'Not at all,' he said. 'I just have somewhere to be.'

'How convenient.'

'I wouldn't lie.'

'Well, let's get some breakfast.'

'I can't.'

'Why not? You allergic to eggs?'

He smiled. 'I am having breakfast, just not in the first-class saloon.'

Martha shook her head. 'You are becoming increasingly mysterious, Mr Beck.'

'Arthur. Call me Arthur.'

'So where are you having breakfast, Arthur? With Captain Smith?'

'Hardly. I'm not at liberty to say, Miss Heaton.'

'Martha,' she said. 'Well, if you're going to stand me up, I'll go console myself with the White Star Line's finest fare. Enjoy your breakfast, wherever it may be. Arthur.'

The way Martha Heaton said the name, her accent, the stress on the second syllable rather than the first, thrilled Beck. She turned and left, and he watched her walk back along the boat deck to the entrance to the Grand Staircase, unable to take his gaze from her, their conversation replaying in his mind. It had been prickly, edgy, awkward and yet utterly riveting. For a few minutes he had forgotten all about what he had seen and who he was looking for.

He wasn't sure that was a good thing.

There was one thing Beck disliked about steerage, and it had nothing to do with the class of people in it. After all, he had grown up in a poor household without wealth or status. In some ways this was his natural class, certainly not the gilded, gilt-edged world he was enjoying – or enduring – in first. Here were honest working people, many of them leaving behind the lives they knew in search of a better future.

The problem with steerages was its depth. The third-class dining saloon was on F deck, still well above the waterline but low down enough to give Beck a sense of being hemmed in. It was unnatural, even though they were closer to the sea's surface rather than towering above it. He thought about the firemen and engineers sweating away in furnace darkness *below* the level of the water and shuddered. It could be worse.

The chief steward had shown Beck to the dining saloon, where he asked to be left alone. No point trying to blend in only to be waited on like a lord. The room was much less fancy than the one in first, but far more pleasant than he had imagined. There were long tables where the diners sat. For breakfast the first sitting was at eight, followed by another an hour later. Beck would remain for both. The room was divided in two, one half for single males, the other for families and women. He would sit in the former.

The first diners started to file in. Beck ordered porridge and some coffee, rather than tea, wondering if Miss Heaton's choice had influenced him. But he needed the stimulation – he wanted to be alert after such a terrible night's sleep.

He scrutinised the face of every man who entered, struck by the diversity of those on board. The majority were Anglo-Saxon, but there were also Italians and other southern Europeans, even a few from the Orient. The man who sat next to him and smiled politely, bowing slightly, appeared to be Chinese. He seemed unimpressed with the porridge until he smothered it with salt, and ignored all offers of a hot drink. he slurped his food loudly.

By nine the room was almost empty, and the waiters were busy tidying away the remains of the first sitting in preparation for the next. There was no one resembling the man whom Beck had seen boarding at Cherbourg from the tender. He ordered another coffee – he had barely touched his own porridge – and sat in wait for the next lot.

The first man through was almost a match. Close-cropped hair, a moustache and beard carefully trimmed, but he was two stones too heavy, and about ten years too old. The man Beck wanted was still in his twenties, and somewhere near six feet tall. Beck knew that because he had seen him, knew his face better than he knew his own. Descriptions in the press were wild and varied and contradictory. He was tall, he was medium-sized, he was slim, he was well-built, he was swarthy, he was light-skinned, he was extraordinarily handsome, he was plain-looking. This aura of confusion, of doubt about the way he looked, seeped into descriptions of his character. He was a cold-blooded killer, or a hot-headed revolutionary; he was kindly and altruistic, or he was savage and sadistic. It was as if people were trying to describe four different men rather than one.

A colleague, older, wiser, more experienced than Beck, had summed it up: 'An enigma wrapped in a riddle cloaked in a raincoat.' To Beck, he had become some kind of will-o'-the-wisp, glimpsed only by a few, appearing differently to them according to prevailing light or the time of day. Had Beck not himself seen the man, and personally witnessed the carnage he had wreaked, he would doubt his very existence. Beck's intelligence-gathering had built up a picture of a cultivated man who had lived in France for some time. He enjoyed smoking, playing cards, and it was well-known he was one of those rare western souls who did not eat meat – vegetarians, as they were known. This kind of detail fed the mystery which had found voice in the popular press, which loved the secrecy and intrigue that surrounded the 'phantom fugitive' and his whereabouts, and which in turn stoked the folklore further. It made the blood pound with anger in Beck's ears. This was no folk hero or freedom fighter; this was a man who in cold blood had gunned down three police officers, and had happily allowed one of his own compatriots to die a lingering, agonising death to prevent his own and his other accomplices' capture.

The men continued to stream into the saloon, old and young, including one elderly man, clearly ill, who moved at a snail's pace. Beck smiled as two waiters went to his aid, making sure that he was tended to. What business had an old man in such a state to be making a crossing like this? he wondered. He glanced across the room. What other stories were there here? Many, he supposed.

The last straggler entered the saloon just as the waiting staff began to clear away. By ten o'clock breakfast had finished – he was no nearer discovering the truth, and too much coffee and not enough sleep had given him a headache.

The doubt returned, as nagging as the pain in his thigh. Had he been mistaken? Yet among all the diners, he saw no one else who was a good likeness for the man he had seen boarding in the half-light the evening before. What if, while glancing up to see what became of the little girl's balloon, he had seen Beck's face peering over the side of the hull and had recognised him? Would Piatkow even know him again? Had he committed Beck's terrified features to his memory on that awful icy night in Houndsditch? Or perhaps he knew his own notoriety and thought it safest to steer clear of public spaces and areas?

Beck could only guess, a feeling he was familiar with. When it came to this man and the hall of mirrors in which he moved, Beck could take nothing for granted.

Martha wasn't sure whether she believed in an interventionist God, though if she had she would have kneeled down and thanked him for the crossing so far. Sure, they had travelled only as far as Ireland, its low green hills visible in the distance as the ship neared its final stop before New York. But so far their first full day of sailing had been blessed with calm seas and good weather, which had allowed her to spend as much time as possible in the open air. She had brought a good book to read, another reason to give thanks. All in all, she was feeling increasingly glad to be on board. Back home, if she had not been chosen for this assignment, she would have been sent to Boston to report on the opening of a new ballpark. Rather here with a book and the scent of a good story than back home in Beantown while some panjandrums christened a glorified playground.

She joined the rest of the passengers as they came up on deck to watch the comings and goings at Queenstown, glancing around hopefully but unable to spot Mr Beck. Her news sense was the one instinct she trusted and that man smelled of news. She had no doubt that he was a police officer or agent, and that his presence on the ship indicated something, or perhaps someone, newsworthy. His secrecy earlier that morning had confirmed it. As did his absence from the boat deck as they moored off Ireland. The question was what he was hiding, and how might she discover it.

She was reasonably certain that he had been tearing up and throwing away pieces of a Marconigram form that morning when she saw him. That might provide her with a lead.

Martha walked forward to the rails just as the sun burst through some thin clouds to bathe the deck in spring warmth. The weather appeared to lift the spirits of everyone around, each of them keen to glimpse their last view of land and get on with the business part of the voyage: crossing the Atlantic as quickly as possible. At breakfast, Darton – she'd been back at her old table, minus Miss Hardee – said he had been told the plan was to push the boat harder each day, and that if she responded well they would try to make New York on Tuesday night. Now this was news she could enjoy. The idea of being in her own bed, in her own apartment, in just a few days' time was a pleasant one. A few others were less pleased, not having made prior arrangements for Tuesday evening.

Darton joined Martha at the rail as the ship came to a slow halt. He leaned slightly too close to her, so that his shoulder nudged hers and she caught the scent of stale alcohol. From that, and his eyes like castle arrow-slits, she guessed he had been one of the last to leave the smoking room the previous night.

'Ah, the ol' country,' he said, gazing across to the rolling landscape.

'You're Irish?'

'Father's side. Came over on a coffin ship in 1863. From Skibbereen. Marvellous place. The Brits have done all they can to ruin it, and its people, but there's a spirit there that can't be quashed. One day they'll do what we managed to do and throw off the imperialist yoke.'

'Maybe,' Martha replied. This was not a conversation she wanted to have. New York was full of men – it was rarely women – like Darton, who had an ancestor who'd once cooked an Irish stew and who became maudlin at the first whiff of stout, sentimentalising about the old country and sounding off against the cruel repression of the English, all the while turning a blind eye to what had been done and was still being done to the American Indians whose land and rights were being trampled on, all in the name of freedom.

She ignored Darton's continued blustering about the Irish Question, focusing her attention on the distant deckside, where two tenders were being filled with people and mail. Even from a mile away, she could see that a fair crowd seemed to have gathered at the water's edge to wave them off. Some of the crowd on deck were leaving for lunch, but Martha vowed to skip it and save her appetite for dinner. She wished Darton would leave, though. His incessant twittering had ceased, and he was watching the two boats ride the churn across to the great ship's side.

'Coming for lunch?' he asked eventually.

'No. I'm not hungry.'

'Hunger has nothing to do with it,' he said with a laugh. 'Mealtimes aboard ship are times for conversation and discussion – they're social occasions.'

Martha gave him a thin smile back. 'I'm fine.'

Darton tipped his hat and disappeared aft, allowing her to breathe a sigh of relief. She turned and cast another look around for Beck, but saw him nowhere.

The tenders were at the side and unloading their passengers, along with sack after sack of mail. It was a reminder of *Titanic*'s original purpose: a commercial vessel designed to transport letters. Once the tenders were unloaded, they were just as quickly refilled with mail intended for Ireland. A few passengers also disembarked, including a young priest whom Martha had seen the previous day taking photographs on board the ship. He was travelling with a young family, whom she could see all crowding the rail of the tender, gazing upwards at the decks above. A young boy in a cap and with a cheeky grin was waving furiously at someone further forward. As the tender ploughed away, she watched the priest turn, his camera raised, to take a last shot of the vessel before they were out of range. It reminded her. Pictures. How were they going to illustrate her piece?

Martha heard screams. Feminine ones. She looked to her right and saw several women, hands to their mouths, shaking their heads. They were gazing upwards, away from the land, towards one of the smokestacks. She followed their line of sight. Rather than screaming, she started to laugh. There, peering over the edge of the fourth funnel, was a face, blackened by soot.

A squat man at her side, all bristling indignation and whiskers, wore a disapproving look. 'Fool,' he said.

'How did he get up there?' The other three stacks were puffing out smoke as the engines were readied for departure. Surely it was as hot as Hades in there?

'It's a dummy,' the man said.

'What do you mean?'

'A fake. The front three are all real stacks. That fourth one is just to preserve the symmetry. Presumably that chap climbed up somehow as some kind of prank.'

Martha looked back. The face had vanished. The tumult around her hadn't. The man continued to gaze up at the empty stack with barely concealed fury. 'Fool,' he repeated. 'I've just managed to convince my wife that we're all safe as houses on this ship, then someone goes and does a stupid bloody thing like that. I should complain.'

'Why would it upset your wife?'

'She thought it was an apparition. The black face, emerging from the flames, so she thought. Thinks it's some kind of omen.'

Martha wondered how shielded from the world you had to be to see a harmless prank as some kind of apocalyptic forewarning. Still, she was glad of the incident, minor though it was. It would add some more colour to the piece she might write.

The swooning women and their men left the deck, so only Martha and a few stragglers remained. She had her book with her and was about to find a bench to sit and read it on, and watch as the boat sailed away from Ireland, but instead decided to stroll along the promenade and take a look at the steerage space. The ship was rumbling to life; there were three piercing blasts from its whistle, and it seemed to alter its course by a few points before juddering into motion. As Martha neared the furthest point of the deck, towards the stern, she heard the sound of bagpipes floating on the breeze. She didn't know the tune but, as it was some kind of mournful lament, she guessed it was Irish.

She reached the rail and looked over the lower decks, where masses of people were gathered. The second-class folk, though their area was sparsely populated, and beyond that the steerage deck, swarming with people. The man with the bagpipes was in full flow and she could hear the sad tune clearly, even above the throbbing of the ship, and could see him wheezing and pushing on the instrument. A group of passengers were waving towards land, though there was no one there who could see them from that distance. Others hugged and kissed and wept. One woman buried her head against a man's shoulder, as if she couldn't bear to look. That is real life, Martha thought: emigrants leaving behind a land they may never see again.

Just then she saw Beck. He was at the rail, leaning back, his hat pushed low over his brow, though she could tell it was him. Among the worn and frayed clothes, his smart overcoat stood out. He appeared to be observing all in front of him, his gaze slowly sweeping around. Martha was tempted to wave but didn't want to make a fool of herself – or bring attention to him, as that would hardly help her cause. She continued to watch him watching the other passengers. Apart from his head, he didn't move. After a few minutes, he changed position and followed the same routine. What was he looking for?

What a great story, Martha thought. The biggest, most luxurious ship ever built, on its maiden voyage, its cargo some of the richest and most glamorous people in the world, and on board a London detective trying to apprehend a criminal before he committed some dastardly deed.

Front page sewn up.

All she needed to do now was stand it up, or enough of it to satisfy her editor, which these days wasn't much. 'Never let the facts fuck the story,' he used to bawl, his motto in Mr Hearst's brave new sensationalist world. Whatever sold papers was more important than what was true. Martha still held to better standards, though. Beck switched his vantage point, moving to the far end of the deck, the furthest point astern a passenger could go, as if he wanted the whole ship in his sight.

Beyond him, a cacophony of gulls, shrieking and swooping above a churning white wake as the ship gathered speed and entered the swell of the open sea. To their right, Ireland, dim and growing distant, its hills melting away, the last sight of land that Martha or anyone else aboard would have for five days.

Beck stood on the poop deck until dusk; Ireland had long been transformed from a blue mass on the horizon to a thin black thread and finally to nothing. Even the squawking manic gulls that had followed the ship all the way from the harbour at Queenstown had given up. Their day, spent feasting on the remains of lunch pouring from the waste pipe into the sea, had been more fruitful than his.

He had looked into so many eyes that afternoon and morning, examined so many faces, that he felt he knew the whole cast of third class. The mournful, yearning for their old homes; the expectant, looking ahead to new lives and futures; the uncertain, torn by both emotions. The Irish had come aboard and immediately transformed the atmosphere into one that resembled both wake and celebration. The music had not ended, just shifted indoors, where the revelry would continue, the streams of whiskey flowing, until the crew put an end to it.

Beck wanted to join them. The distraction would be welcome. The face he had seen the previous day was still proving elusive. Now here he was, under a darkening sky, wondering where to turn next. Having missed lunch, and having been too distracted to consume much breakfast, he knew he should eat and decided to return to first class for a meal. Here in steerage the main meal was at lunch. At teatime they offered only bread and cheese and similar snacks. He needed more sustenance than that.

He turned and looked at the wake whipped up by the ship in the falling darkness. His spirits began to rise as he felt able to lose himself and marvel in the moment. Here he was, a man who had never left England before, let alone crossed an ocean, standing on this mighty vessel, gazing at the vast swell of the sea stretching as far as he could see, towards the dark horizon, making him feel small, insignificant, yet alive as never before to the power and force of nature. The displaced water foamed and fizzed, churned by the force of the three giant propellers which urged the ship onwards, forming a white road that led back home – like trailing a piece of string in case you lost your way.

It was tempting, Beck thought, to forget this business, the face he believed he had seen, get some of this clean salt-sprayed air into his lungs and restore a sense of calm to his life. Yet he knew he could not. That face, those eyes, had been in his head for months and had cost him so much. While he suspected that the bastard was on board he knew that he wouldn't relent. As the light seeped away, Beck lit a cigarette and watched and listened to the water washing below, feeling the ship putting on speed, though that might have been an illusion caused by the increasing darkness.

Beck turned and faced forward, watching the million lights of the ship glimmering through the murk. He looked up towards the second-class outdoor area, where some passengers milled around, a couple of them staring behind at the ship's immense wake.

There the bastard was.

Leaning over the rail. Beck was sure of it. A cigarette in his hand, the same calm, assured round face, the neatly trimmed moustache and beard. Second class. Not third.

Beck set off, walking briskly, not running, eager not to alert him. He walked round the side of the deck so that he was hidden from view by a couple of capstans, increasing his pace until he reached the wooden ladder leading down to the deck below. From the corner of his eye he could see that the man was still there, though from this angle he could only see an arm hanging over the rail, holding the cigarette.

Beck hurried across the deck to a door, above which a sign read '2nd class entrance'. He opened it, hoping to find a stairway that might lead to the promenade deck. Instead he found a steward.

'Sorry, sir, this is the second-class area.'

'I know,' Beck said impatiently.

'It's only open to second-class passengers, sir.'

Oh, spare me the rigid bloody class segregation on board, Beck thought. 'I need to get onto the second-class promenade deck above.'

'That's also only for second-class passengers, sir. The third-class promenade is where you've just come from, the area up on the poop deck, or forward on the well deck, sir.'

'I'm not in third class.' Beck reached into his jacket pocket for his ticket. 'I'm in first.'

The steward's eyebrows rose. 'First, sir?' He paused. 'Are you lost?'

'No. I have been given authority to venture about the ship. I need to get onto the deck above.'

Beck tried to step through, thinking the steward was letting him past. A hand pressed against his chest said otherwise.

Wearily, he reached inside his jacket pocket for his badge. 'I work for Scotland Yard and I need to gain access to the deck above.'

The steward took the badge and stared at it.

'Urgently.'

At last the steward nodded and bowed his head slightly. 'Sorry to have kept you, Officer. Down the corridor here on the port side, then take the staircase going back on yourself.'

Beck was on his way before he had even finished giving his directions, knowing he had given the steward something to gossip about later with his mates. He couldn't worry about that now, though. He reached the stairs, turned and bounded up two at a time, going through the door back into the cool evening air. The light had faded further but was still good enough for him to see by. He walked ahead to the rail where he had seen the man, passing a young couple walking hand in hand.

There was no one at the rail.

Beck looked around. The young couple were just going through the door. At either side of the ship ran two covered promenades. He ran down the port side first, passing another couple but no one else. They must all be inside, preparing for dinner. At the end, he retraced his steps and headed down the starboard side, checking behind every chair and bench, and looking into every cranny. The area was deserted. The bastard must have gone inside.

But now Beck knew he had him cornered.

Martha's plan was simple. She dressed for dinner, delighted to see that her gown was still serviceable, taking as much time as possible to make herself look as presentable as she could. Then she went to the enquiry office where she asked about sending a wireless message. She was told to fill in a form, which they would send by pneumatic tube to the Marconi Room on the boat deck, who would then transmit it into the ether. The man who fed her this information from behind a window was an officious little time-server, and there was no chance of getting him on her side. That left her one other option.

The Marconi Room was in the deckhouse, a white board building behind the bridge, which also housed the officer's quarters. Off bounds to passengers. Or so Martha had originally thought. A close inspection of her map revealed there were several first-class cabins on the boat deck, and some were part of the deckhouse. She climbed the Grand Staircase as the bugle boy blared his call for dinner, going against the tide as people came in from their strolls on the promenade decks to eat. At the top, looking forward, there were two doors on either side of the ship. She took the port side first, finding herself in a small corridor lined with linoleum tiles, which doglegged left. She walked along, passing the doors to three rooms until she reached a dead end. No access there.

Martha retraced her steps and took the door on the starboard side from the hall at the top of the staircase. This corridor was straight; once again there were three staterooms. There was a door at the end. As she neared she could see there was a sign hanging on it that read 'Crew Only'. She was surprised by a man who emerged from the door to Room T. He was in full dinner dress; tall, handsome, mid-forties she guessed from the tinge of salt and pepper in his moustache. He nodded a greeting, and Martha stopped, looking around as if she was lost.

'Can I help you, madam?' Another American. Well-heeled, but his accent carried a hint of New Jersey.

She remembered the letters on the door of the rooms on the opposite side. 'I'm looking for Room X.'

He pointed to a corridor which ran at a right angle from the one where they stood. 'Across the other side. Last door on the left.'

Martha thanked him.

'My pleasure,' he said. 'I thought I was the only passenger in this area.'

She smiled. 'I have a chance to move, if I want. The steward told me to take a look at Room X. I like the idea of being on the boat deck.'

The man returned her smile. There was an outward air of confidence to him but she also sensed fragility, and sadness. As if life had failed to live up to his expectations and it was all too much effort. 'The rooms are rather smaller than some of the others, I am told, but that is more than compensated for by the quietness, from the lack of traffic. Though as we get out to open water the howl of the wind might prove a problem. Of course, there is also the proximity to the promenade. Not to mention the opportunity to descend the Grand Staircase each day for one's dinner, passing honour and glory—'

'And the lifeboats,' Martha interrupted. 'You'll be first on those should anything happen.' She hoped he would move on soon, but she was anxious not to look too eager for him to leave.

He let out a small mirthless laugh. 'I really don't think lifeboats are an issue on a ship such as this.'

'I'm sure,' she said. There was an awkward pause. 'I'm detaining you from dinner. I'd better go and see the room . . .'

'Well, I hope to have you as a neighbour soon,' he said. 'Mrs . . .?'

'Heaton. Martha Heaton.'

'Blackwell. Stephen Blackwell.'

The name was familiar but she could think about why later. Martha turned and walked along the corridor that Blackwell had indicated, hearing him leave and the door close softly behind him. Then she went back, waited a few seconds in case he returned to his room to collect something he had forgotten and, when she was satisfied he had gone, made her way to the door at the end of the corridor, next to his room.

She held her breath as she turned the handle. It was open, as she had hoped, and she exhaled. Beyond the door there was silence. It was also very different in its decor: more spartan, the wood panelling and doors all painted white, so new that she could still smell the paint. She stepped through and closed the door behind her. All the officers on the ship slept and lived here. Some of them might be sleeping between watches and the captain would probably pass this way on his way to eat with passengers at dinner, so dithering wasn't an option. She could walk straight ahead, or she could turn immediately left. She chose to go left, just to see how the land lay. She didn't get very far. The second door she passed bore a sign reading 'Marconi Operating Room'.

Somewhere Martha heard a door close, which again made her jump slightly. She knocked lightly on the Marconi Room's door and stepped back, smoothing down her dress and pushing her shoulders back, the way her grandmother had tried to tell her that a lady should present herself before she gave up on Martha ever being a lady. She put her hands together in front of her and pinched the back of her left hand as hard as she possibly could to try to make her eyes water. A few seconds' pause and the door opened slightly, revealing a young man with a neat, boyish face, his eyebrows knotted with impatience.

Martha looked around and bit her lip. 'I am so sorry,' she said.

The youngster's suspicion became tinged with concern. 'Can I help you, madam?'

'I hope you can.' Not enough, she thought. 'I *really* hope you can,' she repeated. That was better.

His unease was obvious. It was his job to send messages and receive them, not deal with the general public. Like the subeditors Martha knew at work – laconic, cynical and all-knowing in their natural habitat, yet plant them in front of a member of the public and they became stammering, gibbering wrecks.

'What's the problem?' he muttered. As his job was one that involved a good deal of training, Martha assumed him to be a grown man, but he looked more like a boy. Large eyes, ears that stuck out like wing nuts, a pointed chin and thick lips through which she half-expected him to stick out his tongue before slamming the door shut. He didn't. He looked terrified by the tears in her eyes. Which iwa exactly what she wanted.

She put her hand to her mouth, and took a deep breath as if to compose herself. Don't overdo it, Martha, she thought, worried that the poor kid might have a panic attack. 'I'm sorry, it's been a terrible day,' she said eventually.

'Come in, come in,' he said hurriedly, opening the door. Martha could see a large table with some complicated-looking machinery on it. The wireless telegraph, she presumed. On the wall to the right was a panel of levers and switches.

She followed him in. He looked around, nervously, finally pulling out the chair which was at the table and offering it for her to sit on. 'My colleague Mr Phillips is just at dinner,' he stammered. He was wringing his hands, looking everywhere but at her. She guessed his experience of women was minimal; of emotional American women, virtually none. 'Let me go and get one of the officers.'

Martha shook her head. 'No. It's actually you I want to see.'

'Me?' He looked even more bemused.

'Or your colleague. Will he be back soon?'

He glanced at a clock on the wall, which read 6:45. 'He only just went for his dinner. He might be another fifteen minutes or so, though he might stop off and get a few minutes' air outside. Can I help?' His voice rose on the final word, betraying his uncertainty.

'Maybe. I asked at the purser's office but they couldn't help, and said that I would have to wait until morning. I simply couldn't. You see, my husband was supposed to join me on board at Queenstown. He has been in Ireland on some business and I took the chance to visit England. The plan was for me to set sail on *Titanic* and for him to join the ship in Ireland. Yet he has not got on.' Martha bit her lip here again, as if she was about to cry, and could see the panic flare in the young man's eyes once more. 'I didn't receive any advance warning that he wouldn't be coming aboard. As you can imagine, and probably see, I'm out of my mind with worry.'

She could see the young man's head bobbing in agreement. 'Of course, of course. How . . . difficult, awful . . .' His voice faded away.

'I was wondering if you'd gotten a message from him since we set sail? I thought he might have tried to send word that way.'

'Er, of course, he might have.' The wireless operator walked over to the table. There were two piles of papers, each on a spike, not unlike the ones in her own office: the dreaded destination where no reporter wanted to see their copy. He went to the smaller stack.

'Are those the incoming messages?' she asked.

'Yes. We do a tally each night and take it to the purser's office to make sure it reconciles. But we didn't do it yesterday, so this is all the traffic since we left Southampton. What's your husband's name?'

'Quest. Richard Quest.'

'Just a second, Mrs Quest.' He removed the papers from the spike and began to flip through them.

Martha gave a deep sigh.

He turned around. 'Is everything all right?'

She shook her head. 'I'm just so relieved to be finally getting some help. It's been an awful day and I have a splitting headache. I don't suppose you have any tea?'

'We do,' the young man said. 'The officer's smoking room is across the way. Would you like me to fetch you a cup?'

'That'd be very kind of you. Sorry to be such a burden.'

'Would you like me to check for your husband's message first?'

'The tea would be nice. Unless I'm keeping you?'

'We have a backlog of messages to send, but then, we always do. Rarely important. Just people wanting to impress their friends by using the new technology and letting them know they're contacting them from a liner. A few minutes won't harm anyone.' He smiled.

'You're very kind,' Martha said. 'Is there any kind of snack there – something sweet, perhaps – that I could have?'

'I'll see. Give me a couple of minutes.'

'Take as long as you wish.'

The young operator left the room and Martha immediately sprang up, heading to the pile of sent messages. There must have been more than fifty. She licked her finger and flipped through them, ignoring the ones that had been sent later that day. She had almost reached the bottom of the pile when she found what she wanted.

Dective Alec Dunston
Metropolitan Police
c/o Scotland Yard
10 April 1912

ALEC. SUSPEC PP ON BOARD TITANIC. ANY INTEL
TO CONFIRM? AB

The sender's name was written on the form: Arthur Beck. Martha then turned straight to the next pile, the smaller one. There was still silence in the corridor outside, apart from the generator's whirr. The reply from Scotland Yard was there:

NO RECENT INTEL RE PP. GET SOME REST OLD
BOY. A

There was the sound of a door closing. The young man was on his way back. Martha was about to return to the chair when another man appeared at the door. He was a bit older than the other one. He froze when he saw her.

'I'm sorry,' he said, frowning, looking around the room.

Just then the young man came back with a cup of tea and a plate heaped with biscuits. The older man stared at him accusingly.

'I was just fetching Mrs Quest a hot drink, Jack,' he explained. 'She's had a shock.'

Jack looked from one to the other. 'You really shouldn't be here, miss,' he said sympathetically yet with a hint of irritation in his tone.

The younger man squeezed past with the tea and biscuits, which he handed to Martha. 'Her husband failed to board at Queenstown, Jack, and she didn't want to wait till morning for any messages to come in about his whereabouts—'

'Forgive me,' Martha said, interrupting. 'I know I shouldn't have imposed myself upon you like this – and, of course, you're right, I shouldn't be here. But I've been beside myself with worry. Each second is agony. I just wondered if a message had come in which might explain my husband's failure to come on board.'

Jack's expression softened. 'And has it, Harold?'

'I was just about to check when Mrs Quest asked if she could have some tea to help settle her.'

'Well, don't keep the lady waiting, man. Go ahead and see.'

Harold turned to the pile of messages and started to root through them. Jack continued to look at her sympathetically. 'I'm sure that all will be explained, madam.'

'I hope so,' Martha said.

I can't see anything, I'm afraid,' she heard Harold say.

Jack joined him at the table. 'Let me try.'

Both of them started to look through the slips of paper. Grateful for the silence, Martha began to commit the words she had read to memory. Scotland Yard. She had been right. Intel? Intelligence. Beck must be some kind of agent attached to the Yard. Presumably PP was the person he was looking for on board.

Once she'd worked out who PP might be, she'd be in business.

'I'm sorry, madam,' Jack said. 'It appears we have nothing from a Mr Quest, nor anything sent on his behalf.'

Both men looked at Martha apologetically. She took a sip of the tea, trying to work a tear into her eye. But there were limits to her thespian skills. She fell back on that old cliché, the deep sigh. 'I'm sure there's a reasonable explanation,' she added sadly.

'I'm sure there is,' Harold said. 'Do you have an address of a contact – someone who might know your husband, or who he was visiting – to whom we could send a message, perhaps? We're still in contact with land and it wouldn't take long to dispatch it. We could send it now, couldn't we, Jack?'

'Certainly,' Jack said eagerly. 'It would be our pleasure.'

'You're both very kind. But I'm afraid his last whereabouts are unknown to me. I think I'll just to have to wait and see if a message comes in. If not, I'm sure an explanation will be waiting for me when we get to New York.'

'Have you tried the mail room?' Jack asked. 'Maybe a letter from him was brought aboard at Queenstown.'

'Good point. I'll try. Look, I've kept you long enough. You must have lots to do.' Martha put the tea down. 'Thank you for all your help. I appreciate it.'

We'll keep an eye out for that message, madam. Do keep checking with the enquiry office,' said Jack.

'I will.' Martha gave a thin smile, then left. The door closed behind her and she could hear Jack urging Harold to put the headphones on and get back to work. Still, she waited until she had got through the door that led back into the passenger area before dropping the suffering-wife act.

Job done, she set off down the sweeping staircase in search of food and Mr Beck.

Beck fell into a seat in the second-class smoking room and ordered a scotch. He needed it. His hands were trembling, his whole body tense with anticipation, mind awhirl with all manner of other emotions: hatred, foreboding, expectation and vindication. He thought of the widows and children of the murdered police officers and the crippled bodies of those who'd barely survived the killers' bullets.

He had been to see them all for months afterwards. The grieving wives, the bewildered children. Told them of their fathers' heroism. He felt he had to. Then there were the awful feelings of guilt. Why had he survived? Why hadn't he stopped the murderers? Called for more assistance? He hadn't known that another officer, Piper, had knocked on the killers' door fifteen minutes earlier, alerting them to the fact that they had been rumbled, allowing them a chance to prepare.

It was easier to visit the two others who had survived. They understood the guilt. Eventually, as Beck slipped into his personal abyss, he lost contact even with them. His most grievous wounds, it turned out, had not been physical.

It was him. He was certain of it. Peter Piatkow. Also known as Peter the Painter, in the public's consciousness. A man responsible for the biggest manhunt in British criminal history. The leader of the gang that had shot and killed three policemen in cold blood in

Houndsditch, crippled two others and wounded Beck. No one had ever killed more policemen in one act. Then the calamitous events of the Siege of Sidney Street.

The whisky soothed Beck immediately. Piatkow was in none of the public areas. Presumably he had retreated to his hiding place after his twilight smoke.

Every sinew and muscle in Beck's body wanted to search around second class, to break down doors, to invade each public and private space in order to find Piatkow and cast him into the sea. Yet Beck forced himself to remain calm. It was only Thursday. The ship would not arrive in New York until the following Wednesday. There was no rush. To flail around wildly might only alert the fugitive. Then he could turn dangerous, or perform another of his vanishing acts. Better for Beck to bide his time, go through the second-class manifest, narrow his search by a process of elimination, pinpoint Piatkow's berth if possible, keep a watchful eye, and construct a watertight plan to capture and secure him as safely as possible either just before or after they docked in New York.

Beck looked around the room, knowing that he was closer than he might ever have believed to seizing the man responsible for haunting his frantic dreams. The chance to make amends. The warmth of the whisky gave way to a familiar feeling of dread and shame, like cold water poured down his back. The image of the dead girl and mother in his mind's eye . . . he could never atone for that, but he could try to at least gain a modicum of peace.

He thought of Churchill at the Admiralty and how he might react. For the past year, since his move from the Home Office, Churchill had retained a personal interest in trapping and executing the man who had ended up making a fool of him, or so he believed. Following the Houndsditch murders, and the public outrage it created, Churchill had been all over the case and the search for the killer. When news broke, on Beck's tip-off, that those responsible were under siege at Sidney Street he had gone to the scene, trailing publicity and controversy in his wake, neither of which he was a stranger to. Yet it had backfired when his political enemies and the press had accused him of grandstanding. The man they wanted more than any other, the enigmatic leader, had not been found in the burning wreckage of Sidney Street, only two men who might not even have played a part in the slaughter at Houndsditch; Churchill was told to keep his head down and his mouth shut by the Prime Minister – and then the men they subsequently captured who might have been involved in the killings were acquitted. Churchill was moved to the Admiralty where he quietly seethed, his sulk interrupted only by the occasional missive to Beck at Special Branch demanding an update into how the search for Peter Piatkow was going, even though it was no longer his responsibility. For him, like Beck, it was personal: each day Piatkow escaped justice was a constant blemish on the political reputation that Churchill cultivated so carefully.

Beck knew that they all blamed him. All that tumult, all that fire and fury, the eyes of the world focused on them, for so little result, and no justice done. It was never made explicit, but the reproach was there, hanging in the air like a mist.

Stories and rumours about Piatkow – the cold-blooded killer, the anarchist, the ringleader – began to spread. He had fled the scene of the siege dressed as a woman. He was too clever to be caught. His reputation in his absence grew and with it the myth of his powers. While the newspapers condemned the 'aliens' allowed into the country to foment their murderous plans, and the laws which gave them licence to do so, Piatkow became a sort of anti-hero. There was almost a relish and admiration in the way he was described in the press. Beck knew better. The man was a murderer. There was no romance in his methods, just ruthless determination to serve his cause, of funding a revolution in Latvia to throw off the Russian imperialist yoke. A word had been coined recently to describe the actions of Piatkow and his ilk, who acted without conscience, not caring if the innocent were hurt in the pursuit of their own ends, who sought to achieve publicity for their cause by spreading fear: *terrorist*.

Never mind, Beck thought. That was then. This was now. Once Beck was certain beyond all doubt that the man he had seen was Piatkow – and his conviction that it was grew every minute – he would send a coded message to Churchill via the Yard. He might need the politician's help in mobilising the necessary law-enforcement muscle when they docked.

The room was slowly filling up with men, contented and rosy-cheeked after enjoying a good dinner, seeking a brandy and a smoke to ease their digestion. Beck's hunger had gone after his chase around second class. There would be time for him to return to first class later and try out the à la carte restaurant, but for the time being he was enjoying the atmosphere in second class. The room was spacious yet snug, with a warm blue fug from scores of postprandial cigars. He ordered one for himself, and the combination of that, the whisky and his empty stomach made him feel light-headed and optimistic. He sank back into a leather chair, admiring the room's oak beams and panelling, and sighed contentedly. All around him people were doing likewise. There was so much less artifice in here, he thought. Just ordinary folk enjoying some much-needed respite from the hectic, turbulent world that lay behind and ahead.

A young man in a brown tweed suit – no more than twenty, he imagined – pointed to a chair at his table and asked if it was free. Beck nodded that it was. He was in the mood for conversation about matters other than the one which had absorbed him for the previous twenty-four hours, and that would divert him from memories of Sarah. Thinking of her brought up an image of Miss Heaton. Another reason to be cheerful – except that he was wary of becoming involved in any way with a reporter. He simply did not trust them. Their job was a game to them. His own profession often involved life and death.

The young man ordered a brandy and smiled a toothy smile at Beck. 'That was some dinner,' he said, patting his stomach. He was American.

Beck smiled back, not wanting to explain that he had missed it; since he was nursing a whisky, he might be mistaken for a drunkard. 'Some ship, isn't she?' he said.

'Isn't she just?' the other man replied, giving a low whistle. He pulled a cigarette from his pocket and lit it, tipping his head back to exhale a perfect smoke ring. 'I've made a few trips back and forth across the Atlantic and I've seen nothing like it. This place, for example. It's the equal of any smoke room you'll find in first class on most other ships. The same goes for the dining saloon and the library.'

'It's my first crossing,' Beck explained. He offered his hand. 'Beck. Arthur Beck.'

They shook hands firmly. 'Donald Marshall. Well, you picked the right ship. At least in terms of its fixtures and appointments.'

Beck narrowed his eyes. 'Presumably you're referring to its speed, or lack of it.'

Marshall shook his head. 'No. Not at all. She's not as pacy as the Cunarders, of course, but I think she's going to be fine in that regard. Certainly when the daily sweep starts up tomorrow I'll be looking to put my name down for quite a high mileage.'

'The sweep?'

'It's an onboard tradition – about the only form of gambling they welcome. Everyone throws in a shilling and estimates how many miles they think the ship will do on a given day, and those who are closest to the final run when it's posted up the next morning take the pot. Pretty much everyone gets involved.'

'I might give that a go,' Beck said. 'Not that I know a great deal about ships. But you say she should be able to go quite quickly?'

'Yes, her speed isn't the problem. Not for a ship her size, anyway.'

'You speak as if she does have a problem.'

Marshall shrugged, and blew another of his perfect smoke rings. 'Not a physical problem. I can see she's perfect in every detail.'

'You work in the industry?'

'You could say that.' Marshall leaned forward. 'I work for a US naval company. We design steamships.'

'Ah. A spying mission,' Beck said, his eyes gleaming.

'I prefer to call it research.' The young man flapped a hand dismissively. 'It's hardly conspiratorial. White Star know I'm on board. I paid a visit to Harland and Wolff in Belfast and was treated very well. They're making another one, you know, possibly even bigger. *Gigantic*, they plan to call her.'

'Bigger?'

'Marginally so.'

'So what's the problem with this one, Mr Marshall?'

Marshall smiled. 'Are you a superstitious man, Mr Beck?'

Beck thought instantly of the old woman at the dock on the morning they had left Southampton and her muttered words about the ship's size. 'No. Not in the slightest.' He knew spiritualism and the paranormal were all the rage, but he thought such beliefs were ridiculous.

'Good for you. Me neither. Many folk are, though. Have you wondered why the ship isn't quite as full as she might be?'

Beck had noticed. 'I thought that was down to the coal strike. Perhaps not as many people were on the move as might have been.'

'I think it's more to do with the fact this is a maiden voyage, and many people are disinclined to sail on them.'

'Because the ship is new?'

'I don't think it's even as logical as that. It's the idea that disaster is more likely to strike then. The lore of the sea is a law unto itself.' Marshall smiled, obviously proud of his phrasemaking. 'It affects even the hardened realist. I was speaking to a fellow countryman of yours – a science schoolteacher, no less – who seems to be compiling a list of the portents and foreboding showered upon her. I certainly heard a few expressed by the crewmen around me when we had our near miss with the *New York* while we were leaving Southampton. Then there was that business earlier when the stoker stuck his head up and peered from the rim of the dummy funnel.'

'I didn't see that.'

'It caused a commotion among the women. I think most of them didn't know the funnel was false and thought he was appearing through the flames, like some sort of shadow of death.' Marshall rolled his eyes. 'This schoolteacher also told me that he was told that one of the officers doesn't like the ship, and that he has a queer feeling about it. Then there are the stories I was told in Belfast.'

'What stories?' Beck shifted uneasily in his seat and took a sip of his whisky. He wondered what those who believed in omens might make of the news that a murderous wanted criminal whose name had been featured in their morning newspapers for months on end was on board. Even more reason to keep a lid on the news. He winced as he thought of the steward to whom he had flashed his badge earlier. Perhaps he should seek him out and ask for his discretion, even buy it if necessary.

'You know how the Irish are and the yarns they like to spin,' Marshall continued. 'They think the ship is ill-fated. A man died during her construction, pinned and crushed by a falling support during her launch.'

'Surely with a ship this size there are bound to be some accidents? I can't imagine that working in a shipyard is risk-free.'

'Not at all. That's not all of it, though. They also spoke about noises that came from the hull – hammering noises, as if someone was trapped in the double bottom. Unlikely, because on the *Titanic* it doesn't extend much higher than the turn of her bilges. These people I spoke to were Catholic and the shipyard is in a Protestant area, so given that situation you can see why they would bear the vessel ill will. Put it all together, though, and you get the impression of a ship that everyone admires and few love. Not yet, at least.'

'Perhaps after a few voyages that might change?' Beck suggested. 'I certainly don't feel any foreboding. I think she's remarkable and I feel privileged to be sailing on her.'

The American raised his glass. 'Good for you,' he said.

'You don't agree? You don't feel lucky to be sailing on the biggest ship afloat?'

'For now.'

'Your company is planning a bigger one?'

Marshall shook his head. 'Heavens, no. We'll never come up with anything this big. The Germans are brewing up something bigger, though.'

'They would.'

Marshall laughed. 'I don't want to become embroiled in national rivalry, Mr Beck. I know how strongly you and your countrymen feel about the power of your fleet. The Germans have a similar feeling. Their naval industry is becoming enormously productive. There's a bit of an arms race going on.'

'Battleships, perhaps. Not merchant ships like this, surely?'

'Rivalry at sea affects every facet of the shipping industry, not just warships. I think they see a time when it is the Fatherland and not Britannia who rules the waves. A powerful merchant fleet is essential in maintaining and strengthening an empire, as you Brits have shown. And look at what happened when the Germans and Kaiser Wilhelm took the Blue Riband for the fastest crossing. The next thing you know Cunard built the *Mauretania* and won it back. Now we have these enormous vessels like *Titanic*, and what happens? The Germans are about to launch their own leviathans.'

Beck was all too aware of the febrile political situation, and the siren voices and doom mongers back home who foresaw war with Germany. 'I take your point, Mr Marshall, but isn't it the case that your lot pretty much own this ship? By "your lot" I mean the United States. The White Star Line may be based in the UK but I was told it is owned by American financiers.'

'The money may be coming from the States but the pride, the ambition and the public feeling is very much English. If war is on the horizon, as so many feel, then the *Titanic*, *Olympic* and their ilk will be pressed into action on the side of the English, supplying and supporting their forces, regardless of what the Americans feel. War is coming, Mr Beck. Your politicians know it, our politicians know it, and so do the Germans. All this is so much jockeying for supremacy.'

Beck had finished his whisky and cigar. The rumbling from his stomach was reaching critical levels and to carry on drinking without any food to soak it up wouldn't be wise. He said goodbye to Marshall and made his way, light-headed, to first class. Inevitably he got lost on his way as Marshall's words replayed in his mind. The prospect of war was one he had discussed many times, but it had always seemed somehow unreal, a hazy possibility rather than a concrete certainty. Surely Europe's and Britain's leaders, so soon after the barbarity in the Transvaal, would not be so stupid as to engage in war with the modern weapons now at everyone's disposal? It would be mass slaughter.

The à la carte restaurant was still open and busy, not surprisingly since its flexible hours appealed to those who didn't wish to stick to the rigid sittings of the saloon. In the reception room a string trio was playing as Beck climbed the stairs and made his excuses to a member of the waiting staff. He had no booking but since he was alone he was ushered straight in and seated. The room was much cosier than the vast saloon below, but no less grand, panelled from floor to ceiling in French walnut and with a rose-red carpet so soft that someone could lie down on it and get a decent night's sleep.

As Beck sat down, and before looking at the menu, he glanced around, recognising a few faces. Among them was Ismay, who nodded at him barely perceptibly. Beck ordered the roast beef – at least here you didn't have to sit through endless courses – and a carafe of red wine. The food came quickly. The beef was tender and delicious, far tastier than the meal he had eaten downstairs the previous night. As he finished eating, he noticed Ismay leaving his small group and making his way over.

'Are you free to talk, Mr Beck?' Ismay asked.

The tables around were empty. Beck nodded, and Ismay took the seat opposite. 'Some wine?' Beck asked, gesturing at the carafe.

The magnate waved his hand. 'I don't really partake. I trust you enjoyed your meal?'

'It was excellent,' Beck said, patting his lips with a napkin.

''Good. I'm glad to hear it. The restaurant is a concession run by a Signor Gatti. He owns Oddenino's Imperial Restaurant Soho. Do you know it?'

Beck shook his head. 'I should pay it a visit, if this meal was anything to go by.' He could see Ismay almost twitching in his desperation to hear the latest news. There was an awkward pause during which Beck filled his glass. It might have been the drink, but he was quite enjoying the power he exerted over this most influential of men.

Ismay was growing impatient. 'Have you had a fruitful day? Regarding the matter we discussed last night.'

'I have,' Beck said, nodding. 'Eventually. I think the man I'm looking for is in second and not third class.'

'You've seen him?'

'From a distance.'

'And it was him?'

'I'm fairly sure.'

Ismay's dark brows knotted. 'But you're not yet certain?'

Beck shook his head again. He could see that Ismay wouldn't be as patient with the plan of watching and waiting as he was.

'What do you propose to do?' Ismay asked, still concerned.

'I propose to go through every person in second class who's on the manifest and see if I can match him to a name. Then identify his berth. Then we can speak again, once I have communicated with my superiors back in London. If I can be sure it's him it might be best to arrest him just before or after we reach New York.'

Ismay's head bobbed up and down in agreement as he spoke.

'I suppose that would spare you having to decide what do with him and how to detain him for the rest of the voyage.'

'Exactly. After all, now that we have passed Ireland there is nowhere for him to go or escape to until we reach America.'

Ismay stroked his moustache thoughtfully. 'All right. I can see that. Is there any way we can assist you for now?'

Beck thought about the steward. 'I'm afraid in my haste I revealed myself to one of your second-class stewards.' He saw Ismay wince. 'I'm slightly concerned he might gossip about it. I've never travelled on a ship, but I can imagine that once rumours start they can spread and become exaggerated.'

'You don't know the half of it,' Ismay said. 'I'll have a word with Purser McElroy. If he hears of anyone gossiping, then he will be able to smooth it over.'

'That'd be very useful.'

Ismay held up a hand. 'Say no more. Just keep me informed about how things are going and let me know when I can be of assistance – any time, night or day.'

Beck thought back to his conversation with Marshall. 'I was in second class, speaking to a gentleman who works for an American shipping company. He says he's been a guest of White Star and Harland and Wolff in the UK. The Belfast shipbuilder claims that there is a superstition about maiden voyages.'

Ismay smiled tiredly. 'Mr Beck, those who travel on the sea are incorrigibly superstitious. It dates back to a less advanced time, when sailors were at the mercy of nature and luck played a major part in whether they might reach port or not. Given the lottery of the sea, it was little wonder that superstitions, myths and all kinds of irrationalities arose. Some of them have stuck – even now, when we have the wonders of modern technology at our disposal and boats are virtually unsinkable. Wherever there are sailors, though, there will be stories. It all adds to the mystery.' He smiled and rose to leave. 'Goodbye, Mr Beck.'

'Good evening, Mr Ismay.'

Ismay turned back as he made to leave. 'Who was this gentleman you mentioned?'

'Marshall. Donald Marshall.'

A look of bewilderment crept across the magnate's face 'And he says he spent some time with us in Britain?'

'So he says. At your offices in Liverpool and at Harland and Wolff in Belfast.'

Ismay continued to look puzzled. 'The name isn't familiar. Maybe Andrews might know him,' he muttered almost to himself. 'Mr Andrews is our chief shipbuilder.'

'Marshall seemed to know his stuff,' Beck offered.

'Really? How odd. Never heard of him. Thought I might have done if he'd spent some time with us. We're a big operation but I pride myself on knowing what's going on. How odd,' Ismay repeated.

Beck watched as he shuffled away, lost in thought. Something – policeman's intuition, perhaps – told him that Mr Marshall was not entirely what he claimed to be.

In an attempt to shake off his torpor, Sten-Ake had tried to do as much as he could that day. There'd been a breakfast that he could barely eat because the walk to the dining saloon had been so arduous that his whole body was drenched with sweat by the time he sat down. He had tried to eat a smoked fish that the menu told him was a kipper, but the effort of extracting its many bones was almost as tiring as the walk, and he lost whatever appetite he had. He preferred his breakfast fish pickled rather than smoked, and with a dollop of sour cream. What he wouldn't have given for a simple meal like that!

Thereafter a profound melancholy had settled upon him. He went back to his room and lay there for some time, thinking of home, of his youth, of those short yet somehow endless summers when the sun shone all day before it sank briefly and then bounced off the horizon as it rose once more. Back home the snow was melting, revealing the green grass beneath, and soon the land would all be resplendent and lush. Sten-Ake had seen his last Swedish summer and the memories were too bitter-sweet. He had heard that the dying claimed the imminent void made everything more immediate, heightened one's sense of the present, and increased one's appreciation and wonder. Not for him. Instead he was lost in reveries of the past, which brought only an ache in his soul and a sense of futility.

Yet, shaking off his sadness as the engines started to slow for their stop in Ireland, he had forced himself to rise and go in search of the deck. The nearest public area was the forward well deck, between and below the bridge and the forecastle deck. A steward had helped him up the stairs, together with two young men who looked Arabian in their complexion. Once on the deck, the sea air blowing in his face, he felt restored. To his right lay the rolling green hills of Ireland. There were no deckchairs available for those in third class, but someone, a kind young man who babbled in a language that Sten-Ake didn't understand, had found him one, which was placed next to the bulwark on the port side, and he sat and drank in the scenery, making a mental note of every detail. The engines were silent, the sea still and glistening like polished glass. The squawking gulls wheeling and tipping, scavenging while glinting silver in the sun. There was a pencil-thin smudge against the horizon – another boat in the distance. Now he could appreciate what those people meant who spoke of 'nowness'. The beauty was exquisite; he realised that as long as a man could feel the warmth of the sun then life was worth living. Even the constant knifing pain in his abdomen seemed to diminish, as if repelled by the sun's rays.

Sten-Ake had sat there for several hours, long after the ship had upped anchor, the great propellers had sprung to life and they had rumbled away from land. There was a brief halt to drop off the pilot at the lighthouse, followed by a sweeping turn to starboard and an increase in speed as the central turbine cut in. Soon *Titanic* was in the open swell and his heart had beat faster as she'd opened up and ploughed so smoothly through the waves. There was barely a roll or sense of movement, yet the wind in his hair and on his face told him they were working up a decent speed. He felt lighter, younger than he had in years, back out on the sea, a place he would always count as home.

The bridge was behind and above him, and periodically he couldn't resist turning to look at it and the lucky few who got to steer and handle this wonderful vessel, feeling as if they ruled the oceand. There was a man dressed in regal white whom he glimpsed on a few occasions, walking back and forth from the starboard wing of the navigating bridge. The captain, he presumed, a man not much younger than himself, with a snow-white beard that gave him the appearance of St Nicholas. Sten-Ake contrasted him and the other well-fed officers with the stokers and trimmers he saw taking the air on the same deck as him: the 'black gang' seeking respite from the fire and smoke and darkness below, their blackened features twitching and their eyes blinking in the light like those of owls in daylight. He did not envy those men at all. Far better, as when he had been a sailor, to be up and down the rigging preparing the sails, nearer the heavens, than below in the vessel's bowels feeding the fire in such hellish heat. One of the stokers stood smoking next to him, leaning over the edge, his eyes like white holes punched through his soot-encrusted face. Sten-Ake longed to find the words to start a conversation but his spoken English was too poor, or perhaps he was too ashamed of it to strike up a chat with a native speaker, so that all he could do in halting, stuttering words was to marvel at *Titanic*'s size and speed, earning him a grunt and nod. He took the man's offer of a smoke, though, cocking a snook at the physician who had told him to stop to help prolong his life. Why should a dying man forgo any pleasures? Yet all the cigarette did was make him cough and increase his sense of nausea to the point where he needed to return below and sleep.

He woke: it was dark but he was yet again unaware of the time. The steady throb of the engine reminded him where he was – and the pain reminded him, too. You are on the *Titanic*. You are heading for America. You are dying.

There were voices outside, once again English. He was sure that one of them was one of the men he had heard the previous night.

'She's still burnin',' he said.

Whoever replied was a mumbler. It was impossible to make out what he was saying.

'Between five and six,' the first man went on. 'We're trying to get the coal out but it's been a helluva job. She won't go out no time soon.'

The mumbler mentioned something about the bulkhead.

'She's turned cherry red and warped a bit. The wet coal on top is stopping it burnin' through, but underneath it's smoulderin' and it ain't gettin' any better. The wall's holdin' up but it can't help but damage her. Cap'n has said we have to grease it when she's out, but that's only if we get her out. If she's still burnin' when we get to New York they'll have to get the fire boats to come out and douse her and God knows what that'll mean for gettin' 'er back. Bloody cursed, these big 'uns, I tell you. I was on the *Olympic* when she had her collision. Bloody cursed.'

Sten-Ake lay there, the sailor in him sympathising with these men for having to deal with a shipboard fire, and for their superstition. It didn't take much for sailors to take against a boat, and a fire that wouldn't be doused was more than enough reason to spread foreboding. No, *Titanic* was a remarkable vessel, but he was glad that he had spent his time on old-fashioned ones with sails, where fires and coal and soot and darkness weren't needed. Or even thought of.

*B*eck had been the first to the door, as the flames licked from the windows and the smoke billowed high into the dull grey sky. With his good leg, he kicked at the door and it gave way. Flames shot out from within, forcing him back. As the furnace heat warmed his face behind his shielding hands, it was clear that no human could survive such a blaze.

Good, he thought.

He left it to the firemen as they hosed gallons of water onto the fire, waiting until the structure was smouldering, a charred shell rather than a house.

Beck splashed across the ground floor of the building towards a fireplace. There was something there – a pile of burnt rags, perhaps. He moved closer and saw that the rags had once been clothes and were now cloaking a mass that had once been human. It was covered in debris. A fireman began to move it, revealing more. The body appeared to be sitting in some gruesome pose of supplication. There were no legs. No head, either, just the cauterised neck stump. A bone protruded where an arm had once been.

Beck heard a call from behind him. A fireman was wielding a spade where he had been digging through a mound of rubble. He'd found the top of a head, brain matter still attached to it. Not enough to make any sort of identification yet. Beck knew it wasn't Piatkow, though.

Dust rained down on him. A loud cry followed, a warning to get out. Beck ran back into the street to see more rubble cascading down. Someone yelled for an ambulance. His heart leaped. Had they found someone alive? How had they escaped the flames? As he gazed up, a fireman, helmet missing, face soot-black, came out coughing, gasping for help. There was a large gash across his forehead, streaming blood. He pointed upwards.

A wall on the top floor had collapsed, falling on some of his colleagues. More firemen scurried in, returning a few minutes later carrying a couple of unconscious men, one of them in a very bad way. Yet more victims of that bastard, Beck thought.

It was another half an hour until he was able to go back in, past the sitting, half-melted torso. He ignored it and went into the back room. By now it was dark and he was holding a lamp for illumination, glad of the heat coming from it.

Beck saw a second body, half hidden by rubble. He took a deep breath, unsure what he would find, before moving a few bricks with his free hand. He uncovered an arm. The hand and wrist were missing. As he moved more of the rubble he saw a pistol. It looked very similar to the one he had seen pointing around the door at 11 Exchange Street in Houndsditch. The one that had fired rounds into the bodies of Bentley, Tucker and Choate. That had wounded him. Please, he thought. Let it be Piatkow.

As he dug, he was elbowed out of the way by the police surgeon.

'This is no place for you, lad,' the man hissed, eager to guard his territory. So Beck stepped back and waited.

The corpse was a male. The head was again missing. Most of the remains had been consumed in the fire, but the falling bricks had preserved some parts of the body. Beck could see the clothes were of poor-quality material. Not the kind of suits that Piatkow wore. A fireman came forward, carrying a towel in which he'd placed part of a skull and some feet and pieces of limbs like some macabre gift for the surgeon. A carriage had arrived bearing coffins, ready to take the remains away for post-mortem examination.

Beck made his way through the rest of the house, or what was left of it. With a heavy heart, he could see there were no more bodies. Neither of the two dead men were Piatkow, he was sure, even if final confirmation would only come from the pathologist.

He walked back out to the street, where the coffins of the two men were being loaded on carts headed for the morgue.

A voice came from the darkness. A reporter, who had sneaked through the cordon. 'Why didn't you take them alive, sir?'

Beck ignored him.

'Who will pay for all this damage, sir?'

Who would pay? A good question. Everyone but Piatkow. He was mocking them. Beck could picture him, laughing with his friends, laughing at him, free to live his murderous, callous life. Would they ever catch him? While Beck drew breath, he would try. Or die in the attempt.

He carried on walking, away from the smoking ruins, and didn't turn back.

12 April 1912

Martha woke, her eyeballs feeling like they were boiling inside her head – the result of too much liquor the night before, swapping tales with the deliciously indiscreet Miss Hardee, and too little sleep. At one stage, long after midnight, she had looked around the reception room and the two women and their companions – three men, one of them with clear designs on Miss Hardee, which were unlikely to go unsatisfied by the looks of it – had been the last ones standing. When the time came for bed, Martha had had no doubt that she could have had some company in her cabin, but in a rare moment of lucidity she had decided against it. It was one thing to wake up beside some guy after a wild night and kick them out of the door and into the streets of downtown Manhattan, never to be seen again, but do the same thing on a floating hotel and a girl would have to spend the next five days avoiding them morning, noon and night. And that could be awkward.

Her night's sleep had been bad. The vibration of the ship annoying rather than lulling. The feeling of being cooped up had returned, as well as that awkward paranoid feeling that accompanied most hangovers and made a return to unconsciousness impossible. Her only consolation was that she didn't feel nauseous – at least, not seasick nauseous – but the prospect of another five or so days of this caused her to feel queasy. What was there to do? The main reason Martha had chosen to go into journalism was the promise that no one day would be the same as another. Life on board the *Titanic* was the opposite. Each day was the same – the routine, the people, the food, even the scenery. Especially the scenery. And always the same nagging question: how to fill the time? She couldn't carry on drinking like she had last night. And even if she did, that still left a fair few hours to fill unless she fancied staggering around like a lush. She could start writing her article, perhaps even turn it into a day-to-day diary of life on board, but she knew that without the hot breath of a deadline on the back of her neck her words would be flaccid and flabby. Particularly with what felt like a weevil burrowing deep into the front part of her brain.

What she really needed to occupy the dead hours between here and New York was a lead into Mr Beck's investigation. Last night, through the purser's office, Martha had sent a telegram to Donovan Henry, a reporter and friend in New York. Donny was one of the few hacks she knew who didn't use her sex as an opportunity to seduce or traduce her, and the pair had worked on many stories together over the two years she'd been in Manhattan. He also owed her some legwork. She'd asked in as few words as possible – they were charging three bucks per ten words, a racket and a half – whether he could ask the paper's sources in London to discover what cases an Arthur Beck was working on. Once that was sent via Ireland and transatlantic cable there was little she could do but wait. How much time Donny could give it depended on what else he was working on, but she'd asked him to get back to her on board as soon as possible.

There was a faint knock at the door, so timid that it could only be her dreary stewardess, a young woman with bad teeth. She barely said a word, despite Martha's best efforts to get a conversation going, merely smiled and simpered. Martha at first put her down as yet another victim of the British class system, and sought to loosen her up with idle gossip to show they were all girls together and she didn't need to show the same sort of deference to her. It hadn't worked. The poor lass seemed determined to tug her forelock regardless. Yet again today it was the same muttered, 'Good morning, ma'am,' a reminder that the breakfast gong would be sounding soon, and that was about it. She did have a coffee pot, though, which she placed on Martha's small table with a certain disapproving mien, as if she could sniff the decadence in the air. Once she had left Martha grabbed it. She didn't care that it tasted weak and thin, as though someone had taken a coffee bean and held it a few feet away from some hot water. It was still coffee. It still contained caffeine. And in enough quantities it would give her some energy.

As she drank her third cup in bed, Bad Teeth returned, suggesting she might open the porthole and let the fresh air circulate. Rather than telling her to shove the fresh air up her own porthole, Martha smiled and let her do it, glad that she did because she immediately felt better. A reminder of the previous night came back to her through the boozy haze. Of Miss Hardee suggesting they go and try out the Turkish baths, pamper themselves, ameliorate the effects of their excesses. It had seemed like a great idea, even though Martha wasn't sure what a Turkish bath involved. Nor had any time been suggested. She didn't fancy going in search of the other woman who was probably sweating the alcohol from her system right now in a more pleasurable way.

Thinking it might be something of interest to her readers, Martha decided to explore the option herself. Bad Teeth brought her some toast when she asked if she could have breakfast in her room rather than treating her hangover to some company, and, when she asked about the Turkish baths, came back to tell her that they were open to women between ten a.m. and one p.m. However, the prospect of being steamed, stripped naked and scrubbed from head to toe had lost its lustre, while the food, caffeine and fresh sea air had kick-started Martha's recovery. The Turkish treatment could wait until later.

And she'd just had an idea about how she could fill her time.

Beck was in the purser's office going through the ship's manifest when he too heard voices outside. One of them was familiar: American, uncompromising and female.

Martha Heaton.

He left the desk and edged towards the door to hear better. The male voice, quiet and reasonable, wasn't the chief purser's, but belonged to one of his assistants.

'I just wanna have a look,' Beck heard Martha say, as if nothing in the world could be more reasonable.

The male voice was patient. 'We don't allow people to look at it without good reason, madam.'

'Really?' Martha was considerably less patient than the purser's man. Beck smiled. He knew, when all else failed, that making a scene was often the quickest way to shake an Englishman, for whom public embarrassment was the ultimate humiliation. Martha obviously knew this, too.

'I assure you that I'm not being in any way frivolous, Miss Heaton. Unless people have good reason we don't allow them to look at the passenger manifest.'

Beck frowned. Why did she want to look at the manifest?

'Good reason? If you cared so much about it then how come you see fit to plaster the names of all the people in first class on the first-class information booklet? I'll tell you why. Because you want the high and the mighty to know who else is on board so they can gauge their place in the pecking order. Now, if you're going to emblazon that information all across some pamphlet, then how come you won't let me have a look at the same list for second and third class?'

There was silence.

'Isn't the passenger manifest a matter of public record?' she added.

Again more silence. No doubt who had the upper hand here.

'Now, we can do this one of two ways. You can let me have a look at the list, and I will thank you kindly. Or I can carry on this discussion with your boss, Mr McElroy.'

Ask her why, you fool, Beck thought. But he sensed, even with a wall and a door between them, that the air had been let out of the man's balloon.

'I'm afraid, madam, that I'm unable to let you look at it at present,' the purser's assistant said, with a sniff. 'If you would like to come back later then I will consult with my superiors and if they give permission—'

'Why can't I look at it "at present"?'

Another sniff. 'Because it's in use.'

You idiot, Beck thought.

'Well, why didn't you say that? I'll just go and take a seat on that bench over there. Then you can come and let me know when it's no longer in use and I can go and take a look.'

'Very well, madam.'

Beck cursed under his breath. Now she would see him when he left. Did she know? Had she found out? How? Or was he just being paranoid? Perhaps there was another, more innocent reason why she was after the manifest. When it was time for him to leave he decided to pretend he had been in the purser's office on other business. But he knew that that was unlikely to convince Martha. This office was off-limits. An innocent inquiry could have been taken to the public desk next door. She was bound to be suspicious.

Having a reporter on his trail, no matter how attractive she might be, was one thing he could do without.

Beck settled back to studying the passenger list, blocking out thoughts of Martha, forcing himself to concentrate on the names in front of him. He was almost at the end of the second-class list. No names stood out as remarkable. In his notebook he made a list of each cabin and the people in it, even those rooms occupied by families. At some stage over the weekend, he might go from door to door, either late in the evening or early in the morning. He would have to find an excuse, one that was acceptable to Ismay, to explain why he was disturbing people, but there was time to come up with a convincing ruse. His mind wandered beyond the door to Martha, whom he pictured sitting eagerly in a tub armchair, as much to show the purser's assistant she had spoken to that she was not the sort to give up and go away. What could he do about her?

There was a knock and the door opened. Purser McElroy's ample frame appeared.

Oh no, Beck thought.

'Mr McElroy,' he heard Martha's voice sing out.

The purser turned, luckily closing the door behind him, though not before Beck had caught a glimpse of her. Had she seen him?

The conversation between the two of them was conducted far less audibly than her previous one with McElroy's assistant. A few minutes later McElroy re-entered the room, smiling thinly.

'You're in demand,' Beck said.

McElroy raised his eyebrows. 'It goes with the territory. Funnily enough, she wants to look at the manifest.'

'Why?'

The purser shrugged. 'Why do you? It's not my business to ask why. I told her she could come back at one this afternoon. Do you think you'll be finished by then?'

'I should be,' Beck said, feeling a wave of relief. At least that would mean she'd stop hovering outside.

McElroy took off his hat and laid it on the table next to Beck. 'Found what you were looking for?'

'Not yet.'

'Good job I'm not a curious man,' the purser said brightly. 'All these people wanting to look at the manifest. Makes you wonder just who's on board that people are so keen to find.'

Beck wondered how much McElroy knew. He was close to the captain. Had anything been said?

The purser sat back on a small couch and let out a sigh. For the best part of a week he and the other staff had barely slept. And that didn't count the days preparing to set sail. Beck knew the feeling.

'There's a Marconigram for you, by the way,' McElroy said.

'What?' Beck said, spinning around. 'Where?'

The purser reached into his jacket pocket and pulled out an envelope. 'In there.' He tossed it onto the desk.

Beck wanted to rip it open there and then to see who it was from. Alec? But he didn't want to seem too eager. Instead he put it to one side and continued to go down the list, though he wasn't taking in any of the names.

Eventually McElroy stood up, took his hat and said he was needed elsewhere. 'Let yourself out' were his parting words.

As soon as the door was closed Beck ran his finger along the seal of the Marconigram envelope and opened it. He pulled out the form, on *Titanic* headed paper. The message was short.

'Any more news re PP? Have passed word to the Fat Man. Very interested in more details and to provide all help. Didn't mention you. Said news came from an 'agent'. Alec

Beck's first reaction was: why the sudden change of heart? Alec had been so dismissive before. What had changed? Perhaps some intelligence that confirmed Piatkow might be on board?

Then he realised who the message was referring to. The Fat Man. The former Home Secretary. Winston Churchill.

For the rest of the day Beck wandered around the ship, almost in a daze, considering what his response should be. That he would need help in New York, once he had apprehended Piatkow, was clear. How he would get that help was less so; after all, he was the proverbial boy who had cried 'Wolf', discredited and his reputation tainted. Why would they believe him? Now he was being told that Churchill was taking an interest. But only because his name was being kept out of it.

Which all brought back the nagging doubt: 'Are you sure, Arthur? Are you sure?' Until Houndsditch, and the damned siege that had followed, Beck had never doubted his own judgement. Never had cause to. Then it had all unravelled. Before he blew this wide open and set the wires between London and New York humming, he needed to be sure.

He went down into the depths of the ship, to the swimming pool, where he swam length after length, hoping to stimulate some thought and clear his head for the challenges ahead. Then, after changing in his room and washing the pool's seawater from his skin, he dressed and headed for the boat deck and some air. There he prowled back and forth, passing others but not seeing them. The weather was still bright and clear and there was little wind to speak of, though it could have been howling a gale for all the heed that Beck would have paid to it. These people milling around, idling away time on the voyage, a group playing quoits over there, others sitting reading, or walking, entirely unaware that they were potential onlookers to a scene that might become history. If he was right. If. But there could be no if.

This could be a shot at redemption. The saga of the past sixteen months, if not forgotten, then at least atoned for. Justice would finally be served and those affected would be able to move on.

Beck spent some time at the far end of the deck overlooking the second- and third-class areas. Merely standing around looking wasn't going to help him. He needed to be more methodical, yet stealthy with it. He would also need Ismay's unqualified backing, which meant confiding in him about the identity of the man he was seeking. But again, if he was wrong . . . he was damned if he did, damned if he didn't. He didn't want to alert any of the ship's senior hierarchy until he was sure, but he couldn't think of a way to obtain that absolute proof unless he enlisted their help.

Could he trust his own judgement? He had to. The words of the doctor he had seen during his spell in hospital after his episode – a nervous breakdown, he had heard another doctor say – still echoed in his head. 'You have lost trust in how your brain deciphers information,' he had said, with a kindly patrician air. That was how it had come to Beck being unable to get out of bed one morning. Why he'd been told to take leave. Why it had been suggested that he should leave the service. So he could learn to trust in his instincts once more, accept the information processed by his brain, and have renewed confidence in his own judgement. Then he was issued with a writ.

Beck continued to prowl back and forth, like one of the tigers he had seen at the White City exhibition in 1908. He and a friend had visited that gleaming town of white, then walked to the Olympic stadium to watch the remarkable conclusion at the marathon race on a sweltering summer's day. Had he ever been happier? So much had changed in four years. None of it for the better.

The light began to fade and with it the number of fellow promenaders. Beck lit a cigarette and perched himself by the fourth lifeboat forward on the port side. It was only then that he noticed the whole ship appeared to be tilting slightly towards that side. Why would that be? He couldn't begin to guess. But from where he stood he could see the ship's motion, lifting ever so slightly upwards before plunging down as it scythed through the waves, with an almost imperceptible roll as it did so. Below deck these movements were barely noticeable.

He didn't know how long he had leaned against the rail in the lee of the lifeboat. He must have smoked two, perhaps three cigarettes, tossing the butt of each casually into the frothing sea below. In the distance he thought he saw the outline of another ship. He wondered how many were out here on this gargantuan sea. Such a vast and lonely place yet out there, dotted around, were thousands of people on their journeys, to and from new lands, returning or escaping.

Beck stepped back. The deck was by now almost deserted and it had grown distinctly cooler. Up ahead, beyond the barrier of the first-class promenade, he thought he could see movement. Several officers in conversation, one gesticulating, the others looking concerned. He wandered closer to the barrier but the party split up and moved away. His gaze followed one going forward, past the deckhouse, disappearing up some stairs towards what he assumed to be the bridge.

As he watched the officer ascend, he saw another man emerge from around the end of the wheelhouse, on the same deck as Beck, no more than seventy-five yards away. The blood froze in his veins. The man was carrying a mop and bucket, wearing some kind of overall. In the gloaming it was hard to tell, and he was in profile, but the face, the moustache, the height – it all looked like *him*. Beck stepped still closer to the barrier. The man turned, and for a few seconds they seemed to stare at each other. Surely it was him – the same rounded handsome face, looking almost incongruous in workman's wear.

The man disappeared back around the corner he had emerged from. Beck stood there, unable to move, unlike the previous times when instinct had sent him in pursuit. He had surely imagined this. Piatkow, in a crew-only area, dressed as some sort of cleaner? It was preposterous. His breath grew ragged. The same feeling that had led to his breakdown, that had caused the sleepless nights, the long dark hours waiting for the dawn.

'You look like you've seen a ghost.'

The voice snapped him out of his reverie. Beck turned. Martha Heaton. Except this time he was pleased to see her. As she saw him her expression, previously slightly amused, became concerned.

'Are you all right, Arthur?'

He said nothing. He glanced back towards the wheelhouse. Had it been Piatkow? Or was Martha right? Was it a ghost? Had it always been a ghost?

'What time is it?' he said, his voice a croak.

'Almost time for dinner.' She stepped forward, putting a hand on his shoulder. 'Tell me what's wrong. You can tell me.'

Beck shook his head. His mouth was dry. 'I need a drink.'

'Hallelujah. I thought you'd never ask,' Martha said. It was only then that Beck noticed she was dressed in a gown, ready for dinner. He was still in the suit he had dressed in that morning. She seemed to read his thoughts.

'Let's go to the à la carte restaurant. One of the bartenders there fixes a hell of a Martini.'

Beck nodded. He had no intention of telling her what he had

seen, or thought he had seen, or anything else about his search. But right there and then he decided he needed this woman's company, reporter or not.

Trust your instincts, he thought.

Martha had been in this position as a reporter numerous times; sitting across from a potential story, or source, drink in hand, waiting, urging, cajoling them to open up and reveal the goods. Yet rarely had she cared about the person she was interrogating. It was her job to dig for information, and if that meant she had to flirt, or pretend to be interested when she was bored stiff, or find someone engaging when they were dull and pompous, then that was all part of her job. A certain amount of cunning and subterfuge was essential. But here she was with someone who, her news sense told her, offered her the possibility of a sensational story. However, she was more concerned with his well-being. It was a new experience for her. Not for the first time, she heard her grandma's voice, gently mocking: 'Martha, I do believe you have grown a conscience.'

They were in the first-class reception room, waiting for a table in the à la carte restaurant. Around them, the resplendent and well-fed milled and chatted. The orchestra, who seemed to be following Martha wherever she went and were beginning to irritate her intensely with their pallid, ponderous chamber music, were droning away in the corner. The leaden band aside, it was a buoyant scene. Apart from the morose, troubled young man sitting opposite, who had just drained a Scotch and soda in a few seconds and looked thirsty for more.

'How old are you, if that's not too sensitive a question?' Martha asked, if only to get him talking.

'Twenty-six.'

A year older than her, she thought.

He appeared lost, as if he was peering over a precipice into which he would soon be pitched. Just then a waiter passed and he ordered another Scotch, looking at Martha to see if she was interested in another drink. She pointed to her half-full Martini and said she was all set. A faint smile, barely perceptible, flickered briefly on his face. He was handsome, classically so. That wasn't his appeal, though. It was the heavy, hooded brown eyes which seemed to suggest sorrow, yet could also glint with mischief.

'What's funny?' Martha asked.

Beck shook his head. 'The way you said "all set" just then. Never heard that before.'

'It's a New England phrase. Confuses the hell out of a few of my countrymen, too.'

'You're from New England?'

'Boston.'

'But you work in New York.'

'It's where the job took me.'

Talk of her work appeared to darken Beck's mood once more. He fell quiet and sipped at his whisky.

Martha took a hit from her Martini. She could see Lester Darton looking over at them and her heart sank. Please, don't come over, she thought. Thankfully, at that point another self-important blowhard in a dinner suit appeared at Darton's side to divert his attention.

'You can tell me what's troubling you,' she said. Before she could add a qualification to that statement he had snorted quietly.

'To a reporter?'

'To someone who cares.'

Beck glanced at her over the top of his glass. He shook his head slowly. 'Sorry. I've had my fingers burned before.'

'By a reporter? Or by a woman?'

This time he nodded. 'Both. Though they weren't one and the same.'

'Well, unless you have a false identity and are in fact a millionaire and a VIP – which can't be discounted since we're surrounded by them – I don't think your love life would be front-page news. Who was she?'

Beck narrowed his eyes. 'She was called Sarah. We were engaged to be married. I made . . . a mistake at work – a couple of mistakes, if truth be told. That caused me a few problems. Sarah decided she no longer wished to be engaged to me and broke it off.'

It was Martha's turn to snort derisively. 'Sounds like you're better off without her.'

'Maybe. The mistakes were pretty serious, or at least one of them was. It caused me a few . . . health issues. Sarah wasn't prepared to put up with that.'

'That sounds even worse! If you love someone, you stick by them, through thick and thin, particularly when you've agreed to marry them. Otherwise what's the point?'

Beck said nothing, just sat there nursing his drink, looking into it. Eventually he looked up. 'I think she got the feeling that I hadn't quite measured up. And I think she got that feeling because I thought it too. I don't blame her, not for a second.'

'Well, to me, and pardon my French, she sounds like one mean fucking broad.'

Beck's eyebrows nearly leaped off his forehead in surprise. Women simply didn't use language like that. To her right, Martha could hear an indignant 'Tut!' from a rotund woman who was standing while waiting to be seated. Martha ignored it.

'I'm sorry,' she said. 'But I don't see what help it is pussyfooting around these subjects. It sounds pretty damn absurd to hear you blame yourself like that. Folks have a hard time at work all the time, make all kinds of mistakes, and it affects the way they feel and act. But most people hang in there and help out their partners. Not run for the hills at the first sign of trouble.'

The grin was back on Beck's face. 'That's very kind of you to say. It's refreshing to hear a woman express herself with such honesty and certainty. I don't wish to speak ill of Sarah behind her back, but she was often pretty opaque in what she said. I never really knew where I stood.'

'She sounds like the sort of woman who expects perfection. Such a thing doesn't exist, believe me. Before you go around demanding high standards, you should have a look at your own. We're all flawed: some of us accept that, some pretend we're not.'

The drink had brought colour to Beck's cheeks. He seemed less distracted, too. 'And what are your own flaws?'

'That's not for me to say. A blemish to some is a beauty spot to others. I've been called outspoken and unrefined. I don't see the problem with either trait, personally, but if you want to take offence, hell, go right ahead.'

'I admire you for it,' Beck said.

'There you go. The fat duffer on my right doesn't agree with you,' Martha added, indicating the obese woman who had drifted away to a part of the lounge where the language was more decorous. You're a tiny bit drunk, Martha, she told herself. Don't get obstreperous or you'll scare the poor man away. 'I don't play games.'

'I never met a reporter who didn't play games. Their work means that they're dealing with lives and livelihoods, but for them it's just another story.'

'I don't mean in work. I mean in my personal life.'

'So you're not after a story now? You don't see me as a potential lead?'

Martha paused. Beck, who had been leaning forward, sat back almost triumphantly, as if her brief silence proved his point.

'Look, I'd be lying if I said that if I discovered you were involved in a big story, and I got to hear of it, part of me wouldn't want to publish. But right now, right here, no, I don't see any story. I see a guy who needed some company and a kind ear.'

Beck nodded once more, as if that was the right answer. She knew he was too savvy to unburden himself of all his woes and fears. He was a police officer and caution was wired into their personalities. But she had meant what she had said.

'How do you do your job?' he asked.

'I don't follow.'

'What makes you a good reporter?'

'In terms of personality? You need a hide as thick as a rhinoceros's, natural curiosity . . .'

'No, I mean more specifically. How do you know what's newsworthy, for example?'

'It's just a sense you develop. Some people are born with it.'

'But it's crucial to the job?'

'Pretty much. If you can't sniff out a story you're probably not going to go very far.' Martha wasn't sure what he was after.

'Let's just say you got something horribly wrong.' Beck looked into the distance for inspiration. 'Say your news sense let you down, or had been so severely compromised by an earlier mistake that it led you to make a greater one. A mistake that led to someone being harmed or killed. That would shake your confidence, wouldn't it? Something you relied upon, which had got you so far, did not turn out to be quite so infallible as you thought it was. And because of it, people got hurt. How would that make you feel?'

Martha thought for some time. In the past she had got stories wrong. Quite a few. Nothing that had put her career at risk, but one or two that had caused her long dark nights of soul searching as she wondered whether the facts warranted a sensationalist presentation. There was one other example that had been less a mistake, more a cataclysm.

'I know what you mean,' she said.

'You do?' Beck said eagerly.

'I was a junior reporter in Boston. We'd had a report of a local politician who was abusing his position, taking mistresses, not treating them very well. I was asked to follow it up. A few of the guys in the office didn't see the point. What was the problem?

But this guy was pretty nasty and the way he treated the women was horrible. There were rumours he'd threatened one and had her beaten up when she said she would go to his wife and expose the affair. She was willing to go the police but she was scared to. I was asked to root around, see what I could find. Anyway, he turned his attention to me. He was every bit as lecherous as the rumours made out. I spoke to my editor and he said confront him and let's write about it. See if the woman he threatened will press charges. So I did.'

It was a potted version of the story, ignoring the fact that the sleazy politico had half-raped her and it had taken a knee to his groin to get him off.

'And?'

'I told him who I was. He went crazy. Threatened to have me killed. Rang my editor, wanting me fired. He was in the same Masonic lodge as the proprietor, and for a while it seemed touch and go. Thankfully the editor backed me up. The story was dropped, though. That politician's still there, serving the public. The woman refused to press charges. She disappeared completely. And I mean completely. Like she stepped off the edge of the Earth.' Martha paused. 'Or found herself in a shallow grave somewhere. Rarely a day goes by when I don't think about what happened to her. She may be fine. I hope she is. But I know that if we hadn't got involved and stirred it up her life would have been easier, less dangerous.'

'But the politician deserved to be investigated. Such men should not be in public office.'

'Maybe. My experience is that they often are, though. But that it isn't my point. You asked if my confidence and judgement had ever been shaken. They were. I wasn't sure after that that I still wanted to be a reporter, not when I saw how much things are stacked in favour of the big guys against the little ones.'

'But you're still a reporter.'

'That's because I realised that was exactly why I wanted to be a reporter. To help out the little guy. To fight back against the bullies. You get things wrong, you don't always win, but it's a fight worth fighting if it's one you believe in. I don't know what happened to you, but if you believe in what you do, then you need to throw yourself into it with all your heart. We all make mistakes, but the way we can compensate for that is to make sure we do some good. You strike me as someone capable of doing a great deal of good.' Martha took a sip of her drink. 'There endeth the lesson.'

Beck was looking at her with a look she couldn't fathom. Could have been admiration; could have been incredulity. 'You want to tell me what happened?' she asked.

He paused. 'No, I'm not sure enough time has passed. I don't think I can. For now.'

So much for quid pro quo, Martha thought, going down her mental checklist; she had bought him booze, flirted, flattered him, and bared her own soul. Outside of a truth serum there weren't many more tricks left up her sleeve. 'All right,' she said. 'Is it related to what's happening on board here?'

'Who says anything's happening on board here?'

She shrugged. 'Well, the fact that you looked like you'd seen a ghost tonight. The fact that yesterday I saw you checking out the passengers in steerage. And the fact that J. Bruce Ismay, the president of the White Star Line, who is standing over there pretending to be in deep conversation with Sir Cosmo and Lady Duff Gordon, hasn't stopped looking over at you for the past half-hour.' Martha finished her Martini. She needed to eat.

The teasing glint reappeared in Beck's eyes. 'I thought you said you didn't see me as a potential lead.'

'No, I said right now I didn't. That doesn't mean I haven't before. Or that I won't in future.'

Beck said nothing, just continued to stare at her. Martha didn't look away. For a second it looked as if his English reserve and caution might evaporate, but instead he glanced away first. 'The answer is no. The mistake I'm talking about has nothing to do with what's happening on board here. Because I'm just appreciating a leisurely cruise to New York. I'm here to enjoy myself.'

Martha raised her empty glass. 'I will drink to that.' She didn't believe a word of what he'd said. But having painted herself into a corner as the sympathetic shoulder to cry on, she could hardly rip off her simpering mask, accuse him of being a liar, and grill him within an inch of his life. She might have to settle for sleeping with him. It promised to be ample compensation.

A waiter approached with two menus. 'Your table is ready, sir,' he said to Beck, even though it had been Martha who had asked for the booking. She let it pass.

'After you,' Beck said, standing and pulling out her chair.

As she stood, another crew member joined them. But he wasn't dressed in a waiter's uniform and he wasn't Italian like the rest. It turned out that he was from the purser's office.

'Sorry to intrude, Mr Beck. But the chief purser said that you personally requested to be notified immediately should another message come through.'

Beck nodded, slightly abashed. The waiter stood impatiently by with the menus.

'Give me a few minutes,' Beck said to Martha, clearly embarrassed. He probably hadn't envisioned being deep in conversation with her when he'd given his instruction to be told about any messages. She could only wonder what it contained. Insinuating her way into the Marconi Room again was a possible option, but still a ruse that was unlikely to work twice. 'By all means go on ahead without me,' he added.

'I'm actually waiting for a message myself. I'll come with you.'

Beck looked hesitant. The waiter coughed his impatience.

'I'd rather take this on my own. I'm sure you'll understand.' His tone was suddenly formal, stiff. His crisis of confidence in his judgement seemed to have passed. 'Thanks for the . . . talk. It was illuminating. Please, don't delay dinner on my account.'

And eat on my own? Martha thought. No way, buster. She could go back to the dining saloon, she supposed. She certainly wasn't going to act disappointed, not for some mixed-up conscience-stricken Limey. 'Of course. Perhaps I'll catch you later on.'

'Yes,' Beck said. 'Perhaps.' The last word made her feel slightly desperate.

With that he followed the assistant purser out of the room, leaving Martha with the waiter, who seemed to be smirking. She wondered if this urgent message was a response to the one she had read furtively in the Marconi Room the day before.

What had he seen on the boat deck? His face had been drained of all colour, his legs unsteady, his youthful assurance gone. Whoever or whatever he had seen was beyond the barrier, in the section designated for crew only. Was a crew member some kind of wanted man? Not for the first time, the story that Martha's mind started to conjure became wilder than anything reality could possibly live up to.

She turned to the waiter, by now drumming his fingers on the cover of the menu.

'What are the chances of me having a meal ordered to my room?'

The purser's office was closed and the shutters were up. McElroy was either on his rounds or having dinner, so Beck's only option was to take the message back to his berth. His mind was still reeling from his conversation with Martha. The news of the telegram came as both blessing and curse. He had been only a drink, a conversation or a kiss away from telling her everything. Yet he had not wanted to leave her company, not for a second. Could what happened on board stay on board? Unlikely, if he knew journalists. Though he was loath to lump her in with the bunch he had dealt with in London.

However, the news of the telegram had snapped him back into the present and, together with Martha's words, had shaken the self-doubt and depression that had enveloped him since spotting the Piatkow-like figure on the boat deck. Was all this a product of his imagination? Perhaps, but he needed to find out once and for all.

Beck sat on his bed and unfolded the message.

Intel confirms PP last in France. No reply to previous message. Please advise urgently if help required in NY. Fat Man urging all possible haste if so. Alec

He refolded it neatly and placed it in his jacket pocket. France.

Piatkow could have boarded in Cherbourg. But it was a big country with many ports; it proved nothing.

The decision that Beck was so reluctant to make was looming. To answer positively, to tell them Piatkow was on board, would trigger a hurried, huge transatlantic effort, a vast logistical challenge. It would involve both the British and the American governments at some level: arming the port, arranging how Piatkow might be taken ashore without placing the passengers at risk. But that could only be done by apprehending him now.

It also meant blowing his, Beck's, cover. They would know where he was. He would be revealing himself once more.

Beck wasn't sure how much time had passed as he considered his dilemma. Minutes, possibly an hour, but he was no nearer a decision. His sanity couldn't withstand another disaster. Yet neither could he survive seeing Piatkow go free. Beck could see the irony of trying to escape his troubles, only to run directly into them all, but he was in no mood to appreciate it.

Yet underneath it all he knew there was only one option, and it was exactly what he needed to do. 'The way we can compensate for our mistakes is to make sure we do some good,' Martha had said, or words to that effect. All this navel-gazing was selfish and unmanly. It was time to cast it off.

Beck went back to the enquiry office. It was later than he thought, and once more he cursed himself for his self-indulgence. People were gathering in small groups after dinner, saying their goodnights and heading off to bed, while the sybarites set off in search of more pleasure. The clerk behind the counter looked flustered and troubled.

Beck asked for a form to send a wireless message. The clerk, a portly gentleman with a drooping moustache, sighed. 'That's not possible at the moment, sir. I'm afraid the wireless system has developed a fault.'

'Really? A temporary one?'

'I can't say for sure, sir,' the clerk said. 'Be assured we are doing our utmost to repair it. I am more than happy to take your message and it will be dispatched at the earliest possible opportunity.'

Damn, Beck thought. Though it bought him more time. Then a thought occurred to him. An unpleasant one. 'Just when did it stop working?'

'Earlier this evening. I'm not entirely sure of the exact time, sir.'

'And where, out of interest, is the Marconi Room?'

The clerk knotted his brow. 'In the officers' quarters, sir,' he offered. 'I assure you that if you leave your mess—'

'What part of the ship? I only ask out of curiosity.'

The man's brows knotted further, but he relented. 'The boat deck, sir.'

Without responding, Beck turned and headed in search of Ismay.

The two young wireless operators in the Marconi Room looked exasperated. Ismay and Beck had followed them through to a room of dazzling white enamel beside their office, a room that housed the transmitting apparatus for the wireless system. The walls had been soundproofed to prevent the noise distracting them from their work next door and disturbing the sleep of the officers stationed in the adjoining rooms. Not that it was a problem right now because the machine was silent, broken.

Ismay introduced Beck to the two men who manned the room, Phillips and Bride. Phillips was the senior. His face was red, his shirt streaked, his sleeves were rolled up – he'd been delving inside the machine to try to discover the problem. Ismay had explained on the way to the boat deck that neither men were employed by the White Star Line, but by Marconi, which both explained his politeness – Beck doubted whether he would be so deferential to his own employees – and the men's impatience. They earned their money sending messages; any downtime due to a malfunction meant a loss of earnings.

The introductions over, Phillips gestured to Bride. 'Go and update the captain, Harry. Tell him we're no nearer fixing the problem.' Bride, no more than a teenager, looked perplexed but eventually nodded and left.

When he had gone, Ismay closed the door behind him and explained why they had come. 'Mr Beck here is a Scotland Yard detective. He was wondering if anyone had tampered with the, er, the, um—'

'Transmitter,' Phillips broke in helpfully, though he was clearly irritated by the intrusion. He glared at Beck. 'Whatever gives you the impression that someone has tampered with the equipment?'

Beck was prepared for the question, if not for the hostile way it had been asked. 'Just a check. I thought I saw someone here earlier who perhaps shouldn't have been here. Then I heard the equipment was down so I thought I'd pursue it. What's the problem?'

'What do you know of wireless sets?'

'Very little, I grant you that.'

Phillips nodded, wiping his hands on a cloth. 'The simple answer is that at the moment we don't know. I have a feeling it might be the condenser.'

Beck had no idea what that was nor was he seeking an explanation. 'Is there any evidence that the equipment has been tampered with?'

'None that I can see,' Phillips said, sniffing.

'Is the room permanently staffed?'

The technician nodded. 'We work six hours on, six hours off.'

'Day and night?'

'Yes.'

'Busy work.'

'We get well paid for it.'

Ismay piped up. 'The deal is that the Marconi boys send the passengers' private messages, but also receive and send messages on behalf of the ship. It makes sense to have the wireless manned day and night. You never know when people might contact you. Or when you might have to contact them.'

'That reminds me,' Phillips said, turning to him. 'Before it went down we received an ice warning.'

'Did you pass it on to the captain?' Ismay asked.

'Yes. But you said—'

'Excellent,' Ismay said. 'We don't wish to detain you longer than necessary. If you could just spare a few moments more to answer Mr Beck's questions.'

For a brief second Phillip's expression flashed more irritation, but he turned back to face Beck.

'Was there any time this evening when the operating room was unmanned?' Beck asked.

Phillips gave it a few moments' thought. 'Depends what you mean.'

'I mean, was there any time at all when neither you nor your colleague were in this room?'

Beck was experienced enough to know when someone wished to conceal the truth. He could see Phillips was in that position.

'Briefly.'

'For how long?'

'Possibly ten minutes.'

'Possibly?'

'Fifteen, perhaps.'

'When?'

'Earlier this evening. Harold went for his dinner at about seven-thirty or so. I was here.' Phillips paused. 'I had to answer a call of nature. On the way back I got myself a cup of tea.'

'You didn't see anyone loitering around?'

'No.'

'You're sure of that?'

'Certain.'

'Did you notice anything different about your office, or about this room when you returned?'

'Nothing.'

'And the equipment was working perfectly on your return?'

'As far as I'm aware. Harold came back and we had a chat for a bit because we were on top of our work. Then I came to send a few messages and I discovered the system wasn't working.'

'So it could have experienced the malfunction while you were away from your post.' Beck could sense Phillips bridling slightly at the suggestion of negligence. 'By that, I don't mean any criticism of your conduct.'

'None taken,' the technician replied. 'I suppose it could have stopped working during that time. But as I said, I can't see any evidence that it's been tampered with.'

'But it's a possibility?'

'Yes. I suppose it is. Until I work out what the problem is I won't know for sure.'

'What happens if you can't work out what the problem is?'

'Then we won't be able to send any messages,' Phillips said bluntly.

'Or receive them?'

'Or receive them. We have an emergency set that will run for six hours, but after that we'll be radio-silent.'

'Well, let's hope you can fix it,' Ismay said, a half-joking laugh in his voice.

Phillips didn't smile. 'I aim to, sir,' he said with utmost seriousness.

'Once you have fixed it, would it be possible for you to let me know what the problem is? I realise you'll be very busy.'

'Shouldn't be a problem,' Phillips said. 'We don't have much of a backlog. In a few hours' time we'll be out of touch of land and we probably won't make contact until we get further across the Atlantic, so I aim to have her back up and running before then.' He paused. 'There won't be much sleep for us tonight.'

'Well, good luck,' Beck said, and thanked him for his time. He and Ismay left the room and started to walk back to the main part of the ship.

Ismay seemed restless, overwrought. 'What do you think, Mr Beck? Is this the work of the man you are seeking?'

Beck said nothing. The times tallied. Though it could be coincidence. The wireless had failed. Even if it was repaired they were out of reach of land. *If* it was repaired. If not, that would suit Piatkow perfectly. Either way the terrorist had bought himself valuable time, and had confused any plans to capture him. If he was responsible, Beck felt sure Piatkow must have known his presence on the ship had been noted.

Beck knew he might be wrong. But he also knew that he and his country could not afford the cost if he was right and failed to act.

He was so wrapped in thought that he failed to notice that Ismay had stopped walking beside him. When he realised, he turned and saw the magnate standing, hands on hips, eyes ablaze and his moustache almost bristling with irascibility.

'Mr Beck, I demand to know what is going on here. This is my company's ship and I am responsible—'

Beck knew the time had come to take Ismay fully into his confidence. 'I'll see you in your cabin in fifteen minutes.'

'Shall I ask the captain to be there?'

'Yes,' Beck replied.

Ismay's butler brought a brandy for his boss before being dismissed for the night. Beck, wanting to keep a clear head, asked for nothing, as did the captain who was standing by the door as if impatient to return to the bridge. Beck stood at the mantelpiece beside the ornate clock which told him it was twenty minutes to midnight. To Ismay's bemusement, he asked who was responsible for the upkeep of the deck, the boat deck in particular. Ismay, sitting at his bureau, told him it was the deck department and that it would have been the responsibility of an able-bodied seaman.

'I'd like to meet them all tomorrow morning,' Beck said.

'All of them?' Ismay replied in disbelief.

'All of them,' Beck confirmed. 'Every seaman, boatswain, joiner, carpenter and cleaner.'

'But they work a shift system.'

'I don't care. I will need to see them all.'

Ismay pounded his fist against the table. 'Damn you, Mr Beck! I need to know what in goodness is happening here. You force me to take you to the officers' quarters of the ship, to the Marconi Room, areas where I am neither welcome nor particularly comfortable, telling me it's of the utmost urgency. You ask questions about whether the equipment has been tampered with. Then you ask me to muster the crew for your inspection, something once again which is entirely out of my remit. Before we go any further I demand that you tell me just what the hell is going on. Who is this crook you seek? Have you seen him subsequently? And what in Heaven's name has it do with the wireless machine and the damn crew!'

Beck allowed the magnate's anger and bluster to blow itself out, saying nothing, looking down at the floor. He let a few seconds pass before he spoke.

'Mr Ismay, my apologies. I've not been trying to cause you any trouble. I came on board this ship entirely for my own pleasure. The last thing I wanted was to get involved in an investigation.' He paused. 'Everything I tell you now is in the strictest confidence. Can you assure me you will honour that?'

'Of course. You have my word,' Ismay said briskly, as if the mere notion that he would spill any secrets was a grave insult.

'I suspect you have a terrorist on board.'

'A what?' Ismay spluttered. Out of the corner of his eye Beck saw Captain Smith, who barely flinched.

'A terrorist. An anarchist, a cold-blooded killer, a man directly responsible for the deaths of several fine policemen.'

Ismay's gaze scanned the room as he took in the news. 'You don't mean . . . the chap behind the Sidney Street Siege?'

'Peter Piatkow. Yes, I suspect it's him.'

Ismay sat back down in his chair, his face white, his eyes wide with shock. 'I saw in the press that he was never caught. My goodness . . . are you certain?'

Beck had expected dismay but instead saw a prurient relish in his expression – unless that was a consequence of the shock.

'I'm as certain as I can be. I think I've made three separate sightings since I've been on board. While it's not conclusive, it's too much evidence for me to ignore.'

A shadow of concern fell across Ismay's face. 'Do you think he's planning some sort of . . . action, or theft on this ship?'

Beck shook his head. 'I've asked myself that question. I can't be sure. I can't work out what benefit there would be for him in carrying out some action on *Titanic*, or a robbery of some sort.

Gut instinct tells me that he's merely trying to make his way to the United States. Perhaps to meet up with some fellow revolutionaries there. My concern is that he knows he's been spotted. I think I saw him dressed as a member of the crew earlier today. He was near the boathouse around the time when the wireless system failed. It may be coincidence, but it is also possible that he's seeking to stop word reaching land that he's on board.'

'Have you told anyone on land?' Ismay asked eagerly.

'I sent a telegram yesterday saying I suspected he was on board and asking whether there was any intelligence that he might be heading to America. I received a reply saying there was none. A message followed amending that, saying there was information he had been in France. There's been one other telegram.'

'From who?'

'On behalf of Winston Churchill.'

'Churchill. My goodness me,' Ismay said in a hoarse whisper.

'He has a special interest in the case, as I'm sure you're aware. He wants to be informed and he's offered all the help he can. I haven't had time to respond. I was about to when I discovered the wireless was broken.'

It was as if Ismay was cycling through the various stages of grief. Now he was angry. He glared at Beck. 'You have suspected this for a few days and never told me. A dangerous killer may be on board, a notorious villain, yet for all I knew you were keeping your eye on some sort of gentleman crook!'

'I had to try be sure. There seemed little point in alerting you while there was still any doubt. As I said, Piatkow is most dangerous when he's cornered, when he feels threatened. That's when he killed those poor policeman.' Beck cleared his throat. 'I was there. I saw how he acted.'

'You were at Houndsditch?'

'I'm afraid I was.'

Ismay fell silent. 'You think he's cornered now?' he asked eventually.

'I think he feels that his identity has been revealed. It was my hope to sit quietly, narrow down the search, ask for help onshore and apprehend him just as we arrived. I'm not sure that's an option now.'

'So what do you propose?'

'I'm going to try to capture him as soon as I can and then keep him under armed guard for the rest of the voyage. Once the wireless is fixed I'll send a message to London where they can ask for New York to have a police unit meet us. I'm not sure of the diplomatic niceties. It may be that we have to keep him on board and sail him back to the United Kingdom to face trial. I don't know.'

Ismay sat down at the table in the middle of the room and began to chew his nails. Given what was at stake, and his fluctuating moods, he appeared to be handling the news as well as Beck could have expected. Beck was reassured. If he was to capture Piatkow, if this was to work, then he would need Ismay's help and support, as well as his discretion.

'I need your help, Mr Ismay. The British Government and its law-enforcement agencies need your help.'

Beck hoped the patriotic call to arms would further stiffen his resolve. It worked. Ismay thumped the table again, a defiant blow rather than the exasperated slap he had given it earlier.

'Then you will get it,' he said, jutting his jaw out. 'Mr Beck, consider myself, *Titanic* and the resources of the White Star Line at your disposal.'

'I appreciate that, Mr Ismay. As I said earlier, I want a roll-call of all the crew staff at nine a.m. tomorrow. If that doesn't prove fruitful, I want to conduct a thorough search of second class. Then one of steerage, then, if necessary and last of all, of first class. If that fails then I would like to search every other part of the ship.'

'That shouldn't be a problem.'

'Good. How is the ship travelling?'

'You mean how fast is she going?'

'I do.'

'She's improving with each day. Between noon Thursday and noon today she logged 386 miles, which is adequate. However, she looks set to do far more than that in the present run. It is our intention to increase the speed as the voyage progresses.'

'I realise you might not be able to answer this now, so far in advance, but what time do you estimate we'll arrive in New York next Wednesday?'

Ismay fell silent and stared down. For a few seconds, he remained that way, apparently lost in thought. Beck waited patiently for him to respond, aware that everything he had been told might have overwhelmed him. Eventually he looked up.

'The captain and I are still in discussion about this, but because of the encouraging signs of how well she did during today's run I have expressed my desire to have her arrive in New York on Tuesday night, ahead of schedule.'

Beck's face must have registered surprise because Ismay held up a hand, as if to indicate he had more to add.

'The transatlantic route is very competitive, Mr Beck. We cannot compete with our rivals when it comes to speed, so we have built ships that are unsurpassed when it comes to comfort. However, it also helps if they come to be known as quite speedy too. It would be quite a publicity coup if *Titanic* was to make it to New York quicker than her sister ship did on her maiden crossing. If we were to deliver a wanted criminal into the hands of justice, then that would do our profile no harm either.'

Businessmen were the same the world over, Beck thought. They saw a business opportunity in even the gravest of circumstances. 'Arriving in New York at night would be ideal.'

Throughout the entire exchange, the captain had remained silent, as if all matters should be referred to Ismay.

'What do you think, Edward?' Ismay asked

The captain cleared his throat. 'I put my crew and myself at Mr Beck's disposal, sir,' he replied, in the soft voice that was so unsuited to his regal bearing.

'We have spoken about this, captain,' Ismay said, 'but what are our chances of arriving in New York earlier rather than later?'

'Let's see how she goes, Mr Ismay. If she is doing well then I see no reason why we can't aim to arrive ahead of schedule.'

'Yes,' Ismay replied. 'Of course. We can talk about it as the voyage develops. Which reminds me, when we were up in the Marconi Room Mr Phillips talked about ice warnings.'

'Yes, there've been several. To be expected at this time of year, especially after such a cold winter. We'll keep an eye on it. With luck, the equipment will be back in working order soon.'

'Let's hope so,' agreed Ismay. 'Mr Beck would like all the crew mustered at nine tomorrow morning if possible.'

'That shouldn't be a problem.'

'That's very kind of you, captain.'

'Think nothing of it, Mr Beck.'

'Is there any reason why you might be able to get the passengers on deck at some stage? For example, for a lifeboat drill.'

Ismay and the captain exchanged glances. They seemed worried.

'We usually have a lifeboat drill on Sunday mornings,' the captain replied.

'Is everyone involved?'

Again the two men looked at each other.

'It's more for the staff,' Ismay said.

'What about the passengers? How would they know to which boat they were assigned?'

The doubtful looks continued.

'Mr Beck,' Ismay said finally, 'the *Titanic* is designed to be her own lifeboat. Therefore the need to carry sufficient lifeboat space for all those on board is not necessary. We have enough to satisfy United Kingdom laws according to the weight of the ship.'

'I see.' Beck knew what Ismay was hinting at. If all the passengers on board converged on the boat deck en masse they would see there weren't enough lifeboats for them all. Despite all the assurances that the ship was unsinkable, it was likely that a few might panic and they didn't want to cause a scene. 'Don't worry.

I was just trying to find a way to get as many people on deck as possible, so we could have a look at them, and also search down below without inconveniencing them. How about if the different classes perform their drill in staggered fashion, one at a time, so they don't notice the lack of lifeboat provision?'

Ismay and Smith exchanged another look. This time they seemed more hopeful.

'That might be possible,' the captain said.

'I'll get back to you about it. It's an idea we can explore later, perhaps when we're closer to New York. Can I ask at this point that we three remain the only people to know of this? It could cause panic among the passengers if word leaked out, and who knows what reaction that might provoke from Piatkow,' said Beck.

Both of the other men nodded their understanding. 'We can accept more people into the circle, as it were, as and when we need them. But even when we have apprehended Piatkow, I see no reason to let people know his true identity. We can tell them he's a common thief. But we're in danger of getting ahead of ourselves. Captain, when would be the best time to conduct a search of the second-class berths?'

'Do you mean a time when most people are in their berths, or out of them?'

'In them.'

'That would be either early morning or late evening.'

Beck nodded. 'In that case I'll inspect the crew in the morning. During the day I'll search the public areas. In the evening I'll check the second-class berths. If I have no luck, I'll inspect the steerage berths first thing on Sunday morning. If that's fruitless, then we'll have to rethink on Sunday morning and formulate a new plan – perhaps another lifeboat drill on Monday morning,'

'That sounds fine with me,' Ismay said. 'How about you, Captain?'

'I can't see a problem.'

'Excellent,' Beck said. 'Thanks for your help and understanding, and, once again, my apologies that this course of events has unfolded, particularly on this maiden voyage.'

He could see from the glint in Ismay's eyes that his apology was superfluous; the White Star president was wallowing in the whole business. Beck knew that Cunard was offered subsidies by the government to maintain its competitiveness. Perhaps Ismay saw a chance to curry favour and gain some leverage with the authorities. Beck was sure it wasn't merely the prospect of helping catch the most wanted man in Britain that had excited him.

Before he left, Ismay put in a call to the Marconi Room. The equipment was still down. Both the technicians were working on it.

Beck left to go to his room, his mind spinning with thoughts. There was no turning back now. He could only pray that his instincts were right.

A day had come and gone and Sten-Ake had hardly moved. The only meal he had managed was lunch, but he could barely stomach a few mouthfuls of soup. Already his clothes were beginning to sag further, as the weight continued to fall off him. He was feeling weaker and weaker; the previous day's exertion had taken its toll. It was a relief to return to his bunk and to sleep and dream.

This isn't living, he thought. This is just existing.

Some time in the evening – late, he thought, maybe even the middle of the night – he heard someone in his room. It took a while for him to orientate himself and establish what the sound was: a rustling, like someone getting dressed or undressed. He heard a sigh. The light in the cabin was off so he was unable to see. There was a smell of something familiar in the air, a chemical. Carbolic acid, maybe.

'Is someone there?' he asked.

The person paused. He said something in a language he didn't understand. It sounded almost Russian. It was only then that Sten-Ake realised he had asked the question in his own native tongue.

'Who's that?' he asked in English.

'Go back to sleep, old man,' the voice replied. It was low and sonorous, heavily accented; the voice of a young man, he guessed. 'I have been moved here. Sorry for disturbing you.'

Sten-Ake thought of his jacket, and the savings that were stitched into its lining. Where had he put it? He turned his head, his eyes now growing used to the darkness. He could see the outline of a man sitting on the bottom bunk of the bed opposite. He seemed to be wearing some kind of outfit, though Sten-Ake couldn't tell what. Was he crew? Perhaps he was a fireman or a trimmer.

'I am dying,' he said bluntly, though he meant it as a warning, an apology in advance if this man was to be sharing with him.

There was a pause. 'That's all right. You won't be having too much trouble with me.'

Sten-Ake licked his lips. They were dry and cracked and he needed a drink. 'You're Russian?'

'No,' the man said swiftly, angrily almost. 'Certainly not.'

'I am Swedish.'

The man didn't respond to his statement. 'Go back to sleep, old man,' he repeated. 'It is too late to talk.'

In more ways than one, Sten-Ake thought. Then he remembered his jacket, and where he had put it. It was at his feet, propping them up.

13 April 1912

The next morning it was as though a fog had cleared from around Beck. He felt renewed, brimming with purpose. There was no going back on what he had said, and it felt as though a burden had been taken from him. He also had a plan; one that didn't involve him running around in circles like a dog chasing its tail.

He attended a roll-call for the deck department on the forward well deck as planned. They were a fine collection of men, though a few of them seemed unhappy to have been called away from their beds after a long shift. Chief Officer Wilde called the muster and Beck walked beside the captain – who was gazing proudly and benevolently at his men – making sure he took in every face. Piatkow, as he had expected when he woke that morning, was not to be seen among them.

Once they had finished, he thanked the captain and his men for their time and went in search of Martha Heaton.

Martha was on her way into breakfast when Beck caught up with her, putting a hand on her shoulder. There was a flush to his face, a sense of energy and health that contrasted with his listless and morose demeanour of the night before. What had been in that telegram? At least he had been lucky to receive his. She had been to check that morning to see if Donny had replied, only to be told the system was down. What that meant for any messages being transmitted, she didn't know, and neither could the enquiry office tell her. Would the sender keep trying until their transmission was received, or would they just give up?

''You look very sprightly,' she told Beck.

'I had a good night. Mind if I join you for breakfast?'

'Feel free. Be warned: my dining companions are hardly stirring company.'

He waved her concern away with a dismissive hand. 'Actually, I'm quite intrigued to meet them. Mr Darton in particular.'

'But he's a terrible bore. He loves the sound of his own voice.'

Beck did not seem deterred. Instead, he ushered her through the door into the bustling dining room, his arm resting gently across her back. 'No need to apologise. I know the type.'

The others were already seated, some already well into their breakfasts. Darton was holding court, his face red as a ripe tomato, presumably from the previous evening's excesses. He stopped talking as they took their seats, Beck taking the place vacated by Miss Hardee.

'Nice of you to rejoin us, Miss Heaton,' Darton said, not without sarcasm. He looked at Beck, who nodded a greeting at him and the others.

'Good morning,' Beck said politely.

Martha could see Darton's piggy eyes glisten with amusement as he saw them arrive together at breakfast and reached a hasty conclusion.

She made the introductions, leaving Darton to last. 'This is Mr Beck, a friend.'

The rest of the group either nodded or smiled, whereas Darton stood, reached across the table, and pumped Beck's hand vigorously. 'My pleasure, my pleasure,' he said.

They ordered – Martha some grapefruit and oatmeal, Beck the kippers – and sat for an awkward period of silence. At least, it was awkward for Martha. For the first time, with Darton's beady eyes on them, she found herself unable, or unwilling, to chat with Beck, something which had previously been easy for her. Nor could she work out why he had been so keen to join her and her table for breakfast. Had it just been her company that he wanted, he might have suggested the à la carte restaurant.

'So, Mr Beck, what's your line of business?' Darton asked, pushing a half-eaten plate of eggs and bacon to one side.

Martha sipped her coffee and waited, with some eagerness, for Beck's answer. 'I'm in the publishing business.'

She almost spat her coffee across the table. Thankfully, Darton's resounding, overly enthusiastic 'Really!' cloaked her surprise.

'Yes. This is just a holiday, though. Not business.'

'Which part of the publishing business? Books, journals, magazines?'

'Books. Antiquarian books predominantly. I'm a sole trader, in that I travel around seeking out the books which I buy. Some I keep, others I sell on for a small profit.'

'Fascinating,' Darton said.

Kimball, previously detached, seemingly more interested in his porridge, was nodding eagerly too. 'Truly very interesting. How does one source such books?'

'I have contacts,' Beck said. 'People who visit fairs, second-hand bookshops, but nothing can substitute for going to these places yourself. I travel as much as I can. Much of the skill comes in knowing the right book and right edition for certain collectors.'

'Is there money in it?' Darton asked. Martha saw Kimball raise his eyes at the vulgarity of the question.

'I do all right. Every now and then one comes across a book that is of great value, to the right collector, though the seller might not be aware of it.'

'Aha!' Darton said, chuckling. 'Business is business whether one sells books or bath attachments.'

'Is that your line of work, Mr Darton?'

'It is,' he said, with a sense of pride. 'And a lucrative one it is, too.'

'Good for you,' Beck said.

Kimball interrupted, obviously not wanting the conversation to detour into the world of faucets and mixers, 'So, Mr Beck, what is the holy grail of the antiquarian book market?'

Beck, his kippers barely touched, sat back and folded his arms. Martha watched and waited, starting to believe on the evidence of this performance that Beck would make a first-class ham – and therefore a decent news reporter if he continued to grow disillusioned with detective work.

Eventually, he replied. 'The answer depends on who you speak to. The consensus among some of us would probably be the Gutenberg Bible of 1456, the first book ever printed.'

'How much would that fetch?' Darton asked. Kimball rolled his eyes once more.

'Somewhere between two and three million dollars,' Beck replied. Darton let out a whistle.

'However, the chances of finding one are slim. Hence the price tag. Of the books that are rather more freely available, I'd quite like to get my hands on a first edition of the collected works of Shakespeare. There are some that exist from the early years of the seventeenth century that I would kill to get my hands on. Though I'd probably have to lay out somewhere near a million pounds.'

Darton gave another whistle. Even Kimball gasped.

'I am in the wrong racket,' Darton said emphatically.

Martha said nothing, just picked at her grapefruit and wondered from where on God's Earth Beck was plucking these facts, and what it was all in aid of. Had he lost his mind?

'It's a very competitive world,' Beck continued. 'People think of books and booksellers and they think of dusty old shops, yellowing paper, musty leather-bound books, silence, the smell of old print. In fact, it's as full of chicanery and sharp practice as any other trade I can think of.'

'Is that right?' Darton asked.

Beck nodded. 'For sure.' He leaned forward. Kimball, Darton, the women, all followed suit. Even Martha. His voice dropped to a conspiratorial whisper. 'I only recently discovered that one of the most sought-after and valuable books in the world is on this very voyage. My heart almost stopped when I found out.'

'What is it?' Kimball asked, any proprieties gone south by now.

'It's a copy of the *Rubaiyat of Omar Khayyam*.'

There was a pause, even a few gasps from the ladies. 'I've never heard of it,' Martha said.

Beck didn't even look at her. 'It's a translation of a collection of Persian poems written around the turn of the twelfth century.'

'Wow, that's old,' Darton said.

'The edition itself was only recently printed. However, it is one of a kind. The most remarkable specimen of binding ever produced. It is festooned with more than a thousand precious jewels, thousands of separate leather inlays, and took more than two years to produce. It was sold recently at Sotheby's of London for an unnamed amount, and is being transported to its new owner in the United States. I've made it my mission on arrival to find out who has bought it, and see if they will let me have a look at it. Who knows,' he said, sitting back, dabbing his mouth with napkin, 'perhaps I can put in a bid. I know of quite a few people who would be willing to part with some serious money to own it.'

'Well, I'll be damned,' Darton said, shaking his head. 'What a story. It's on this ship?'

'It sure is. I've seen the cargo manifest. Where it is is less certain. Presumably under lock and key. At least, I hope it is. My guess would be the specie room. I think that's where the most secret, expensive and official parcels and packages are kept. Though I could be wrong.'

'The specie room,' Kimball said. 'Sounds very exotic.'

'Yes. Who knows what else lies therein?' Beck said, rather overegging it by now, Martha thought.

Whatever his purpose, it had been a convincing performance. Darton and Kimball would be telling the tale to everyone they met.

It was then that Martha realised what Beck was up to, and why he had been so keen to join her for breakfast.

One by one, their fellow diners left, until Martha and Beck were alone. He had still barely touched his breakfast.

'Not hungry?' she asked.

'Not really. I had breakfast earlier.'

'Oh, really? In your room?'

'With the crew, actually. Some of them, anyway.'

'So why were you so keen to breakfast with me and my gang? And what was all that with the shaggy-dog stories? You're no more an antiquarian book dealer than I am a Broadway actress.'

'Isn't it the case when one is on holiday that one can pretend to be who one wants to be, if only for a short time?'

'If one is full of bullshit. You wanted Darton to hear all that baloney about the book.'

'Who says it's baloney?'

'You're telling me it's true? There's a priceless bejewelled book on board?'

'Let's just say I took a thread of truth and spun it into a rather wonderful yarn. Something that, as a journalist, you probably know more about than most.'

'Touché,' Martha replied. 'What bits are true and what bits aren't?'

'The book exists, though some of the jewels are semi-precious. It isn't priceless; it sold at auction for £405 – a decent sum, but hardly extortionate.'

'Why did you want Darton to know about it?'

'He strikes me as a man of rare breeding, with a heightened sense of culture.'

'Now I know you're full of it. The only culture he knows is the one growing between his toes. You want him to spread the word about this book, don't you? Because he will. By this evening the whole of first class will know about it, and it will be worth billions by then.'

A smile spread across Beck's face, revealing two slight dimples in his cheeks.

'You should smile more,' Martha said. 'It suits you.'

Beck shrugged.

'Now are you going to tell me what the deal is with this? Why you want the whole world to know the *Titanic* has a fabulous book of incalculable value in its hold?' She paused. 'Unless you're trying to encourage some kind of heist.'

Beck said nothing, merely wiped his lips with a napkin once more. He picked up his cup and drained the remnants of his tea.

'You can include the story of the *Rubaiyat* in your piece. Maybe you could even help me track its owner on our arrival. Might make a nice story for your paper.'

'Thanks. I'll leave it to our fine-arts correspondent. I'm after bigger fish than that.'

Beck got up and straightened his jacket. He glanced towards the window, where light was streaming in. 'Well, if you're after big fish, what better place to be than in the middle of the ocean. Sorry, I need to be elsewhere. Thanks for inviting me to join you for breakfast. Always a pleasure.'

Martha watched him leave, a spring in his step, wondering whether she didn't prefer him when he was downcast.

Martha idled away much of the morning, checking periodically with the enquiry office to see if there were any messages. According to the clerk, the wireless system was working again but the backlog had prevented them sending any new messages for several hours. She was more interested in what was incoming, but he was unable to enlighten her about those.

She climbed the stairs to the boat deck. The weather was still clear and bright but noticeably cooler. She did a few laps, taking care to have a look at the second- and third-class decks below to see if she could spot Beck loitering, but he was nowhere to be seen. Breakfast still baffled her. He had been so impish and mischievous where previously he had been intense and distracted. He wanted word of the book to spread. For whose ears? The man he sought, presumably. A thief of some kind. Whatever his reasons, it seemed to have worked. She overheard a group playing quoits – a dumb game if ever she'd seen one – talking excitedly about the priceless jewelled book on board.

After taking some air, Martha went back to her room and read. The lunch bugle sounded but she ignored it and carried on reading. When her eyes grew tired she napped, and woke feeling refreshed. Another check at the enquiry office revealed that there was still no message for her. Meanwhile, there was an excited murmur among the passengers, and it wasn't about priceless books. The 'run' for the previous day between noon on Friday and Saturday had just been posted on the passenger bulletin board and people were crowding around it. 519 miles had been logged. Some of the chatter was speculation about who had won the daily sweep estimating how many miles they had travelled; but the rest was about how fast the ship was going, the marked increase in distance from the previous day, and whether the rumours of them arriving in New York on Tuesday might possibly be true.

Not wanting to go back to her room, Martha took her book, as well as some paper and pencils in case her muse struck her, and went to the reception room on D deck, still crowded with the lunchtime crowd. She sat and read near a window on the port side next to a grand piano, behind a large potted plant, and the area gradually emptied as peopled drifted off to fill their afternoon. By two, the room was agreeably silent for reading, save for the distant throb of the engines.

Martha was so involved in her book that she took some time to notice that two men had sat down at a table near her. Eventually she tuned into their low voices and looked up. One was the captain, in full regalia, the other was Ismay. The only other person she could see in the room was a stout woman in a green dress sitting at a table beyond the two men; she appeared to be engrossed in letter writing.

She turned back to her book but the words didn't register any more; Martha knew there was no chance she could avoid eavesdropping. Luckily, for her curiosity, Ismay had one of those clipped voices that carried even when he was trying to speak quietly, though Captain Smith's was much softer in tone and consequently harder to make out. The conversation seemed to be about nothing in particular until Ismay brought up the day's mileage.

'We had a good run,' he said.

The captain pursed his lips and nodded.

'A very good run,' Ismay added. 'Five hundred and nineteen

miles. That's only five less than the *Olympic* managed on the same day and it is so much better than the previous days.'

Captain Smith nodded his assent. Martha wasn't sure if he was aware of others being present and wished to be discreet, or whether he was staying quiet in deference to his boss, but he seemed reluctant to speak. Ismay was not as reticent.

'She seems to be standing up very well indeed. We are very, very impressed with her, and I dare say we will make a better run tomorrow. The boilers are performing well. I think we can put a little bit more pressure on them now and increase her speed even further. The weather is good and looks set to stay fair.'

Captain Smith murmured a few words that Martha could not make out.

'I'm sure the obstacles ahead will not prove an impediment. There is a real chance here for us to beat the *Olympic*'s time and get into New York on Tuesday. We will increase her speed from here on in. The coal reserves are adequate, I trust?'

Captain Smith nodded.

'Excellent. So, God willing, Tuesday it shall be. If we need to, we should think of lighting the auxiliary boilers and connecting them to the engine. We don't want to thrash the engines – they are new, after all – but it would be good to know exactly what she's capable of.'

It was news to make Martha's heart soar with delight. In four days' time she would be back in Manhattan. It was all she could do to resist shouting out, 'Full speed ahead, and get us there on Monday!'

The woman in green stood up, smoothing down her dress, and

waddled off towards the door, leaving a steaming cup of coffee and her papers and books on the table. Ismay watched her go, as if waiting for her to be out of earshot. He turned back to the captain and leaned forward.

'I have not seen our friend since this morning. He seems to have changed his strategy somewhat. I think we have no choice but to trust his judgement.'

Again, Smith's brief reply was inaudible.

"Yes, but it would be an enormous coup if we were to be responsible for helping to bring him in. You can imagine the press going very big on it, not only back in the UK, but in the United States, too. I don't need to tell you, Edward, of all people, that these are very competitive times in the transatlantic trade. Publicity is everything, and while we might shy away from some of the more vulgar tactics of our rivals, the sort of coverage we might receive is priceless.'

Martha tried to make herself as small as possible in her chair. She had a sudden urge to cough but managed to repress it. She wanted nothing to stop Ismay talking.

'It makes arriving in New York as soon as we can absolutely paramount,' Ismay said. 'Has the wireless been fixed?'

Smith nodded. He mumbled some more.

Ismay responded: 'Well, of course it is entirely your judgement. It is not for me to tell you how best to pilot this ship. But I'm glad to hear that the warnings are unlikely to hamper our progress. Considering what we have to gain by getting to New York on Tuesday, it would be a terrible shame if we were to be slowed down in any way. Especially when you consider how well the ship is performing and how much she has in reserve. It seems to us that she will prove to be a much faster vessel than the *Olympic*. I have spoken to Mr Andrews and he concurs. He is delighted with her in almost every aspect.'

He paused. The captain spoke, once again too softly for Martha to hear.

Ismay replied: 'No, as our friend asked, I have not told him yet. Nor do I intend to unless it is necessary. Not that he would mind. Andrews is entirely focused on how well she runs and how she works and looks, even down to the coat hooks. Some might say he's obsessed. The least interesting things to him on this ship are the passengers.' He let out a small chuckle. 'Which reminds me, he was going on about some complaint about the squash courts. I have to say I was rather distracted. My mind is on more serious things but it will serve us well to check out what he says. You know how impatient he can be.' There was another small laugh.

At this point the ample woman in green returned to her seat. The two men fell silent as she sat down. Finally Ismay spoke up.

'So we are agreed. We shall increase her speed each day and see what she can do. We will light all her auxiliary boilers when necessary and connect them to the engine.' Smith nodded and Ismay stood up. 'Come on, captain, we will get somebody and go down to the squash courts.'

Both men left. Martha was left to ruminate on what she had overheard. Her professional opinion was that she had a minor scoop. *Titanic* was likely to make it into New York in faster time than her sister ship had on its maiden voyage. Hardly hold-the-front-page stuff, but it was a line at least.

Of greater interest was the hushed conversation about 'bringing in' someone, and the publicity this would garner. Martha knew this was linked to Beck's activities on board, and it explained the anxious glances that Ismay had kept shooting at him in the restaurant reception room the night before. 'Our friend' had to be a reference to him, and the 'strategy' he spoke of being changed was, if she was a gambling woman – and she only was after a few drinks – connected with the performance that Beck had put on that morning.

She wondered where Beck was now. Spreading more hokey rumours, probably. After eavesdropping on the conversation between Ismay and the captain, she was in a position to start gossiping herself. It was tempting to go in search of Darton if only to lord it over him about what she had learned. But that could wait. What she wanted more than anything was a message from shore that might give her a starting point for the bigger story. The fact that Ismay had alluded to the America press, which was notoriously insular as she knew from experience, going big over this mystery crook on board indicated that the fugitive was even more important then she had first thought. Add to that the stated desire to increase the ship's speed to its limit and dock in New York early, despite the inconvenience that might cause to some of the passengers who were prepared for a Wednesday arrival, and she knew this was a copper-bottomed front-page award-winning scoop.

The sort that made careers.

The loud, high-pitched whine of the rotating spark disc within the Marconi Room's main transmitter told Beck that the equipment was working once more. The dark rings that circled Phillips's eyes also told him that fixing the problem had been hard work.

According to the senior operator – his assistant Bride was catching up on some sleep – it had taken them all night to solve the problem.

'That was the hard bit,' Phillips said with a rueful smile. 'We had almost taken her to bits. I thought it was the condensers but they seemed to be fine.'

'What the was the problem?' Beck asked, happy to be playing the role of a detective seeking information once more rather than the on-board gossiper-in-chief. His performance at breakfast had been the first act of three. The second had been at lunch in second class, where he had joined the young man Marshall with whom he had shared a smoke on Thursday night. Exactly the sort Beck was seeking. The type, like Darton in first class, who was no more capable of keeping quiet about a valuable piece of gossip than Churchill was of keeping away from the centre of action. He knew that their personalities would compel them to spread the word. It helped that Marshall had fallen in with a group of other young men in second class, all of whom had sat rapt while listening to Beck.

The only uncomfortable moment came when one, a young Englishman with a chippy air, put down his knife and fork and asked Beck how he knew all this information about the book. Beck had replied that a member of staff had told him, and that he had seen evidence on the cargo manifest – which was a lie, as there was no mention of the *Rubaiyat* on the official list. It was probably lumped in with the other books that had been brought on board.

'Sounds like the stuff of myth,' the young man sniffed, picking up his knife and fork again and tucking in to his roast pork.

'I don't see any reason to lie about it,' Beck said. 'My source is a good one.'

The meal continued, the talk moving on to other subjects, including a rumour that the ship was increasing its speed in the hope of making an early arrival in New York. This created a faint sense of alarm within Beck: he wondered where the rumour was coming from and whether it was related to last night's conversation with Ismay and Smith. As he was discovering, it wouldn't take much, only a passing comment, for news that there was a crook on board to fly around the ship and create mass panic.

The third act was due to be played out in steerage, but before then he had made a detour to the wireless cabin to question Phillips, who was looking at the equipment with some disdain.

'The problem was a short,' he said eventually, matter-of-factly.

Beck had no knowledge of electrics. The new technologies were a mystery to him. Science altogether baffled him. Yet he knew that it was playing an increasing part in detective work. He was no Luddite: fingerprinting, the analysis of evidence under a microscopic lens, and the recent classification of blood groups, which allowed the linking of blood found at a crime scene to that belonging to a suspect, were all welcome advancements. It was simply that much of the detail of how they worked went over his head. He was glad that police work still relied on hard work, logic, instinct and skill.

'A short?'

There was a hint of impatience in Phillips's tone. 'A lead from the secondary in the transformer somehow came into contact with the metal part of the equipment. Once we realised that, we fixed it with some insulating tape. It wasn't a big problem. In the end.'

He might as well have been speaking in Swahili for all that Beck understood of it. But it didn't matter. More urgent was the answer to the next question. 'You said "somehow" – does that mean you don't know how the short happened?'

'Well, it happened because the wire in the coil was exposed, maybe because of a heat build-up, so it burned though and touched the casing around the transformer.'

More Swahili, thought Beck. 'Is it possible that someone with a basic knowledge of electrics could have sabotaged the equipment?'

Phillips didn't seem to be in the mood to discuss theories. 'Most people would know that if an exposed wire comes into contact with metal it will create a short.'

'Is it more likely to have happened naturally?'

'Things like this happen frequently, yes. But I'm puzzled as to how it came to touch the casing.'

'So there's a chance that someone came in, exposed the wire and caused the short?'

'A chance, yes.'

Beck wondered if Piatkow knew anything about electrics. It wasn't in any file he had read, nor had it cropped up in any of the interviews with the terrorist's acquaintances. But as Phillips had said, even a cursory knowledge of electrics was enough to know what caused a short. If Piatkow was responsible, why hadn't he merely cut the wire, or another wire, rather than exposing it? It would have made fixing the machine harder, and would have put the transmitter out of action for longer, if not for the whole voyage, assuming that the idea was to thwart any messages being sent to and from the ship. Once again, a worm of doubt nestled in the back of Beck's mind, but he pushed it away.

'Has the malfunction affected the flow of messages?' he asked.

'Not too badly. I cleared a bit of the backlog an hour or so after we got it working again. There're a fair few outgoing messages to be sent. But I'll wait until we get in touch with land tomorrow night to send those out – the non-urgent ones, anyway. There're messages coming in, and that takes up most of our time.'

'Messages for the passengers?'

'Chatter from other ships, mainly for the captain, wishing him and *Titanic* well, weather updates, ice warnings, that sort of thing,' Phillips said.

'There's ice ahead?'

'Apparently. Presumably not on our track. Which reminds me, I must get back.'

'Of course,' Beck said, and they returned to the operator room. Bride, bleary-eyed, had just surfaced, his thick hair sticking up in spikes. He nodded a greeting. Phillips slipped his earphones back on, the spike next to him piled high with messages.

Beck wondered if London had sent another message. He had yet to respond to their earlier communications and considered sending a Marconigram now, even thought of dictating it directly to one of the operators. But he decided it was too early for that, and he needed time to see if his plan would work.

Any message could wait until they were in touch with land, when it could be passed directly and with greater confidentiality.

And when he hoped they would have Piatkow in custody.

The evening meal was just entering its second course when Martha chose her moment to leave, explaining that she felt faint and needed some air. Mrs Kimball offered to come with her to make sure she was all right, but Martha explained it was probably nothing, just a passing flush, a hint she took in the ladylike fashion Martha expected of a woman of her class by saying nothing, avoiding eye contact and staring primly at her sole meunière.

The dining room was full, conversations at their most animated, and Martha had to swerve round the waiters weaving in and out of tables with silver salvers and carafes of wine. She passed Ismay at his table deep in conversation, no doubt purring about the speed of his ship and the headway they were making. There was roast beef in front of him so he was still several courses away from finishing his meal. As she left the room the band was just launching into a new number. It felt as though they were following her around. One morning she would awake and they would be there, serenading her morning ablutions. She was sure they were good, but she liked her tunes with a bit more jaunt and bounce.

As she had hoped, the reception room and the hall beyond were quiet. The whole shipboard routine revolved around meals. Few people missed them.

Martha made her way up the Grand Staircase to B deck, turning left immediately and avoiding eye contact with anyone in the enquiry office, but the murmured voices of the staff, happy to be given a few moments' peace to idle and chat, drifted along behind her. The sound of their conversation faded, leaving just the throb of the engines, which she had long grown used to. She wasn't sure but their vibration seemed to have increased, as if they were running faster, straining harder. But that might have been her imagination, influenced by what she had overheard earlier.

She passed through a pair of double doors. If she was correct, Ismay's room was here on the right. She knocked lightly on the door. No answer. She knew he had an assistant with him and a manservant, but hoped they might be allowed some time to eat too. She waited for the door to open – if she had to, she would apologise for having picked the wrong room. Glancing up and down the corridor she saw no one approaching. The stewards might well have seized the chance of respite from their wealthy clients too, and were probably having a well-earned cigarette in their quarters. She knocked once more, louder. No answer. She tried the door. Like all the others, including her own, it was open.

Inside, the room was warm, with a hint of cigar smoke in the air, mingling with the scent of cologne. Martha looked at the door. No catch or lock. Across the other side of the room she could see a set of glass doors which appeared to open out onto a private promenade. She smiled. Ismay was hardly slumming it. A perk of owning the ship. It also gave her an escape route if the worst happened.

The room was neat and ordered, the opposite of hers, where every available space was scattered with clothes, papers and books, despite the best efforts of Bad Teeth to maintain order. Ismay's man was obviously more successful. Or Ismay was less of a slob than her. Not difficult.

Martha walked over to the table in the centre of the room. There were a pile of papers, a few books. What was she looking for? She wasn't sure. Something, a note, draft of a telegram, with the details of what Beck was up to. Cocking an ear for any sound from outside, which didn't come, she leafed through the sheaf of papers. There was a memo from someone called Andrews, listing a few defects with the ship. There was a telegram warning of ice. There were a few notes, presumably in Ismay's own hand, about the ship's performance and a scribbled heading 'Suggested Improvements for *Gigantic*'. Another ship, she guessed. None of it what she was looking for.

She froze. There were voices in the corridor. Male voices. She headed for the glass doors and tried to open them but they were stiff. Instead, she slipped behind the long drapes designed to cloak them. She listened, heart hammering against the walls of her chest. The voices seemed to have died down. Moved on, Martha hoped. She gave it a few more seconds. What was she doing? This was madness. If she was caught she'd be taken ashore in handcuffs. Was it worth it?

She stepped out from behind the curtain. The only other object of interest was to her right. A bureau strewn with random papers. There was a letter, a few pages long, to Ismay's wife. Reading his personal mail was a step too far. Oh yes, Martha, she thought, give yourself a pat on the back for ethics while you ransack the cabin you've broken into. There were a few more letters, some completed, one addressed to Harland and Wolff in Belfast, another to the White Star Line's offices in Liverpool. She scanned them. Nothing of interest, just shipping business scrawled in a neat, precise hand.

Martha stopped to listen once more. Only a few more minutes, then she'd be pushing her luck. She glanced around the desk but there was little else, just a well-stocked box of cigars. They looked expensive. She thought of taking one. Though she hated the taste, she adored the smell, and she was sure she could find someone who would appreciate the treat. But theft was something else she baulked at.

There was a drawer on the right-hand side of the bureau. Martha slipped it open quietly. It was empty save for a small pad of paper, similar to the one she wrote in. It was closed. Without taking it out, she raised the cover. It was filled with Ismay's scrawl, less readable than the one he used in his correspondence. Only a few pages had been filled. The first was about J.P. Morgan and it was clear after a few sentences that she was reading a rant, or some kind of moan at least, about the American owners with whom the White Star Line and Ismay had entered into a business agreement. There would be a short piece of copy in that, perhaps, but not one she wanted to write. The workings of business bored her profoundly.

The third page of the notepad grabbed her immediately. It had been split into two columns: pros and cons. There were only a few points under each heading.

In the cons, it read: 'Can Beck be trusted?' Underneath it were the words 'Is it worth the danger?' Under pros, it said: 'Very beneficial publicity if caught.' Beneath that Ismay had written

'A chance to ingratiate with HMG.' The final con was 'Smith uncomfortable – me too.' Across the page, underlined several times in a heavy hand, were the capitalised words 'PATRIOTIC DUTY'.

That was it. It raised so many more questions. Martha's heart pounded again at the sound of voices in the corridor. She was about to slip back behind the drapes when she heard them fade. People would be leaving their tables soon. Some would be heading straight to bed. The halls would be full. That was enough trespassing for one night, she decided, and headed to the door, listening carefully behind it for a few seconds before opening it slowly. Popping her head around she could see two men along the corridor running aft. Their backs were to her. There was no one forward, not that it was easy to see because of the baize doors. She stepped out and closed the door behind her, expelling a deep breath.

A man, young, handsome, with an amused smirk on his face, burst through the hallway door. It made her jump. The man held up his hands.

'Sorry,' he said, his smirk turning to a look of concern. 'I didn't mean to scare you.'

Martha raised a hand. 'No need to apologise. I'm a bit . . . a bit lost.'

She felt sure her guilt was written all over her face. The man smiled. If it was, he was too stupid to read it.

'Where are you trying to go?'

'I should be on C deck,' she said. 'Came up one floor too high, it seems.'

'An easy mistake to make,' he said, not without a hint of

condescension. 'Please, let me escort you back to the stairway.'

'Thank you, but it's fine,' Martha said hurriedly. Perhaps too hurriedly. He seemed affronted. 'It's been a long day.'

He nodded. 'She's a big vessel. Easy to get confused, especially when one is tired. Goodnight,' he said, flashing her a smile on full beam.

'Goodnight,' she said, lowering her head and making her way through the double doors. Behind her, she had a sense that the young man was about to go through the door opposite Ismay's. Oh God, Martha thought. Perhaps he knew where she'd been. She went into the area near the stairs, across from the enquiry office. She needed a drink and dark place to have it. Give herself time to think. Ponder what she had read, and lie low.

'Miss Heaton!'"

She was about to go up, get some air and have a smoke when she heard her name called. Once again, her heart started to beat as if it was trying to leap out of her mouth. Had she been caught?

Martha turned, smiling as innocently as she could. It wasn't the man she had just passed outside Ismay's room, nor was it an official-looking purser or steward. It was a young bellhop, bright-eyed and eager.

'A message for you, madam,' he said. He was holding out an envelope. She didn't say anything, just looked at him for a few seconds as her heart rate slowed. 'From the Marconi Room,' he explained.

'Oh,' Martha said. 'Thanks.' She patted her dress as if she might have change for a tip, but the bellhop had turned on his heels and gone before she could make any apology.

She walked up the stairs to the boat deck, ignoring the glorious light from the overhead chandeliers that bathed everything around them in a soft golden glow. By the time she reached the boat deck she had the message opened. It was from Donny, dated earlier that day, addressed from the office.

SCOTLAND YARD OFFICIAL SAYS AB NO LONGER WORKS FOR THEM. SOURCE CONFIRMS HE WAS SACKED. MORE FOLLOWS SOONEST.

Martha read it three times, standing at the top of the stairs. No matter how many times she looked the words didn't rearrange themselves into an order she understood.

Beck was no longer employed by Scotland Yard? Then what was he doing on board acting as if he was?

The door leading to the deck opened, letting in a cool draught and the ozone waft of the sea. She looked up.

There stood Beck.

The specie room lay behind a sealed wooden hatch that prevented anyone gaining access from the hold. It was concealed by the heaped first- and second-class baggage located in the bowels of the ship along with a few other pieces of more valuable cargo, like a Renault motor car which was encased in a wooden crate and housed in a room of its own on the Orlop Deck.

Anyone seeking to reach the specie room – which, Ismay had told Beck, also contained a large consignment of opium on its way to the United States for pharmaceutical use – would have to walk down the stairs from G deck. There was no other way in. If anyone came this way intending to steal anything or simply to case the joint, Beck would see them.

There were boxes and chests piled everywhere, and the smell of leather and dust lay heavy in the air. Beck couldn't help but wonder what gifts and treasures lay inside them. Those moving to America would be taking all their worldly possessions. He had only one bag and it was in his cabin. But he planned to return to the United Kingdom. One day, at least. A day that might come sooner rather than later if he pulled this off.

He reached into his pocket. The chunky, reassuring feel of a gun. Captain Smith had taken him to the officers' quarters, a secure area, where he had handed it to him gravely, asking him to take as much care as possible.

Beck had made a promise that it would only be fired as a last resort. He wanted Piatkow alive, not dead. Smith had not seemed too reassured, but they couldn't risk the chance of Piatkow being armed. He had shown himself more than willing to use a gun in the past.

Beck rested back on a chest, hidden slightly by a stack of bags but still able to see the stairs. He took out the pistol and checked that it was loaded. A Webley double-action revolver. He had handled one before. It seemed a strange choice to have on board. Most seamen were inexperienced with firearms. The Webley was very powerful, almost too powerful, its recoil so strong that it would cause all but the best-trained shooter to fire wildly and inaccurately. He wondered under what circumstances a ship's crew would have to use firearms. Situations like this one, maybe – or perhaps crowd control in an emergency?

He put the gun back in his pocket and checked the stairs. No one. His pocket watch had told him it was just after ten. This could be a long night, he thought. At dinner he had eaten well, drunk lots of hot coffee and steered clear of liquor to make sure he was alert.

Then, after dinner, he had gone on deck for a smoke and to take in some air, to clear his head further, Lighting a cigarette down here, with all these bags and papers, would be a bad idea. It wasn't as if there was a hatch or porthole he could smoke out of, either; it was well below the waterline. The thought gave him the creeps. Below him was the tank top, the lowest level of the boat. Beneath that was the double bottom that was rumoured to be haunted by the ghost of a trapped construction worker. Beck shook his head.

The sea created myths and fables as surely as it made waves.

After finishing his cigarette, and half-frozen from the dropping temperature outside, Beck had gone back inside to prepare for his vigil. There he had bumped into Martha Heaton. The encounter was an odd one. The poor woman seemed troubled – a result, he presumed, of whatever it was she held in her hand. A telegram or letter of some sort. It must have been bad news because her troubled manner was in stark contrast to her usually assured and confident demeanour.

'Are you all right?' he had asked, thinking at first it was a shame that he had ever seen Piatkow. In other circumstances, he and Martha might have had some fun together – or as much fun as you could have with a journalist.

She had nodded hesitantly, looking everywhere but at him, when previously she had kept her blue-eyed gaze on him at all times, sometimes disconcertingly so. Beck was used to men looking at him fair and square, but it was damned disconcerting coming from a woman. 'Yes,' she had said softly. Then she'd cleared her throat. 'Yes, I'm fine. I just need some air. It's been quite a day.'

Her smile was thin and forced, not the open, beaming one he so admired. It was as if she was ill. He knew better than to stand between an ailing woman and some fresh air, so he let her pass. 'Perhaps later,' he had said, trying to rekindle some of their earlier spark, but she had not acknowledged his comment or even turned around. He had watched her go through the doors and out on to the deck.

Very odd, Beck thought, looking back. Maybe there had been some bad news from work. The snooper in him was tempted to march up to the Marconi Room and, citing police business, demand to see all the messages which had come in and find out what was wrong. But there wasn't time, and he respected her privacy too much. Respecting a journalist's privacy. He chuckled to himself. If only they held the same standards.

Beck put Martha and her troubles from his mind, or tried to. The memory of their conversation the night before was still clear. Not only because it had given him strength, allowed him to see what was truly important and how he should proceed, but because of how close he had come to confessing everything to her. His reasons for being on board, for fleeing England, all about Piatkow. That would have been a grave error of judgement. Her first loyalty was to her newspaper colleagues and she would have turned to them first.

A thought, an old vague sense of uneasiness, settled upon him, but he quickly fought it back. He needed his wits about him here and now, not in the past, recent or not, and he could do without any woman troubles either. What mattered was trapping Piatkow.

Once more Beck glanced at the stairs. There was no sign of anyone. The boys in the mail room would be working all night somewhere nearby, sorting through three thousand letters. The black gang in the boiler rooms and coal bunkers would be toiling away and so would the officers on watch. But soon, room by room, light by light, the ship would grow dark and quiet, even as it was propelled onwards faster and faster. The last conversation he'd had with Ismay earlier that evening had confirmed that the engines were working well and would be tested further, and pushed harder, and the ship would continue to raise its speed towards its maximum. Ismay thought, on the advice of the captain and the chief engineer, that she might be able to reach twenty-six knots by Monday, a figure which meant little to a landlubber like Beck but was spoken with hushed reverence by the White Star Line president.

A Tuesday arrival was a distinct possibility. Beck might well be here for much of that time, though there'd been talk of asking another of the crew to spell him on watch to help him rest. A bunker hold was empty and had been earmarked as a secure place to hold Piatkow when he was captured. It was a room below the waterline with a metal padlocked door for access; a perfect place to imprison the terrorist until they docked and the ship was cleared. Then he, Beck, would remain on board and await further orders from London. Perhaps even accompany his notorious quarry back home, to a hero's welcome for Beck and a raft of snivelling apologies from those who had sought to prosecute him and had doubted his sanity.

Beck woke with a start. The dream. He must have been asleep. For how long, he wondered? He checked his watch. It was coming up to one a.m. He looked around. Nothing. The bags covering the hatch to the specie room were still in place. He breathed a sigh of relief. Not enough coffee, obviously.

The dream, though. Why now? Why not at dawn? It was as if it was determined to force itself into his sleep, even when he planned *not* to sleep. The two bodies on the floor, the thousand-yard stares in their eyes, the blood oozing slowly from the gaping wounds in their throats. A mother and daughter united in bloody, gruesome death.

And always no sound. The scene bathed in sepulchral silence. Then the fading darkness that ended it, that stole up on him like slow death. Then he woke.

A dream, he called it. But it was more than that. A dream was conjured, a work of the imagination, not real. This *was* real. It had happened. It was a true memory, a perfect recreation of the worst moment of his life, a culmination. A horrible, terrible ending.

And here he was seeking salvation.

All of a sudden, it seemed futile and stupid. What was he doing in this hold full of bags and chests? On this vast tin tub? He had no right being here, and he had no right sucking all these people into his own personal vortex. On what basis had he formed this plan? On the evidence of his eyes and his judgement, both of which had proven to be disastrously fallible. The gloom which he had been fighting to stave of all day broke through, spreading out from his chest and across his whole body, which ached with tiredness and shame. What was he thinking? What had he done? He felt the gun in his pocket. It was solid and comfortable in his hand.

Beck stared at the revolver. He hadn't noticed before but hot tears were starting to spill down his cheeks. Maybe this was where a lack of belief in God got you. No one or nowhere to turn to.

What of Piatkow?

Beck remembered the killer's face. The absence of all emotion as he had pumped bullet after bullet into unarmed policemen. There was no way Beck could leave this unfinished. Not after all he had experienced.

There was a clank. It had come from the stairs. He paused. There it was again. He held the gun at his side and crouched beside a pile of bags.

Someone was coming down.

When Martha fist saw Beck in the hold he was crouching by a pile of luggage, holding a revolver in his hand. As she came down another step he stood, raised the gun and pointed it at her. Her stomach lurched with fear. Involuntarily, she raised her hands.

When he saw it was her, he lowered the gun slowly.

'What are you doing here?' He seemed twitchy and uneasy.

Martha replied in a croaking whisper. 'Couldn't sleep.' She cleared her throat. 'I thought what I needed to do was walk all the way to the bottom of the ship to a dusty baggage hold. That'll help.' She smiled weakly, hoping the joke would relax Beck, show him she had come in peace. It didn't work.

'How did you know I'd be here?' He seemed brittle, almost defeated.

The gun in his hand worried her. 'Kinda hard to talk when you're holding that thing. It's a bit of an impediment to amiable conversation.'

'Oh,' he said, frowning as if he'd just noticed it was there. 'Sorry.' He put it down on top of a chest.

Martha breathed out in relief. 'That's better. In answer to your question, I knew you'd be here because of your little performance this morning at breakfast. You wanted the world and his manservant to know about this book so that whoever it is you're looking for would come looking for it too. And you'd be waiting.'

Beck said nothing. Just stared at the floor.

'I take it you've had no luck, then?' Martha asked.

'No luck?' he said, looking up, as if it was the strangest question he'd ever heard.

'In finding your man?' She glanced around. 'Unless you have him locked up in one of these chests.' She smiled again to let him know she was joking. All his sharpness, his humour, seemed to have evaporated completely. She was looking at a broken man.

'It'd probably be best for your safety if you left me here,' he said solemnly.

'Because of this guy, or because of you?'

Beck said nothing. Martha walked towards him, to be nearer, to lessen the distance emotionally and physically. He watched her, took a deep breath, and said, 'It could be dangerous and I will not allow a civilian to become involved—'

'You're not what you claim to be,' she interrupted.

His eyes narrowed. 'What do you mean?'

'What do you do?'

'I'm a police officer, Special Branch.' His stare flicked around, revealing his agitation.

Martha shook her head. 'No, you're not.'

A flash of anger flickered across Beck's face. Before he could speak, she pulled the message from Donny from her pocket and tossed it onto the chest beside the gun. They both stared at it. The hold was filled with the sound of the engines' furious throbbings. The vibration seemed worse down here, maybe because the ship was moving faster. Martha felt a faint wave of nausea, and a nasty metallic taste in her mouth. Whether these were the first signs of seasickness or symptoms of nervousness at the situation she was in it was difficult to tell. Beck reached for the message, unfolded it, scanned it quickly, refolded it and handed it back to her.

She waited for his anger to show but he remained calm – outwardly, at least. Though she was learning that with him it was very difficult to gauge what was happening under the surface. 'You've been checking up on me,' he said quietly, almost matter-of-factly.

'Consider it research.'

'So I was always the potential subject of a story. Nothing else.'

This was a bit more like it, Martha thought. A sense of spark, a gleam in his previously dead eyes.

'What can I say? I'm a reporter. It's my job to follow my instincts. It struck me from the start that you were up to something. It was clear that you were carrying more baggage than this hold, too. I asked my office to run a check on you. Of course, they couldn't do that because you aren't what you claim to be.' She paused. 'So the questions I have are these: who are you really? Why have you taken a false identity? What exactly are you running away from? And what does all that have to do with the guy you're trying to arrest on this ship?'

'No comment.'

'Off the record?'

'I don't believe there is such a thing.'

'There is for me.' Martha shook her head. 'Look, I meant what I said to you yesterday. This goes beyond any news stories. I want to help. The research, the telegrams – they were curiosity. That was Martha the reporter. This is me as a human being. A human being on a big floating tin can, with a guy who's posing as a cop when he isn't any more, who's obviously in some kind of pain or turmoil, who is trying to find someone on board who is so dangerous that he feels the need to carry a gun. That does not strike me as a particularly safe recipe for a pleasant trouble-free voyage. Now you can tell me here just what the fuck is going on and I can try and help you.' She paused.

'Or?' he asked, his eyes narrowing again.

The gun had diverted her attention. Martha was sure this guy had nothing to lose. When she'd started her lecture she hadn't been sure she would end up threatening him, but it seemed now that that was what she was about to do. And it might not be the safest option. To hell with it, she thought.

'Or I can tell J. Bruce Ismay that the Scotland Yard detective whose tune he's dancing to isn't who he claims to be.'

Her breathing was shallow and she felt sick, nervous at what Beck's reaction would be. He said, 'You're threatening me?'

'You say threaten. I view it as encouraging you to open up.'

His laugh was bitter, sardonic. He shook his head. 'That wouldn't be wise.'

'What? Me telling Ismay, or you telling me?'

'Both,' he said.

'Well, there're more than two thousand people on this liner. Who's going to speak for them?'

'So now you're going to cloak yourself in sanctimony.'

'I'm a journalist, baby. That's what we do. But look at it from my perspective. A ship full of people, a guy claiming to be a detective running around with a gun, some kind of dangerous criminal, the ship being pushed to its maximum speed . . .'

'Who says it's being pushed?'

'This afternoon I overheard Ismay agree with the captain to do just that,' Martha said. 'He's desperate to get into New York early, for all kinds of reasons, not least the publicity coup he thinks he's going to land when you deliver whoever this criminal is you're hunting. I think he'd be interested to learn you're not who you claim to be.'

Beck looked down at the floor again, scratched his head, and then looked at her, a sort of resigned grin on his face. 'All right, then.'

'Meaning you'll talk to me?'

'Yes. But not now. Not here.'

'When? Where?'

'Let me see out the night here. I was going to ask for a master-at-arms to replace me at dawn, so I can get a few hours' sleep. After that, mid-morning. Let's say eleven a.m.'

'Your berth or mine?'

'Yours.'

Martha nodded, surprised that he had agreed. 'Great.'

'Off the record.'

'Sure. This stands even if you trap this guy you're after?'

'Yes.'

She nodded, aware that he might be stalling. 'If you haven't been to my place by eleven-thirty then I'll go and see Ismay.'

'I'll be there. Don't worry.'

'Good. In that case, I'll go. Unless you need my help in any way?'

Beck shook his head. 'Go and get some sleep. Tomorrow could be a long day.'

'All right.' Martha turned. Then she remembered something. 'One thing. This guy you're searching for. Is he definitely on board this ship?'

A long pause, during which the engine's throbbing seemed to grow even louder. Martha was looking forward to getting back above the waterline. It was dry as a bone down here but it also felt cold and clammy. He, Beck, whoever he was, was looking at her. It seemed to take an age for him to speak.

'I don't know,' he said.

Sten-Ake couldn't sleep that night. A new feeling for him. It was as if he'd had all the rest he needed. But while his mind refused to rest, his aching, ailing body refused to move. He lay on his bunk, slightly on his side where the pressure caused less pain to his abdomen, and gazed at the porthole. All he could see was the sea, still as a boating lake.

His room-mate had slept for most of the day. Snoring like one of those new motor cars starting on a cold morning. During the early evening he had got up and disappeared for a few hours before coming back with a plate of food – plain vegetables and a sauce of some sort. The remains were congealing on a plate on the floor by his bed. Sten-Ake had asked if the meat had run out, but the man told him he hated the taste of flesh and never ate it. Now he was pacing the floor of their room, as though he was trying to wear a hole in the carpet. Sten-Ake could ignore it no more.

'What is it with you that makes you walk the floor so?' he asked.

The man stopped. He exuded a manic nervous energy when he was awake. Sten-Ake had lived a bit, and he had seen the type before. Restless, questing, never happy. The sort who would burn himself out in no time.

'I am thinking, old man,' he said. He was much more confident in his English than Sten-Ake was. He had a smoothness to his manner, too, a charm. Sten-Ake didn't even mind being called 'old man'. In fact, he quite liked it.

'A man can think just as well without moving.'

'It depends on what he's thinking about.'

Sten-Ake pushed his head nearer the edge so he could peer over the side and get a clearer view. 'And what thoughts are these that force you to pace so? I feel tired just watching you.'

'Nothing that would interest you, old man,' he muttered.

Fair enough, Sten-Ake thought. But there was something about this handsome young man that intrigued him. He wanted to know more. Because of the pain and the exhaustion, which had made him retreat into himself, he had barely spoken to another human being in any meaningful way for what seemed to an age. But he wasn't tired now and the agony had abated. He wanted to talk.

'Where are you from?' he asked. The man showed no willingness to answer. 'Russia?' Sten-Ake added.

The man shot a look at him, one of fierce anger. 'You asked me that before. No, I am not damn Russian!'

Sten-Ake raised a calming hand. 'Sorry, I forgot. It's difficult to tell. You sound eastern European and I just thought—'

'Latvia,' the man said suddenly. 'My people are from Latvia. A country that has been torn up and mutilated and destroyed by the Russians. And by your people, too.'

True. Sweden had once owned Latvia, but not since Peter the Great had taken it for the Russians.

'I would like to say sorry for the actions of my countrymen, but it was a long, long time ago. If it's of any interest we Swedes don't like Russians either. Their empire includes not only your nation but our neighbour Finland. Their presence so close makes us feel very nervous.'

'So it should. They are pigs.' The Latvian had sat down on his bunk but still radiated anger. It was almost tangible. 'Murdering pigs.'

'It sounds as though you speak from experience.'

He said nothing. 'I know people who have suffered.'

'Were they killed?'

'Killed. Maimed. Tortured. I have known a man who had his fingernails pulled out one by one by those bastards. Then they punctured his eardrums and tore off his genitals.'

'Jesus,' Sten-Ake muttered.

'Yes, well, as I said, they are pigs.'

'Are you exiled? You speak good English.'

'I left some years ago. I was in London. I will go back to Latvia one day, though. The people's passion cannot be denied. Soon we will be free.'

Sten-Ake smiled. The idealism of youth. The hope and the optimism. It had long since died in him. Growing old was merely a series of deaths. 'I hope you are right,' he said. He paused as he caught his breath. 'What takes you to America?'

The Latvian sighed. 'You ask too many questions, old man.'

'Do I? I am sorry. But I probably have precious few days left on this planet and most of them are spent in excruciating pain. Most of the time I am too ill or tired to talk. But today it is a distraction. A pleasant one. Indulge me. You don't even have to tell the truth.' Sten-Ake gave a little laugh, which caught in his throat and turned into a coughing and wheezing fit that racked his whole frame with pain. By the time he'd finished a sweat had broken out on his brow. The Latvian was standing beside him with a small cup of water. Sten-Ake took it eagerly and drank. He wiped his mouth on his sleeve and thanked the other man.

'You should rest,' he said.

'I do nothing but rest,' Sten-Ake said dismissively. He was glad that the pain had eased once more and there appeared to be no lasting effects of his coughing spasm.

'What takes you all this way in your condition? I presume you have travelled from Sweden?' the Latvian asked him.

'You presume right. I have family in the States, in Pennsylvania. My wife died and I have nothing left in Sweden. I haven't seen my grandchildren so I wanted to make the journey to see them before the end. I have a cancer so that will be soon. I decided to make the journey rather than sit and wait for death to come to me in Sweden.'

The other man didn't respond immediately. Sten-Ake wondered if he'd grown bored, but when he peered over the side of his bunk he could still see him sitting on his own bed.

'I admire your determination, old man,' the Latvian said eventually. 'And your dedication to your family.'

'Do you have any children?'

'Not yet. I am not married.'

'You should. It is the greatest thing a man can do. To raise a child to be a man or a woman. The hardest but most rewarding work of all. We only had one child, but she was the best thing I ever did.'

'I would like to one day,' the other man admitted. He sounded

calmer now, less agitated. 'But there are other things I would like
to accomplish first.'

'Of course,' Sten-Ake muttered, beginning to feel the first
familiar waves of exhaustion. He remembered a time when the
days were endless and the song of all things was still being sung,
before the world became so bewildering and the span of his life
had spun away. 'Well, make the most of it, young man. Life is
precious. We are a long time dead.'

'You don't believe in a higher being, an afterlife?' There was a
note of surprise in his voice.

'No,' Sten-Ake said. 'I never have. Though I wish I did. It
would make what I face right now a damned sight easier.'

'You will make it to America. Seeing your grandchildren will
give you some energy, no? Something to live for.'

Sten-Ake settled his head back on the pillow, feeling sleep
beckon. 'I suppose I will,' he said. 'If we make it.'

'What do you mean?' the Latvian asked, agitated.

Sten-Ake smiled, his eyes closing. 'I joke. I overheard two of
the stokers talking about a shipboard fire. Their accents were
thick but I think some of the coal in one of the bunkers was
burning.'

'Is that bad?' the other man asked tentatively. 'I have a strange
feeling about this ship myself. I feel that we may never reach New
York. What you have just told me convinces me further that a
terrible fate awaits us.'

Sten-Ake was beginning to drift off. 'She will be fine. Well, no
fire on a ship is good news. But I dare say this one can handle it
better than most. They can't have been too concerned or they

would have turned back. Just pray there is no collision, because it's bound to have weakened her.'

'I thought you didn't believe in any God. What good would prayers do?'

Sten-Ake smiled, slipping into consciousness. 'You are very sharp, young . . . what is your name?'

There was a long pause, a gap in which sleep came before the Latvian had a chance to tell him.

*B*eck was in bed at his apartment in Marylebone when he heard the loud rap on the door downstairs. He sat up immediately. He had not been asleep. He had barely slept for weeks. Each night was the same: he would stay up as late as he could, fall into bed when he was exhausted, but as soon as the lights went out and the silence came with it, it was if his brain awoke and tumbling thoughts eddied and billowed across his mind.

The knocking was loud and insistent. Despite sharing the apartment building with some other detectives, Beck knew immediately it was for him and that it wasn't good news. Night-time calls never were. He slipped on some clothes and walked downstairs.

There was a young uniformed officer, holding a lamp, behind the door.

'Sorry to wake you, sir,' he said.

'What is it, Officer?'

'You're requested to accompany me, sir. I have a hansom cab waiting.'

Beck could see the driver sitting on his perch, the horse's breath steaming from its nostrils in the fresh night air. It was autumn and the nights had grown colder.

'To where?' he asked, though deep down, and to his growing horror, he realised he already knew the answer.

The constable paused. 'To Barlby Road, sir. North Kensington.'

Beck's fears were right. Without asking any more questions, he followed the officer and climbed into the cab. Through deserted night streets, they made their way west as he gazed from the window and tried not to be sick. As they passed Paddington the first signs of dawn began to bleed into the sky. The officer beside him remained tight-lipped, making no attempt at conversation. They turned left off the Harrow Road and down Ladbroke Grove, passing over the railway line, and then taking a right on Barlby Road, past the Pall Mall Deposit towards the terraced houses which were their destination.

As the cab pulled up, Beck could see officers fanning out across the entire area. A few early-bird locals, or those who had been woken from their sleep by the commotion, had formed an interested crowd, being held back by some constables in their long cloaks. He stepped gingerly out of the cab, feeling weak and light-headed. He took a deep breath and summoned as much strength as he could.

'Follow me, sir,' the young officer said.

'I know where we're going. You can leave me now.'

The constable hesitated. It was obvious that his orders were to deliver Beck directly to the scene. But he desisted and nodded, melting into the background.

Beck went down the street, past the crowd behind the cordon, his gaze fixed on the policeman standing sentry at the front door. As he approached, a plain-clothes detective stepped out onto the street, deep in conversation with a uniformed officer. As he saw him draw near, the detective stopped talking and straightened up. They knew each other, having worked on several cases together, both before and after Beck became Special Branch.

They nodded. The detective, only thirty at most but already with greying hair and whiskers, looked at Beck tersely.

'In there,' he said. 'Tread carefully.'

Beck nodded, and stepped across the threshold. It was all unravelling like some horrible and twisted dream. Yet he knew this was real.

Another detective was inside, scribbling notes. From the back came the loud air-sucking whump of a photographer's flash mechanism, followed in a split second by a blaze of light that left them momentarily seeing spots in front of their eyes. The snapper was at the kitchen door. Beck squeezed past him, noticing the lines of blood on the floor.

There, by the small table, was a man's body. The sleeves of his shirt were rolled up and soaked with blood. Two deep gashes along the main veins in his forearms were visible. Suicide. Beck's heart lifted momentarily.

'They're upstairs,' a voice behind him said softly. He turned and saw it was the same detective he had seen outside. His face and tone extinguished the brief flicker of hope that Beck had just experienced.

Beck nodded, and made his way up the narrow steps, past the fading, peeling paper on the walls, catching the smell of damp and must. At the top, more uniforms. The group parted silently for him. One of them gestured with a slight movement of his hand to a door that stood ajar. Beck stood for a second, inhaled deeply, and then pushed it open.

The curtains were slightly open, letting in the steel-grey light. The top sheet and blanket on the bed were peeled back. The two bodies lay entwined, in each other's arms, their nightdresses stained ruby red. Mother and daughter united in death's embrace. They had sought comfort in each other from the frenzy and the pain and the sheer horror of what the man had been doing to them.

And Beck could have stopped it. Should have stopped it. They would have been alive now. Not lying here stabbed and shredded.

He turned, headed down the stairs, stumbled into the garden and vomited copiously on the damp soil.

14 April 1912

Sunday morning, brilliant and bright outside, was all about wasting time for Martha until Beck was due at her cabin before lunch. As the conversation at the table drifted around her at breakfast, she scoured the room for him but saw him nowhere. She found herself checking the faces of Ismay and the chief purser for signs of stress, some indication that something momentous or dramatic had happened overnight. But they seemed to act normally.

Once breakfast was over, the captain entered the room, and people started to gather.

'What's happening?' she asked Mrs Kimball.

In return she was given a look that her mother would have described as 'old-fashioned'. 'It is the Sabbath,' Mrs Kimball replied crossly.

'Oh,' Martha said, catching on slowly; there was to be some kind of service. Damn, she thought. She had almost lost track of which day it was on board the ship, since each was so similar to the last. It was Sunday. She hated Sundays. The dreary piety of it all. The denial. Everywhere and everything closed. The way it seemed that all the bad thoughts of the past week crept up on you as the day ebbed away and the new week rolled around.

She thought about hightailing it back to her cabin, but changed her mind. The service might keep her occupied as she watched the clock tick away to eleven-thirty. Plus, while she was no fan of religion, she did love hymns. Surely even the deadheads in the band couldn't butcher those?

Martha scanned the room as it filled; she was unable to see Beck anywhere. She remembered the gun in his hand and shuddered. Surely he wouldn't have been so stupid? But she didn't know the depth of the abyss he'd seemed to be peering into. Why hadn't she stayed with him? She had barely slept, apart from a few hours before dawn, thinking of him down there.

The captain, in that soft, mellifluous voice of his, started the service. Everyone bowing their heads as he delivered a prayer, one which, since it wasn't the Lord's Prayer, Martha wasn't familiar with. This one seemed to be addressed directly 'for those in peril on the sea', asking to grant them some kind of calm and peace. Perhaps Beck should be here, she thought.

There followed some hymns, few of which she recognised and which were spoiled anyway by Darton's tuneless bellowing beside her. The whole painful half-hour was brought to an end after thirty minutes by 'O God, Our Help in Ages Past', a tune that Martha knew and actually liked, and at whose ruination Darton truly excelled. By the end the only stormy blast from which she wanted shelter was the one which blew from his whisky-soaked mouth.

Despite her cynicism, she came away in high spirits. The nervous fluttering in her stomach was familiar to her from other times when she'd been about to get to the nub of the story. She went upstairs to the boat deck, only to find instantly that she wasn't dressed for it. The temperature was markedly cooler. The next time she ventured up there she'd wear a coat.

Back at her room, she asked Bad Teeth for a jug of water and two glasses and then told the girl that she was expecting a guest and wasn't to be disturbed after he arrived. The smirk on the insolent girl's face when she gave away the sex of her visitor didn't bother her. Let her gossip, Martha thought.

She sat down, counting the minutes to eleven-thirty. The appointed time came and went. Eleven-thirty-five rolled around and she started to get impatient. She really did not want to have to track down Ismay, explain who she was and how she had found out that Beck wasn't who he claimed to be, and deal with all the hassle and strife that would ensue. She never liked the feeling of being a snitch. Perhaps Beck was sleeping? Maybe she should go to his berth and see. Or could he be in conversation with Ismay? Again the image of him with the gun in his hand flashed across her mind but she forced it away.

It was as Martha stood up, resolving to do something even if she wasn't yet sure what that should be, that there was a knock on the door. She smoothed down her skirt, walked over to the door and opened it.

There he was. Dark rings around his eyes, skin the colour of ashes, hair dishevelled. It was obvious that he hadn't slept. In his hand he was holding a hat. He nodded, his lips closed tight.

'Hello,' Martha said. 'Come in.'

Beck stepped in hesitantly, saying nothing. She pointed at an unused bunk, still made up to look like a sofa, and he sat down heavily.

'I can get some coffee,' she offered.

'Please,' he said, not looking up.

Martha left him, tracked down Bad Teeth, slipped a few dollars into her hand, and asked for hot coffee and lots of it. Then she went back to her room, followed a few seconds later by her stewardess.

Once the girl had gone, Martha poured the coffee and handed a cup to Beck. 'How did it go?'

He shrugged. 'It didn't.' His voice sounded weary. There was an unsteadiness to his movements, too, though whether from emotion or exhaustion it was difficult to tell.

'He didn't show?'

'No.'

'Maybe he saw through the ruse?'

'Maybe he isn't on board at all,' Beck shot back.

Martha paused. 'We can come to that. First of all, please, finish your coffee.'

He sipped away, looking down at the floor. She knew from experience that you got no information if you rushed someone. Sure, she had held a metaphorical gun to his head to get him here, but now that he was she wanted him to move at a pace that he was comfortable with.

'It's cold outside,' he said.

'It is. Much colder. I went up on deck earlier and half froze.'

'There're reports of ice. I heard Ismay being told about it.'

'That'd make sense, given how cold it is.'

There was another awkward silence, one that Martha didn't want to leap into or fill. She had time. The next two and a half days of her diary were looking pretty free.

'What do you want to know?' Beck said eventually.

'We can start with why you left the force.'

'Off the record?'

Martha nodded. 'I suppose you're a source now. Which means I guard your identity with my life.' She smiled. He didn't. Boy, he could be hard work.

Beck said, 'I am a detective. I did work for Special Branch. Until last November, to be exact.'

'What happened then?'

For their entire exchange so far his gaze had been cast down to the floor. For the first time he looked up, his blue eyes staring at her coolly, almost detached. 'I suffered from what the doctors called shattered nerves.'

'A nervous breakdown?'

'You know people who have suffered from it?' Beck seemed eager to know that others suffered from his malady.

'I'm a journalist. I live in New York. That means I'm surrounded constantly by kooks and freaks.' Martha realised how that must have sounded. 'Sorry, I didn't mean to cause offence.' You idiot Martha, she thought.

But Beck was smiling again. 'Don't apologise. I find your honesty and directness refreshing. Whenever this has come up among my friends in England, everyone goes quiet and looks at the floor. It's like admitting you are weak and, well, feminine.'

'Did that include the woman you spoke about? Sarah?' Martha paused. 'She does exist?'

Again the smile. 'Yes, she exists. Though often I wish she didn't. At least, not in my orbit.'

'I'm sure you don't mean that. My grandfather used to tell me that you had to lose a couple of fights to appreciate what it's like to win.'

'I didn't lose. I got humiliated.'

'Yeah, well, it means that victory will taste even sweeter. As I said, she doesn't sound like the sort of girl you should lose any sleep over. But I fail to see why your shattered nerves and broken heart have led you to leave England and sail to America. Are you on the lam?'

'The lam?'

'The run. From the law.' Even though you *are* the law, Martha thought. Or *were*, at least.

'I'm not a wanted man.' Beck let out a bitter laugh. 'You could say I'm the opposite – the unwanted man. Apart from a civil claim which may cost me everything I have. The *little* I still have.'

'A civil claim for what?'

'Last October, I was working at Kensington as a detective.'

'I thought you were Special Branch?'

'I was. I had been . . . moved sideways, so to speak. Anyway, looking back I can see that I was in no fit state to work. But I had little option. On my second day at my new posting I was asked to turn my attention to a case in North Kensington. There was a man who had been acting strangely. A few reports that he'd been heard threatening his wife and neighbours with violence. He'd also been heard making similar threats in his local pub.'

Beck stared over Martha's shoulder. 'I went around there and made a few inquiries. The man was a nasty piece of work. That much was clear. But I didn't think much more of it. The wife had a black eye. I tried to ask her what had happened. She wouldn't tell me. I talked to the drinkers in the pub and for the most part they spoke well of him, but said that he was a swine when he had drunk too much alcohol. He had strong opinions – about the world going to the dogs, women wanting the vote, that sort of thing. It seemed an ordinary enough story of everyday London domestic strife. Nothing much I could do really. Unless someone made a formal complaint and even then all I could do would be to issue a caution. I left it alone.'

Martha waited for him to continue, knowing that the story couldn't end well. She remembered their conversation on Friday night, when he'd been despondent. This must have been the case he'd been alluding to.

'A few days went by and I didn't think anything more about it. Then word came through that a woman had been found murdered, her body dumped under the arches of the railway that runs through the area. The woman, a local prostitute, was well known for being vocal and quite forthright. We managed to find a few of her clients.'

'Your man the abuser was one of them?' Martha asked.

'Yes. I called him in, like I did the others. I spoke to him. He was aggressive and hostile but very bright. A clerk to a trader in the city. He was honest and said he had used her. It was blatantly clear that he had a problem with women. I marked him down as a strong suspect but that was it. There was no physical evidence to put him at the scene. His alibi seemed solid. It was provided by his wife.' Beck stopped and shook his head, offering another jaundiced laugh. 'What was I thinking?' he added rhetorically.

'You knew he beat his wife?'

'I knew he was a tyrant. He fitted the type of man we were looking for. I should have followed my hunch and kept him in. He was clearly on the edge. He might have confessed, or at least given something away – enough to charge him with. We searched his house while we had him. But no, I was paralysed by doubt; I couldn't make a firm decision. Even worse, I let slip that we'd had a complaint about his recent behaviour. He immediately started asking me if it was his wife who had complained. I denied it but the damage was done. He was seething. But still I did nothing. It was as if I couldn't force myself to make a judgement call. I just couldn't.' As Beck spoke that last sentence he spread his arms wide.

'What happened?'

'That was a Sunday. The following night he murdered his wife and daughter and then killed himself.'

'Jesus,' Martha exclaimed.

'Exactly. Two innocent people died in a horrible fashion because of my failure to do my job properly. I deserve all the bad things which come to me.'

'You were fired?' Martha asked, her mind racing through everything that Beck had told her. She knew now why he had been so low the other night. Anyone would have had to be superhuman to recover from such an error of judgement.

'I resigned. Not immediately. I had a relapse, and, rather than offering me support, this time they asked for my resignation. Then the details of what had happened – or rather, what hadn't – appeared in the press. The blame was pinned entirely on me. The family of the murdered mother and child then filed a civil suit seeking damages and compensation.'

'Why weren't you in a fit state?'

'What?'

'You said earlier that you weren't in a fit state when you were moved to Kensington. Then you just said you had a relapse, which indicates you'd suffered a similar episode before. Was it because your relationship fell through? Was it that which triggered your collapse?'

Beck shook his head slowly. 'No. Sarah left after my first collapse.'

'What caused that?' In the distance, Martha could hear the bugle sounding for lunch. It could wait, she thought.

He sat there, pulling at his chin thoughtfully. She feared he might decide that he had said enough and clam up right now.

'What caused that?' he repeated slowly, still stroking his chin, showing the first shadow of a beard. He sat back and folded his arms across his chest. 'Have you heard of the Siege of Sidney Street?'

Sten-Ake could feel the change in temperature. Old bones are quicker to protest at fluctuations in heat and cold than younger ones. So he knew before his eyes opened, from the ache spreading across his body, a pain separate from his cancer, that the weather had changed. Lifting his head so he could see through the porthole, the bright blue sky confirmed that the day outside was clear and crisp.

Ice, he thought.

Around Sweden and its shores, across the Sound and the Baltic, the outer reaches of the North Sea and on into the wide, bitter North Atlantic, he had sailed through, past and around ice fields and icebergs. The signs were clear. The plummeting temperature, both in the air and in the water. Then there was the smell, a clamminess in the air that the experienced sailor knew meant ice. Looking out across the still blue sea, just above the waterline, Sten-Ake could see no evidence of it yet, though. From the forceful throb of the engines it felt as if they were going faster, and he knew that wouldn't be the case if they were near ice.

He sensed movement below. The fiery young idealist. The man spent a lot of time in his quarters for one so young.

'Open the porthole, could you?' he asked politely.

There was a moan of impatience. 'It is cold outside, old man.'

'Not for long. I just want some of that cold air in here. I have plans to get out of this bed and it may help invigorate me.'

'Whatever you want,' the Latvian said sardonically and went to the porthole and opened it. There was a blast of cool salt-sprayed air. 'It doesn't matter to me. I'm going.'

'Lunch?'

The young man started to put on his coat, hat and gloves. 'Perhaps.'

'But you are putting on your outdoor clothes. A stroll on the deck first?'

'Perhaps.'

'You are not so talkative today.'

'I have things on my mind, old man. Places to go.' The Latvian hoisted a bag onto his shoulder.

'You are leaving? For where?'

'There is something I need to collect.'

'You will be back?'

'I don't know.'

Sten-Ake thought he seemed impatient, edgy.

'So long, old man,' the Latvian said, and it sounded like a permanent goodbye.

'Goodbye,' Sten-Ake said and watched him leave.

The old Swede lay there for a while, wondering what it was about today's youth, and their inability to be at rest. Always moving, always searching. No patience to speak of. Had he offended the young man during their chat the previous day? He could think of nothing he had said which might have upset him. They had merely shared some stories about each other. Quite amicably, he thought.

Sten-Ake rose slowly to a sitting position. Then he got down off the bed and stood up. He would empty his bladder, then think about going to get some food. He even had an appetite, albeit a meagre one. Still, it was a good sign. If he felt all right after eating, he might go out on deck and get some of that icy Atlantic air in his lungs.

He sat down to put on his boots, wincing at the soreness in his arthritic knees that had been brought on by the cold. But his thoughts were mostly on the young Latvian hothead. He reviewed their conversation once more. The young man had spoken of his desire to throw off the Russian imperialist yoke. Sten-Ake wondered if his response had been patronising. He hoped not. He admired the idealism of youth, even if it seemed futile once you were old. Maybe Sten-Ake could learn from the Latvian's passion and fight this cowardly cancer with more fervour. Yes, it would kill him, but it need not make him into such an invalid.

He stood up, feeling renewed. Now, where was his jacket? He had left it hanging from the end of the bedstead. He felt a faint sense of panic when he saw it wasn't there. Then came relief, as he saw it at the other end of the bed. Still, he couldn't remember leaving it there.

He picked it up and put it on. It felt lighter than before.

The panic returned.

His savings.

Sten-Ake snatched open the jacket and checked the lining. There was a small hole just along the hem. He put his finger inside.

The money was gone.

Martha needed no lessons on the Siege of Sidney Street. It had been big news in the American press, and not all of the coverage had been complimentary to the Brits. The deployment of a large part of the British army and the destruction subsequently wreaked had seemed something of an overreaction. Like using a cannon to kill a sparrow.

'You were there?' she asked, intrigued that Beck had been involved.

'Do you know about the events leading up to it?'

Martha could recall them vaguely. 'Some anarchists shot and killed some cops.' 'You were there, too?'

Beck nodded. 'Houndsditch, December 1911. I'd been on the trail of the ringleaders of a group of Latvian nationalists who were hiding out in London. There were rumours that they were planning some acts to raise funds for the cause back home, seeking independence from the Russians by whatever means they could devise. Most of them had been arrested – some of them tortured – by the Russians before they'd fled. I was put on the case after the Tottenham Outrage. Two of their men had tried to rob a wages clerk at gunpoint. They shot and killed a cop and a small kid – ten years old. Both victims died. I was put on the team to try to find out who else might have been involved. I was on it for a couple of years – monitoring and surveillance. Tough work because the men we were watching just came and went. They were very slippery.'

Beck sighed. Martha said nothing, waiting for him to continue. The ship's vibration seemed more noticeable, as if its engines were straining. She ignored it. It was strange: everything beyond this boat, this room, had ceased to exist. Now it was just her and this troubled young man and his story. He went on: 'It obsessed me for some time. But despite all that work we didn't see what was coming. One night I'd been at Liverpool Street railway station. A few of the men we had been watching were there to meet some people and we wanted to have a look at them. Once we'd done that we let them be and I went to the police station across the road, where I'd left a few things. It was the City of London police, a separate force, but we had good relations with them. The chief inspector was there, plus a few other beat policeman. There was some excitement because there were reports of noises coming from a house behind a jeweller's – sawing, hammering, that kind of thing. Not what you'd expect to hear at eleven o'clock on a Friday night. The area was quiet because it was the eve of the Jewish Sabbath and it was a Jewish quarter. There was more than one report. The chief inspector was quite animated because a bit of door-knocking had told them that there were some foreigners in the area. He wanted a team of officers to see if they were making the commotion. A few were at the scene already. He needed someone to take that message to those at the scene. I volunteered. I was curious about who these foreigners were and whether they were related to the men we had been tracking.'

Beck swallowed hard, though he appeared to be in control of his emotions.

'It was a cold night,' he continued. 'Freezing. The wind bit into you. I reached the road where the noises had been reported and found the officers. They had moved quickly and had the area surrounded. We didn't know it then, but another officer had already knocked on the door of that house in Houndsditch about ten minutes before and alerted them to our presence, a warning. There were four cops and me. We went to the house, a tiny little terrace in a cul-de-sac. We knocked on the door. There was no answer. We knocked again. Eventually one of them answered, went back inside. We sat on the steps. The lead officer pushed the door open. We didn't know it but the rest were out the back where they'd been trying to attach a pipe to the gas and blow the jeweller's safe open.

'Just then, the door to the backyard burst open and there he was. Peter Piatkow, the leader of the whole group. I'd never seen him before. I wasn't even sure he existed. Everyone spoke about him in hushed reverential tones, as though he was some kind of devil.' Beck paused and shook his head. 'Turns out they weren't far wrong. He had a gun. Before any of us could react he shot the lead officer, then turned the gun on the rest of us. I was hit in the thigh and knocked back onto the street. Three of our group were killed. Me and another were wounded. One of the gang was killed, the rest got away.'

No wonder he was troubled, Martha thought. To have been caught up in a massacre like that, to watch good men cut down. 'You were armed?'

'None of us were. The only reason we took down one of them was because one officer, Choate, was so strong that he managed to wrestle one of their chaps down and when the others came to put a bullet in him he managed to flip the guy in front of him so they shot their own man.'

Again Beck paused, eyes moistening, voice a hoarse whisper so that she had to lean in to hear him above the throb of the ship's screws. A flicker of anger flashed across his face.

'I watched as Piatkow, a smile on his face, with Choate lying on the ground bleeding heavily, pumped three bullets into him from point-blank range. He never stood a chance.'

Beck stopped there, tears rolling down his cheeks. Martha got the feeling that it was the first time he had ever talked about this in such detail. How could he have when he lived in a society that disapproved of any show of emotion or weakness?

'How badly hurt were you?' she asked.

'Not too badly. The bullet went through my thigh and out the other side. It missed the bone. I was lucky.'

That wasn't the word Martha would have used, but in the circumstances she saw his point.

'If only I'd told them to wait. I could have made a few more inquiries. Got some backup. Armed, if necessary. Instead I let them walk straight into the arms of death.'

'You had intelligence that these were the men you'd been trailing?' Martha asked.

'None.'

'So what could you have done? The orders from the policemen's boss were to go and knock on the door.'

'But I should have done something!' Beck spat.

Martha said nothing. He held up his hands. 'I'm sorry.'

'There's no need to apologise. You went through a lot. I can see why you'd blame yourself.'

'You can?'

'Yes. But you shouldn't. Those guys were police officers. They were carrying out their duties. No one was to know that the men behind the door were armed and dangerous.'

Beck said nothing but she could see he wasn't convinced. Martha wondered how she might have reported it. Someone would have to be blamed. In journalism, there always had to be someone to point the finger at.

'Maybe,' he said wearily.

'What happened then? You took some time off to recover?'

'No. That was the sixteenth of December. I was back at work on the twentieth.'

'That's insane. You'd been shot.'

'It was my job to find them. I knew them. I had contacts. The force needed me and wanted them found. Piatkow especially. I had his face in my mind the whole time. The way he seemed to smile as he shot Choate. I worked every day over Christmas and New Year.'

'You must have been in pain.'

'At least I was still alive. Unlike Bentley, Tucker and Choate. When it was tough I pictured that bastard standing over Choate, shooting him like a dog. Anyway, over New Year I was given some information from a trusted source that Piatkow and a few others were hiding out at a house in Sidney Street. Hence the siege.'

'Wasn't the army involved?'

Beck nodded. 'Hundreds of them. They even brought in field

guns. Half the street was destroyed. And yet, in the rubble, all we found were the dead bodies of two men who were in the gang but hadn't even been at Houndsditch. Piatkow got away. The powers that be weren't very happy that such a large public show of might and destruction had reaped such pitiful rewards.' He paused. 'I took much of the blame.'

'Why you?'

'It was my information they had acted on. But my source was good. Piatkow had been there. He must have somehow slipped away without us noticing.' He grimaced. 'He did that a fair bit in the weeks that followed.'

'You were involved in the search for him?'

'For the next six months. I barely slept. It consumed my every waking moment. My nights, too, because he was in my dreams. Trying to find him, to bring him to justice. I went all over the country, spoke to thousands of people, but he was always one step ahead of us. I thought I saw him lurking in every corner. I became obsessed . . . Eventually, my body rebelled. I fell ill. I took to my bed to recover.' Beck was looking down at the floor once more, his voice a low mutter. 'I didn't get out of it for a month.'

'A month? Did anyone help you? Come to see you?'

'A few friends and family. No one at work wanted to know. Eventually I saw a doctor. He suggested rest, a holiday of some sort. It was then that Sarah left me. She had had enough, I suppose. I was hard work.'

'You'd just gone through an unbelievably traumatic experience. One that you were never given a chance to recover from. Instead you continued to work. The only surprise is that you didn't break down sooner.'

Beck seemed to ignore Martha's words of consolation. 'I was ashamed. I hid from the world. But I had no source of income, no real savings. I had to work. So I went back. That was when they switched me to Kensington and asked me to prove myself.'

'Prove yourself? You were recovering from a breakdown.'

'I don't think they saw it like that.'

And Martha thought she worked in a ruthless industry. She had seen reporters burn out through overwork, and receive little sympathy. But they had not been shot at or asked to make life-and-death decisions. This man should have received help, been told to stay away from work and given a chance to talk about his problems. Instead he had been driven close to exhaustion, all kinds of demons in his head, and when he had made a tragic error as a result of his own shattered nerves and confidence the force appeared to have hung him out to dry.

No wonder he had fled.

But there was still one question left unanswered.

'Who is it you think you've spotted on board?'

Beck said nothing.

'It's Piatkow, isn't it?'

Still no words. Just staring at the floor. Then he nodded.

Martha felt a lurch in her stomach, an entirely involuntary reaction – nothing to do with the motion of the ship and everything to do with her news sense. The most wanted man in Britain, possibly the world, on board this glittering ship, hunted by the man he had wounded.

Before she got too excited, she remembered her source. A man who had admitted having seen the shadow of the man he sought in every corner. Who had been driven almost crazy by the search for him.

'You *don't* think it's Piatkow you saw?'

Beck rubbed his face.

'Arthur,' she added. The first time she had used his first name.

He jolted as if he'd had an electric shock. She repeated her question.

'The simple answer is that I don't know,' he replied. 'I *was* convinced but, as I said to you before, I have lost all faith in my judgement. I felt certain that if I spread word of the book around the ship he wouldn't be able to resist trying to steal it. It's the sort of windfall he would dream of.'

'What if he doesn't want to risk getting caught? What if his main objective is to arrive in New York and hook up with some people there? A ship is a pretty dumb place to carry out a robbery – there's nowhere to escape to.'

'I thought of that. He may well try later in the voyage. The only alternative is to search the entire ship, top to bottom. But there are so many places to hide, so many things that could go wrong if he panics and he's armed. I wanted to flush him out.'

'How many times do you think you've seen him?'

'Three times. Once when we stopped at Cherbourg – I thought I saw him board from a tender. The second time was on Thursday, just before dinner, smoking on the second-class deck astern. The final time, though I'm still not sure it was him, was on Friday. But then he was in the staff area on the boat deck.'

'The staff area?'

'Yes, by the officers' quarters. He seemed to be dressed as a sort of deck crewman, a cleaner of some kind. I made an inspection of all the staff yesterday morning and he wasn't among them.'

'What time did you think you saw him?'

'Around six, perhaps six-thirty p.m.'

Each time had been around the time the sun was setting and the light was deteriorating, she noted.

'You don't believe me, do you?' Beck asked.

Martha decided to be honest. 'I don't know. How can I be sure when *you're* not even sure you can trust what you have seen? You've checked the passenger list?'

'Yes. Nothing that fits Piatkow or any of his known aliases.'

'What did you plan to do next?'

'The master-at-arms is in the hold now. I've told him there was a report that someone might try to steal the book. He's armed, but I don't think Piatkow would try to steal it in the middle of the day. I plan to get a few hours' sleep and go back there later this afternoon. Beyond that, if it doesn't work, I haven't really thought much. I've told London he might be on board, though they don't know the information is from me. By this evening I'm told we'll be in contact with land by wireless so I should be able to send an update. They can arrange for armed cops to meet us at New York. To watch the passengers disembark and then search the ship if Piatkow doesn't get off . . . Of course, that means revealing myself, putting myself in the hands of the New York police, and facing the consequences if he happens not to be on board. But that's a risk I'm more than willing to take. I'd appreciate it if you waited to wire your office until after I have wired mine.'

'Of course,' Martha agreed. Though since she was already on board, all she would need was a photographer; rather than transmit this sort of information across the air, and risk tipping off her rivals, she would simply ask for one to meet her at Pier 59, without giving a reason.

Which would also cover her if Beck's suspicions were mistaken. There was nothing an editor hated more than having his hopes raised for a scoop to trump them all, only for it to be killed. Disappointments like that were rarely forgotten in a newsroom.

'Can I help?' she asked.

'You can promise not to reveal the details of this conversation to Mr Ismay. In return, I'll try to keep you posted.'

It sounded fair. 'Deal.'

'Deal,' Beck echoed. 'Now I need to sleep.'

He got up slowly, as if his body was aching.

Martha didn't want the conversation to end like that, with some kind of transaction. 'Arthur, what happened to the woman and her daughter was truly awful. That can't be denied. But these things happen in your line of work. The simple fact is that you should have been nowhere near a police desk, not for many, many months after the shootings in Houndsditch. Not until you were fit to return. Asking you to come back was barbaric. I don't think that under the circumstances, you have anything to feel ashamed of. You were only guilty of wanting to do your job.'

As she spoke, Beck stared at her. He looked as if all the energy had been sucked from him. But her words appeared to stir him.

He smiled sadly. 'Thank you, Martha,' he said, putting a hand on her shoulder. 'You're very kind.'

She put her hand on his. It was her turn to feel a jolt. His hand was warm, firm. She looked at him, experiencing an emotional charge she had rarely felt.

'I must sleep,' he said eventually. His eyes were red-ringed. 'Thank you for listening.'

He took back his hand, and smiled again, but then looked away. Martha wanted to tell him to stay, to sit beside her, to talk more, but something stopped her. This guy was broken. Throwing herself on him might not be the wisest move.

She heard the door close behind him and wondered what the next few days would bring.

Beck stumbled from Martha's room feeling exhausted and spent, yet also unburdened and free. There might be consequences from spilling his heart out to a journalist, but it felt as if he had crawled out from under a dark, heavy rock into the light. He might even be able to sleep. He needed to.

Before that, he decided he'd have a cigarette on the boat deck. He expected to find it swarming with people walking off the effects of their lunch, but found few there. It took only a few seconds for him to work out why. The temperature was more like December than April. The air was bright and clear, but the chill was bitter, exacerbated by the wind created by the ship's motion as it steamed westwards.

Beck smoked and walked, wavering between sticking to his plan to entrap Piatkow or risking a Marconigram to London asking them to take charge and organise the terrorist's capture at New York. He passed a few hardy souls wrapped up against the cold, their cheeks and noses reddened. He guessed the public rooms would be busy that day.

As he turned at the furthest point astern, aiming to scurry back and warm up in his berth, he saw Ismay approaching. Despite the falling temperatures, the magnate was wearing neither hat nor overcoat, just a blue serge suit. He appeared to heading straight for him.

'Good afternoon, Mr Beck,' he said briskly.

Beck nodded. 'Mr Ismay.'

'Do we have any news?'

'Not yet, sir. I'm just about to grab some rest. Mr King is in the hold as we speak. I shall relieve him in a few hours' time.'

'Good, good,' Ismay said. Beck thought he seemed distracted.

'Is everything all right?'

'Fine, splendid,' Ismay said sincerely. 'The ship is proving to be a wonderful mover. She's already making twenty-one or twenty-two knots, which, while it isn't that fast, is more than acceptable when you consider we still have a few more boilers to light. We're going to put two more on this evening. I have every confidence we're going to show the world what she can do and arrive in New York on Tuesday evening.'

'Good,' Beck said, not entirely certain why Ismay was sharing this information. 'I'm glad.'

'We logged 546 miles between noon yesterday and today. Again, a very encouraging sign. More than the previous day and we expect to log even more between noon today and tomorrow, once the extra boilers have been started.'

'Good,' Beck replied once more.

'The only downside is that we are about to enter an area of icebergs,' Ismay said.

'That would explain the cold.'

'Yes, I suppose it has grown noticeably cooler, hasn't it?' the White Star president replied, looking around at nothing in particular. He reached into his pocket and pulled out a piece of paper that Beck could tell immediately was a Marconigram. 'Have a look at this,' he whispered.

With slight trepidation, Beck took it from him and unfolded it. It was from another ship, the *Baltic*, timed at 1:40 that afternoon, only an hour or so earlier. He read twice:

> Captain Smith, Titanic. Have had moderate variable winds and clear fine weather since leaving. Greek steamer Athinai reports passing icebergs and large quantity of field ice today in latitude 41.51 N, longitude 49.52 W. Last night we spoke (with) German oil tanker Deutschland, Stettin to Philadelphia, not under control, short of coal; latitude 40.42 N, longitude 55.11 W. Wishes to be reported to New York and other steamers. Wish you and Titanic all success.

The information remained impenetrable to Beck so he handed it back.

Ismay had a strange, almost fervent gleam in his eyes.

'This is on our track,' he said. 'We should be up around it about nine this evening. But don't you fear. We shan't let it slow us down.'

'I'm glad to hear that,' Beck said, still puzzled. He wondered if in his exhaustion he was missing some special import or meaning in the telegram relevant to him and his search for Piatkow. 'What about this *Deutschland* ship?'

'Oh, that is no business of ours. We are too busy for that.'

Beck realised then that Ismay was merely demonstrating his dedication to the cause. Despite ice, despite cries for assistance from other ships, *Titanic* would not be thrown from her senior staff's determination to reach New York at the earliest possible time.

'I see. Well, there's no need to take an undue risk,' he said.

Ismay took back the message, folding it neatly and replacing it in his jacket pocket.

'No need to fear that, Mr Beck,' he said jovially. 'The captain is very experienced. It might mean we make a minor adjustment to our course, one that enables us to miss the worst of the ice, but it won't in any way affect our chances of getting to New York ahead of schedule. Now, is there any other way I can be of assistance to you?'

Beck was too tired to think. He shook his head. 'I can't think of anything.'

'Well, don't hesitate to ask.' Before Beck could thank him, Ismay skipped away. As Beck reached the stairs leading back down to first class, he turned and saw the White Star president in conversation with two women sitting on deckchairs in readiness to watch the coming sunset. He was speaking in animated fashion, gesticulating wildly.

As he opened the door, he found the ample figure of Purser McElroy filling the doorway. He seemed out of breath and anxious.

'There has been a call from a Mr King, one of the masters-at-arms. He wishes to see you in the hold on Orlop Deck immediately.'

King was at the bottom of the stairs leading down to the hold when Beck arrived. He was a burly man, and tall, the ideal build for someone whose job was to maintain discipline and police the ship. He was also used to following orders without asking too many questions. When Beck, backed by a word from Ismay, had asked him to keep an eye on the hold and to report back to him if he saw or heard anything suspicious, he had agreed without needing any further explanation. Nor had he looked surprised when Beck had said it might be a good idea if he armed himself with a pistol.

As Beck reached the bottom of the stairs, King started to speak.

'Thanks for coming, sir.'

'What did you see, Tom?'

'Something and nothing, sir. I was at the post you specified, by the chest. I heard footsteps on the stairs. I called out, friendly like, not wanting to startle anyone.'

'What did you say?'

'"Who goes there?" Not in a stern voice, I must say, but a soft one. Anyways, I got no answer so I stepped forward and repeated myself. As I came forward I saw a man standing there, halfway down the stairs. When he saw me he turned and went. Quickly, like. As if I had caught him somewhere he shouldn't have been. I went half up the stairs and he had disappeared. I asked a few lads in the post office if they'd seen him but they said they hadn't. It's pretty quiet down here.'

'Can you describe him to me?'

'Tall, wearing a cap – brown, I think it was. He had a round face but not fat. A moustache. He was tall, maybe five feet and ten inches, and he was well built. He was wearing a brown coat and trousers.' King thought some more. 'The most interesting thing was his bag.'

'He was carrying a bag?'

'Yes, sir. A battered brown holdall.'

'Did he say or do anything when you saw him?'

'No, sir. He just turned and headed back from where he'd come. Quite quickly with it, as I said.'

'Is there any reason why anyone would be down in this part of the ship?'

'None at all, sir. It's off-limits to any passengers who don't have express permission.'

'I suppose someone could end up here after getting lost.'

'I see no reason for that, sir. Unless they had some reason to visit the mail room. But they would go to the post office first if they had a query.'

Beck knew that King was right. The chances were that it had been someone enticed by the rumours about the book. The description King had given certainly fitted Piatkow.

Had his plan worked, Beck wondered, and had they missed their chance even so? Or had the man whom King had seen just been casing the hold and was planning to return later? Beck cursed himself for leaving his post when he had. A few more hours and he might have been able to positively identify Piatkow. As it was, he hadn't slept and it was unlikely that he would be able to now.

'What do you want me to do now, sir?' King asked.

Beck thought for some time. They would need to keep someone here. Would his time be best spent watching the hold, or was now the time to search the liner?

Just then, there were footsteps on the stairs. Both men spun around straight away. It was a steward.

'What is it?' King barked, irritated by the intrusion.

'Excuse me, sir. Mr Brown, one of the assistant pursers, requests your presence in the third-class berths forward. One of the passengers has reported a theft.'

Beck followed King and the steward out of the hold, up a few decks, then forward along a vast busy passageway used only by the crew that seemed to run the entire length of the ship. At the other end they reached some third-class berths next to those used by the stokers and trimmers. The steward led them past some communal toilets to the starboard side of the ship and a poky room containing four beds. Sitting on one of them was an old man who was staring at the floor. A tall gangling man in an assistant purser's uniform and with a grim look on his face stood there. He nodded at King as they entered.

'Mr Brown,' King said by way of greeting. 'What have we here, then?'

'Mr Gustafson, this is Mr King, the master-at-arms. Please tell him what you have told me.'

The old man looked up. His face was gaunt, the skin of his face tight, his eyes yellowing and downcast, his neck thin and scrawny. He still had a fine head of grey hair but it was about the only thing about him that seemed to be in good condition. His clothes were a size or two too big and hung from his body.

'I have been robbed,' he said mournfully in a Scandinavian accent.

'Of what, may I ask?'

'Most of my savings. I had stitched them into the lining of my jacket for safe keeping. Or so I thought.' He sounded rueful rather than angry.

'How much are we talking about, sir?'

'I had them converted into dollars before I left Sweden. There was around six hundred dollars.'

Beck thought of the money he had stitched into the bottom off his bag, sitting there right now in his room. It was about the same amount as the old man had brought, the sum of both their lives' earnings. He felt tremendous sympathy for him.

'Do you have any idea who might have taken it, Mr Gustafson?'

He nodded sombrely. 'I do,' he said wearily. He winced.

'Is everything all right, sir?' King asked.

'Fine,' Gustafson said, waving a hand. 'I am ill.'

A glimmer of concern spread across King's face. The old man must have seen it.

'Don't worry, don't worry. I have a cancer. It is nothing contagious.'

'Oh. I'm sorry to hear that, sir.' King paused for a few seconds, as if waiting for a suitable time to lapse before he ploughed on with his questioning. 'But you said you think you know who took your money.'

Gustafson nodded. 'I shared a room with him.'

King looked at the assistant purser.

'We have no record of anyone else in this room sir. It was to be left empty. Mr Gustafson was moved here because of his condition. He had previously been sharing a compartment with some others in the after part, and it was felt he would benefit from having a room to himself. I have asked the stewards and other staff and no one is aware of anyone else who was allocated this berth.'

'You won't find him,' the old man said balefully.

'What makes you think that, sir?' King said.

'Call it an old man's intuition,' Gustafson said, a faint smile on his crumpled face.

'Well, would you mind telling us about him so we can at least give it a go?'

'For sure. He was young, perhaps the same age as that gentleman there. Similar height, too.' He was pointing at Beck. 'He was handsome, dark hair, a moustache – and a round face. He wore a cap – a navy-blue suit, and he had a battered brown holdall that appeared to have all his possessions in it.'

As Gustafson outlined each part of his description, Beck's heart beat harder. 'Did you speak to him?' he blurted out, even though technically it wasn't his business to.

'Sure,' the old man said in his matter-of-fact way.

'Did he speak to you about himself?'

'Some things.'

'Would you tell us what he said?'

The old Swede shrugged. 'He was from Latvia.'

Beck resisted the urge to punch the air in vindication. After all, Latvia was a fair-sized country.

'Go on.'

'But he had been living in London. He was very angry about what the Russians were doing to his countrymen. And his friends. Some of them who had been tortured – their fingernails ripped out, that sort of thing. You could see he harboured a great hatred.'

Each detail was like a tick on Beck's mental checklist. It all made sense. Seeking to lie low, Piatkow had come to this cabin, in this remote part of the ship, which housed only a sick old man. For some reason, he had left, to move on elsewhere, knowing he had perhaps spoken too much. But not before he had robbed the old man of his savings. Then, it seemed, he had gone to check out the security in the hold ahead of planning a raid on the book.

He should get back there, Beck thought. They had left Bailey, the other master-at-arms, on guard. But first he needed more information.

King, perhaps slightly disgruntled that Beck had started asking questions, muscled back into the interrogation. 'Did he give you a name?'

'No. I did ask. But I think I fell asleep before he gave it to me, if indeed he did.'

'And did you tell him about your savings?' King asked.

The old man scoffed. 'Of course I didn't. I wouldn't be so stupid.' A mournful look fell across his pallid face. 'I told him I was emigrating to America, going to see my daughter and grandchildren before I died. He must have thought I might be taking my savings with me.'

'Did he tell you anything else? What he might be doing on board? Where he might be going? If he was travelling with anyone else?' Beck asked.

Gustafson shook his head. 'He said only that he had friends in America.'

'We will get on the case immediately, Mr Gustafson. Your description is a good one to go on. I give you our word that we will pursue him vigorously and tenaciously. We hope to get your money back to you.'

'Thank you,' Gustafson said quietly.

King turned to leave. Beck waited at the threshold, scouring his mind for something, anything he might ask that would confirm it had been Piatkow. The old man had let his head hang down, and Beck did not want to bother him further. He headed for the door. But it was the old man who summoned them back.

'I remember one more thing.'

'What?' Beck and King asked in unison.

'The man didn't eat meat.'

A vegetarian.

Beck was now certain that it was Piatkow.

It might have been the cold, or it might just have been because the women were reaching to the backs of their wardrobes where the dresses were less knockout, possibly even in deference to the Sabbath, but Martha found dinner that evening was a less glitzy affair. Before eating, she had been out on deck but had lasted for only a few drags on her cigarette. The air was cold and the breeze cut through her flimsy shawl, and when she inhaled she could feel the cold air sting her throat.

At her table Martha really wasn't in the mood for either small talk or big food. Her mind kept returning to her conversation with Beck. She had heard nothing from him since, and she wondered if he was down in that lonely hold, shivering and waiting while the demons in his head crowded in. She thought of going down there but resisted the impulse. Maybe later.

The talk at the table, most of it coming from Darton's mouth along with various fragments of food, was of the speed of the ship and how well she was doing. People now seemed sure that they would arrive in New York on Tuesday. Darton was even wondering if he might get a late table at his favourite restaurant. Martha made a mental note of its name and vowed never to go anywhere near it.

Other talk was of the temperature outside. She had experienced it herself and had no wish to discuss it in detail, so she amused herself by casting her gaze around the room, keeping a close eye on the major players. Ismay, laughing loudly, seemed so carefree that she didn't think that Beck could have found his man. The chief purser was regaling some more folk with his stories. The captain was nowhere to be seen. Darton said he was a guest of the Wideners in the à la carte restaurant, with a few more of their more illustrious fellow passengers.

The time crawled by. The whole journey now seemed to be dragging. Martha wasn't sure she could stand even two more days of this boring routine. Never mind latitude, they should record the *lassitude* of these journeys. She tried to remember to make a note of that wordplay later when she got back to her cabin, perhaps use it in her piece. Fat chance her subeditors would keep it in, though, she thought.

Bored, glassy-eyed and full of rich food that her stomach was rebelling against, she did what any good woman would have done. She decided to get loaded. Sabbath or not, once dinner was over she would go in search of Miss Hardee and see if she would be a willing colleague. Then, emboldened and warmed by booze, she would go in search of Beck. If she was a little bit fresh, she might even take the chance of trying to revive his spirits physically. Lord knew he was taking his time in making a move. Curses on these English gents and their proper way of doing things. Right now she wanted something improper.

After speaking to Gustafson, Beck had gone back to the hold with King. There had been no sign of Piatkow returning. He didn't expect him to. The Latvian would want to lie low for some time after his act of petty theft. It didn't rule out an attempt to steal the book before the voyage ended, but instinct told Beck that Piatkow might tread carefully, particularly after he had seen that the area was guarded and had guessed that the book was bait in a trap.

Bailey, the second master-at-arms, had been left there just in case, though there was talk of giving the task to one of the seamen so that Bailey could take up his usual duties. King said he was going to conduct a thorough search of the ship and said he was happy for Beck to tag along. Beck decided to warn him about Piatkow's nature.

'The man we are searching for, if it is who I suspect it is, will not come quietly. In fact, he's likely to raise holy hell if we corner him.'

'You sound like you know him.'

'I do. Sort of. I know what he's capable of. Our first duty is to the other passengers on the ship. We can't endanger them in any way. So let's step carefully.'

'What do you suggest?'

'Let's cover as much of the ship as possible, looking deck by deck for anyone who might fit the description. But if we do find someone, we do nothing unless we're in a private place. If it's public, we lie low and we watch and we wait for the right time.' Beck paused. 'Be prepared to use your pistol.'

King nodded, his apprehension clear. He was more accustomed to putting the frighteners on boisterous drunks than chasing a hardened criminal while carrying a gun. But he seemed like a good man to have by your side and Beck was glad of the extra set of hands and eyes, as well as another pistol.

'Should we take the old man with us for a positive identification?'

Beck shook his head. 'Not necessary. To begin with Gustafson is too ill. It would be barbaric to drag him all around the ship. I can vouch for a positive recognition.'

'You've seen our quarry?'

'On land, yes.' Beck thought it best at this point to keep the story of the Houndsditch shoot-out to himself. 'I know as much about him as I do about some of my friends. If we capture him, we can always get the old man to confirm it's the same man who shared his cabin and stole his money. Now, are you ready?'

King nodded once again, with more conviction this time, a look of quiet determination on his face. On their way back to the hold, they had swapped some small talk. King had let slip that he was a widower; his two children were staying with his mother.

'You don't have to do this, you know,' Beck offered. 'It could be dangerous. You have two children to think of. They depend on you.'

King's response was emphatic. 'No way. This is my ship. I'm in charge of discipline. I'm part of this.'

Beck smiled. He had known that King was a good man. If things got dangerous he would find a way to try to get him out of the firing line. He had enough fatherless children on his conscience without adding two more.

It was dinner time and they headed first for the third-class dining saloon. It was busy, but there was no sign of Piatkow. They went through to the smoking room where an impromptu party seemed to be taking place, inevitably led by the Irish. The drink was flowing, a makeshift band was in full swing – who would've known that bagpipes, harmonica and piano went together so well, Beck thought with some amusement – and people were dancing and reeling in the warm fug. At one point, a rat ran across the room, creating uproar among the women. Beck couldn't believe it at first, but King assured him that rats were commonplace on board most vessels.

'They'll be the first ones overboard if we go down,' he joked.

From there, they moved to the third-class deck, almost deserted because of the cold and the attractions of the knees-up down below. The sky was a magnificent sight: a thousand stars pinpricking the moonless canopy. The air was still, and the sea also. The glitter of the heavens seemed to extend for miles. Beck told King about the reports of ice he'd been told of.

'It's not uncommon at this time of year,' King replied. 'The captain's an experienced hand. He knows what he's doing. Anyway, on a clear night like this when the visibility is so good we should be able to steer clear of trouble. There's certainly no sign of the ship slowing. In fact, it seems to me we're getting faster.'

They explored as many of the outdoor areas as possible before conceding defeat and heading inside, glad of the warmth. Next stop was second class. The dining saloon was full, even though the main sitting was over. In a less ribald echo of what was going on in steerage, the second-class passengers had also gathered together but this time for a hymn session. A priest with silver hair, and a manner that indicated he was no stranger to public speaking, was regaling those present with the stories behind several hymns. Beck could see from the rather glazed expressions on the faces of the assembled throng that most of them would prefer singing the hymns to being given a sermon on their origins, but even his godless heart swelled when the group joined in song. As he walked around the room, trying to see as many faces as he could, he couldn't help but wonder whether any faith in God might have helped him during the travails of the past few months. Perhaps, he thought. But how do you find faith? Maybe one day he might be blessed with it.

The song ended and the priest went into another of his rambling monologues. Beck was too busy scrutinising faces to listen to much of what was being said, but the holy man appeared to be talking about a hymn which offered solace to those in trouble at sea. It certainly seemed to grab the attention of those present more than his other introductions had.

'We may not be in peril,' the cleric declaimed, 'but there are sure to be others out there who are.'

As the voices rose and echoed off the panels and balustrades, Beck was satisfied that Piatkow was not there. He met King by the exit and the master-at-arms spread his hands to show he had seen no one fitting the description either. They left the congregation and headed for the less crowded smoking room, occupied by those who were devoted to more earthly pleasures. Piatkow was not among them, either.

Before they moved into first class they went back to the hold. Bailey had not seen a single soul. They carried out a search of the other holds and the mail room before moving on to the general stores area, the squash court, the swimming pool, the Turkish baths, the galleys, the pantries and the linen rooms. Then they walked the entire length of Scotland Road – all without luck.

There were a few decisions that Beck needed to make. He had to decide when to send a Marconigram to London telling them that Piatkow was confirmed as being on board and they would need to summon an adequate force to meet and capture him on arrival. He also had to see if there was a sketch artist or similar on board who might be able to draw a likeness of Piatkow, based on the old man's recollections, and post it among the staff and enlist their help. The consequences of that caused him to shudder. But without a hundred sets of eyes to help him, the chances of finding Piatkow during a general search were slim.

Beck checked the time. It was after ten in the evening. The search had been going on for five fruitless hours. The adrenalin surge from the old man's revelation was starting to wear off and the lack of sleep was beginning to take its toll on him. His limbs ached, and his head felt as if it was filling with water. Every part of him craved rest but he knew he couldn't give in to it yet.

They searched the forward well deck and forecastle deck. Beck was glad to be in the crisp night air once more. He lit a cigarette, eager for the stimulation. There was no one around. All he could hear was the sound of the ship tearing through the water. Looking up he saw the skies were even more glorious than before, almost unreal, like a giant black stage backdrop studded with sequins.

He extinguished his cigarette. He was losing the feeling in his fingertips. He knew then that it was time to update Ismay. He arranged to meet King by the purser's office in fifteen minutes for a final search of the upper decks and first class. Then, if that was in vain, he would rest and telegraph London in the morning. Then he would take a final decision on the sketch. Nothing could be gained from him stumbling around half-dead.

Ismay was in his room, about to turn in for the evening. He answered the door in his dressing gown. There was a hint of irritation as he opened the door but as soon as he saw that it was Beck, he ushered him in.

'You look exhausted,' Ismay said. 'Coffee?'

'No, I'm fine.' Beck stayed standing. If he sat down he felt as if he would fall asleep. 'Look, there's no need to detain you as I can see you're about to go to bed. Just to let you know there was a theft in steerage earlier today. I think the culprit was our man.'

'Really?' Ismay said, with some delight. 'What sort of theft?'

'Money stolen from the lining of an old man's jacket. Quite a decent sum, too. But his description fits exactly with that of Piatkow, as do a few personal details. With Mr King I've searched the third- and second-class areas, as well as some of the private and staff rooms. We are about to go through first class and the upper decks and maybe the deckhouse, if we have time. Though we might have to pick it up in the morning.'

'Of course, of course.'

'But we may need to speak then – early, I'm afraid – with the captain if possible. I may have to shift tack. It may be an idea to hold the drills we spoke of, perhaps tomorrow. People may be less inclined to report for them when we're only a day or so out from New York.'

'Whenever you say. The captain and I will be there.'

'Let's say seven a.m. Here is as good a place as any.'

'Splendid.'

'If anything happens in the meantime, I'll let you know.'

'Please do, regardless of the hour. If there's any other help you need, don't hesitate to ask.'

Beck thanked Ismay and left, making his weary way to the purser's office. He would give it until midnight before he called the search off until morning.

Then he bumped into Martha Heaton.

Martha had needed air. Too many Martinis with Miss Hardee and her companions had left her light-headed. One of their group, a stiff young Englishman who was rather too pleased with himself, kept saying the word 'Marvellous', only his plummy accent rendered it as 'More-vahl-arse', and about the tenth time he said it Martha had got the giggles. Excusing herself, she said she needed air but would return. Then she went back to her room, trying to appear as ladylike as possible, to get a coat, and headed for the highest deck to get some of the cool Atlantic air and a nicotine fix.

As she approached the Grand Staircase she saw Beck. He looked like a corpse in a suit.

'My God, you look awful!' she said.

'Thanks. You're the second person who's said that.'

'Sorry,' she mumbled. God, Martha, you're drunk. Try not to slur your words. 'What's happening?' She spoke as slowly as she could, which probably made things worse. Beck merely glanced around nervously. Whether from discretion or the shame at being seen talking to a lush she wasn't sure.

'There have been developments.'

'Oh. Good-oh,' she replied, and immediately regretted it. 'Sorry. I've had a couple of drinks. I was just on my way to the boat deck to have a smoke and get some air. You could join me and we could talk?'

'I'm a bit busy.'

Yet another brush-off. He was giving her a complex, Martha thought.

'I'm not brushing you off.'

'I said that out loud? Jesus. Sorry.'

'You're apologising too much. We'll make a Brit out of you yet.'

'Sorry. Sure you can't be tempted to come upstairs with me?'

Beck shook his head. 'I really am busy.' He glanced around. There was no one on the corridor. 'I've had reasonable confirmation that Piatkow is on board. We're just following a few loose ends now. I should be able to let you know more in the morning.'

'Sounds fascinating.' Hell, Martha, she thought, everything you say sounds like it's coming out of the mouth of a teenage girl. She paused. She had definitely only thought that one.

'Well, as I say, tomorrow I'll find time to update you, but you may have to wait until I've cleared a few things with Ismay and the captain. Now I must go.'

Beck left, the baize doors swinging behind him. Martha carried on walking until she realised she was moving away from the staircase. Retracing her steps, she went through the same doors and found Beck in conversation with a tall, thickset man by the purser's office. A clock on the wall said it was just after ten-thirty. Without looking at him, she carried on up the stairs towards the boat deck. The ship was quiet. Most people had drifted off to their cabins, leaving only the pleasure-seekers behind. Given how she would feel in the morning, Martha wondered if she wouldn't be better off pursuing a more puritanical regime. In the morning she might search out the Turkish baths and lay off the liquor for a night or two.

One thing was for sure: after this cigarette, she would go back to her cabin and sleep. Not go back to the Palm Court cafe and carry on drinking. Though maybe one more wouldn't hurt. It would be rude to disappear like that after promising to return.

She opened the door and was met with an icy, sobering blast. But what with the warmth from her coat and the booze in her system she felt no discomfort. A couple of fellow addicts were hanging around, having a last smoke before turning in. She walked straight to the rail, and lit up, feeling better already. Yes, tomorrow she would turn over a new leaf. A healthier me, she thought. And, with luck a good story to go with it.

Martha couldn't wait for morning to come.

Disappointment doesn't linger, not when it's become a part of your soul. Sten-Ake sat on the bottom berth, the lights out and the freezing air pouring through the porthole, unable to sleep knowing that sadness and disillusionment would be his lot to his dying day.

His dying day, he thought. That wasn't far off. He looked at the porthole. Not wide enough to squeeze through. But he knew that the icy waters would offer him a swift end. If he put on his lifejacket he would float and not drown, while the shock of the water's cold would numb him from pain and death would be mercifully quick for someone of his age and in his condition. His heart might give way immediately.

But he was no coward. He would complete the voyage. See his grandchildren. Who cared about money, anyway? It had been never been a love of his. Just as well, because he had never possessed a talent for making any.

Sten-Ake continued to stare out of the porthole. The sky was as clear as on any night he had experienced while at sea. And despite the draught created by the onrushing ship – he had never dreamed a ship could travel so fast, he guessed they were making upwards of twenty-two knots – there was little other wind to speak of. Still, lingering in the air was the clammy damp scent of ice.

He sat and he watched, and sometimes he stood. He put on his jacket, the one that the young Latvian had stolen Sten-Ake's money from, to ward off the chill. Still he kept watching, unable to take his eyes from the starlit sky and the placid sea, black as oil. The lights in his cabin had been off all evening so he was accustomed to the darkness outside, and was able to see a good distance. At one stage he thought he saw the foremast light of another ship but it might just have been a shooting star.

Then he did see something. A shape, somewhere in the distance. He stood and went closer to the porthole. A blue-black mass perhaps half a mile to the north. There was a small white swell at its base. A berg, he thought. More likely a growler, like a berg but lower, less easy to see, more dangerous even. Aha! he thought. I knew I could smell ice.

On the bridge, and up in the crow's nest, Sten-Ake pictured them passing on the messages. He heard no warning bells but he knew they would be in communication. There would also be a lookout at the ship's bow whose eyes, like his, were accustomed to the light, and lower down than those of whoever was in the nest and so better able to judge distance.

But why were they still going so fast? They must be mighty sure of their ability to swerve around the bergs. It was a clear night and visibility was good, but there was no moon to light their way, and the lack of wind meant the swell at the base of any bergs would be difficult to see unless you were less than a mile away. Sten-Ake knew from experience how they could creep up on you unawares. Ships rarely hit them. He couldn't think of any he knew which had. But that was because you always took greater care when the threat of ice was real.

A minute or so later he thought he saw another berg, this time further away. Perhaps they had picked a path that ran through the middle of them? These new ships could pick up warnings from others, and the charts and things they had were probably far more advanced than any of the equipment his vessels had used. Maybe they had told them the position of the bergs so they were better able to avoid them?

His eyes felt heavy. He should sleep. But Sten-Ake knew he couldn't. He would continue to watch and wait for the dawn.

At sea, in the presence of danger, if you slept, you died.

Beck and King walked the entire length of the covered first-class promenade on A deck, and then made it up onto the boat deck as a distant bell tolled six times. Eleven o'clock, the master-at-arms explained. The bell not only marked time for those on board, it told the crew on watch how much of their four-hour shifts they had completed. Eight bells at midnight and then the next watch would take over.

His breath frosting on the air, Beck pitied the poor souls whose job it was to work on deck during freezing nights like this, in particular the men in the crow's nest with no shelter. When he mentioned that to King he told him that the lookouts only did two-hour watches, and they did them in pairs so at least they could talk to each other. Still, Beck thought, rather them than him.

The cold pierced and revitalised him, even though he was wearing the large woollen overcoat which King had found for him. Their plan was to check the boat deck going anti-clockwise, starting at the forward port-side first-class entrance and walking aft, checking as many areas as possible.

King flapped his arms across his broad chest. ''It would take someone very brave or very stupid to hide up here on a night like this.'

Beck knew that Piatkow wasn't stupid. But he wouldn't rule anything out. In truth, he just wanted to get this last search of the evening done, then try and get some sleep, and tackle the problem with renewed vigour in the morning.

They walked slowly, the lights from the first-class lounge blazing across the yellow pine decking. Not everyone had called it a night. Beck wondered if Martha was still up. There had been a strong scent of alcohol on her breath and she'd seemed rather unsteady on her feet. He smiled. Not the sort of girl you'd wish to take home to meet your mother, perhaps, but one that your mother might like; that was, if she could see past the cursing, drinking and smoking.

They reached the end of the first-class promenade and went through the barrier to the engineers' area, where a few of the black gang were having a smoke. King nodded at one, his face bathed with sweat. The cool air must come as a relief for those sweltering in the Hades heat below, Beck thought.

'She's going well,' King said.

'All twenty-four boilers are going now,' the man said eagerly. 'Now we'll really see what she can do.'

As they passed through into the second-class area, the cold began to reach Beck's extremities. His feet were heavy and the tips of his fingers, despite being plunged into the coat's voluminous pockets, were beginning to go numb.

The second-class deck, which they had checked earlier, was deserted save for one man, silhouetted in the light cast from the entrance to the ship below. Beck's heart surged with excitement. The man, his back to them, was leaning over the side at the far end of the promenade, beyond the furthest lifeboat, overlooking the poop deck not far from where Beck believed he had seen Piatkow last Thursday at twilight. Beck and King quickened their pace, their stares fixed on the figure ahead.

About three or four yards away, King stopped. 'Evening, sir,' he said. His hand was in his pocket.

The man spun around. He was clean-shaven, mid-forties, his features angular.

Beck glanced across at King and shook his head.

'Good evening,' the man said, appearing friendly, though with a hint of uncertainty in his tone. He was probably alarmed at being crept up on at such a late hour.

King grinned broadly. 'Cold, isn't it?'

'It most certainly is. I was just about to go back and get warm in my cabin.' The man pointed to the heavens. 'Amazing sky. I'm a keen astronomer. You can see all the constellations tonight. Ursa Major, Draco, Polaris, Cassiopeia. I don't even need a telescope. They're just there for us to admire. A stirring sight.'

Both of the other men looked up, Beck once again taken aback by just how *many* stars there were. The whole sky appeared to be aglow. In foggy, smoke-shrouded London you would be lucky to see a fraction of this illumination.

'It certainly is a stirring sight,' King said.

The three of them stood there for a few seconds, admiring the cosmic display, until the man said his farewells and disappeared through the nearby entrance. Beck walked forward to the barrier and looked below and across at the poop deck. Another man appeared to be pacing back and forth across the deck, but King explained that it was one of the quartermasters. The lights would be out in third class now. Beck wondered if Piatkow was down there, hidden in the vast bowels of the ship.

The port-side amidships and aft now covered, Beck and King rounded the starboard side. Beck lit another cigarette for them both, realising that their night's work was almost complete and that their energy would be best saved for the next day. He could hear the churn thrown up by the propellers, but beyond their white wake the sea was as flat and still as a boating lake.

They finished their smoke and continued their walk.

'Once we reach the end of the first-class promenade on this side we'll call it a night,' Beck said.

'I agree. Not sure what else we can do tonight. Do you want to meet in the morning?'

Beck nodded. 'I have a meeting at seven so let's say seven-thirty at the purser's office. We can talk a few things through first.'

As they they passed through the other side of the engineers' promenade, the sound of the bell echoed through the air. Ding-ding, ding-ding . . . Seven times. It was 11:30. Beck was looking forward to a warm bed and the chance of some sleep.

A minute later they had reached the first lifeboat on the first-class promenade. Beck was about to speak when he heard a cry. Sort of muffled.

He turned. 'Did you hear that?'

'Yes. Sounded like it came from the lookout.' King pointed. Beck looked. Ahead of the bridge, perched at least another twenty feet in the air, was the crow's nest.

'I think he said there was something ahead,' Beck said.

Both men moved to the side and craned their necks to get a view, but there was only starlit darkness.

A few seconds passed.

'Well, I can't see anything and she hasn't changed course,' King said, leaning on a lifeboat.

'Must have been mistaken.'

Just then there was a thud. The sound of something hitting wood. Beck looked at the lifeboat. The noise had come from in there. King had heard it too. His head turned to face the boat. He looked back at Beck. Neither man spoke.

Beck put a finger to his lips. He crept towards the white boat. As he grabbed the protective canvas cover, it flipped back. A figure appeared. A man.

Beck stepped back, surprised. King shouted something. The man got to his feet on the edge of the boat, ready to jump. A cap was pulled low across his forehead and a bag was in his hand. There wasn't enough light to see his face. Beck and King moved forward in a pincer movement as the man leaped, arms out, straight at them. Beck was knocked backwards, his arms grasping at cloth. His back hit the cold deck and a flailing foot struck his mouth.

The man scrambled to his feet. His face was caught in a shaft of light cast from the small window of a stateroom.

It was the same face that Beck had seen on an equally cold night sixteen months before.

Beck got to his feet. King had been knocked over too, but was also getting up. Piatkow glanced left and saw that the route aft meant passing the burly King. Instantly, he turned right, towards the small barrier barring access to the officer's promenade. In one movement he vaulted over.

King shouted for him to stop. Beck set off in pursuit. Piatkow landed and stumbled but stayed on his feet. Beck followed, clearing the barrier but falling to his knees on landing. He got up and started running after the sprinting fugitive.

Piatkow was fast but Beck was faster. As the anarchist reached the end of the promenade, Beck was closing in.

Got you, he thought. Piatkow was at the bridge.

Piatkow turned left. Beck followed. Now they were both on the bridge.

As Beck turned he saw Piatkow barging past an officer in a large overcoat.

'What the hell!' the officer said.

'Stop that man!' Beck shouted. 'I'm police. Stop him?'

The officer turned as Beck flew past, only a few feet from Piatkow who had reached the other side of the bridge. A door flew open and two more seamen piled out. Piatkow hesitated about which way to turn. Beck took his chance, leaping forwards and bundling him to the floor.

One of the seamen who had left the wheelhouse jumped on Piatkow too. But the anarchist started to convulse his body, trying to break free.

From inside the wheelhouse there came the sound of a phone ringing.

The young seaman had a hold on Piatkow. The other, an officer, was unsure what to do. Another was in the doorway of the wheelhouse. Then the first officer they had seen arrived.

'What is going on?' he asked in a clear Scots accent.

Still the phone rang.

Beck ignored the officer and leaped onto Piatkow's body, helping the young sailor. Piatkow was thrashing like a fish in a net, his angry breath billowing from his nostrils, but two were enough to hold him down. Where's King? Beck thought.

Three clear bells rang through the air. Not the ding-ding that marked time. But three separate urgent tollings.

'Shit!' the Scots officer said. The other, younger officer went back into the wheelhouse and picked up the phone.

'What do you see?' he asked. A pause followed. Beck heard him saying, 'All right.' He looked at his senior officer. 'Iceberg dead ahead, sir.'

'Shit,' the officer said again, hurrying into the wheelhouse. The young seaman on top of Piatkow started to get up.

'Stay!' Beck said.

'Hard-a-starboard,' he heard the Scots voice bark.

Even Piatkow seemed to have stopped struggling, as if he wanted to see how events would unfold. Here, on the floor behind the wall of the bridge, Beck's view was blocked. The ship started to turn right.

'No. Hard-a-starboard,' he heard the Scots voice shout. 'Turn her to port.'

'Hard-a-starboard,' a wavering voice came back.

The liner appeared to change direction, turning to the left now rather than the right.

The young seaman holding Piatkow couldn't bear it any longer, and jumped up to take a look. The anarchist took his chance, the weight off his body, mule-kicking his legs, catching Beck in the face with his boot. Instinctively Beck raised his hands to protect himself and felt the warm metallic tang of blood in his mouth. He got to his feet. Piatkow was running down the port side of the deck.

'We're going to hit it!' the Scots officer said.

Beck turned. The ship was veering sharply left. Ahead, outlined against the night sky, was a dark approaching mass, towering high.

Jesus, he thought. It looked as if the ship would strike it but the *Titanic* continued to turn to the left. Beck couldn't wait. He turned and started to sprint after Piatkow, just as he heard the Scots officer cry 'Hard a-port!' again.

As Beck reached full speed, the deck seemed to shake slightly beneath his running feet and undulate briefly, as if it had rolled over a line of logs. He lost his footing and fell forwards onto his knees. As he got up he looked to his left. Over the top of the deckhouse he could see the shadow of the looming icy mass, at least another thirty feet above. But the bow was clear. The worst had been avoided.

Beck vaulted over the barrier but couldn't see Piatkow anywhere. He must have dived into first class. He went through the entrance and down the staircase. Down one deck. No sign. He went down another. Nothing. He went back up to A deck. A few of the male passengers had come out of the smoking room.

'Have you seen a man in a brown cap running this way?' Beck remembered that the cap had fallen off. 'No, he wasn't wearing a cap. He was dark-haired, moustache, quite plainly dressed, carrying a bag.'

The men shook their heads, nonplussed.

Shit and damn, Beck thought.

'What just happened?' an Englishman in evening dress asked.

'What do you mean?' Beck was breathless from his exertions.

'It felt as though there was some kind of collision.'

'There was an iceberg. I'm not sure we hit it. If we did, it was just a glancing blow.'

'Thank goodness for that,' another man added emphatically. 'Gentlemen, back to our game.'

They went back inside. Beck stood for a few seconds, wondering what to do. They had had Piatkow. But then the iceberg warning had distracted those who'd been helping Beck. What had happened to King? He should go and look for him.

Beck went back to the boat deck, noticing only then that the ship was slowing, the vibration and hum of the engines starting to lessen.

Why were they stopping?

It was the loud grinding noise, like a giant serrated knife being drawn along the keel of the ship, almost directly below him, that Sten-Ake heard first. Then came a violent juddering that pitched him forwards onto the floor. As he lay there, ice – great blocks of it – came pouring in through the porthole, scattering across the floor. As he looked up through the opening he had a glimpse of a glistening blue-white wall passing by, and smelled a sulphurous whiff in the air.

He lay there for a short time. It could have been seconds, or it might have been minutes. There was no doubt what had happened. They had hit an iceberg. Not head on – the bow would have been crushed and Sten-Ake with it – but some kind of glancing blow to the starboard side, or even to the bottom of the boat. In the five or six minutes or so leading up to the collision, he had noticed, looking out of the porthole, the ship altering direction a few points to starboard and then abruptly switching course to port. Dodging bergs, he thought. He knew that most captains when faced with ice put their trust in a good lookout and crew and steered around the obstacles. That had been in a different age. At the speed they were travelling, on a vessel this size and so cumbersome? Madness.

There was the sound of doors closing and opening. Passengers started to gather outside in the corridor. Sten-Ake could hear their questions. What had happened? Someone said they had hit another boat. Another said they were dropping anchor. Then why is my bloody room like the North Pole with ice everywhere? another said. There were other voices, some in languages he couldn't understand. Slowly, he rose to his feet, crushing shards of ice beneath him as he did.

A steward had appeared in the corridor and was being bombarded with questions. He didn't have any answers. 'I don't know what happened. I'm sure it's nothing to be concerned about. Just keep to where you are and we will see.'

Sten-Ake could have told them what had happened. What he had been seeing through the porthole during the past hour or so. But he was distracted. He had noticed another thing. The ship was stopping, her engines going silent. Their tremor, a constant companion since Southampton, was gone. Sten-Ake tried to work out what it meant. Presumably the crew were assessing the damage.

He stepped towards the door, to hear what else might be said. His foot landed in something wet. The ice has melted quickly, he thought, looking down.

But it wasn't ice. It was water. And it was flowing across the floor.

Martha had been drunk and the hot whisky she was drinking wasn't going to sober her up. Hot whisky? Every other drink she'd had was over ice. Now she was drinking grog. Well, they *were* on a ship.

She was just about to stand up and announce, for the fourth time, that she was going to bed, and this time she wouldn't be persuaded to stay by the promise of another drink – especially if it was hot – when there was trembling motion, as if some omnipotent hand had briefly grabbed the boat and given it a small shake. It was barely noticeable; Miss Hardee and her beaus didn't even stop the word-association game that was causing them endless amusement but that had started to bore Martha rigid.

'Did anyone feel that?' she asked. No one had. Maybe she was just too loaded.

Martha got up and left the à la carte restaurant where they had set up camp, watched over by two very bored waiters who wanted to sleep. She went out through the door onto a landing, to be met by two men in dinner jackets, who seemed almost as worse for wear as she was.

'Did something just happen?' she asked, surprised by how clear and measured her voice sounded. She was starting to think that she might have drunk herself sober.

'I really don't know,' one of the men said, in one of those prim clipped English voices that she always thought sounded vaguely villainous. 'We were just wondering the same. It felt as if the ship had struck something. The engines appear to have stopped. David here thinks that one of the propellers might have snapped or developed a fault.'

David nodded. 'Be a damn nuisance if so. We're two days out of New York and if we've dropped a screw it could mean we limp in.'

Please, God, no, Martha thought. Two days seemed like an eternity. More than that and she would surely die of tedium.

As they spoke, a young man, fresh-faced, colour in his cheeks, and a broad grin on his face, appeared. He had a large block of ice in his hand. He saw their looks of curiosity.

'It's all over the forward well deck. The steerage lot are playing with it. The word is that we brushed an iceberg.' He left them, bound no doubt for his pals in the smoking room. Martha made her way up to the boat deck. She walked out, almost losing her breath as she went from the comparatively warm air within to the arctic cold outside. The two dinner-jacketed men had followed her up. On deck a few other people were milling around, including one man in his dressing gown, obviously woken from his bed. He'll be back in it with pneumonia, Martha thought, unless he gets changed into something warmer.

She saw a group who were at the rear end of the promenade, leaning over the rail. They were laughing. She saw what they were looking at. A group of steerage passengers tossing lumps of ice around as if they were snowballs. Martha's reporter instinct, buried beneath a lake of booze, bubbled back to the surface.

'What happened?' she asked, of no one in particular.

A rotund man with a round friendly face turned to her, smiling.

'We hit an iceberg, they say.'

'Who says?'

'Some of the other passengers. Apparently one chap said he saw it passing by astern. A hundred feet high, apparently. That's why the ice is all over the deck in front. Must have winged it and broke some off.'

Suddenly Martha was aware that she was no longer just a passenger. She was in the middle of a story. 'Ship on maiden voyage clips iceberg' would be worth more than a line or two.

Some more details, some facts, and it could be dressed up into a lucky escape and a candidate for the front page. Scratch that – a cert, given the company on board. Throw in the Piatkow tale and this could be the trip of a lifetime. She took a deep breath, relishing the cold and the way it cleared her mind. She needed to find someone official, someone who might know what had happened, rather than some boozed-up clowns with tales of towering icebergs.

Purser McElroy was her man.

Martha was about to step back inside when she stumbled. Not because of the booze, woozy though that was making her feel as it lay on both her head and her stomach. But she felt as though the floor beneath her was sloping away to the right.

Then she realised it wasn't her that was listing. It was the ship.

B eck was on the bridge. The Captain was there, face bled of all colour. Ismay too, his head twitching anxiously, the bottom of his striped pyjamas peeking out from underneath his long overcoat. King was in the officers' mess. He had turned his ankle when Piatkow had leaped out of the lifeboat and straight into them. Just a sprain, they hoped. But Beck cursed King's absence at the crucial moment. Had he been there to help restrain Piatkow then the terrorist would be in custody now. Instead, once again, he was roaming the ship, able to find another place to hide. Nothing had changed, except for the incident with the berg.

Before going to the bridge, Beck had briefly returned to the boat where they had surprised Piatkow. There were a few belongings and some bags that weren't Piatkow's, some containing money, plenty of it. He'd been busy on board and the lifeboat had obviously been the chosen place to stash his swag. Where safer and less populated than a lifeboat on an unsinkable ship?

The captain asked Beck and Ismay to follow him through into his quarters. Beck shut the door behind them. The time on the clock on the wall was just after 11:50 p.m.

Ismay was like a dog on a tight leash. 'What happened?'

Smith was more restrained, but grave with it. 'We have struck ice.'

'Is it serious?' Is she damaged?'

'It could be. There is some damage. I have sent the carpenter to sound her out and see exactly what the extent is. The good news is that in the third-class area on G deck near the bow, where it seems the impact was, there seem to be have been no injuries to any of the passengers.'

'Good,' Ismay said. He paused. 'How did we manage to hit the berg?'

Beck saw the captain glance briefly at him before he answered. 'The circumstances are still somewhat unclear.'

'Didn't we see it?' Ismay asked

'As I said, it is still unclear. However, from what I am told, the lookout saw a dark mass on the horizon immediately after seven bells. The men on the bridge were then distracted when the gentleman Mr Beck has been seeking burst onto the bridge with him in pursuit. Some of the men then helped him apprehend the suspect. The lookout appears to have been phoning with a warning but in the melee his call went unanswered. Then he rang three bells and everyone's attention turned back to the bridge. This time the phone was answered and the iceberg was reported dead ahead.'

Ismay had put his hands to his face. The captain continued. Beck knew how bad it sounded.

'There was still time to avoid the berg, and Murdoch called "Hard a starboard!". However, in the panic the quartermaster responded to his order as if it were a tiller order, and turned the ship to starboard, rather than to port. By the time the confusion was cleared up, and the helm was turned to port, we were too close to avoid a collision. Mr Murdoch did what he could and tried to port around the berg, but it appears to have clipped the starboard wing.'

There was silence. Ismay's face stayed in his hands. He eventually brought them down. He looked at Beck. 'Your suspect Piatkow – do you still have him?'

Beck shook his head slowly. 'Mr King was incapacitated. I had Piatkow under control with one of the seamen but after the report of the iceberg came through he lost control of him and Piatkow managed to struggle free. As I gave chase we struck the ice and I was sent to the floor. He got away.'

Ismay inhaled deeply. For a few seconds he didn't say anything. Then he spoke. 'For now, we must not breathe a word of this to anyone. Captain, you must instruct your crew who witnessed the event to say nothing about it. The implications of people leaving their posts, ignoring the lookout's ice warnings, could be disastrous for this company.'

'I understand,' Smith replied.

'I heard the second officer Mr Lightoller say earlier that it was a difficult night for sighting bergs, with no wind or moon. We will say the berg was too close to avoid.'

'I understand.'

'In the meantime, what are the chances of getting *Titanic* under way and heading for land?'

The captain's eyes opened wide. 'I wouldn't advise it until we've done a thorough search of the vessel to see how badly she's damaged.'

'Do you think she's seriously damaged?'

'I'm not sure at this moment, Mr Ismay.'

'But we know she's unsinkable. The pumps will be able to help expel any water she's taken on. In the meantime let us head for the nearest land. Where would that be, Captain?'

'Halifax, Nova Scotia, around 450 miles north-west of our present position. We should arrive there on Wednesday, God willing, though it depends on our speed. It also seems we are on the edge of an ice field, so we may not be able to take the most direct route. At least, not by night.'

'Then let's head for there, drop our passengers safely and this suspect of Mr Beck's into the custody of a police force. A train can be chartered to transport the passengers to New York. Then we can get *Titanic* back to Belfast for repairs. We're not going to be reaching New York ahead of the *Olympic*'s maiden-voyage time, for now. But we can show that, after a chance encounter with an iceberg, as this was, she is still strong enough to make it to land and deliver her passengers safely to shore. If anything, it will prove the invincibility of our ships. Once we are nearer land we can consider how we should present our story for the press about how the accident happened, but if we are delivering one of the most wanted criminals in history to justice it will make our job a damned sight easier.'

Beck could see that the captain was reluctant, but it was also clear who was in overall charge of the ship. It wasn't the man in uniform, but the one in pyjamas.

'Very well, sir. I shall instruct them to go slow ahead.'

There was a knock on the door. Smith looked at Ismay, who nodded.

'Come in,' Smith said.

The door opened. An intense-looking man, with a bushy moustache and worried eyes, was at the door.

'Mr Bell,' the captain said. 'You have news to report? How is she?'

'She is taking in water, sir. But we think the pumps can handle it. I was wondering if it might be possible for the watertight doors aft of boiler room five to be opened.'

'Is five not flooded?'

Bell shook his head. 'We would like to get into those spaces and rig the suction lines to hold the flooding forward of that compartment.'

Smith appeared to brighten. 'Of course.' He turned to Beck and Ismay. 'Excuse me for a few moments, gentlemen.' Smith left for the bridge with Bell.

'Excellent,' Ismay said after he left. 'If the chief engineer is asking for the watertight doors to be opened she can't be too grievously damaged. It will be a longer journey now, but we will make it.'

Beck felt that he needed to apologise. 'I'm sorry we interfered with operations on the bridge. Piatkow took us by surprise and bolted in that direction. I feared he would get away so I called for assistance. That was an error.'

Ismay waved a dismissive hand. 'Well, we can talk about that in the days to come. We just have to make sure we get him next time.'

'I hope so, sir.'

The captain slipped back into the room. 'The engines have restarted. She is going to go ahead slow. I will pay a visit to the wireless room and see if we can get a message out that we have been in collision with ice, that all is well for now, and that we will be making our way to Halifax. They will need to make arrangements. I've asked one of my officers to go and find the ship's carpenter and report to me as soon as possible about any damage. In the meantime, we shall get her back under way.'

'Excellent. If you don't mind, Captain, I will stay around for the next few minutes. Unless I'm in the way?'

'Be my guest, Mr Ismay.'

Smith left once more. Ismay clapped his hands together. His earlier agitation seemed to have eased. In fact, yet again he seemed to be relishing the situation.

'You see, Mr Beck? Unsinkable.'

The water was sloshing around their feet. All around Sten-Ake men were collecting their luggage and moving, aiming to get higher up in the liner. He stood at his door and watched them.

'You coming, old man?' one asked

'Where to?'

'Anywhere but here,' came the response.

At that moment, the strange silence that had settled on the ship since the crash was broken. The growl of the engines rolling back to life. Obviously she was making water. Sten-Ake could see the evidence of that soaking his trousers. But if they were moving once more it must be that the pumps were working, that this would be as wet as she got. Presumably they were going to steam in search of help, or the nearest land. He sighed. It would be a long time now until he reached the station at Harrisburg.

At least, he thought, we are still afloat. He could not think of many ships that could survive a collision with an iceberg. The advance publicity was right. Yet Sten-Ake wasn't entirely at ease. The fire he had heard the stokers gossiping about. The collision. Now they were steaming ahead again. He hoped something wouldn't give.

It took a while, but he hauled himself onto the top berth, away from the water. He looked out of the porthole. *Titanic* was definitely listing, he worked out, checking against the sea and the sky. And down a bit by the bow if he wasn't mistaken. But at least she was moving. If she was seriously wounded they would be stationary and the crew would be getting the passengers off in boats as quickly as possible. No word had come for them to report to their lifeboats, wherever they might be. There had not been a drill, or if there had been, he had slept through it.

The gentle motion of the ship, far slower than before the incident, lulled Sten-Ake. He rested his head, exhaustion breaking over him like waves on a shore. He would get some sleep. When he woke up, he might have enough energy to go and ask some questions. He remembered the earnest young man, Beck, and his vow to return his money. There was something about that boy which made him believe it, an intensity and fervour.

As the ship started to move, and his companions in this part of steerage continued their exodus towards the stern, Sten-Ake drifted into unconsciousness.

'Come on, old man!' There was a hand on his arm, jolting him back into the present.

He looked up. It was the steward who had found him the room. He was smiling. 'Come on,' he repeated. 'This place is water-logged. We need to get towards the stern where it's drier.'

Sten-Ake shook his head to rid it of sleep, and eased himself up, a dull ache gripping his tired bones. 'Is she sinking?' he asked.

'Probably not,' came the reply. 'But she's taken on some water and the forward part is flooding somewhat. Should be fine but we need to get people to where it's dry.'

Sten-Ake climbed down slowly, helped by the steward. They

got his bag and started to walk. he hoped there was a bed wherever they were heading.

'Is she badly damaged?' he asked.

'I'm no sailor. The word is she'll be all right. We may end up limping into port, though.'

They walked aft, to the door that opened onto Scotland Road, the long corridor that seemed to run the entire length of the ship.

'You get to take a short cut,' the steward said, holding the door open.

As Sten-Ake was about to walk through the door, thanking the steward, there was a noise behind. He turned. Three stokers, drenched head to foot.

That isn't a good sign, he thought.

Martha went back to her room, looking to change into something less glitzy and more practical. When she had left, the corridors of her section of the ship had been beginning to fill with people, some of them in their nightclothes, wondering what had happened, grabbing hold of stewards and quizzing them or other passengers, knocking on the doors of their friends or family to alert them to what was going on.

As she made her way back to the Grand Staircase, she saw the man she wanted to see: Purser McElroy, outside his office, surrounded by passengers. He was still wearing his white dinner jacket from earlier that evening. His face was a picture of calm, beaming the same easy smile she had seen all voyage.

'I assure you, there is nothing to worry about,' he was telling them. 'We hit an iceberg but the ship appears to be fine. I suggest you return to your rooms until such time as we get further information. But it's probably just that we need to ascertain any damage.'

The group around him appeared to be satisfied by his calm assurance and moved away. Martha saw her chance.

'Miss Heaton, can I help you?' he said in a soothing voice. If there was any reason to panic, you would not have guessed it from either his tone or his bearing.

'Did we hit an iceberg?'

'It appears so, madam. But, as I was just saying, there is no need to panic.'

'How did we hit it?'

He raised his eyebrows in surprise. 'I have no idea. I'm no sailor.'

'Is *Titanic* taking on water?'

'I can't answer that question.'

'It's only that on my way here I overheard a gentleman saying he had been down to the mail room and apparently it is pouring in there. The workers have started hauling sacks of letters up to a higher deck to save them.'

A look of concern flickered briefly across McElroy's face. 'I don't know anything about that, Miss Heaton. All I know is that we struck a light blow with an iceberg. The damage is not thought to be too serious. The engines, as you can feel, have started once more, and whatever repairs can be done are being done. I'm sure the captain wouldn't start the ship unless he was sure she was in a good condition.'

Martha wasn't convinced. 'Have you spoken to the captain?'

'Not yet. As you can imagine, he is rather busy.' The purser's patience was wearing thin. 'You obviously have many questions. As do all of you.' Martha looked around. A few more passengers had encircled her, hungry for information too. 'All I can do, tedious as it may sound, is to repeat that at the moment there is no reason to worry and that you should all return to your rooms. If you don't wish to, I have asked if they can reopen some of the public rooms. I realise some of you might not be quite ready to go back to sleep.'

Martha was about to ask one more question when McElroy announced that he had to take care of urgent ship business. He slid behind the door of his office, where he probably lit a cigarette and wiped his brow.

By now the corridors, vestibules and landings were beginning to fill with the curious and the concerned. Most people seemed satisfied that restarting the engines meant there was nothing much to worry about, reassured by the throbbing, even if it was only half as perceptible as it had been before the collision.

Martha decided to head back to the deck to see what was happening.

Ismay and Beck were sitting in the captain's quarters when the door opened and the captain himself bustled in. If his expression had been grave before, now it was positively lugubrious. Beck glanced at the clock. It was a couple of minutes before midnight.

Ismay spoke first. 'What is wrong, Captain?'

'The flooding might be more serious than we thought at first. Mr Andrews is on his way. We are going to tour the site of the damage. He should be here presently. We are venting off steam pressure to avoid an explosion in the boilers.'

'Let me go and get changed,' Ismay said. 'I will return.' Some of his ebullience appeared to have gone. He left, head bowed in thought.

Beck wondered what he should do. He was of no use here, but until he learned what was happening to the ship there was little else he could do. If they were unable to reach land and had to wait for help, he would need to know the condition of the ship and their destination before he wired any news to London, or planned how to restart his pursuit of Piatkow.

There was a knock at the door. 'That will be Andrews,' the captain said.

'Do you want me to leave?' Beck asked.

Smith shook his head. 'I fear we may need your advice shortly.'

Beck wondered what he might mean.

The man at the door wasn't Andrews. It was an officer named Boxhall. He was gasping for breath. 'The mail room is filling fast with water, sir.'

'The mail room?' the captain said incredulously.

Boxhall continued, his agitation clear. 'I was on G deck, at the top of a staircase which allowed me to look down to the mail room. The water was up to within two feet of the deck I was standing on. Bags of mail are floating everywhere. I thought it best that I report it, sir.'

The captain nodded slowly. 'Thank you, Mr Boxhall. Your watch is almost done.'

Boxhall left. At that point, another man appeared. Smartly dressed, cropped hair, a brisk and efficient manner, but the same worried look that Beck was getting used to seeing. The first prickle of fear crept up the back of his neck.

'I'm just off to tour with Mr Andrews,' Smith said. 'We will return.'

Beck watched them go. As they did a huge hissing sound broke out on deck. He went to the door. It was deafening: the high-pitched scream of gushing steam. He looked back and could see the blasts billowing from the funnels.

He went back into the captain's room. It was a minute or so past midnight. He stood staring at the clock, wondering what might happen next, when Ismay burst in, this time wearing a suit under his coat.

'Any news?'

Beck explained that the captain had left on a tour of the ship with Andrews and told Ismay what Boxhall had reported about the mail room. Ismay, eyes ablaze, stroked his moustache. 'Is it serious?' Beck asked.

'I fear we may not be able to reach land. I saw Chief Engineer Bell on the way to my room. I asked him if *Titanic* was seriously damaged. He said that she was. But he also said the pumps should be able to keep her afloat.'

'I offered to leave – after all, it's not really my place to be here – but the captain said I might be needed. I wasn't sure what he meant.'

Ismay said nothing, lost in thought. The seconds trudged by, Ismay brooding on events, Beck wondering how they would try to catch Piatkow if they were forced to abandon this ship and be taken the rest of the way in another. Might there be two ships? In which case, how would he guess if the one he chose was the right one? Would the rescue ships have wireless? But he decided to save these questions until the situation was clearer.

Ismay broke his silence. 'The ship is stopping,' he said.

He was right. The movement of the ship was slowing. Beck went to the window and looked out. It was too dark to tell. Though he could see that the ship was beginning to tilt forward.

The door opened to let in a blast of cold air. The screaming sibilance of the escaping steam grew louder. The captain and Andrews walked in, even more sombre than before.

'Why have we stopped?' Ismay asked.

Andrews spoke, in a clipped voice that betrayed a hint of Ireland. 'The forward motion of the ship has pushed water into the bows. There was a danger that the fire-damaged bulkhead might burst. As it is, *Titanic* is making water in six of her compartments, far more than the pumps can handle.'

Beck could not take his gaze from the captain. Smith's face was sapped of any colour. His rheumy eyes were sad and downcast. Beck knew then it was trouble.

'What are the implications of that, Mr Andrews?' Ismay asked, drawing himself tall, pushing back his shoulders as if bracing for an impact.

'The implication is that she will sink, Mr Ismay.'

The words, spoken almost casually but with utmost seriousness, seemed to hang in the air for several seconds.

Ismay cast around for a reply, but it was as if his capacity for speech had gone. His mouth flapped open but no sound came. It was the captain who spoke.

'I am going to go to the Marconi Room and ask them to send a call for assistance. I have asked Boxhall to calculate our position.' He left.

'How long has she got?' Ismay's voice was a hoarse whisper.

Andrews tilted his head each way to indicate that he wasn't sure. 'If the bulkhead holds, she may last until morning. If it doesn't, a few hours. At best.'

Ismay sat back on a sofa, his head in his hands. Beck felt numb. The ship was going to sink. What had he done?

There was more agonised silence until the captain returned. Ismay didn't even look up. 'We must start to get the passengers away in the lifeboats,' Smith said. 'With luck we will find out there's a ship nearby. There are reports of lights in the near distance. The wireless lads are trying to make contact.'

Andrews nodded his agreement. 'But we have a problem,' he said.

'I know,' replied the captain. 'Mr Beck, has your police work brought you into contact with crowds?'

Beck's earlier sense shock had gone. Now he was calm, searching for a way to salvage something from this sorry mess. He would need to watch as many passengers as possible get off the liner, study the faces in each lifeboat, and see if Piatkow was among them. The question caught him by surprise.

'Not for some time. Why?' There had been a crowd at Sidney Street, though not one he had controlled.

The captain looked at Ismay, who was still holding his head in his hands. 'We have lifeboat capacity for less than half the people on board.'

Beck remembered his many walks on deck, and seeing how few lifeboats there were. 'Why?' he asked, almost involuntarily.

'We have the minimum we are required to by law. A ship like this is designed to be its own lifeboat. Alas, that has not proved to be the case. So we have a problem. If we allow everyone up to the boat deck believing there is enough space for them, we might have a panic on our hands when they realise there is room for only half of them. We can't allow that to happen.'

The seriousness of the situation hit Beck like a hammer. If no ship had arrived before *Titanic* sank then half their passengers would go down with her.

'You will need to find a way to filter people onto deck.' An idea came to him. 'I suggest you evacuate women and children first. Few decent men would argue with a proposal to save the weakest and most vulnerable. We would need to control it carefully.'

Ismay had taken his hands from his face. His eyes were moist and red-ringed. Yet it was the captain who spoke. 'That's the best idea,' Smith said.

Andrews beside him was nodding vigorously. 'I agree. We must encourage as many passengers as possible to put on their lifebelts, without panicking them.'

'I will go and instruct two of my senior officers to swing out the lifeboats. Mr Beck, would you be so kind as to help patrol the deck and maintain discipline.'

'I will.' In his mind Beck cast around the deck. The boats were spread far and wide. Keeping an eye on each side of the liner would not be easy. 'Can I just add one thing?'

'Yes,' the captain said.

'If there aren't enough lifeboats for all on board, and people do get on deck despite our efforts, the chances of a panic and some kind of disorder are likely. There's a good chance they could overpower your officers and force themselves onto the boats. That raises the spectre of the boats becoming overcrowded and sinking themselves, with inevitable consequences.'

'What do you suggest?' the captain asked.

'I suggest you ask your senior officers to equip themselves with firearms. With any luck they won't need to use them, but they may help restore order if discipline is lost.'

As Beck finished speaking, a doleful silence spread through the room. He could sense the disbelief among the other men that their prized ship, this majestic voyage, had reached the point where they were openly discussing arming the crew, with the dire prospect of having to open fire on its passengers.

'Of course, let's hope it doesn't reach that stage.'

'I will help, too,' Ismay said, standing up suddenly. He appeared dazed, the irascibility, anxiety and nervous energy that defined him had evaporated quickly.

'Just one more thing,' Ismay said, as they were about to leave. 'Can I reiterate that after this night the events which have taken place, as we know them, must go no further than this room? Captain, you will need to find time to talk to members of your crew about this.'

Smith nodded. As did the others, including Beck. He was interested in two things only. Saving as many people as possible – and making sure Piatkow didn't make it off the liner. Having women and children in the lifeboats would mean that he shouldn't be able to sneak onto one, though Beck would need to watch the situation vigilantly.

Whether Beck himself made it off alive was irrelevant.

15 April 1912

On deck the sound of escaping steam was overwhelming. Conversation was impossible. Martha didn't know which was more alarming: the din or the angle of the ship. Only on deck, able to use the sky as a guide, was the tilt visible. It didn't look good even to her landlubber eyes.

It seemed that more of her fellow passengers had not been soothed by what little information they had been given. More and more were appearing on deck, braving the cold, wincing at the blasts of steam gushing into the frozen night.

Then Martha saw that the ship had stopped once more. This can't be good news, she thought. All these people, and so few answers. She believed that one of the duties of the press was to make sure the little guy stayed informed. While a bunch of pampered millionaires – one woman she could see was clutching her lapdog – hardly constituted the little guy, they and the rest of the suckers on board still needed to know what was going on.

Martha walked forwards along the port side towards the barrier on A deck dividing the officer promenade from the first-class one. As she reached the gate she could see an officer, thickset, square-jawed, with a white cable-knit sweater under his jacket, pulling the canvas from one of the lifeboats. You'll do, she thought.

'Do you know what's happening?' She had to shout to make herself heard over the racket.

The officer turned, appraising her coolly. 'The captain has asked that I swing out the lifeboats and prepare them for launching.'

'Is that because we're sinking?'

'Now, madam – don't get ahead of yourself, please.'

Martha winced inwardly. Please don't patronise me, she thought.

'Sorry, I didn't realise I was. I just saw that you were preparing the lifeboats and blithely assumed you would be asking people to get into them.'

The officer continued with what he was doing. 'We will be asking people to get into them – the women and children, that is. It is merely a precaution. There is nothing to be concerned about.'

Some precaution, she thought. 'Why only women and children?'

'It is the natural order of things,' he replied crossly.

'But what of their husbands and fathers? What if the women and children don't wish to leave them?'

'Look, the captain has ordered us to fill the lifeboats with women and children first. It would be a good idea if you returned to your cabin, put on your lifebelt and came back to the deck. Now, if you would kindly let me continue about my duty.' The officer turned away from her ostentatiously.

Martha decided to leave him alone. She had turned to head towards the bridge when she saw Beck making his way hurriedly along the deck on the other side of the officers' promenade. He seemed preoccupied and only recognised her when he got to the barrier. He stepped over and grabbed her arm tightly before she could speak.

'Martha, go down below and get your lifebelt. Then come back up here and get on the first lifeboat you can.'

She freed her arm from his grip. It wasn't quite the physical contact from him that she'd had in mind. 'You're the second person to tell me that in the last few minutes. Except the first one didn't sound as urgent as you.'

'Who?'

'Him,' Martha said, gesturing at the officer, who had now removed his jacket.

'Well, it *is* urgent.'

'Really? Care to explain?'

'The ship is going to sink, Martha. The only question is how long it takes.'

'Oh, Jesus,' she said.

'They tried to steam on to land, but all that did was let in more water. Had she stayed still . . . who knows? She may well have been holed badly enough anyway.'

'I thought she was meant to be unsinkable.'

'Obviously not. Apparently she can cope with anything up to four of her watertight compartments being flooded. But now six of them are. She's doomed.' Beck paused. 'Please go and put your lifebelt on and then get off the ship. They are letting women and children off first.'

'So I heard. Seems crazy to me, splitting families up like that.'

Beck looked around nervously. 'They have to have some kind of system.' His voice fell to a whisper, or as low as it could go yet still be heard over the venting steam as he leaned in towards her. 'There aren't enough lifeboats to hold everyone on board.'

Martha couldn't believe what she'd just been told. 'You *are* kidding me?'

He shook his head gravely. 'I wish I was. Therefore it's only right that women and children go first because they would be the least able to fend for themselves if *Titanic* does go down. They have radioed for assistance. I don't know if anyone has answered that call.'

'What will *you* do?'

'I'll be here until the bitter end.' Beck went quiet. She could see that he was wrestling with some problem. Eventually he carried on talking. 'Look, this is off the record, but the public should know. We found Piatkow. He was hiding in one of the lifeboats on the starboard side. We were searching the deck and we obviously spooked him. He jumped out at us and ran to the bridge. I followed him. I managed to catch him with some help from the crew up there. As that was happening, the lookout was trying to warn them of an iceberg ahead. They received the warning but in the confusion the man at the wheel turned the wrong way.'

'The wrong way?'

Beck nodded. 'Under tiller orders, which they still use, turning the wheel to starboard turned the tiller right but the ship left. An order to turn one way steered you another. But with these new ships now if you turn the wheel left, then the rudder goes left too and so does the ship. However, they still use the old tiller orders even when some sailors are trained under the new commands.'

'I don't follow.'

'The hard-a-starboard emergency order actually meant turn the wheel to port. But in the panic, or because he was used to new orders, the man at the helm took it literally and turned the wheel to starboard. By the time he corrected his mistake and went to port it was too late.'

'They could have avoided the iceberg?'

'It seems that way. What a mess.'

Martha couldn't believe what she was hearing. 'What about Piatkow? Did you get him?'

'No. Once the cry went up about the iceberg he got away. I chased him but I fell down when we hit the ice.'

It was almost too much for her to take in at one go. The unsinkable ship was sinking. There were not enough lifeboats for the passengers on board, who were blithely unaware of that desperate fact. And the reason the *Titanic* had collided with an iceberg was because key crewmen had been trying to capture the most wanted criminal in Britain. It all threw up more questions than it answered.

'But why – if there were icebergs around – were they going so fast? Why not stop?'

'That's one question I can't answer. Look, I've said too much already, Martha. Please go and get your lifebelt. You need to get off this ship.'

Martha looked back down the deck, which was beginning to slope upwards even more. People were spilling out of the first-class entrance. Many of them were wearing lifebelts, or holding them. Beck followed her gaze.

He looked back at her imploringly. 'They are telling people to get their lifebelts and get on deck. Soon they will swing out the lifeboats. Try to get on an early one, Martha. Once people realise there isn't enough room for them, then who knows what might happen.'

'I'm a reporter, Arthur. This could be the biggest story of my life. I ain't running away from it. It's that simple.'

'If you don't get off the ship then there will be no story.'

'You said yourself that they had asked for assistance. Surely a ship can make it here and pick us up.'

'Maybe. But I heard the chief designer tell the captain it may only be a matter of a few hours, even less, before *Titanic* goes down. The Atlantic is a big place, Martha. Who knows how far away help is?'

'I'll take my chances.'

Beck looked sombre. 'I can't even begin to tell you what a mistake that may be.'

'Well, don't, then. I'm rough enough and tough enough to look after myself. Please, spare me your outdated notions of chivalry and concern.'

'I *am* concerned, Martha. I like you.'

'I like you, too. But we can pick up on the mutual admiration another time. What are you going to do now?'

'I'm going to try to monitor each lifeboat that gets away, and see if Piatkow tries to sneak onto one.'

'That's a big undertaking.'

'Not as big as it would be if they had a full and proper complement of lifeboats.' He smiled grimly.

'What's with the steam?' Martha asked.

'They have to vent it to prevent it building up in the engines and causing an explosion,' Beck explained.

'But really, how are you going to be able to keep tabs on the lifeboats on both sides of the ship? Do you have some help?' Martha asked.

'I have King, the master-at-arms. He's hurt but I'm hoping he can help me pick up the slack.'

'How about if *I* help?'

Beck hesitated. 'I'm really not sure . . .'

'You can give me a roving brief. I'll move around and, if I see anything suspicious I'll let you know. Deal?'

'I'd much prefer it if you got away in a lifeboat.'

'That isn't going to happen. Not yet, at least.'

Beck looked back down along the deck. It was beginning to look crowded. 'All right,' he said. 'I'll be near the boats. Come and find me if you see anything. But promise me that when the last boat is ready to leave, you'll be on it.'

That sounded fair enough. 'You have my word,' Martha said.

The ship was dead in the water. Apart from drifting on the current, the only direction the *Titanic* was going was down. Beck could see water creeping up the bow. He was no seaman, but he sensed the end would come sooner rather than later.

As he stood beside the crew members who were swinging out a lifeboat on the port side, just by the first-class entrance, he saw the captain in animated conversation with one of his senior officers. Beck hurried across, stepping over the barrier. Those demarcations seemed pointless now. The captain gave a small nod of greeting as he approached.

'Has there been any response to your calls for assistance?'

'Yes. The *Carpathia* is fifty-eight miles away.'

'How long will it take for her to reach us?'

'Four hours.'

'Is that soon enough?'

'I fear not. A bulkhead has just given way. Mr Andrews thinks we may only have an hour and a half. However, there are reports of two masthead lights on our port side, which could be those of another ship. We are trying to contact her, both by wireless and by other means.'

Beck thanked the captain and returned to the deck. The orchestra was setting up by the first-class entrance. It might even be possible to hear them. Beck wasn't sure if his ears had simply grown accustomed to the cacophony, but the noise from the venting steam seemed to be subsiding. Though, as he reached the lifeboat, he could see the crew still communicating with hand gestures to avoid being misunderstood.

The deck was still much emptier than he had anticipated. A few men stood smoking. Not many of them were wearing lifebelts. Beside them their women glanced around anxiously, watching the crewmen prepare the lifeboats. Beck walked through the entrance hall at the top of the Grand Staircase and out onto the starboard side to be met with a similar scene. If anything, there were even less people here. Again there was little sign of panic. If passengers had had the information to which he was privy he knew that the atmosphere might be different.

He watched as Murdoch, the officer who had been on the bridge at the time of the collision, supervised the preparation of the lifeboats. The covers had been removed, the masts cleared, while other crew members brought forward tins of food and lanterns. Once they were loaded in, and the cranks fitted into the davits that held the lifeboats in position, the boats were ready. Slowly the cranks were turned and the rescue vessels swung in stiff, jerking motions out from the deck and were suspended above the calm, black waters of the Atlantic.

Beck walked along the entire length of the starboard side, checking as many faces as he could. Then he crossed to port, retracing in reverse his earlier route when he and King had found Piatkow. He passed through the second-class area and noticed the same outward calm among the passengers. By the time he reached first class he could see Lightoller, the senior officer charged with launching the lifeboats on the port side, with one foot in a boat that was swinging precariously off the side of the hull.

They hadn't started to fill the boats. What was the delay? Beck crossed once again to the starboard side and saw more action. Most of it provided by the agitated figure of Ismay. Beck walked towards the White Star president as he chivvied the men preparing the lifeboats. 'Come on!' he was urging them. 'There is no time to lose!' He saw Beck and strode up to him.

'There is no time to lose!' he repeated. 'We must start getting them away!'

'And you must remain calm,' Beck replied.

'Yes. Yes. At last!' Ismay pointed to Murdoch, standing near a lifeboat dangling over the side. He was summoning people to come forward. Ismay set off and Beck followed him. As they approached, another officer was calling for a group of women to get in a different boat. He had jumped in, as if to show how safe it was. The women edged forward uncertainly, followed by their men. None of them showed any obvious desire to escape.

'We'd really rather stay on the ship,' one woman said. 'It seems safer here than down there on the sea in that little thing.'

'She's as sturdy as they come, madam,' the officer said cheerfully. 'It is just a precaution, believe me. You'll be able to come back on board when all is well.'

'Are you going to give them a pass for that?' one of the men joked.

It was all Beck could do not to let his impatience show in the same way as Ismay's. He wanted to scream, 'Get on the bloody boat! The ship's going down!' He wondered if the officer knew the full truth. Probably not. The women still dithered.

'I'd rather stay here,' one of them said defiantly.

'Me too,' added another.

Further aft, Beck could see more women getting on the lifeboat that Ismay was flustering around. The officer near him had noticed, too. 'See, they are boarding down there,' he said.

Now that someone else had been brave enough to step into a lifeboat, it seemed to overcome their resistance.

'Please get on dear,' one man urged his wife. 'It's only a precaution. You'll be back on board for breakfast.'

'If you say so, Henry,' she replied.

'I do.'

Henry's wife stepped into the lifeboat, waving goodbye, blowing kisses. Her husband waved his hand in embarrassment at this display of affection. Some more women climbed aboard gingerly, glancing down nervously at the murky sea that was a skyscraper's height below. A child was passed in, and more women came forward, though many more still hung back against the sides, some shaking their heads, the light and warmth of the huge vessel giving them more reassurance than a wooden lifeboat and the pitch-dark night.

The lifeboat that Ismay was fussing around was now being lowered. It was only then that Beck noticed there were men in it. He hustled over and found Murdoch, who was ordering the men to turn the crank and lower the boat steadily.

'There are men in that boat,' he said indignantly.

Murdoch sneered. 'What if there are? What is it to you?'

Obviously he had not forgiven Beck for what had happened on the bridge earlier. Beck did not blame him. But that was no reason not to carry out orders.

'The orders are for women and children first.'

'Don't tell me what the orders are. I know more about them than you do. Now, if you would kindly let me do my duty?'

'Why are there men in there?'

'Because there were not enough women to fill her up by themselves, so I told the men they could accompany their women. What do you want me to do? Send a half-empty boat off? I will put those who come forward on a boat. I can't coerce anyone.'

Murdoch turned away and watched as the boat slipped from view. Beck turned away in disgust. It was only the first lifeboat to be launched and already the system was falling apart. He saw Ismay watching anxiously, biting his nails to the quick.

Beck went over. 'Murdoch is letting men on. The orders were for women and children first. That lifeboat wasn't even full. He could have waited and filled it with more women. We need to get the message across that people must get off the ship.'

He switched his attention to the other lifeboat, by now almost loaded, the faces of those on board cold and showing fear. A small boy, no more than five, wept softly, buried in the crook of his mother's shoulder. On the liner's deck, the men stood, some waving, others smoking. Why weren't they getting aboard the lifeboats if that was now the rule? There was no method to it.

As the boat swung from its davit, causing the child to wail loudly, Murdoch urged the other officer to get in and take charge.

The officer, Lowe by name, started to turn the crank, lowering the boat slowly.

Ismay lost his patience. 'Lower away! Lower away!' he shouted.

Lowe stood up, pushing back his shoulders. 'I will do if you'll get the fucking hell out of my way,' he spat.

Ismay's face froze in shock. For the first time in what seemed an age, Beck wanted to laugh. Did Lowe know whom he was swearing at? Ismay got the message, though, and backed away. Then he turned and walked off, head bowed, towards another lifeboat.

Beck scoured every face in the boat. Piatkow was not there. Beck left the starboard side and went back to port. The first lifeboat on that side was about to be lowered. In stark contrast to Murdoch, the ship's second officer, Lightoller, was turning every man away, insisting that it was for women and children only. Which might have explained why there were only a couple of handfuls of people in the boat. Beck had been told that they could hold more than sixty. There couldn't have been more than sixteen in it. A few more women came forward, pushed by their men. Even then one woman wouldn't have it.

'I simply refuse to leave. I shan't. I have made up my mind,' she said firmly.

'Then lower this lifeboat,' an officer standing by it said. And so it swung out, no more than a quarter full, Beck guessed. What a waste. Perhaps they would stand by and take on more survivors as the night wore on – or what little of the night might remain before the icy waters sucked the *Titanic* down? Who knew? All he knew was that no one seemed to have a clear idea about how to fill the lifeboats and in what order. It was as if everyone – crew and passengers alike – was in denial, and evacuating the ship was just a minor inconvenience.

He looked around the deck. The number of people was swelling. The majority of them were from first class. Where were the others? The masses down in steerage – had they even been told? Beck guessed not, otherwise the decks would by now have been swamped. Their absence made Beck's job easier, but he couldn't help wondering what was happening to those poor souls below, the crew and passengers on the lower decks with the water pouring in. Although the ship's engines had stopped, the lights from all the windows still blazed brightly. That meant there were still those down below who were feeding the fires to keep the generators going and the lights burning. When would they be told?

Beck's anger grew. Not with himself, but at the damned idiots who would send a ship out to sea without enough lifeboats to save everyone aboard in an emergency. It was immoral. He had seen Martha's horrified expression when he'd told her. At least if she got off and wrote her story the world would know that the planet's finest ship had provided barely enough resources to save half her passengers. Maybe then something would be done.

Behind him, a blaze of light soared into the night. Beck turned to see a glistening tadpole shape shoot ever higher until it exploded in a cascade of sparks, causing a chorus of 'oohs' and 'aah' as though it was Bonfire Night. Almost all those around him stared as the rocket's embers fell slowly towards the sea. Some gazed in delight, but others watched with looks of growing horror on their faces.

Now Beck could see the truth sinking in with them. The ship

was not simply wounded. The damage it had suffered was so grievous that they needed help. And they needed it so urgently that they were signalling out across the ocean for any passing ship to see.

Martha paced the deck, as Beck's words replayed in her mind, trying to reconcile the awful truth with the phlegmatic, unruffled appearance of those on deck. It was the same story where the second-class passengers were gathering. She wondered about those in third class. Only a few were on the poop deck, milling around, some with bags and belongings presumably salvaged from the flooding decks below. Yet there were no lifeboats back there. When would they be allowed up to where there was some small hope of rescue?

Then there came the explosive noise that grabbed everyone's attention. The rocket flaring in the sky. People's expressions changed. Some began to weep and even those who didn't started to show real fear. Awareness of the grim reality spread: loading the lifeboats wasn't a token gesture but a vital necessity.

Martha went to her room, walking forward as if down a gentle slope. There she got her lifebelt and the few things she valued and would need: some money, a notebook, some pencils, a necklace that had been given to her by her grandmother. She put on as many extra layers of clothes as she could, without hampering her movement. She wished she had a quart of whisky to sip for internal warmth. That could wait.

There were still many people who preferred the warmth of the ship to the cold of the lifeboats. She followed a group to the dining saloon to find it half full of passengers. They could not have seen the flare of the rockets but word of the dire situation must have spread, as must the news that the women were to be let off *Titanic* first. All around Martha some of the richest and most powerful men and women in the world were reduced to emotional wrecks, all equal in the face of death. If anything, it was the men who were the most febrile. The women seemed to be in shock, pale and cowed, while the men moaned and blubbed. She saw one man pounding the walls with his fist in agitation.

Not all of them had lost their heads. One shouted out, 'You must go out on deck. The women must be loaded onto the lifeboats before they go.'

Yet his words were drowned in other cries of anguish.

Just then a group of men burst in, their grimy faces looking wild and incongruous under the brilliant lights in the gilded room. A bunch of stokers. If they were fleeing to the upper decks the water must have reached the ship's heart. Some of the women screamed in shock at the sight of them. The two groups stood looking at each other across the thick carpet. The refined and the rough.

One man, his face and clothes coated in grunge and soot, looked around the trembling men and women, his face betraying no emotion whatsoever.

'I think a few of you need to get yourselves together,' he said slowly, but reasonably. 'You need to make sure your ladies get off this ship safely, rather than cowerin' in here feelin' sorry for yourselves.'

His plain words had an immediate galvanising effect. Men who had previously been in a funk started to talk, turning to their wives, asking them to accompany them to the decks.

'You must go, darling,' Martha heard one man saying. 'I will be all right. If you stay with me, you will only endanger my chances further. I have my lifebelt and if I have to keep you afloat then saving myself will be all the harder.'

Feeling that she was intruding on private grief, Martha decided to leave. It was heartbreaking to see and hear those husbands and wives parting, knowing that they might never see each other again. Martha could not help but be distressed by the very idea of men agreeing to let their wives and children be separated from them. She would have been more impressed had they marched out on deck and demanded to get into the lifeboats with them. There was something about their resigned acceptance that chilled her. The bovine deference to a misplaced notion of duty and doing the right thing. It would make more sense to rage against fate than stand by numbly while your life was extinguished.

When the end came, she would find the stokers and their counterparts. She guessed their will to survive would be greater than the passive majority in first class. But she was unable to think of her death yet. She would find a way off this damned, cursed ship even if it killed her. She smiled inwardly at the irony.

Martha went back to the port side of the boat deck, where the crowd was growing. The air seemed even colder, if that was possible, the ship's list more pronounced, while stars in the brilliant sky seemed to gleam brighter. Distress rockets were still being fired, but the mood seemed to have lifted among some of the passengers. There was talk of a boat nearby, its lights visible in the distance, that the captain had instructed the officers loading the lifeboats to tell those rowing to head for. Martha wondered how, if a boat came, people would be transferred to it. At least it would give them something to swim for if the ship did go down. The only problem for her was that she couldn't swim.

She put her lifebelt on. It was heavy and uncomfortable. I'll take that if it means the difference between life and death, she thought.

A hand tapped her on the shoulder. Lester Darton. He looked smaller, less full of himself than she had seen him. But who wouldn't be diminished by the night's events?

'Miss Heaton, you should get in a lifeboat. They are calling for ladies.'

'Rules me out, then.'

He didn't smile. 'This is no time for levity. The ship is foundering. I don't know how long she will stay afloat, but the fact is that if she does go down then the vortex she creates will suck everything nearby down with her. It would be best to board a lifeboat now and have a chance to get as clear as possible when she does slip beneath the surface.'

Martha glanced around. The steam had now stopped. All she could hear above the hubbub of voices was the sound of rockets being fired, and the band playing some ragtime. Great, she thought. Music to drown by.

But where were the steerage passengers? She paced up and down; the majority of those on deck, she guessed, were from first class, with some women from second class thrown in. Were the steerage people still below?

There was one way she could find out, though it meant going down onto the lower decks.

*

If it was to end, Sten-Ake could take comfort that it would take place under the type of glorious night sky that you can only witness at sea. It was almost breathtaking enough for him to believe in some kind of God. The same God to whom many of his companions in third class were now praying. Everywhere he had hobbled, he had seen groups bent in prayer: in their berths, in the saloon and now here on deck.

Their very predicament could be taken as proof of a vengeful God, he thought, sitting wrapped in his layers of clothes on a bench on the poop deck. Smite the ship to punish mankind for daring to believe they could master nature and for claiming that a vessel was unsinkable. Though, of course, that was nonsense. The *Titanic* had been stricken because those in charge of the ship had chosen not to slow down when surrounded by ice. He had seen the bergs, many of them. It was arrogant to think you could just weave past them at high speed, believing that the ship you had constructed was invincible. That was just stupid.

Sten-Ake had been taken along Scotland Road into the main section of third class. The atmosphere was charged. There were those praying for their souls mingling with those who were seeking to raise hell before they went there. Stewards came through, handing out lifebelts, though there were still many who were left without one. Sten-Ake had handed his to a terrified-looking young man who had babbled incomprehensibly. But he'd had a child with him. Sten-Ake had no use for it, anyway.

Wanting to get away from the others, he'd ventured out onto the deck and braved the cold. The ship, he could see, was more clearly doomed than he'd thought; it was listing to starboard and was well down by the bow. Here on the poop deck, he guessed, would be the last part of the vessel to slip under. Which meant that on this bench he had the best seat in the house. All around him people were fussing and panicking. From his elevated position he could see more of the boat deck than before. The lifeboats were being launched from there. Why these people weren't forcing their way kicking and screaming to those decks baffled him.

'How are you doing, old man?'

Sten-Ake knew the voice instantly. The accent. He turned. Yes, it was him.

'You!'

The man held up a quieting hand. The peak of his cap cast a shadow across his face, but Sten-Ake thought he could see a bruise or welt under his left eye. 'There is no need to become agitated.'

'You robbed me,' the old Swede hissed.

'I did. I apologise.' The Latvian reached inside his coat pocket. 'Here you go.' He handed him the bankroll.'

Sten-Ake took it and stared at it.

'Put it away, old man. There are others round here who would want that and they wouldn't return it.'

'Why have *you* returned it?'

'I am not without a conscience. Anyway, where we are going I'm not sure there will be much use for it.'

Sten-Ake continued to look at the money.

'It is all there. Count it if you don't believe me.'

The old man shook his head. 'Keep it.' He gave it back.

'What do you mean?'

'You can atone for what you did and the misery you caused me when I thought my money had gone. Now it doesn't matter. I will not survive. You are younger, stronger – there is a good chance you will make it.'

'How?'

'How can you atone or how can you make it? If it's the latter, I suggest you try to get into one of those lifeboats up there. That may prove tricky. In which case, grab hold of a deckchair or some other item and throw—'

'No,' the Latvian interrupted. 'How do you want me to atone?'

'If you make it, I want you to make sure that you give it to my daughter. She lives in Harrisburg, Pennsylvania.' He reached into his inside jacket pocket. On a piece of paper he had written her address. 'This is where you can send or take it. I don't care how. Just make sure it gets there.'

The Latvian appeared too stunned to speak. He said nothing, but put the bankroll back in his pocket. 'I will do that,' he said.

'Thank you.'

There was silence. They watched the rockets explode in the night sky.

'I told you this ship wouldn't see New York,' the Latvian said.

'You were right. She is going down. There are men pursuing you, you know?'

The young man nodded. 'I am aware of that.'

'You stole from a dying old man.'

'I know. I am sorry. When you said you were moving to America I assumed you had brought your savings with you. I checked the lining of your jacket. What can I say? It is what I do.

I raise money for the cause. I usually pick bigger targets. That's why I have returned it.'

'And if we weren't sinking?'

The Latvian shrugged. 'Does that matter? All that matters is that we are heading for the bottom of the ocean.' He placed his hand on Sten-Ake's shoulder. 'Well, good luck, old man.'

Sten-Ake wanted nothing to do with farewells. He reached into his jacket once more and handed a small package to the other man. 'Just make sure you get the money to my daughter if you survive. You can show her these if she doesn't believe your story. They are my identification papers.'

Beck stood at the end of the second-class promenade. The lifeboats were taking an age to load and many were leaving barely half full. The whole thing was a farce. He put a cigarette in his mouth, struck a match and cupped his hands around the flame even though there was not a cough of wind. Down to his right he could see a lifeboat pulling away nervously and slowly on the glassy sea – away from the boat, away from the light blazing from her deck and portholes, into the inky darkness. He scanned the dark horizon. The only lights he could see were from the stars, not from any boats steaming to their rescue. The game was surely up.

Still no sign of his nemesis, though. He smiled. No nemesis, though there had been plenty of hubris.

Beck exhaled strongly, smoke and steaming breath billowing from his nostrils. Then he saw him. Saw *them*. Talking.

The old man and Piatkow.

This time Beck knew the way. He went into second class and down the stairs, bounding down them two at time, fighting his way past the crowds coming up to the deck. He raced down to C deck on the starboard side, turning left onto the second-class promenade just as a lifeboat descended haltingly past him, the worried look of those on board, huddled together for warmth, level with his gaze.

He ran forward, down the stairs that led to the aft well deck. It was swarming with steerage passengers, as if they had filtered out here, unaware where they had to go. He fought his way through them, his route made more difficult by the ship's listing angle which made it an uphill climb. Finally he reached the stairs that led up to the poop deck.

Once there he found that it was equally crowded. People had been attracted by the illusion of safety, the point furthest from the water, heedless that when the boat started its final plunge the deck would become a cliff face.

Beck found the old man. But Piatkow was gone.

'Where is he?' Beck shouted.

The old man looked alarmed. 'He gave me back the money.'

'I don't care. Where is he?'

'He just left. He went forward.'

As the Swede lifted a finger to point, Beck saw Piatkow, down on the well deck, looking over his shoulder anxiously. He was almost at the entrance to second class. Beck started running, trying to stay low so that Piatkow wouldn't see him in the crowd, hoping to steal up on him. As he went down the stairs he saw his quarry go through the door, allowing him to race across the small deck. An arm went across Beck's path as he reached the door.

'Sorry, sir, that's second class.' The speaker was a tall, well-built steward.

'Get out of my way!'

'Only women allowed past, sir.'

'I just saw a man pass through.'

'I must have missed that. Only women and children now though, sir.'

Beck couldn't mess around. He pushed the steward out of his path and grabbed the door. The steward took a tight grip of his forearm.

'Now, sir—'

Without thinking, Beck turned and punched the man in the face, sending him staggering backwards. Then he opened the door and hurried towards the second-class foyer outside the library. The door was open and he could see Piatkow weaving his way past the columns, quickening his stride. Beck followed. The room was empty save for one man in a corner sitting reading a book and calmly smoking a pipe, his lifebelt tossed casually onto a chair opposite.

Piatkow went through another door, forcing Beck to run; there was a staircase beyond and he wanted to see if the terrorist took it. As he reached the door he checked his pocket, feeling the cold steel of the gun in his hand. He opened the door to see

Piatkow scurrying down to D deck, going deeper into the stricken ship.

Beck followed. At the bottom Piatkow turned. Beck bent his head and tried to conceal his face against the wall but it was too late. Piatkow had seen him. The Latvian darted away.

'Stop!' Beck cried, pulling the gun from his pocket. He started to run. Piatkow was going forward. Beck barged through the double doors into the empty first-class dining saloon. Piatkow was ten yards ahead, weaving his way past the tables that were set for a breakfast which would never be served. Beck started to gain on him, given momentum by the forward lean of the ship. Given a clear run he felt he could catch him easily, but Piatkow was closing on the door to the reception room. He burst through, flooring a steward standing behind it. As Beck raced past the felled man he was lying on the floor, gasping for breath.

The pursuit continued across the reception room to the Grand Staircase, with Beck getting closer with each stride. Piatkow turned left on to the stairs, which led to down to the Turkish baths, the swimming pool, F deck and a dead end. Exactly what Beck wanted so that he could corner him and put a bullet in his head. Maybe three. One for each copper that the terrorist had killed.

But rather than carry on downwards to E Deck he turned left and lunged for a small door on the port side. It took him into the long staff passageway, rather less busy than when Beck had been last there. Piatkow knew his way around, he'd give him that. He must have done plenty of exploring during the past few days.

Rather than running back towards the stern, Piatkow continued towards the sinking bow, his feet slapping against the wet floor. The water was rising higher. Beck sprinted along the corridor, his lungs bursting. Piatkow was fit. Perhaps fitter than Beck, who had spent most of the past six months lying in a bed or sitting on his backside.

As they reached the forward end of the corridor, Beck felt the water reaching his knees, slowing their progress, soaking his trousers. Piatkow continued to fight his way onwards, the water getting deeper, until it rose to their waists.

Beck turned right. A wave of water hit him immediately, forcing him back, the cold stinging like pins stuck in his skin. He got up. The whole area was flooded, up beyond his waist. He began to feel his feet grow numb.

Beck looked around. There was no sign of Piatkow anywhere. The water swirled past. This was dangerous. A wall could break, or a window, or, worse, another bulkhead and he would be sucked down into the icy depths, trapped in the ship's bowels. He waded forward, knocking debris out of his path – bags, cups, pillows, a cigarette case, a chamber pot, a host of other items all washed away by the water. Looking left he could see from an open porthole that he was no more than a few feet above the waterline. Soon he would be below it. But he couldn't turn back. Not until he knew what had become of Piatkow. He carried on searching, holding his gun above the water. He saw nothing but debris.

At that moment, directly in front of him, Piatkow rose from the water like a creature from the deep. Before Beck could react, the terrorist had punched him in the face, sending him falling back into the water, the gun spinning from his hand so that it too was now submerged. His head went under and he struggled to find some purchase on the floor.

The water was so cold that it made him gasp. Beck felt around on the floor for the gun, hoping it was nearby. He could feel nothing. He came up for air. There was Piatkow standing in front of him. A gun pointed at his head.

He saw those same dark, dead eyes that he had seen on that cold December night in Houndsditch. The same eyes Choate had seen as he lay wounded on the ground before he was cast into the void.

There was a click and Beck braced himself. But the gun didn't fire. He opened his eyes. There was emotion in Piatkow's eyes now: dismay. The gun was too wet and its mechanism wasn't working. Click, click.

Just at that moment the front of the ship seemed to dip and a great wall of water rushed around the corner. It slammed into both of them, washing over them, knocking Beck off his feet. Instinctively he put his hands up to protect his head, fearing that he would be thrown against a wall or column. He was at the mercy of some unnatural current, unable to force himself in the direction he wanted, to reach the surface, or even to work out where the surface was. His lungs were beginning to burst. With all his strength, he pushed himself in a direction he hoped was upwards. Eventually his head broke the surface, and he sucked in great lungfuls of air.

As the wave of water had retreated it appeared to have sucked him deeper into the bows. He didn't know where he was. It was difficult to tell. There were only a few feet of space between the rising waterline and the ceiling. It looked as though he was in some kind of corridor. He needed to find a way to get back up the ship. He checked around. No sign of Piatkow. He waited, watched as the water rose. His leg was being pulled down. Still no sign.

Beck's heart was beating hard. He was very cold, his arms and legs were heavy. He took a deep breath and went under, forcing himself to swim, beating away all kinds of flotsam as he did. He fought as hard as he could against the water, which tried to suck him back and further down. He must have been under for thirty, maybe forty seconds, possibly more, when he needed to get more air. A few more strokes, then he kicked upwards, reaching with his hands, hoping to break through to the surface. Finally he did and once more emerged gasping.

He was in the long passageway again: Scotland Road. The water had risen higher but was less likely to trap him here. A few more strokes forward and his feet were able to touch the bottom. He waded towards the door through which he had followed Piatkow. Where was he? Beck turned. There was no sign of the Latvian. He cursed. He needed a body, some confirmation that Piatkow was dead. That wouldn't happen now. If the terrorist had drowned he would go to the bottom with the ship. But rather than catharsis and closure Beck now had confusion. Piatkow might, like he had, have escaped and swum to safety. It was unlikely but possible.

Beck opened the door and the sea poured through. A few seconds later he might not have been able to open it because of the weight of water. He could see another wave washing through, and in the distance there was the sound of wrenching and twisting. There was just time for one last look. Piatkow still wasn't there.

Drenched, exhausted and numb with agonising cold, Beck began to climb the stairs to the decks above.

'**M**adam, you must get in the boat!'

The voice was stern and unyielding. Martha turned and saw that its owner matched it. An officer, tall and broad, his face fixed in concern.

She gave him a smile, or the closest thing she could muster to one in the circumstances. 'Not yet,' she said.

'Miss, the lifeboats are leaving one by one. You should get in one of them. If you look around you will see that most passengers of your sex have taken the opportunity.'

Yes, but they're going unwillingly, Martha thought. The officer was right, though. She looked around. All across the boat deck all she could see were pockets of men. The only woman was dear old Mrs Strauss, shivering beside her husband having refused to leave his side. As she looked the pair of them got up and went past the orchestra, back inside the ship, presumably in search of warmth.

'I will. I will, I promise.'

The officer shook his head. 'I'm afraid I can't take a promise for an answer. Allow me to escort you to the next boat. There are only a few more left to be launched and the women from second and third class are coming up as we speak.'

Because you've held them down there, Martha thought. She had been down below. Most of the passengers had been sitting in prayer; no one was instilling any urgency in them. The ones who had tried to get up to the top decks had been stopped by a steward and threatened with a gun if they tried to break through. From there, they had drifted out onto the furthest deck astern, milling around, gazing longingly at the higher decks and the wealthy travellers who had the boat deck to themselves. Then word had come through that women and children were to be allowed up, and Martha had gone with them, or had been about to when she saw Beck rush past in pursuit of Piatkow. She watched him go through a door, and then saw him send a steward spinning across the deck with a right hook. She tried to follow the hunter and the hunted into second class, but they were too fast. When she walked through the ship there was no sign of them, and the fear of meeting the rising water forced her to turn back and head for the boat deck and wait to see if Beck would return there.

He hadn't. And now she was being browbeaten into a lifeboat. She wasn't ready to leave the ship, but she took this serious young officer's word for it when he said he wouldn't allow any refusal or evasion.

'There is one thing I need to get from my room.'

'It isn't worth it, miss.'

'It's a present left to me by my father. Before he died. It's very precious to me.'

That appeared to appeal to the officer's manly soul.

'Very well. Where is your berth?'

'Why?'

'I will go and fetch it for you. It is getting rather dangerous down there.'

'It's only on B deck. Near the stairs. I would rather get it myself. Thanks for your offer.'

'All right. I will wait here. Please be quick.'

Martha went to the first-class entrance and ran down the stairs. Only a short way down she could see and hear the water washing across the floor below and hear the sound of objects falling and breaking. Though she knew it was futile, she decided to check the public areas that were still safe to see if Beck was there.

She retraced her steps. By the time she reached the Grand Staircase the water below was already a deck higher. She looked in the public areas; the restaurant was full of cowering staff, a steward at the door standing guard. She went into the smoking room. Two card games were still going on, their participants smoking and playing as if it was the first day out at sea rather than their last few seconds on earth. No one gave her a second look.

Beck was nowhere to be seen. She went to his room, the list of the ship now so bad that she had to use her hands on the walls of the corridor to support herself and make her way there safely.

Martha didn't knock. As she had suspected, he wasn't there, either. But that wasn't the only reason she had come here. The room was neat, tidy, as if it had been empty for the past few days. All she found were his clothes hanging in a wardrobe and stowed in a few drawers. She took off her clothes and most of her underthings. Then she went to a drawer and found a pair of trousers. Thank goodness she was tall for a woman, she thought. But she still had to turn up the bottoms. Then she found a button-up shirt, a waistcoat, and a jacket. Because there was no other coat she put on another jacket and a scarf. She then piled up her hair, secured it with a clip and put on a trilby that she hadn't seens Beck wearing but believed he would have looked pretty fetching in. Then she checked the mirror. Her features were still too soft but she pulled the hat down so that most of her face was in shadow. The clothes didn't fit – at all – but that was a good thing because they still concealed most of her shape. It would have to do.

She turned. There Beck was in the doorway, drenched and exhausted, one eye blackened. Despite his condition, he was grinning. 'I always knew there was something strange about you.'

Martha realised what it must look like. Her standing there admiring herself in a mirror and wearing half his wardrobe. 'I needed a disguise. They wanted to frogmarch me into a lifeboat.'

'You should go.'

'I will. I just wanted to wait and see what had happened to you. I saw you chasing Piatkow. I didn't want to leave . . . what happened?'

'I caught him. Below decks. The water was rising. We fought.'

'Where is he?'

Beck shrugged. 'I don't know. Drowned, I hope. He'd got the gun. He tried to shoot me. The pistol didn't work and then a wave of water engulfed us. I came up eventually. He was nowhere to be seen.'

His lips were blue and he was shaking.

'Get out of those clothes. You're freezing.'

'I would but someone's wearing my spares.'

'Have them.' Martha slipped off the jackets and started to unbutton the shirt. He took off his jacket and shirt. Soon they were both dressed, Martha in her own clothes once more.

'The floor is wet,' she said. If the water was reaching this high up the ship the end must be nigh, she thought.

They stood and looked at each other for a few seconds. Martha didn't know what to say. Eventually she spoke. 'Do you have a cigarette? I'm dying for a smoke.'

Beck reached for a silver cigarette case on his bureau and handed it to her. She noticed that it was engraved with his initials. She went to take one out.

'Keep it.'

'Excuse me?'

'You'll have more need of it than me.'

'What are you saying?'

'I'm saying you'll be off on a lifeboat. I may be getting wet and I'm not sure how waterproof it is.' Martha felt the first flicker of panic at the danger they found themselves in. Beck seemed to sense her disquiet. 'You can always return it later.'

She smiled gamely, and stuffed the cigarette case down the front of her top, beneath her underclothes. 'Well, let's get on deck.'

The officer had gone, obviously fed up with waiting for her. But most of the lifeboats had gone too. The ship was even further down by the bow. The forecastle deck was awash, and the water was creeping towards the bridge and the boat deck.

'I think there may be one or two lifeboats still to go,' Beck said, looking aft along the boat deck. He held Martha's hand firmly.

'I'm only getting in a boat if you get in too.'

He turned and frowned. 'Don't be stupid. You hardly know me.'

'I'm deadly serious.'

Beck said nothing, just tightened his grip on her hand and led her forward. Martha couldn't believe how empty it was on the starboard side, as if the liner's list had forced people over to port. They went forward to where a small group had gathered, Beck quickening his stride as he got near, though it was difficult to move swiftly while wearing the heavy lifebelts.

Too late. The boat was already halfway down the ship's side. Beck stopped abruptly. 'My God,' he gasped.

'What?' Martha thought at first that he had seen Piatkow. She checked the faces on the boat. Some were faces she recognised from first class, others looked as if they had come from second and third. Mainly women, but a few men. Then she realised what had made Beck halt in his tracks. One of the men was Ismay.

'The yellow-bellied bastard,' Beck hissed.

'He's saving himself. Big deal.'

He shot her a look of pure anger. 'It is his ship!'

'And he's a human being.'

Beck didn't look convinced. Instead he followed the boat on its slow swinging descent with a stare of pure malevolence. 'Jump in.'

'What?'

'It's not too far. Come on, it's your last chance.' He grabbed Martha's arm as if he was going to pitch her over himself.

She shook herself free. The boat was thirty feet below them. No way was she going to risk that. She'd rather take her chances in the sea. 'No!' she said.

Beck saw she was serious and his expression relaxed. They ran around to the port side, where a large crowd had gathered. It was impossible to get through. A barrier seemed to have been formed by a group of crewmen to stop male passengers surging forward and trying to get on a lifeboat. It couldn't be seen on the davit so it had to be on its way down. Beck shouted, 'I have a woman with me – let me through!' but the in the maelstrom of screaming and weeping, and people trying to fight their way through to jump in the boat, he couldn't make himself heard.

'Come with me,' Martha whispered, and this time it was her turn to drag him. They went back across to the starboard side, where the chaos and panic was less.

'What about that boat?' she said, pointing. On the roof of the officers' deckhouse, just behind the bridge, there was an upturned boat which seemed to be bound to the roof.

Beck looked around. He glanced down towards the bridge and the rapidly rising water. 'Wait there,' he said.

He climbed onto the roof, helped by two officers and some more men, and struggled with the bindings. Eventually the boat was free and it bumped down onto the deck with a loud crash, just as the ship itself seemed to tilt further forwards, causing Martha to lurch and lose her balance. She steadied herself and looked back up the deck. The stern was now rising clear of the water, a mass of humanity scrabbling around on it, seeking safety away from the water. Just then, from one of the entrances amidships, a huge crowd seemed to surge outwards and spread across the deck. From their clothes Martha guessed they were steerage passengers – men, women and children – who had been held below decks all this time, emerging from the sodden bowels of the liner only in time to see that all the lifeboats had left the ship, apart from the one that had been tied to the roof and was now on the deck being readied by Beck and his desperate cohorts.

Some of the crowd saw them grappling with the boat and started to run towards it, while others turned, saw the great mass grouping on the poop deck and headed aft, searching for safety in numbers. With a sinking heart Martha could see that enough people were heading towards them to ensure that if the boat did get away it would be swamped and would sink.

'Arthur,' she cried, urging Beck to pull away, wanting them to take their chances elsewhere. But more crew arrived and soon they were swarming over the boat, trying to ready it.

He didn't respond, too engrossed in his work. Martha looked back at the approaching horde. At their front, running fast, was a tall man. As he came nearer she could see that his clothes were dripping wet. He must have fought his way up from the flooded deck below, but those behind him seemed to be dry. Then she recognised his face. The man Beck had chased across the well deck. His eyes were cold, his face devoid of all emotion.

He was carrying a gun. He slowed to a walk. The mob behind him caught up, crowding the boat, scores of them, which didn't help Beck's group who were still trying to prepare it for launching.

'Arthur,' she yelled again. Her cry was lost as the ship lurched forwards once more and a first wash of water swept up the deck. The small boat still sat on the deck and some fools even started to try to climb into it, unaware that their weight would make it practically impossible to launch.

A shot rang out. Martha screamed. Piatkow had fired. A man in front of him fell. Beck looked up and saw her. She shouted once more. Piatkow looked across at her, his face as dead and calm as the sea that surrounded them. Martha saw him lift the gun. Was he firing to clear his way to the lifeboat or was he pointing it at Beck? She couldn't tell.

Another shot sounded. This time it had been fired by Murdoch. He had seen Piatkow and aimed at him, but the bullet had hit a man in front, who fell to the deck in a spray of blood.

Martha stared at Piatkow. His gun was still raised. No one else seemed to notice him, or make an effort to stop him. He fired once more.

Murdoch staggered towards the rail and fell backwards. As Piatkow got the shot off, Beck dived forward through the crowd of men scrambling to get on the boat.

There was a huge roar beneath Martha's feet and she fell down. Across from where she lay she could see Beck and Piatkow grappling on the deck. Beck was underneath, Piatkow on top, but his hand holding the gun was twisted and bent. Martha lost sight of them for a few seconds but then she saw Beck had wrestled himself on top, his face twisted and contorted with effort. She screamed out his name once more as the ship seemed to tilt even further forward. Martha rolled onto her back, and was briefly able to see that *Titanic*'s stern was now rising precipitously out of the water. Another shot rang out and she twisted her head. Both men were still battling on the deck: Beck was gripping Piatkow's arm. The gun must have fired into the night sky. There was yet another lunge forward and more water surged, then more, washing her down the deck. The bridge was now totally submerged.

The ship slipped further down, bringing with it a wave that

washed over Martha completely, so cold that it seemed to suck all the life and warmth from her in one instant. All she could think of as that icy water engulfed her was that if this was it for her, she wouldn't know if Beck had survived. She tried to fight but the water had her in its grip, and she knew that to struggle would cost her valuable strength and energy. So she held her arms against her side, shut her mouth tightly and put her faith in a lifebelt and the mercy of a God in whom she didn't believe.

Sten-Ake had watched the disaster unfold, awestruck.

A young man, seeing that the old Swede didn't have a lifebelt, had offered him a rope, which Sten-Ake used to tie himself to the rail at the stern. He had considered going back inside the liner but he wanted to see his end come, to die under this beautiful panoply of stars and not be pitched around like a rag doll. This way it would be brief and, as the last seconds arrived, he could fill his mind with all the memories and moments from his life that were worth savouring. He had lived a long life and it was too late to change much now. But what of all these younger men and women, even kids, whose hopes and dreams would stay unfulfilled? He knew that the great ship would suck many of them down with it, while those lucky enough to escape its vortex would perish soon enough in the icy waters or drown unless help arrived.

The lifeboats had all gone – there'd been space for less than half of the people on board, it seemed – and the boats' occupants had nearly all been drawn from first and second class. It didn't surprise Sten-Ake. That was the way of the world. The rich had always looked after themselves.

The forecastle went under and the water lapped at the wings of the bridge. The orchestra, whose music had wafted through the ship, had given up and its members were now heading for the stern. Remarkably, crowds were still spilling from doorways – the steerage folk who had fought their way up, the engineers freed from their duty. Yet still, Sten-Ake marvelled, the lights blazed, which meant that those down in the depths were still at their stations. Had they been told? They were sailors. They must have known. Yet they had chosen to remain at their posts, ensuring that those above weren't plunged into darkness.

He checked the rope that tied him to the stern railing. It was secure. Just as well: the bow made a further lurch downwards and a vast wave of water swept over the bridge and the boat deck, washing away a group that had gathered there. All around him, the hordes who were scrambling to reach the point furthest from the rising water, began to scream as the stern rose higher. Sten-Ake looked to his left. Two men who were holding on to the railing shook hands before jumping into the sea below.

Sten-Ake turned and looked back down the unsubmerged length of the ship. The water was surging up the boat deck, pulling the bow down still further. There was a vast creak, the sound of twisting metal. Then the first funnel wobbled and swayed before it fell slowly, a spray of soot and sparks cascading from its torn base, landing in the sea on the port side where many of the swimmers were trying to get away, crushing them and creating a wave that swamped others.

The submerged bow sank deeper. A great roar seemed to come from the ship, like the death cry of some harpooned leviathan. As her tilt grew steeper, people started to lose their hold on the wires, capstans, ropes and rails and to slide inexorably towards the sea and floating pieces of wreckage from the disintegrating vessel. Some fell so hard that they must have been killed on impact.

Any screams were lost in the deafening rumble from the ship's guts as the engines and boilers were wrenched loose and smashed down, destroying all in their path.

The *Titanic* was close to the vertical by now. Sten-Ake dangled from the rail, one hand loosely gripping it when he heard again the horrible mangling sound of wrenching, heaving metal. Gouts of flame began to spit and shoot out from amidships. Some of those around the old Swede climbed onto the rail and the exposed ridge of the liner's keel to stay on her, while others fell or jumped into the heaving maelstrom of the sea. The tearing sound turned into a thunderous explosion, and the boat became almost perpendicular. Sten-Ake's hand lost its grip and he swung from the rail, suspended only by the rope. But the knot he had tied, learned during his years at sea, was strong enough to hold. He braced himself for the inevitable fall and the death by drowning that would follow. But all of a sudden, as he dangled in mid-air, the stern seemed to halt its rising tilt. He managed to look down. The ship had broken in two, its bow already gone beneath the waves.

A remarkable thing happened. The stern began to fall back. Sten-Ake was able to grab hold of the rail again. It continued to settle back in the water, shifting towards the horizontal. With the water-filled bow now wrenched away, the after part was able to float. Unbelievable, he thought. Perhaps we are saved.

In the aftermath of the ship's dying bellow, all he could hear were the cries for help of those in the sea. Then the stern started to rise again. Quicker this time. His previous hope had proved unfounded. The half-ship was filling with water. It could not float.

Sten-Ake lost hold of the rail again and knew that this was the end. He thought of Malin, their first date, their first kiss, an eye-popping midsummer's evening when the sun shone almost all day and night and the world seemed full of infinite possibilities. The birth of his daughter. The death of his father. His first day at sea. Weeping over the dead body of his beloved wife. The imaginary pictures he had created in his mind of the grandchildren he had never seen. Would now never see.

The stern had tilted fully to the vertical, pointing up at the sky. Then, with barely a noise, it slid down into its saltwater tomb. Sten-Ake's heart started to beat wildly and it felt as if a tight band was being wrapped around his chest, squeezing the life and breath from him.

He saw the water rushing towards him. He didn't even bother to take a breath. Just let the water wash over him and waited for the arms of death to enfold him.

Martha was sucked deeper and deeper, down into the freezing sea. She did not resist or try to fight her way back to the surface. That was strength she would need if she was to get out of the vortex. If. At one stage she felt a blow to her face, from a piece of debris that had also been sucked down.

Down and down she went in the blackness, water rushing past her ears. Her lungs felt as if they would burst. Then the grip from the suction seemed to loosen. Sensing her chance, Martha kicked and kicked, and pushed with her arms. She started to rise, the natural buoyancy of the lifebelt taking effect. She broke the surface and sucked in great lungfuls of air. As she burst out of the water, Beck's cigarette case catapulted out from her cleavage.

Her joy at being able to breathe was short-lived. All around her the sea was full of people, screaming and thrashing, a chorus of despair and agony. Although not from the poor soul floating next to her, clearly dead in the water, blood seeping from a gash across his brow.

But all Martha could think of for a few fleeting moments was the cigarette case. She wanted to return it to Beck. She stared intently across the water. Nowhere to be seen. She felt an ache of disappointment. No point crying over it, Martha, she thought.

Despite the fact that the cold cut into her like spears of ice, that she couldn't swim, Martha felt calm, knowing that panic would be a sure route to death. Had the ship gone? She paddled around in a slow circle until she spotted the *Titanic*. The liner made a pitiful spectacle. Her back was broken. The rear of the stern was clear of the water, the enormous propellers silhouetted against the starry sky. The lights on board went out one by one until she became a dark twisted mass.

Then the *Titanic* started her final descent. Sliding gracefully beneath the surface. In a few seconds she was gone, making no more noise than the splash of a pebble in a pond. Once the sea had closed over her it was as if that enormous vessel had never been there at all. There was just sea and sky. And the tormented wails of the dying.

Martha knew the way to survive was to get away from the struggling mass. The lifebelt kept her afloat while she paddled forward doggy-style towards where the boat had once been, not away from the site as so many others seemed to be heading. The cold was already numbing her extremities, her feet mere blocks of freezing flesh of no use to her. But methodically, breathing as regularly as she could, she started to make some headway. Towards what it was too dark to tell.

Debris floated past. Martha saw a deckchair and held on to it, buying some time to rest. Yet she knew her enemy wasn't the effort she was having to make: it was the temperature. A body could survive only so long in a sea so marrow-chilling. A few more bodies, killed in their falls from the ship, their heads bloodied, floated around.

She paddled on, her heart hammering against the inside of her chest, losing momentum. She could no longer feel her legs and her clothes seemed so heavy that just keeping moving took a monumental effort. She was feeling weaker by the minute, an insistent pounding in her head, her arms leaden, the feeling in her hands and arms gone . . .

I can't go on. I *must* go on, Martha thought. She saw more bodies bobbing past, this time with no sign of wounds, their heads tipped back, mouths agape. She looked upon them without emotion. Her body was now devoid of feeling and somehow she still moved on. But all she really wanted to do was stop and sleep.

She heard a voice, not a scream, more a word of warning. It shook her from her frozen torpor. Some kind of rescue? She looked around and saw nothing. But then it came again. From some kind of raft. Men had piled onto it, some standing, some lying down, others half on, the rest of their bodies in the water. Martha paddled towards it, boosted by a shot of hope.

The men on the edge had the dead look of the exhausted. She felt sure that one of them *was* dead, staring glassy-eyed over the side, his body twisted and contorted. No one noticed Martha. There was no space for her. She felt the life draining from her, the weariness creeping up on her again. She tried to call out but the words stuck in her throat.

AThen she glimpsed a gap, no more than the width of two wooden slats but something she could get hold of. She fought her way forward, expending her last drops of energy to cover a distance of just a few feet. Once there she put her hands on the raft. She would need to get out of the water or she'd be done for.

'Help me,' Martha croaked. No one reacted.

Her eyelids grew heavy. Her head felt as if it was filling with water. She just wanted sleep. But she forced her eyes to stay open.

'Help,' she repeated. Louder. A hoarse whisper.

A hand reached out and grabbed Martha's forearm. A strong grip. Then a pull that dragged her body closer. Another pull brought her hips against the edge of the raft. A few more and she would be on – or most of her would be.

Martha lifted her lolling head to see the helpful stranger. She thought briefly not just of her own survival but also of Beck's. Had he made it? Was he too on this makeshift craft?

Another wrench and she was half out of the water. She saw the face of the man it belonged to who was helping her. Looked into his eyes.

They were dead and cold, bled of all emotion. Her frozen, exhausted brain took a few seconds to work out who the man was. On the boat deck, holding a gun, Martha screaming to warn Beck, and this man looking right at her exactly as he was doing now. With hatred.

Piatkow.

He smiled, a mirthless, joyless smile.

Piatkow let go of Martha's arm. She pawed at the slippery edge of the raft but started to slide off slowly. All the time he watched her with those dead eyes.

'Goodbye,' he said, in a thick European accent. Then he looked away.

Martha had no strength left. She slipped back into the water.

Her head went below the surface and she was enveloped by a warm, numbing blackness as dark as a womb.

Beck saw the boat as he came to the surface. He was groggy and his head ached. He remembered the wave slamming him against the deckhouse and that was it. But now he was here, floating, and there was the samll boat he had been trying to launch until Piatkow had started shooting and the sea had claimed the *Titanic*.

He hauled himself in, feeling a spasm of excruciating pain searing up from his ankles. He let out a scream. He wasn't the only one. Nearby he could hear the sound of a thousand people flailing and thrashing in the water, struggling for their lives, their heartrending cries filling the night-time air.

'*Help me! God help me!*'

'*My baby! My son!*'

'*I want to live! For the love of Christ, I want to live!*'

The boat was half-filled with water. Icy cold. To lie down would be no different from being in the sea. Yet Beck couldn't stand because of the pain in his ankles. He knew straight away that at least one of them was broken, perhaps both. Instead he lay back.

He lay there shivering, turning once to vomit over the side of the boat, feeling as if he might lose consciousness. As he hung his head over the side, he saw a shoe float past, an empty lifebelt, and a silver cigarette case very much like the one he owned.

He did not notice other survivors climbing into the boat. Soon it was almost full.

A man, tall, looming large in the darkness, spoke, his voice loud enough to be heard above the din of the dying.

'We shouldn't take anyone else on board,' he said. 'Look at the water level. Any more and we shall sink and be at the bottom with them.'

'But those poor people,' a woman said, sobbing.

'We can't help 'em, madam,' the man replied sombrely. 'All we can do is save ourselves. They're in the hands of the Lord.'

They fell silent. The only noise the cacophony of screams and entreaties. Was Martha out there among them? Had she found a boat? Beck hoped so with all his heart. And what of Piatkow? At the bottom of the ocean, he hoped. But he might never know.

He turned his head and looked at the sea. A man, gasping for breath, was swimming to the boat's side. But as he reached them, one of the occupants was there to push him away.

'Sorry, old chap. No room, you see.' For all the world as though he was explaining that the last table for dinner had gone and he was frightfully apologetic.

Rather than putting up a fight and trying to climb in, the swimmer pushed away and carried on his search for rescue. Why weren't more coming? Beck wondered. But between the pitch darkness and their blind panic, it was unlikely that many of the survivors knew the boat was there. And as he now knew, trying to swim in one of those damned heavy life jackets was a nightmare. Good for keeping you afloat but terrible for allowing you to swim for your life.

Beck tried to block out such thoughts as he continued to look at the sea. The cries were beginning to die down as one by one the swimmers were overcome by the cold, or cast off their lifebelts and let themselves sink to the bottom of the ocean.

He could join them. Simply roll over the side. Then it would be over. This horror. The pursuit of one man that was going to lead to the death of hundreds.

How could he ever recover from this?

Yet, even in his despair, something stopped Beck. Some atavistic urge to live. For what purpose, he didn't know. Whether news of this ever came out he didn't care. He just hoped that Martha and the others had lived. But the screams of the dying, becoming less frequent, indicated otherwise. The cold was claiming them, as it would surely claim him too before the night was over.

The cries and screams eventually ceased, leaving behind an awful silence broken only by sounds frosm the boat.

There must be others out there but it was impossible to see. In the boat there was another man, injured like Beck, who moaned incessantly. A woman wept without pause for her two sons, who were missing. Beck ignored it all, gazing at the sea and then at the heavens, his wounded feet numbed by the icy water that they were resting in.

And what a show the heavens provided. A reminder of nature's beauty as well as its cruelty. Aurora borealis, the Northern Lights, throwing the mesmerising green-blue shapes of spectral light across the night. Beck followed each dance of glowing and undulating light with awe. They started to fade and once more he contemplated throwing himself into the sea. Looking across that dead calm water as the first faint signs of dawn crept over the horizon, he could see the looming shadows of icebergs. There seemed to be hundreds of them.

More guilt: why hadn't Ismay and Smith told him that there was so much ice ahead and this tragedy was possible? But Beck knew they had not even considered it themselves. Ismay was intent on steaming ahead, and the captain had been confident of his ability to steer clear of danger. But neither had reckoned on Beck and Piatkow arriving on the bridge as they reached the ice.

You might well live, Beck, like it or not, but there are hundreds of people out there, or already at the bottom of this pitiless ocean, who have been denied that chance. Ismay too may survive, he thought, remembering him sitting hunched and shamed in a boat full of women.

But what about Martha? Time would tell, sure enough.

It was slowly growing lighter, revealing the haggard and distressed features of his boat-mates. Each lost in their own private thoughts and torment. Survivors unable to revel in their good fortune. How could the sun rise after such an event? A dawn that so few would see. Someone should have told it to stop. Yet more evidence to Beck that no benevolent God existed.

He seemed to fall into a reverie. He was shaken from it when his boat stopped its aimless drift. They had come across another rescue vessel. A lifeboat that was filled with more people and was dry. The occupants must have been those who had been let off when the *Titanic* was still afloat. A crewman asked Beck to move and the pain erupted from his shattered ankles. At least he *could* move. Unknown to him, a few souls in his boat had perished from exposure. While he was gently eased into the crammed dry boat, the dead were left behind and set adrift.

Beck was laid flat. A kindly woman smiled thinly and gave him some clothing, presumably her own, to provide a makeshift cushion for his head. He murmured a thank-you, but his mouth was dry and the words wouldn't come. He desperately needed a drink, but no one offered him one.

It took a few minutes to compose himself, to muster the strength, but eventually he managed to croak in a cracked, hoarse whisper: 'Is Martha Heaton on board?'

The woman who had helped to comfort him repeated what he'd said to the other people in the lifeboat. Twice she called out the name. There was no response.

Beck fell back into his sullen self-absorption, ignoring to the whispers of the others on board, the sniffs and cries of those who had been left wondering about the fate of their loved ones.

If they knew he had been partly responsible for the decisions that had caused the collision he felt sure they would tear him limb from limb.

He would have done little to dissuade them. He envied the dead their peace. There was none for him. Only the dishonour of survival.

Dawn continued to arrive slowly, bleak and hopeless. Then one of their number gave an excited shout. Beck felt nothing. The same voice had claimed to have seen lights in the distance when it was still dark. But this time a few others joined in.

'A ship!' they yelled.

Beck forced himself up on his arms to see over the side of the boat. Once again astonished to see the still-calm sea studded with icebergs of all sizes. There was also debris from the stricken ship which now lay at rest in the depths below. Deckchairs, chairs, tables, bottles, cups, boxes and chests, a vast array of mundane material.

There were bodies, too. A woman clutching what might have been a lapdog. A man in a dinner suit slumped over a deckchair. Beck was almost dead from the cold but a hot tear spilled onto his cheek.

There, approaching, was the definite shape of a steamship.

'It is the *Carpathia*,' someone said. 'We are saved. Praise the Lord.'

So, Beck thought, I will live. For now, I will live.

Beck came to. He was in a cabin. Not on board the *Titanic*. Then came the awful realisation of what had happened. The sinking, the coldness of the sea, the feelings of utter despair. He turned and felt a searing pain in his ankles. He had forgotten about those. Glancing down, he could see they had been bandaged.

A closer inspection revealed it to be a professional job, neatly done. Splints of some kind had been inserted to prevent him bending the joints concerned. It meant that both of them must be broken. His head felt woozy, and he wondered if he might have been given some kind of medication for the pain, or to allow him to sleep while they attended to his injuries.

Beck looked around the room. Whose was it? They must be on the *Carpathia*. He had no idea what class he was in. It was nice enough, but nothing compared to the *Titanic*. Not that it mattered.

That liner was at the bottom of the ocean now. Her fancy fittings and sleek design would do her little good there.

He didn't how long he lay there. An hour or so, perhaps. A young man, all brisk and efficient, came in to check on him. A doctor. He said that Beck had broken both ankles. There were also signs of frostbite. He needed to lie and rest until they got to New York. Beck asked whether he had been the one who'd dressed his wounds. The doctor nodded gravely and Beck thanked him.

'Think nothing of it,' he replied.

'I suppose there are others who are injured.'

The doctor nodded. 'A few. Mainly exposure, the occasional bump and bruise like yourself. But on the whole those who made it are doing well.'

'Those who made it.' The finality of that phrase hung in the air. Even the doctor seemed shocked at the starkness of it.

'How long have I been here?' Beck asked.

'Two days,' the doctor answered. 'You were out cold for the best part of the day. We gave you some medication for the pain and it helped you to rest. One of the passengers gave up their berth for you. So did a few others, for the rest of the injured.'

'And the uninjured survivors?'

'They're bunking down in the saloons.'

Martha, Beck thought. Had she made it?

'Can I speak to Ismay? Is he available?' He had seen him leave the ship by boat before the sinking. He could think of no reason why he wouldn't be.

There was a pause.

'Mr Ismay was incapacitated.'

'With what?'

The doctor seemed reluctant to speak.

'I'll see what I can do. He has asked not to be disturbed.'

The doctor left, promising to come back and check Beck's injuries before they reached New York.

A few minutes later there was a timid knock at the door. Beck asked whoever it was to come in and Ismay appeared, his hat in his hand. His expression was lifeless.

'Are you all right?' Beck asked.

'I'm fine,' Ismay mumbled. 'You?'

Beck said he had broken both his ankles. 'Damn lucky compared to some.'

Ismay winced. 'Of course.'

'I wish I hadn't survived,' Beck said.

Ismay said nothing. He knew that Beck had seen him in the lifeboat. The shame was etched on his face.

'How many have survived?'

Ismay swallowed. 'Around seven hundred.'

'How many lost?'

'Approximately fifteen hundred.' The White Star president looked down at the floor.

The sheer scale of the loss of life took Beck's breath away.

'We really shouldn't have survived,' he said.

'Yes, well,' Ismay said.

'The captain?'

'He went down with the ship.'

So should we, Beck thought. 'Do you have a list of the survivors?'

Ismay nodded.

'Do you have it on you?'

Ismay reached into his pocket. 'I have it here.'

The list consisted of several sheets of paper, folded together. 'I'm not sure it's one hundred per cent complete yet. People were scattered all over the ship.'

Beck's mouth was dry. He took the list from Ismay and started to look down it. There was no system to it, no class differentiation, just a list of names, neatly written. He used his finger to keep track as he worked his way down each sheet, hoping and praying for Martha's name to be there.

It was nowhere to be seen. Beck ignored Ismay and went through it again, the ache in his heart growing sharper. He reached the end once more.

Martha was gone. Tears welled in Beck's eyes but he did not wish to break down in front of Ismay. He handed the sheaf of papers back to him without even looking up.

Beck felt numb. There had been so much sorrow and disappointment in his life. It was as if he was full to the brim, and there was no room for all this new grief. He had the rest of his life to come to terms with it.

'Look,' Ismay said, 'I have spoken to the crew. Those who survived, anyway. No word of what really happened will get out. Murdoch is dead. Andrews too. No one else would have known.' His forehead was beading with sweat, even though the room was cool. 'I trust I can count on your discretion.'

Beck didn't care. Had Martha made it he would have wanted her to publish and be damned. 'I suppose.'

Ismay nodded, reassured. 'There will be many questions but I think we can handle them. You won't be brought into it.'

Beck wanted Ismay to go. In fact, right there and then, he didn't care if he never saw the man again. This was some horrible nightmare. He would wake up from it soon and find it was all unreal.

Ismay went on: 'I have wired my offices in New York. I've asked them to hold one of our ships, the *Cedric*, until Friday in order to take the crew and myself back to Southampton. I don't think it's wise to spend too much time on American soil. There is likely to be a hullabaloo. I can guarantee you a berth on the boat if you wish.'

Beck had stopped listening. He couldn't think of the future. The past was too painful. All he had was the present, and it was horrific.

Had Piatkow survived? How could Beck find out? He was an invalid, unable to get up and walk about, to look at the faces of the survivors. All he wanted to do was die. The only name on the list that had meant anything to him was that of the old Swedish man, Gustafson. Beck supposed it was good for him and his loved ones, but it seemed a waste that a man nearing the end of his life had survived while those at the start of theirs had perished.

'I can't think about it,' Beck said. 'Not now.'

'Of course,' Ismay muttered. 'Well, I'll be off.'

He let himself out. Beck didn't say a word as he did. He looked out of the porthole. The sea was the same. As was the sky.

Yet he knew nothing else would ever be.

The smoking room was too full of the sleeping bodies of others, so for the second night running the man's bed was the open deck. The ice field was long behind them now, and while the deck could hardly be described as warm it was preferable to topping and tailing with a bunch of strangers.

And it lessened the risk of being identified. There was a better chance of anonymity here under the open skies. A few other men had thought likewise and had bunked under the stars, many of them wearing the same stiff salt-encrusted clothing in which they had been rescued. A storm was brewing, though, and he feared they might all be driven into the crowded rooms below, where people filled almost every available space and the queues for the public toilets stretched down the corridors. It was a comedown for the high and the mighty who were used to the luxuries of the ship that had sunk, the man thought bitterly. Sleeping on floors. Despite the shock that he felt – it still seemed so unreal – he smiled bitterly when he thought of it. That great ship and all of the money lavished on it, now a useless pile of tin at the bottom of the ocean. Man could not cheat nature.

The man leaned over the side, watching the dark, bruised clouds massing ahead. The coming storm promised to be a wild one. He felt in his pockets for some cigarettes. In the chaos below it had been easy pickings. These people had no possessions – all their belongings had sunk – but some had cigarettes and right now it was the only swag he wanted.

He felt his inside pocket. The large billfold of dollars was still there. Slightly damp, but still very much usable. It would be useful in New York.

As he lit a cigarette, another man joined him. Young, bedraggled, clearly a fellow survivor. He knew what the newcomer wanted, so he simply pulled out a cigarette and handed it over, then lit it. The other man sucked in the smoke eagerly.

'Speak English?' he asked in a halting accent.

He nodded.

'*Titanic?*'

Again, he nodded.

They stood in silence. A silent gash of lightning tore across the sky.

'Bad,' the other man said.

'Yes. Bad,' he replied. Whether the other fellow meant the tragedy or the coming storm he wasn't sure. He was right on both counts.

'English?'

He shook his head.

The other man pointed to his own chest. 'Germany.'

He had never been there. Didn't want to go, either.

'You?' The German was looking at him.

Eventually he answered.

'Swedish,' he replied.

'Ah, Sweden.' The German nodded eagerly. He pointed to his chest once more. 'Olaus.' He held out his hand.

He felt a surge of communal spirit, a bond of shared experience. He shook the other man's hand firmly and smiled.

'Sten-Ake,' Peter Piatkow told him. 'I am Sten-Ake Gustafson.'

Acknowledgements

This story could not have been told or published had it not been for my editor Jack Fogg. I'd like to thank him, Briony Gowlett and the team at Arrow for all their hard work and inspiration.

As always, my agent Araminta Whitley, Peta Nightingale and the good folk at LAW were all excellent sounding boards and helped improve the book immeasurably.

I'd also like to thank those posters at the excellent www.encyclopedia-titanica.com for answering my questions patiently. Nick Barratt was another good source of *Titanic* wisdom at the start of this project. Of course, any mistakes are entirely my own.

Finally, ultimate thanks go to my family for their patience and understanding while I immersed myself in all things *Titanic*. Cheers and love to Maya, Dougie, Vinnie and my wife, Seema.

Bibliography

There has been, and will continue to be, a vast amount of written material about the *Titanic*. I consulted many of them while researching this novel. Here are those that I found the most useful.

Websites
www.encyclopedia-titanic.com
www.titanic-titanic.com

Titanic Inquiry Project
www.titanicinquiry.org

Publications
Barratt, Nick. *Lost Voices from the Titanic*. Arrow, 2009.
Bartlett, W.B. *Titanic. 9 Hours to Hell, the Survivor's Story*. Amberley, 2010.
Beesley, Lawrence et al. *The Story of the Titanic as told by its Survivors*. Dover Publications, 1960.

Behe, George *On Board RMS Titanic. Memories of the Maiden Voyage.* Self-published.

Behe, George. *Titanic. Safety, Speed and Sacrifice.* Transportation Trails, 1997.

Beveridge, Bruce et al. *Titanic: The Ship Magnificent. Volume Two: Interior Design and Fitting Out.* The History Press, 2009.

Brown, David G. *The Last Log of the Titanic.* International Marine, 2001.

Davie, Michael. *The Titanic. The Full Story of a Tragedy.* Grafton Books, 1987.

Eaton, John P. and Haas, Charles A. *Titanic. Destination Disaster.* Patrick Stephens Limited, 1998.

Eaton, John P. and Haas, Charles A. *Titanic. Triumph and Tragedy. Patrick Stephens Limited, 1998.*

Lord, Walter. *A Night to Remember.* Holt Paperback, 1983.

Lord, Walter. *The Night Lives On.* William Morrow, 1986.

Lynch, Don. *Titanic. An Illustrated History.* Hodder and Stoughton, 1992.

Maltin, Tim. *101 things you thought you knew about the Titanic but didn't.* Beautiful Books, 2010.

Patten, Louise. *Good as Gold.* Quercus, 2010.

Rumbelow, Donald. *The Houndsditch Murders.* The History Press, 2009.

Wade, Wyn Craig. *The Titanic. End of a Dream.* Wiedenfeld and Nicholson, 1980.